MUSIC TO SACRIFICE VIRGINS TO

KRISTOPHER TRIANA

BAD DREAM BOOKS

ISBN: 978-1-961758-25-4

Edited by Lisa Lee

Cover art by Tery Ramdhany

Cover wrap design and interior formatting by C.V. Hunt

Interior "Guitar Skeleton" art by Imperial Skulls

For signed books and merchandise visit:
TRIANAHORROR.COM

Praise for Kristopher Triana

"Like the bastard son of Faulkner and Barker, Triana trudges a literary lane all his own."

—Nick Roberts, author of
The Exorcist's House

"Kristopher Triana is without question one of the very best of the new breed of horror writers."

—Bryan Smith, author of *Depraved*

"Triana's masterful, gripping storytelling will not let go… I'm blow away with what he can do and will read just about anything he puts out."

—Scream Magazine

"Kristopher Triana writes beautiful nightmares, horrific fairytales, and intoxicating horrors, and however depraved and damaged his characters, you get to know them well… whether you want to or not."

—Tim Lebbon, author of *The Last Storm*

"One of the most exciting and disturbing voices in extreme horror in quite some time. His stuff hurts so good."

—Brian Keene, author of *The Rising*

"Kristopher Triana's prose is unapologetic and totally without restraint or mercy. There's no denying it. Triana is the Master of Extreme Horror!"

—Ronald Kelly, author of
Southern Fried & Horrified

"Triana is a master of affecting, distressing, and immensely powerful horror."

—Jonathan Butcher, author of
What Good Girls Do

for Gregg
the most metal friend I have

"We must live for the rock 'n roll underground. It can be dark and dangerous again. It can be threatening to our society as it was meant to be."

—GG Allin

"Lucifer dwells within us all."

—Richard Ramirez

ONE

DEVIL WORSHIP IS THE OLDEST of all religions.

Nearly every faith in history, dating back to their most primitive origins, tells of a powerful, evil entity. The demon is the backbone of all faiths because human beings respond to fear with submission and worship. When early man first felt thunder shake the earth, he needed something to blame it on. Lacking an understanding of the temporal world, humanity assigned responsibility to dark forces and spiteful deities. These entities had to be appeased. Like landlords coming to collect the rent, the gods demand obedience, worship, and sacrifice. And like mobsters, appeased deities promise protection—*from them*. The spirit world is bloodied by their baffling vanity. And the less man understands, the more he worships.

Asher didn't feel like he understood anything about his life.

When his troubles began, he had no religion to fall back on, no idols to pray to, and no devils to blame. It would have been a relief to lay fault upon something other than himself. He might have taken comfort in having a god to ask for guidance. But Asher Benton had not been raised with faith. He'd never said a prayer or even meditated, having only been in churches for weddings and funerals, and while he had no qualms with others using religion as a crutch, he'd never found solace in their bibles or sanctuary in their cathedrals. Though he'd not chosen atheism, his refusal to believe in things he could not see, hear, or feel had chosen it for him. So when things fell apart, Asher's only saving grace was himself, which was no safety net at all. There was no one to carry him. No guide to follow. He'd forged his own path, time and again, but the results left him wondering if free will was everything it was cracked up to be.

"Unbelievable," he muttered as he wheeled his suitcase up the front porch.

The house looked the same as it had when he'd moved out. The past six years had done more to change Asher than the one-story home he'd grown up in. Same bland beige color. Same manicured lawn, the grass matching the house now that autumn was ending. The first freeze of the season had been announced, and the plants in Mom's garden were shielded by black bags. A wooden craft's fair sign hung upon the front door—"Join the Harvest" above the image of a cornucopia vomiting vegetables. Though the windows were sealed tight against the cold, Asher could smell Mom's homemade chicken soup on the stovetop inside. Under different circumstances, he would have found the aroma comforting, but he felt only embarrassment.

Twenty-five years old and moving back in with Mom, he thought bitterly.

He looked over his shoulder for any old neighbors witnessing his shame. The street was empty. At least the kids he'd grown up with had all become adults and moved away.

Unless they're a fucking loser like you.

Grumbling in self-disgust, he reached for the spare housekey on his keyring, but the door came open without his help as his mother appeared. The sight of her gave Asher pause. She'd been going through a lot of transformations since separating from his father, finding her way back to the gym and the beauty salon, but her recent body modifications left her son uncomfortable. Having always been a flat-chested woman, Mom had splurged on breast implants several months back, giving her an ample C-cup that appeared bountiful even under her thick sweater. Yoga pants hugged her legs, which were toning nicely from her afternoon bike rides. She'd dyed her hair blond and grown it out, the straightness ending in curls at the center of her back. A fresh tattoo—her first, as far as Asher knew—was wrapped around her right wrist like a bracelet of rose petals. All these changes combined seemed to strip a decade off her fifty-one years.

There was no doubt about it. Mom had become a M.I.L.F.

The thought curdled Asher's stomach.

"Hey, honey," Mom said with a smile.

Before he could finish saying hello, she wrapped him in her arms, her firm new boobs pressing into his ribs. Her hair smelled like lilacs. When she pulled back, Asher realized she was wearing eyeshadow and lipstick. Mom looked as if she'd been expecting a gentleman caller, not her only child.

"Jeez, Ma," he said. "You got a hot date or something?"

Her smile soured. "Let's not start, okay?"

"Start what? I'm just sayin' …"

"I know what you're saying, mister, and I'm not in the mood. I understand it's still weird for you, but your father and I are nearly finished with our divorce. I'm entitled to date. It's healthy for me to."

"I wasn't saying otherwise," he told her, irritated before he'd even crossed the threshold. "I was just saying you look like you're ready to hit the town."

He shuffled inside. While the outside of the house remained the same, Mom had changed the interior, moving furniture around and swapping out wall art. There were more trinkets and crafts, more merchandise professing a love of wine and a "you only live once" attitude. All traces of Asher's father had been peeled away like sunburned skin, transforming their old family home into that of a newly single, middle-aged woman.

"I put some soup on," Mom said. "Chicken noddle with carrots—your favorite."

"Thanks, Ma." He didn't have the heart to tell her he'd already shoved a Baconator from Wendy's down his throat on the way over. "I'm just gonna get set up in my room first."

"Take your time."

Entering his old bedroom, a cold sorrow moved across the remains of Asher's heart. He'd almost expected Mom to have renovated this part of the house too, but the guest room remained the same. The walls were bare, the décor sparse. There was a queen-sized bed with a hand-quilted comforter. A stout dresser with four drawers. An old couch-chair in the corner. A bookshelf cradled more kitschy knickknacks. If she'd been storing anything else in here, Mom had graciously cleared it out before Asher's arrival. The closet and dresser were as empty as he was.

Removing his parka and beanie, Asher sat on the bed with a long sigh. The last time he'd slept on this, Rebecca had slept beside him. They'd been visiting for Dad's birthday and drank too much to drive home. Feeling naughty, they'd quietly fucked in his childhood bedroom, feeling like teenagers sneaking around. Rebecca was always down for any naughty business, anywhere, at any time. Her constant arousal was one of the many things he was going to miss about her, though he hated to admit he'd miss anything about a woman who'd treated him so poorly. Regardless, it was still difficult for Asher to think of Rebecca as his ex-girlfriend, even now that he'd moved out of their apartment at her insistence.

He ran a hand through his shaggy hair, thinking of the boxes he needed to haul inside. He'd amassed so little—mostly clothes and video game cartridges. The furniture he'd shared with Rebecca had been handed-down gifts from her folks, so it all stayed with her.

At least I have my own car, Asher thought. The fifteen-year-old Honda wasn't much to brag about, but it did its job and would enable him to get out of the house when his mother inevitably got on his nerves or—worse yet—brought a date home. Just the thought made Asher seethe.

He managed to avoid his mother while going to the car for the moving boxes. The sky had gone white in a nod to the coming winter, the branches of the front yard's maple tree seeming to rake across it like claws. A nip in the air made Asher wish he'd left his coat and hat on, but he was already outside, so he just zipped up his hoodie as he shuffled down the driveway. It was a quarter past noon, and already, he was thinking about washing down some edibles with a cold beer— anything to escape his pathetic reality. Lately, he'd been relying on weed and alcohol more than he should, but he gave himself a pass given all he was going through.

As Asher drew a box from the Honda's back seat, a dark figure moved across the corner of his vision. Turning, he gazed across the street at what used to be the McMillan house. They'd moved upstate over a year ago, but Asher couldn't remember if Mom told him anything about the house's new owners. He hadn't been curious before, but seeing this girl exit the side door, Asher's interest sparked. She looked a few years younger than him, short yet slender, soft with femininity. Her platinum-blond hair came with two black streaks and black bangs, matching her all-black outfit. Without being flashy, her appearance grabbed his eye, even though he couldn't make out her body under that faux leather trench coat.

The girl walked down her driveway, and Asher briefly imagined she was coming over to say hello to him. Instead, she went to the mailbox, either ignoring or not noticing him as he stood there watching her with a box of random crap in his hands. The goth girl gave him only a perfunctory glance, as if for her own safety. Getting a closer look at her, Asher wondered if she were still in high school. He decided not to say hello.

After bringing all the boxes inside, he grabbed the mail. He'd already had his forwarded to his mother's address, and while he wasn't expecting anything good, he wanted to make sure it was being delivered. He sifted through the stack as he returned to the porch. Most of it was junk mail addressed to his parents. There was a letter from Mom's attorney and a small package from Amazon. Only the last piece of mail was addressed to Asher. He squinted at the plain, white envelope, not recognizing the handwriting. There was no return address.

Probably some bullshit from Rebecca, he thought. *Maybe she had her new boyfriend write it out for her.*

Asher sucked his teeth, picturing Rebecca snuggled up on their sofa with the new guy she swore didn't exist, the two lovers writing out a letter to Asher so she wouldn't have to contact him in real time via a text or phone call. He couldn't imagine what the letter would be about, but Rebecca was always finding new avenues to hurting him.

"Soup's on," Mom called from the kitchen as Asher closed the front door behind him. "I warmed up some Hawaiian rolls for us too."

"Thanks."

He itched to get to the letter but didn't want to keep his mother waiting any longer, so he joined her at the table, folding the letter into the pocket of his hoodie.

"Just saw our new neighbor," he said. "The girl in the old McMillan place."

"Which one?"

"I dunno. She was a young blonde dressed like Darth Vadar."

Mom placed an ice cube into his steaming bowl. "That's Violet. The younger one's Kelly, I think."

"Violet … that's a pretty name."

"Well, she's a pretty girl. Did you introduce yourself?"

"Nah," he said, shrugging it off. "She looked a little young for me."

Mom smiled. "Sometimes I forget you're not a teenager anymore. I suppose that'll be even harder with you back in your old room." Asher couldn't help but cringe. Realizing her words had stung, Mom changed course. "Violet's probably only a few years younger than you, though. Maybe nineteen."

"Guess I just considered any girl still living at home to be too young for me. But now I'm living at home again, so …"

"Don't be so hard on yourself. Things happen. This is just temporary. I mean, you can stay as long as you like—you know that—but you won't live at home forever."

"Nothing's forever. I've learned that these past few weeks. I mean, I was with Rebecca for over two years and then *bam*—it all ends, just like that."

Mom gave him a sympathetic frown. "Honey, couples break up. I mean, just look at me and your father. You think the end of a two-year romance is hard, try a thirty-year one."

Asher almost told her pain wasn't a contest but didn't have the energy to start an argument. He dipped a roll into the broth. Today, his favorite soup might as well have been poorhouse gruel.

"I know it's hard, honey," Mom said, "but maybe it's all for the best. You never know. Someone even better might come along, and now you'll be free to date her."

"Is that why you want me talking to the girl next door?"

"It couldn't hurt, right? Even if she's too young for you to want to date her, it'll be good for you to talk to a pretty girl. Sharpen your flirtation skills after being in a long relationship. Build your confidence back up."

"You gonna give me a makeover too?"

She narrowed her eyes at him. "Is that a shot at me?"

"No," he lied. "I was just joking."

"There's nothing wrong with wanting to look good. When you're depressed or going through difficult changes, it helps to not forget about hygiene and exercise, and sometimes a whole new look can give you a whole new outlook on life."

"You sound like a hairdresser."

"Now I *know* your making fun of me."

"Okay, I'm sorry, Ma, but *c'mon*." He gestured to her. "I mean,

6

look at you."

Her eyebrows drew closer together. "Are you saying I look bad this way?"

"No, you look great. Maybe a little too great."

She put her spoon down on the table. "So, you think a woman my age shouldn't look this way? That I'm too old for tattoos and breast im—"

Asher threw up his hands. "No, no, no. God, I'm sorry, all right? Please, let's just let it go."

"I'm just saying that—"

"I already know what you're saying."

"Well, I think you're just struggling with your parents' divorce, so maybe we should talk about—"

"For Christ's sake, I just don't want to talk to *my mother* about her big fake tits, okay?"

He regretted these words as soon as they left his mouth. They were an invitation either to an argument or silent anger, and he'd had enough of both from Rebecca.

Mom returned to stirring her soup, no longer looking at him. "Fine."

"Ma ..."

But he didn't know what else to say—to her or anybody.

"I've got to get some work done on my laptop," Mom said, cradling her bowl as she stood. "I'm gonna finish this in the den."

Asher knew he should apologize just to keep the peace, but he just didn't have it in him. His emotional battery had been sucked dry. Alone in the kitchen, he poured the rest of his soup down the garbage disposal, grabbed a beer from the fridge, and retreated to the familiar isolation of his room. As he stretched out on the bed, the envelope in his pocket crackled, reminding him it was there.

Asher opened it. A single page was inside, handwritten just like the address on the envelope. Though unfamiliar, the handwriting was jagged and crooked, suggesting a male author. It addressed him by his first name only. Asher read it closely, his curiosity growing.

Hey Asher,

If you're reading this, it means I'm dead. I arranged for my stuff to be distributed, and I'm leaving you the things that were the most special to me. I know we didn't really know each other, but that wasn't my choice. Anyway, I never married or had a family of my own, so you're as close to an heir as I'm going to get. It's

7

important to me that your inheritance ends up in your hands but the only contact info I had on you was your parents' address. You must be in your twenties by now. Hopefully your folks pass this letter on to you, and your mom is cool with this, considering I'm gone.

You can pick everything up at Stowaway Storage on Bristol Road, unit #6. Ask for John. The code for the lock is 0-8-44. Bring a van or truck.

Treat my things well, dude. Use them wisely and I guarantee they'll give you everything they gave me and more.

Keep rockin, buddy,

Uncle Rex

Asher read the letter three times. So many things about it perplexed him. It was not only vague but entirely unexpected. He knew of his uncle but had no memories of him, though Mom had a few pictures of her estranged brother in yellowed photo albums, including a few of him with Asher when he was barely a toddler. The man had been tall and lanky, towering over the other adults in the pictures. He had long black hair, a unibrow, and bushy sideburns, and was always wearing heavy metal band t-shirts, black jeans, and a motorcycle jacket. But it was his eyes Asher remembered most. He'd never seen anyone with bags under their eyes that purple and all-encompassing. If he hadn't appeared that way in every photo, Asher would have thought he'd just lost a fistfight.

Rex was rarely talked about. Mom never explained why she and her brother had not spoken in over twenty years. To Asher, he was just one of those distant relatives that had no role in his life and was therefore forgotten. The man had never reached out to Asher before. That Rex left him anything came as more of a surprise than his death, even though he must have died young, being only a couple of years older than Mom.

A sad thought struck him. Did Mom even know her brother had died?

Rising from the bed, Asher took the letter into the den. Mom was on the sofa with a blanket and her laptop, working while watching one of her true crime shows.

"Uh, Ma," he said, not knowing where to begin.

"What is it?" she asked, still watching the show.

Asher held up the letter. "Uncle Rex wrote to me."

Now, she turned to face him. Her brow lowered, mouth opening in shock. "Rex? He ... wait, what? He *wrote* to you?"

She stood up, reaching for the letter, but Asher didn't give it to her just yet. He could tell Mom didn't know about her brother's death and figured he would break it to her more gently than Rex's blunt text.

"Well, what did he say?" she asked. Her eyes darted. She almost seemed afraid, which confused Asher. "What the hell does that bastard want after all these years? Why is he writing to my son?"

She tried to snatch the letter away from him, but Asher took her hand in his.

"I'm sorry, Ma, but according to this, Rex is dead."

Mom's face paled, her nervous outrage giving way to a stunned expression. She said nothing as her eyes fell to the floor, but her hand tightened around Asher's so hard he winced and drew it away.

"Are you okay?" he asked. "Maybe you should sit down."

She gingerly slid the letter from his fingers. As she read, she put her hand to her mouth. "Jesus. So he's finally gone."

"*Finally?* Had he been dying for a while now? Did he have cancer or something?"

Her eyes didn't leave the page. "I ... I don't know. It's been a long time since I've known *anything* about Rex and ... I don't think anyone really knew him anymore."

"What do you mean?"

Finally, she folded the letter and looked up at her son. "Asher, I need you to listen to me. Don't go and pick up whatever it is he says he left to you."

"What? Why?"

"Just don't. Trust me."

Asher shook his head. "C'mon, I know you guys didn't get along, but if he left me something special, I'd like to know what it is. It might be money or something worth money. I'm strapped and need all the help I can get."

"Listen to your mother. Your uncle went off the deep end years ago. He was completely estranged from everyone else in the family and didn't even show up when our parents passed away." She took a deep breath and pulled the blanket around her shoulders like a shawl. "Rex was a sick man. A *bad* man. And judging by how he chose to live his life, I doubt he had anything of value to hand down to you."

"Okay, but he did say this stuff was special."

"Anything that was special to my brother is something you don't want in your life."

9

"You don't even know what it is. It can't hurt for me to check it out, right? If it's junk, it's junk. But if it's worth money, I'll sell it and add funds to my savings for a new apartment."

Her eyes tightened. "But at what cost?"

"Jeez, Ma, you talk like he's gonna hurt me."

"Hurting people is just what Rex does."

"Not anymore. The guy is dead."

"Or so he says," Mom said, hugging herself.

Asher paused before replying. "You think this is a trick?"

"I don't know what to think."

"Man, I never realized things were so bad between you two. But why would he break a twenty-year silence just to lie to me about his death when he never really knew me?"

"I told you I don't know. Maybe he is dead. He probably is, but the letter doesn't even say anything about funeral services or last wishes or anything." The tears she'd been holding back began to fall, but there was more anger in them than mourning. "I suppose I have a few phone calls to make."

"Oh, I can handle that if you want."

"No, that's all right. I'm his next of kin. It's my responsibility to notify the family, even if Rex didn't notify me directly." She ran her sleeve across her wet nose. "Sorry. This is all so sudden. Maybe I am overreacting, but I still don't want you having anything to do with him, dead or alive."

"I hear you, but it's not him, it's just his stuff, whatever it is. I'm just gonna check it out. No big deal."

Mom nodded. "Well, like I said earlier, sometimes I forget you're not a kid anymore. I've got to let you make your own decisions, even if they're mistakes."

Asher made a halfhearted effort to reassure her everything would be all right, but his mother was already walking away from him.

Two

DIEGO'S PICKUP TRUCK PULLED AROUND the back of the storage facility. Riding shotgun, Asher counted the unit numbers until they reached the sixth. Despite what his uncle's letter said, no one named John was employed at Stowaway Storage, according to the manager. Asher figured the guy must have quit the job after Rex made the arrangements because the computer still had a note on file to admit Asher to the unit, so the manager allowed them in unescorted. Not knowing what they'd be loading, Diego backed the truck up so the bed was facing the rolling door. As they got out, a biting wind struck their faces.

Asher's best friend put the hood of his coat up. "Damn. Shit got cold fast."

"That's New England for you."

Though Mexican, Diego was born and raised here in New Hampshire but still seemed shocked by winter's touch. Unlike his parents, he preferred beaches to these mountains. When they were eighteen,

Asher and Diego had gone to Fort Lauderdale for spring break, and Asher had never seen him happier, and not just because of all the drunk girls in bikinis.

"We should've come here at noon instead of dusk," Diego said. "Once that last bit of sun is gone, we're gonna freeze our asses off."

"It's not that bad. Besides, this shouldn't take too long."

"Thought you said you didn't even know what we were picking up."

"I don't."

Diego laughed. "You asshole."

They approached the unit, and Asher took the lock in his hand. He'd been excited on the way over, imagining all the different things that might be awaiting him. Maybe his uncle was one of those eccentric recluses who didn't trust the banks and had left him a mattress stuffed with cash. Maybe he had jewelry, a coin collection, or collectible comic books in great condition. But now that he was standing at the threshold of his inheritance, his mother's warning ricocheted through his mind, making him a little nervous. What if she was right and Rex really was playing some horrible prank, one he'd set up before his death as one final jab at his sister? Asher had a sudden vision of the storage unit exploding, the lock having some hidden trigger wired to a dirty bomb. It was ludicrous, but his mother's paranoia had a way of seeping into his thoughts. It was one of her many traits that annoyed him.

He dialed in the code: 0-8-44.

The lock popped open.

"Let's see what's behind door number one," Diego said, raising the door.

Asher stepped back to take it all in, but the unit was shrouded in darkness. Finding a dangling string, he pulled it, illuminating the unit in a boozy, yellow glow, revealing several cube-shaped plastic totes and one large, wooden shipping crate. None were labeled or had windows to reveal their contents. Aside from these containers, the unit was empty.

"Guess it won't take long after all," Diego said, approaching the crate. "Long as this big one ain't too heavy." Diego was only five foot six, and the crate came up to his chest. "Glad I brought the dolly."

"Yeah, good call," Asher replied, staring at his uncle's vaulted belongings, which were now his. "I appreciate the hand."

"Don't forget that sixer of Michelob you're gonna owe me. And if this stuff does make you rich, just remember your old friend Diego and how he was always willing to help you."

"Wait … who're you again?"

The friends grinned, always happy to bust each other's balls.

Diego slapped the top of the crate. "So should we open these suckers here or what?"

"I didn't bring a crowbar. Didn't think I'd need one. You don't happen to have one in your truck, do you?"

Diego shook his head. "No. Not all Mexican are thieves."

Asher lowered his brow. Diego chuckled.

"Let's just get them to my mom's," Asher said. "Hopefully, she doesn't have a conniption."

He'd explained to Diego about his mother's aversion to the inherited goods so it wouldn't be a surprise to him if she flipped out. Asher had been friends with Diego since the ninth grade. Mom had always liked him. Hopefully, that would help somehow when they came home with Rex's stuff.

The crate was heavy, but with the dolly, they managed to move it without any problems. The totes were hefty too, but the young men easily carried them to the truck one by one. There were thirteen in all.

"We should at least pop one of these babies open," Asher said. "But the tops are screwed into the base. No easy entry."

Diego hunched his shoulders against the breeze. "I'm good with waiting. I'd rather open them in a warm house than out here where I'll freeze my dick off."

"No big loss. Emphasis on *big*."

"Bullshit. I've got a can of corn down there."

"More like a can of cat food, judging by the smell."

Diego cracked up, causing Asher to do the same. They closed the tailgate, and within the hour, they were back at Mom's place. Seeing her car missing from the driveway, Asher exhaled with relief. Even if she were out at some single's bar showing off her cleavage, it was preferable to her having a meltdown while they unloaded.

The friends hauled the totes into Asher's room first, then worked together to roll the crate through the front door and down the hall. It just barely fit, but they managed to get it through the bedroom doorway at an angle.

"Probably should've opened the damn thing before bringing it in," Diego said. "If you don't want what's in it, we'll just have to haul it out again."

Asher shrugged. "I'm gonna grab some tools."

He returned from the garage with a prybar and power screwdriver. They looked brand new. His father had taken his tools with him when he'd moved out, so Mom must have made a trip to Home Depot.

"Here goes," Asher said, wedging the prybar into the slats of the crate.

"Just open it already, man. The suspense is boring me."

Jamming the bar in, Asher put his weight onto its side. The wooden planks began to separate. Diego reached into the gap with both hands and tugged as Asher repositioned the prybar. Packing peanuts rained down from the openings, revealing a large black mass covered in shrink-wrap.

"Is that an amplifier?" Diego asked.

It was too soon to tell, but Asher could see what his friend meant. The mass was rectangular with some sort of perforated material on one side. Looking closer, Asher saw it was not one piece but two identical ones. With another shove of the bar, the front panel fell to the floor, and the rest of the packing materials spilled out, revealing a third piece taller than the other two. Diego tore at the shrink-wrap, peeling it away to reveal Asher's inheritance.

"Hey," Diego said. "It's a stereo."

This time, he was right. Through the clear wrapping, Asher made out a vintage stereo system with black paneling and tall, immaculate speakers. At the top was a turntable with a glass covering, all without a single smudge. The turntable was covered by a blood-red slipmat that bore a black design of a three-headed serpent. Though hardly an audiophile, Asher knew how collectible vintage stereo equipment was, and this set appeared pristine. He tore at the remaining wrapping, Diego helping him unspool it until the stereo was revealed in full. Its midnight-black body caught the gleam of the light overhead, making it shine like a wet tarmac. Something about it struck Asher as sexy. He bit his bottom lip.

"Not bad at all," Diego said, admiring Asher's prize. "One guess what those totes are full of."

Taking the power screwdriver to the first tote, Asher removed the screws at each corner and lifted the top off. As his friend hinted, the tote was stacked with vinyl records. He pulled one out and examined the cover. The artwork created a hellish scene of skeletal forms writhing in flames with a demonic creature hovering over them. It read: *Samhain III: November-Coming Fire.* He showed it to Diego, who only shrugged, as unfamiliar with the album as Asher was. He drew two more from the tote to get a better look—Slayer's *Show No Mercy* and Venom's *Black Metal.* These, too, had demonic, horned figures on their covers.

"Your uncle was a real metalhead, huh?" Diego asked.

Asher drew others—Judas Priest's *Painkiller,* Black Sabbath's *Heaven & Hell,* Morbid Angel's *Blessed are the Sick,* Acid Mammoth's *Caravan.*

"Sure seems like it," Asher said.

"Think all thirteen of these boxes are full of records? There must be hundreds of them."

Asher recalled the pictures he'd seen of Rex in his shredded jeans and studded leather jacket, the greasy hair and unruly muttonchops, and those wild, haunted eyes.

"*This* is what my mom wanted to keep out of my reach?" Asher said. "A bunch of albums by old, geezer metal bands?"

"Back in her day, they blamed heavy metal for teenage suicides. All that devil shit, you know? Maybe that stuck with her."

Asher shook his head. "I dunno. Mom listens to rock like Nirvana and Guns N' Roses. She even saw Metallica live in ninety-seven—I know because she still has the ratty old t-shirt."

"I don't listen to much of this stuff, but I know Slayer, and it is *nothing* like Nirvana."

"I know that. I'm just saying it doesn't seem like her to get bent out of shape about *any* kind of music. She never tried to keep certain bands from me when I was growing up or anything."

"Maybe because you weren't listening to records like these."

"Yeah, maybe. She's never been the God-fearing type, though. She's not even religious."

Diego shrugged. "You'll drive yourself crazy trying to understand women—even your own mother."

"Fair enough."

They opened more totes, finding records in each one. Though Asher and Diego were unfamiliar with most of the bands, their names and the album art assured they belonged to the heavy metal genre.

Asher read off some of the band names. "Possessed, Sorcery, Pentagram … I'm sensing a theme here."

Diego smirked. "What? Cocaine?"

"That and Satan."

"I told you—it's devil music. My cousin Ximena listens to this shit. You know she's been wearing only black clothes for about five years now? Got a bunch of creepy tattoos too. Snakes and skulls. I love her, but she's a fuckin' weirdo."

"Sounds like your typical goth girl to me. But what about my Uncle Rex? I mean, am I to gather from this he was a Satanist?"

Diego shrugged again. "I'm sure plenty of people who don't worship The Devil still enjoy Judas Priest and Black Sabbath. Those are big bands that have been around for half a century."

"True. But if he was a Satanist, that could explain why he was excommunicated from the family."

"You make it sound so official. Like he was cast out of town on horseback with his hands tied behind his back."

"Honestly, I don't even know if he still lived here in town—or even in New Hampshire anymore. I don't know anything about this guy."

"Except that he took very good care of his stuff," Diego said, admiring a vinyl removed from its sleeve. "These covers are worn, but the records themselves don't have a scratch on them. If you do end up selling these, you could charge near-mint prices. And if any are out of print, you'll see a fat payday. Vinyl is a collector's market."

Asher ran his fingertips over the top of the stereo, the sleek glass and cold steel sending chills across his flesh.

"That stereo too," Diego said. "People pay out the ass for vintage equipment like that."

Asher heard his friend but wasn't fully comprehending. As his fingers danced across the stereo, his mind drifted into sublime blankness, making him fall silent.

Diego cleared his throat. "That is, if you *want* to sell it."

Asher came back to Earth. "Oh … I mean, yeah. I need the money, so …"

"Up to you, man," Diego said, as easygoing as ever. "Either way, congrats. This is a hell of a score—no pun intended."

Asher flipped through the next stack of records, revealing more images of demons, skeletons, and violence. "Want to listen to some of these?"

Diego snorted a laugh. "Nah, man. You know me. I prefer hip-hop to all that yelling and screaming."

"I'm not a metalhead either, but aren't you curious?"

"Well, maybe you should play them just to check the quality before you sell them."

16

But it was more than that. Though Asher never really knew his uncle, the man had left him a valuable collection which must have taken years, if not decades, to amass. Whatever beef Mom had with Rex was between them. Asher should at least honor the man's memory by listening to some of the music, considering it meant enough to Rex to pass it down to his only nephew. As far as quality was concerned, he was curious about the stereo. He had a small boombox to stream music but had never owned a sound system like this. It was rare for him to even see one in person. The black stereo was gorgeous and would probably sound even better than it looked.

"Anyway," Diego said, rising from the chair, "I've got to head back. Fernanda is making her salsa chicken tonight, and no way I'm missing that."

Asher forced a smile, trying not to let his envy show. Diego's relationship with Fernanda had gone right in all the ways Asher and Rebecca's had gone wrong. They'd been dating for over three years now and had moved in together last spring. Being almost thirty, Fernanda was older than Diego and his friends, but she was an attentive girlfriend with nice looks, a good job, and talent in the kitchen. Having always been a ladies' man, Diego was now firmly in Fernanda's grip but seemed overjoyed to be there. From the beginning, Asher believed the two were destined to marry and start a family together. Now that Fernanda was six months pregnant and they'd gotten engaged, it all was coming to fruition. Diego was progressing into adulthood, whereas Asher was tumbling backward. His friend never framed things that way—never boasted or bragged to feel superior—but he didn't have to. His obvious love for Fernanda said more than words ever could.

Sometimes, it was difficult for Asher not to hate him.

"Just one record?" Asher asked. "Just a song or two, from whichever album you want."

Diego shook his head. "Sorry, but I've heard enough of that twentieth-century devil rock to know it's not for me. No offense to your uncle."

"Okay," Asher said, unsure why he'd even wanted Diego to hear the music. "I'll let you know if I find anything interesting." But it all seemed interesting to him right now. "Thanks again for taking me to get it all. Let's get that beer. And I've got some cash I can give you for gas money."

Diego waved him away. "Forget about it—at least until you make a fortune selling this stuff."

"You sure?" Asher asked, mostly for show. He needed the money but felt obligated to offer it. "I have a few bucks."

"I said forget it, man. I knew what I was getting into when I bought the truck. When you own one, you become a free U-Haul for all your friends."

Diego nudged Asher to show he was just kidding around, but Asher found it difficult to be cheerful when his rotten position in life was humbling him. Though he wasn't destitute and had relatives and friends to fall back on, he couldn't help but see his lot in life as one of poverty. After dropping out of college, much to his father's chagrin, Asher had only ever worked low-paying retail jobs. He'd worked his way up to assistant store manager at Bookworms bookstore but was laid off when the small regional chain folded just a few days before Rebecca decided she didn't want to be with him anymore. Asher was not lazy, only lost. He was willing to work hard for the things he wanted but was constantly surprised with unscalable obstacles on every course he tried to pave for himself.

"C'mon, it was just a joke," Diego said, sensing Asher's shift in mood. "I don't mind giving you a ride. I'm happy to help."

Asher shrugged it off as if he weren't wallowing. "I know. Thanks, man. I appreciate it."

Diego patted his shoulder before leaving the bedroom. Asher walked him to the front door. The night wind had grown meaner, its icy touch like the burn of a freezer, causing Diego to hug himself on the way to his truck. It gave Asher a small chuckle as he closed the door, but his thoughts remained in the same grim cauldron they'd been in since Diego mentioned his girlfriend cooking dinner for him in their happy home. Depression had a way of blackening every moment.

Seeing friends should help Asher escape from his troubles, not worsen them with envy. Inheriting an expensive stereo system and hundreds of records was an unexpected windfall. He knew it should be elevating his mood more than it was and cursed himself for being incapable of joy. If he was ever going to get his shit together enough to find a job and a new girlfriend and a place to live without *his fucking mommy*, he'd have to alter his attitude.

Asher Benton needed to make a lot of changes.

Returning to his childhood bedroom, he closed the door behind him and started setting up his new stereo. He was alone now, and the house was silent and peaceful.

It wouldn't be much longer.

THREE

THERE WERE EXACTLY SIX HUNDRED and sixty-six records.

Asher had to laugh. He almost didn't believe it but didn't want to bother counting them all again. *The number of the beast,* he thought, recalling the term from *The Omen* or some similar horror film. *Nice attention to detail, Rex.* One tote even contained a few DVDs of popular horror films—*Rosemary's Baby, The Exorcist* and its sequels, *The Prophecy,* and all four films in *The Omen* series. There were more obscure movie titles as well, including *The Devil's Rain, Antrum, Häxan,* and *The Devil's Partner.* The tote with the least number of records also contained a black figurine of a winged demon with goat legs, bull horns, and human breasts. An internet search revealed its purpose as a turntable topper. Also inside were some additional mats, which Asher learned were used to shield the surface of the record to prevent damage, as well as enhance sound fidelity by dampening resonances— whatever that meant. The online forum was full of comments about this giving the listener a "warmer" sound, but Asher didn't understand how sound could have a temperature. To him, this just sounded like a pretentious way for these guys to justify spending so much money on music.

And what music it was.

Asher had put on a record while counting. The band was called Death; the album *Scream Bloody Gore*. The directness of the band's monicker and the overkill of the album's title amused him, but the songs were too heavy for his taste, with their raging guitars, pounding drums, and roaring vocals. He soon switched it out for Dio's *Holy Diver*. While still metal, the music was groovier, and the frontman could actually sing. The same went for an album with the same skull on it as the Samhain record, simply titled *Danzig*. Asher recognized one of its songs from playing *Guitar Hero* when he was a kid. He sampled records by Mötley Crüe, Lucifer, Witchfynde, and others, and the more he listened, the more he started to enjoy them in a strange way, or at least appreciate them. The songs were lyrically darker than he was used to, and sometimes the tempo was too fast, but Asher was surprised by the variety of different styles, revealing metal to have many different subcategories—hair metal, death metal, black metal, grindcore, doom, and others. Most of the records were from the '80s and '90s, but some were as old as 1970, and the newest ones had come out just last year. Each one he checked was in pristine condition, but he'd only flipped through the bulk of them to do the count, not inspecting each or even noting the album names.

Mom ran the furnace nonstop in the wintertime, and Asher worked up a sweat arranging everything, so he cracked the window to let in the morning's cold November air. With Mom at work, he didn't have to worry about the music drawing her attention. He still hadn't told her he'd picked up his inheritance. Would it relieve her to see it was just records and stereo equipment? Asher hoped so. He had to keep Rex's stuff here if he were going to sell it online.

He was tempted to keep the stereo, even though he could attach a hefty price tag to it. It was just so attractive in every possible sense. The sound was exquisite, and every bit of equipment was slick as if it were brand new. Owning something this luxurious would be a welcome change and make for one hell of a centerpiece once he got a new place. It was worth thinking about.

Tomorrow was garbage day, so Asher broke up the remains of the crate, bagged all the packing materials, and dragged the can out of the garage. The day was grayer than a gravestone, with a dampness that threatened snow. He was halfway down the driveway when he realized he was still hearing music. He'd left the window open a crack with a record spinning. Parking the can on the curb, Asher looked up and down the street. All was desolate. Everyone else had places to be. They had careers, families, lives. At least his uncle's music couldn't bother anyone.

Turning back to the house, he glanced across the street and noticed a small, black shape growing taller. It was the girl—Violet—standing up from the tree stump she'd been sitting on. Her black clothes had camouflaged her against the backdrop of the black minivan in the driveway. Asher wet his lips as she started walking toward the street, toward *him*. The closer she got, the more beautiful she appeared, a dark angel coming on as graciously as a creeping fog. Youth made her pale face a work of art.

"Hey," she said with a small wave, her hand half covered by the sleeves of her frayed sweater. She remained on the edge of her property but offered a smile. "How's it going?"

Asher struggled with what to say, not wanting to blow this first impression, certain he would.

"I'm good," he managed to get out, hoping to sound chill. "What's up? I'm Asher."

"Violet Vincent. And not much. I was just admiring your taste in music. Not everyone knows Son of Sam."

He'd already forgotten the name of the band currently playing. Luckily, she'd said it for him. "Oh, yeah. They're one of my favorites."

"Totally. Sucks that they only made two albums, but they're both bangers."

"For sure. I've got them both on vinyl." He wanted to say more but didn't know anything about Son of Sam.

"You collect vinyl?"

"I've got over six hundred records."

Her eyes went wide. "Holy shit."

"I didn't realize I'd left the window open. I'm glad the only neighbor who heard the music likes it."

"Are you kidding? I *love* it. I heard you playing Alice Cooper too. Figured I'd say hi to a fellow metalhead." Her smile was earthshattering. "Are you related to Mrs. Benton?"

"Yeah," he said, hating to admit it, hating to be talking about his mother at all right now. "I'm her son."

"Oh, okay. She's a really nice lady. Are you visiting for Thanksgiving?"

He almost said yes before coming up with a better lie. "Actually, I'll be here a while. The house I'm buying is being renovated, so I figured I'd kill two birds with one stone and stay here through the holidays to spend time with her."

"That's cool. I've seen you around the past few days. You know, it's funny, but I never would've guessed you for a metalhead." Asher was wearing an old American Eagle hoodie with gray sweatpants and house slippers, a stark contrast to how his uncle used to dress. "Not that you have to look a certain way or anything."

"Do you always dress in black?" he asked. "I couldn't even see you sitting over there."

"I just like to hang out outside when its gloomy like this. And yeah, mostly, I wear all black. Not religiously, but habitually."

"Well, it looks good on you," he said, daring to flirt a little. It annoyed him to realize he'd taken his mother's advice.

Violet looked away at the compliment, and Asher wasn't sure if it was due to bashfulness or annoyance. He hoped he hadn't turned her off. Things had been going unusually well.

"So what's your situation?" he asked to keep the conversation going.

"What do you mean?"

"You live here with your family?" He also wanted to know her age, so he found a way to ask if she were still in school without asking that. "Do you work in town?"

"Yeah," she said with a shrug of self-deprecation. "I still live at home. I'm *between jobs,* I guess you could say. Been taking classes at the community college. Just trying to find myself, you know?"

College, Asher thought. *She's at least eighteen—and legal.* The thought made his loins stir. There was a lot he'd like to do to that lithe, prime body of hers, especially after fucking the same woman for so long. Sleeping with someone else was also a surefire way to help get over an ex, something Asher desperately needed to do.

"Want to check out my record collection?" he asked.

Violet didn't give a straight answer at first. She seemed interested yet hesitant, seeing as she'd just met Asher, even if she did like his mother. But living just across the street must have given Violet a sense of security because they were in his room a few minutes later.

Side A of Son of Sam's *Into the Night* record had ended, and the stereo gave off a low, electric hum, its ON button glowing crimson. Violet looked upon it with silent awe. She marveled at the totes on the floor, squatting down to peruse the titles.

"Damn, you must have every Iron Maiden album ever made in here," she said, flipping through the collection. "Do you have the complete discoveries of other bands too?"

Asher wasn't sure. "Some but not all. Can I, um, can I get you something to drink?"

She smiled up at him from the floor, and seeing her face level with his crotch, Asher couldn't help wetting his lips, though it was Violet's mouth he was thinking of.

"No, I'm good," she said, her eyes returning to the records. "I just want to check out this killer collection you've got."

She drew one from the tote—*Rites of Black Mass* by Acheron. Asher hadn't seen this one yet, but it, too, had Satanic imagery on the cover. With most people, he would have worried about them discovering the evil theme of Uncle Rex's collection, but Violet seemed excited by it.

"I don't even know some of these bands," she said, "but now I want to hear them all."

"Want me to put something on?" he asked. She nodded emphatically, looking spooky-cute and delicious. "Which one do you want to hear first?"

"You decide. I thought I knew metal, but looking at your collection, you clearly know more than me. Introduce me to something heavy and wicked."

He didn't have the slightest idea what that would be but figured he could fake his way through it, given the records at his disposal. They were all heavy in sound and wicked in lyrical content. He pawed through them, holding up a few to ask if she was familiar with them, and when she was, he drew another.

"C'mon," she said when he held up a Cannibal Corpse record. "You're not even trying now."

"What do you mean?"

"I know who Cannibal fucking Corpse is," she said with a giggle. "I mean, they're only one of the most famous death metal bands of all time. Give me some credit."

"*This* is too mainstream?" he asked, pointing to the grotesque cover art of zombies ripping a dead baby from a woman's eviscerated carcass.

"You might as well be showing me Marlyn Manson or Rob Zombie," Violet said. "C'mon, give me some of the obscure stuff. Introduce me to something really dark."

He nodded, still faking his way through. "Okay. The Cannibal Corpse album was just a test—to see if you're ready."

Asher pawed through the next tote, hoping luck would be on his side for once, but deep down, he knew he was blowing this first impression just as he suspected he would. That he was a heavy metal novice would soon be obvious to Violet, and then she would label him a poser, even if she were too polite to say it to his face. He would cease being cool and interesting to her, and she would never come over again. She'd be just another woman laughing at him like all the others.

The sound of a cowbell jarred Asher out of his self-deprecating thoughts. Violet reached into her pocket and withdrew her phone, the cowbell clanging as she received another text message.

"Shit," she said, reading the message. "My mom's asking where I am. I told her I'd be in the front yard." She got to her feet. "I'd better get going."

Asher deflated. "Do you have to?"

"She's not a controlling mom, if that's what you're suggesting. But she does worry about me like I'm still fourteen."

"I wasn't suggesting she—"

"My dad must be wondering where I am too, then. It's not like he'll be mad or anything. He just watches cable news too much, and my mom's true crime podcasts don't help. They get anxious is all."

Violet was out of the bedroom before Asher could even get to his feet. He followed her down the hall, her scent wafting back at him like a witch's love potion. He admired her petite form from the back, imagining grabbing her, bending her, entering her. Erotic daydreams raked across the hemisphere of his brain—Violet's hair between his clutching fingers, one pale ass cheek between his teeth, his semen slick upon the girl's cherub face.

"Maybe we could get together later," Asher dared to suggest.

She stopped at the front door. "I have plans. But hey, this'll give you time to dig through your collection and find me something good—or evil, I guess I should say." She opened the door before he could do it for her. Smiling, Violet gave him the horns salute, a hand gesture synonymous with heavy metal. "Rock on."

Then she was gone.

Asher went to the bathroom, locked the door, and drew his mother's body lotion from the cabinet. It'd been a while since he'd masturbated, and the fresh images of Violet Vincent added fuel to his fantasies, making him cum quicker than usual. As sperm channeled out of him, Asher imagined it gushing down Violet's throat while she looked up at him with those enchantress eyes. It was still a possibility. She'd suggested she'd be back.

Washing up, Asher looked at his reflection in the mirror with a modicum of shame—not for jacking off but for not getting further with Violet while she was still there. It's always a delicate dance when a man gets a woman alone. Most women want to feel safe and secure, so a man can't move too fast, but if he doesn't attempt intimacy, she might think he isn't interested or, worse yet, that he's not manly enough to make the first move. Some women want a man to dominate them, to *do* rather than *ask*. Asher knew this but sometimes struggled to find the right balance, especially in these sensitive times when making any kind of move on a woman was a dangerous gamble. But mostly, it was the sting of Rebecca's rejection that had chiseled away at his confidence. He knew this too but just wasn't sure what to do about it.

Returning to the bedroom, he sat on the floor with the totes, determined to find that rare record that would make Violet Vincent squeal. She'd given him a key to her lock—now he just had to find it.

He pushed aside the bands he'd heard of, going for ones Uncle Rex only had one or two albums by because, as with Son of Sam, it probably meant the band had a limited number of recordings. These would be the more obscure bands. Whenever Asher thought he'd selected something with esoteric appeal, he researched the band online to get a sense of their history and following. He discarded any bands that were still active. If finding their merchandise was easy, the bands were disqualified. If they had large social media profiles—even just fan pages—Asher knew Violet would just roll her eyes when presented with their music. This was his one chance to impress the girl. He had to be thorough and selective.

Searching through so many records caused all the scary artwork to lose its effect. Desensitized to such imagery, the horned demons and mutilated corpses failed to grab Asher's attention. It wasn't until he came across a blank, black slate of an album cover that his curiosity was triggered. He drew it from the tote for a closer look. Both the front and back were entirely black. Asher looked at the spine. There were words printed on it—black letters on the black backdrop, difficult to read. On either side of the words were red inverted crosses. He raised the spine to the light until the letters caught the glare, revealing the title.

Music to Sacrifice Virgins To.

Asher chuckled. These words seemed to apply to his uncle's entire music collection, but that someone had given this name to their album was pretty goddamned crazy. It seemed like deliberate black comedy. Perhaps one of these death metal bands decided on it as a self-deprecating joke on the entire genre.

Drawing the record from the sleeve, Asher deftly turned it between his fingers. The sticker at the record's center was blood red with the image of a black goat's head inside a pentagram. An inverted cross sat in the center of the goat's forehead. Surrounding the image in a perfect circle were the same words: *Music to Sacrifice Virgins To.* It seemed to be the name of the album, but who was the band? Was it a compilation? He tugged the inner sleeve from the cover, but it was just plain, black paper. No text or images. No record label. Not even any copyright information.

"Oh, this is promising," Asher said to himself.

An internet search offered no explanation. There were plenty of articles on the history of human sacrifice and occult hymns, but no mention of an album with this name. He could not find it on any music streaming service nor locate a physical copy to purchase, not even a used one. The album was as lost as a recording could get. Violet would not have heard of it because *no one had.*

Asher placed the record on the turntable and set the needle.

It began with the sound of wind and thunder, with a lone church bell ringing slowly—very Black Sabbath-like, from what he knew of them. As the wind sound grew louder like an oncoming storm, chanting voices played in reverse rose from beneath the surface and bounced from speaker to speaker in a haunting cycle of stereo sound. Just when Asher thought this was a Halloween sound effect record, the first musical note chimed in, if it could be called that. The heavy drone of an electric guitar made the walls tremble. It was a retro riff, slowly played with a deepness beneath it. The guitar went on solo for several minutes in a crunchy, doom-laden dirge before the first snap of snare drum was heard, followed by steady percussion and rumbling bass. Though it had a sinister edge, it didn't sound much different from Uncle Rex's other music. The song continued without any vocals other than the reversed chanting that came and went as if playing hide-and-seek with the listener.

After several minutes of this, Asher took another look at the record and noticed there were no lines on its surface to mark where one song ended and another began. Side A's track was an ongoing piece, but as it played on, the melody changed, more like one song segueing into another without a break. There was groove to it now, and he found himself nodding his head to the distorted rhythm. It was like loud ambience in a way, a song that didn't engage the listener as much as it hypnotized. Asher sort of liked it, much to his surprise. Was he really developing a taste for heavy metal?

His bedroom door came open, giving him a start.

Mom stood in the doorway, her brow furrowed, lips pale. Asher turned the volume all the way down. The floor around him was decorated with the Satanic metal albums, fanned out like magazines in a waiting room, images of demons, goats, and ritualistic murder welcoming his mother in a hellish tableau.

"Hey, Ma," Asher said, rising to greet her.

His mother scanned the records, then stared at the stereo with wide eyes.

"Were you knocking long?" Asher asked. "The music was probably too loud for me to—"

"Rex," she muttered, as if the name might choke her. "My fucking brother left this shit to you. I knew it would be this. I just knew it."

Asher tried to shrug it off. "It's just records and a stereo. No big deal."

"No." Her gaze bore into him. "It's a *huge* deal."

"Okay …"

"I want this devil shit out of my house, Asher. I want it gone—*now.*"

"Since when are you so religious?"

"I'm not. I don't have to be to know evil when I see—or hear it."

Asher smirked. "It's just music. These singers aren't warlocks, Ma, they're just playing a role in their songs. Don't you think you're overreacting?"

"There's no such thing as overreacting where Rex is concerned."

"But you like some heavy metal too—"

"Damn it, Asher! It's not about the music. Not exactly. It's much more than that. It's a collective thing."

"What? You mean, like, the collection of records he left me?"

She shook her head. "You just don't understand."

"Then explain it to me. I mean, since when are you some censor of the arts?"

"It's not the art and not the music. It's Rex and everything that comes with him." Her face had flushed with anger, but now her eyes grew wet with something like fear. She crossed her arms under her new breasts. "I want all these records and that goddamned stereo out of here."

Asher glowered. "And what about what I want, Ma? Huh? I mean, shit, you know I'm broke. Now look, I've been researching, and some of these albums are worth a lot of money. There's out-of-print stuff and rare bootlegs and live show recordings. I've got one by Warzwolf worth thousands and a Paradoxx one worth even more."

"Stop it, Asher."

"No, I'm serious. Look it up."

"That's not what I meant. I mean stop talking about Rex's collection."

"But why? What's the big problem? I know you two didn't get along, but that shouldn't affect my inheritance."

"*Didn't get along?*" She scoffed. "You have no idea how much you're understating it."

"Maybe because you refuse to tell me anything."

Mom shook her head and wiped a tear away.

"What is it?" Asher asked. "Do you think I won't be able to understand or that I won't believe you?"

She swallowed hard. "Both."

A cold silence hung between them then. Finally, Asher broke it.

"Ma, just let me hold on to this stuff long enough to sell the bulk of it, okay? If I can just sell ten of the rarer records, I'll have more than enough money to move out. Then you'll never have to hear them ever again."

"I don't want to hear them *now.*"

"Okay, fine. I'm only playing them to make sure there's no damage before I list them for sale online. I can do it when you're not home or buy some headphones."

His mother wouldn't look at him. Her voice was barely above a whisper. "What was that one you were playing when I came in?"

Something told Asher he shouldn't tell her the truth. With a name like *Music to Sacrifice Virgins To*, the album would only underline her point.

"It's just Black Sabbath," he lied.

She shook her head again. "No it isn't."

"Hey, it's not like 'Iron Man' or 'Paranoid.' It's one of those rare albums I was talking about. Much more obscure than any of their hits you might know."

"I know far more than just their hits, and that was *not* Black Sabbath."

"How would you know if you've never heard it before?"

Her eyes flashed. "Because I think *I have* heard it before."

Asher tried not to look in the direction of the turntable. The record was still on it, and Mom could easily walk over to the stereo to look. Instead, she'd given him a chance to be honest with her, and he'd chosen to deceive. How much did she know about *Music to Sacrifice Virgins To?* Should he ask her about it?

"Look, Ma," he said, "I don't fully understand why you're getting so heated, but I accept it, okay? Like I said, I'm gonna sell all of this off, I promise. Just give me some time. I swear you won't have to hear another note." He gave her a moment to respond, but she didn't. Growing irritated, Asher grimaced. "I'm not just gonna throw away stuff this valuable! It's my inheritance. I've a right to it. I know this is your house, so if you want me to see if I can stay with one of my friends for a while instead ..."

"No. I'd rather you be here where I can at least ..." She sighed instead of finishing the thought. "Besides, you've nowhere else to go. If you did, you never would've come home."

Though Asher didn't want to hear it, his mother was right, and that irked him most of all. He felt on the verge of a tantrum, like he really was a teenager again. Dealing with his mother's passive aggression always left him petulant, but being back in his old room made it even worse. He was about to tell her off, but she stepped out as if accepting defeat.

"You're all grown up now," she said. "You must choose your own path. I can't make this decision for you. Only you can decide what things in life you'll reject and which ones you'll allow in. But you're still my son. I'll always want to protect you, even if it's from yourself."

She'd said something similar before, but Asher still wasn't sure what she was talking about. But he also didn't want to argue any further.

"You've got one week to get it all out of here," Mom said, though she did not threaten any consequences. "One week and that's it."

Taking a deep breath, Mom walked down the hall with her back to her son as if she could no longer bear to look at him. Asher let her go, though he still wanted to understand her strong feelings about all of this. Had she really heard *Music to Sacrifice Virgins To* before, or had she been mistaken? He wanted to know how their relatives had responded to the news of a death in the family. Most of all, he wanted to know about his uncle, Rex Von Spades, and what had drawn the man to Satan.

FOUR

"THIS IS SERIOUSLY HEAVY," VIOLET said as the record spun on.

She didn't know just how right she was. For Asher, *Music to Sacrifice Virgins To* was not just heavy but *heavier* the second time around. The music was the same yet somehow different, the guitars more gravelly, the backwards chants more snarling and lustful.

"I'm not even sure how to the classify this," Violet added. "Doom metal meets black metal with something else I can't quite identify. But I kinda like it."

Asher smiled knowingly, pleased to have impressed her, but more than anything else, he was just glad to have gotten her back in his bedroom again, especially with Mom working late. It was early evening, but with the sun going down by five now, darkness had fallen in full, which helped set the mood. Asher had picked up a red party bulb to enhance the atmosphere, and it bathed the room in a crimson glow like a darkroom, but he imagined it more like a scene from a surrealist horror film. He and Violet sat on the floor together with their backs to the bedframe. Her flesh was pink under the bulb. Something about that made Asher desire her even more.

While at the store, he'd also picked up a pair of black jeans to go with his one black shirt, hoping to better look the part. Violet wore a black hooded dress with a thick, black leather belt around her waist. The skirt only came down to her thighs, revealing stockings with a spiderweb pattern, topped off with her studded boots. She wore black lipstick and heavy eyeshadow that turned her eyes into smoky caverns. When she leaned forward to look through records, he noticed gray shapes on the spine of her dress—a full moon with crescent moons on either side, a donut-shape with another crescent moon on its side above the donut, and a series of spirals shaped like fidget spinners.

"What're these?" he asked, touching her back with one finger and dragging it down slowly, unsure where he'd gotten the confidence.

She did not recoil from his touch. "They're symbols. There's the triple moon, the horned god, and the triple spiral."

"Horned God? You mean The Devil?"

"No. Common misconception. They're Wiccan symbols. The Horned God is one of the deities but not an evil one. Like most things in Wicca, he represents nature. He's the lifeforce of the wilderness and all its creatures. But yeah, he kind of looks like The Devil, what with the horns and everything."

"So you're Wiccan, then?"

"Well, sort of. I mean, I celebrate Mother Earth, just not in some lame hippie way. Wicca is complicated. I've met with others in the local group, and not every Wiccan believes the same things. But I like the ideas behind it and practice the lifestyle."

"So … witchcraft?"

She smirked. "In a Stevie Nicks sort of way. Don't worry, I don't have a cauldron or fly on a broom. I don't think I have any magical powers. I just enjoy tarot cards, horoscopes, and making moon water—stuff like that."

"I see."

"It's no big deal, Asher. I just believe you have to find the magic in life."

They locked eyes then, and while Asher normally would have gone hollow in the stomach when this happened with such a pretty girl, instead he felt a sudden surge of cocksure desire. That he was broke and living in his childhood bedroom completely left his mind, and he suddenly felt masculine for the first time in months. When he scooted closer to Violet, the music intensified like it was his own personal soundtrack, cheering him on. He placed his hand on her bare knee. Violet flinched a little but giggled it off, laughing at herself, not at him. She seemed a little flustered, but Asher did not let that deter him. He inched closer, titling his head so their faces were inches apart.

Violet looked away. "This music is tripping me out. I don't know … it's like …"

He put two fingers beneath her chin and turned her face toward his. The guitars grumbled as the backwards choir screamed in harmony. Asher's tongue entered Violet's mouth, and she reluctantly accepted him, her leg trembling beneath his grip as he slid it up her thigh without breeching the underside of the skirt—yet. Already, an erection was pressing against his fly. The smell of her hair, the taste of her saliva, and the velvet of her flesh made his blood pulse hot. When he breathed on her neck, Violet's skin rippled with goosebumps.

"I don't usually …" Violet said, trailing off into heavy breaths as Asher's fingers climbed her inner thigh. "That feels so …"

The music thrummed and wailed, growing impossibly loud. The bass shook Asher's bones. Kissing Violet, he guided her to the floor, and she arched her back so he could slide her panties off. Her eyes were closed, mouth open, hot breaths escaping her as he slid the first finger in. Though part of him was amazed he'd gotten so far so fast with such a lovely creature, the newfound confidence flooded him with testosterone. He curled one finger inside of Violet until she was sopping wet, then went at her with two.

The alluring smell of her tight pussy filled the air between them. Asher began kissing her inner thigh. The flesh made him carnivorous, as if he could devour the girl like a rare steak. He bit her legs gently, and when she responded with moans, he bit a little harder. He'd never chewed on Rebecca like this, nor any other girl. Horniness had struck him like a possession. He allowed it complete control of his body as he lowered his head between Violet's thighs until his mouth pressed to her labia. Asher could almost feel them pulse, almost hear the girl's blood redirecting even above the roar of the music. Though these sensations were peculiar, he welcomed them.

Violet shuddered with his tongue against her clitoris, his fingers curling deeper within her while her fingers entered his hair. She moaned loudly, but as he went down on her, Asher began hearing other voices coming through the speakers. These weren't played backwards, and they weren't singing. Beneath the music, there was a deep, distorted voice overlapped by a high, feminine one, speaking in unison to say the same thing.

"Behold the return of Astaroth ... the resurrection of Beelzebub, the dark one ... the rise of The Morning Star, herald of the dawn."

Violet's body went taut as she began to climax. She bucked like a mad bull, legs gripping Asher's skull. He felt as if she might break his neck, but he did not stop pleasuring her. Her orgasm empowered him. Asher couldn't recall ever making Rebecca quake like this. It wasn't that Violet came easier; it was as if he'd acquired new abilities as a lover. He could anticipate what her nerve endings needed at each moment to take her to the edge of ecstasy, then shove her over it with intense force.

The album's messages continued. *"In the glorious name of Satan, ruler of the Earth, pain of the world, we summon the forces of The Prince of Darkness so the trinity may ascend once more."*

Asher undid his jeans and entered Violet in a sudden thrust that shook her. There was no hesitation, no talk of condoms or other contraception. There was only the raw and screaming, irrefutable impulse to fuck her as hard as he could. He pulled her hair, manhandled her breasts, and placed his hand on her throat. He'd never been so rough while making love, even though he'd fantasized about it and secretly enjoyed rough-sex porn. He'd been too apprehensive to make moves like this, especially with a new lover, and Rebecca hadn't encouraged him to dominate her the way he was now dominating the girl next door.

"From the ninth circle ... from the pit of sulfur ... from the blood pool of the virgin ..."

There was a grunt and a wheeze. Violet's face was like a beet. Asher realized he was choking her now, but he didn't stop. Her eyes watered and the veins in her neck stood out, but still, she did not resist him. Asher's cock felt forged in iron, a rock-hard erection he pummeled her insides with, their sex going on for nearly forty minutes with the music somehow never stopping. Violet shuddered in orgasm after orgasm, and for once in his life, Asher didn't cum until he decided he was ready to. He was that in control of his body, that attuned with his flesh. The music grew more distorted as he climaxed inside of Violet, the sinister voices breaking through the noise in direct messages.

"You belong to your father, The Devil, and you want to carry out your father's desires."

FIVE

"I'M TELLING YOU, DUDE, IT was like a fucking drug the way the music affected us," Asher said as he and Diego brought beers to a pool table at Kirby's Place bar and billiards. "I mean, I've had great sex before, but this was on another level. This was *wild* in the true sense of the word."

Diego started racking the balls. "It's always crazy when you have sex with someone new after the end of a long relationship."

"No, this was more than that. The music … it, like, *fueled* our fucking."

"I never took you for one of those guys who puts on music in the bedroom," Diego teased.

"That's not how it happened. Like I told you, this chick came over to listen to the records, and we just ended up fucking, just like that. I mean, it was only the second time we'd hung out. I made a move, then another, then another. She just submitted to me completely. It was so fucking hot. And you should see this chick, man. A seriously cute goth girl. Young and petite. Pussy tighter than a nun's."

Diego chuckled. "You're an absolute pig."

"Not a pig—a man. Feels so good to be one again."

"What're you talking about? You never stopped being one."

"Rebecca made me feel like half a man at best."

"That's on her, not you. You were always a man, Asher."

"Not like this. Not like I was last night. Seriously, I fucked this chick better than I've ever fucked anybody. Made her scream and thrash. I bit her, manhandled her—even choked her—and she took it all like a good girl."

"You're a maniac," his friend said. "How old did you say this girl was again?"

"Nineteen."

Still smiling, Diego shook his head. "You are bobsledding straight to Hell."

His choice of words gave Asher pause. Diego offered to let him break, but Asher told him to go ahead. Diego knocked the cueball into the pyramid, cracking it apart. Kirby's Place was close to empty tonight. Asher found its darkness more inviting than usual.

"Look, she's legal," Asher said. "I'm not banging jailbait here. But the great thing is she looks like jailbait. She's got the beauty of youth, and her smallness makes her look even younger than she is."

Diego gave him a curious look. "Shit, man, just how young do you want your girlfriends to be?"

Asher felt suddenly cornered. He'd thought his best friend would be excited for him, perhaps even envious. He wanted to celebrate a victorious sexual conquest, but Diego seemed to want to shame him for his preferences. Instead of taking his turn at the pool table, Asher stood holding his cue stick, staring at Diego.

"She's only six years younger than I am," Asher said. "You don't have to come at me like I'm some kind of pedo."

Diego seemed caught off guard by the comment. "Hey, nobody's saying that. I was just bustin' balls."

"You're just jealous I nailed such a hot piece of trim."

"How could I be? I haven't even seen her yet! Besides, I'm perfectly happy with the relationship I'm in."

"Oh, that's right. How could I forget? You and Fernanda have the perfect little love life. You made a point of throwing that in my face the whole time my relationship with Rebecca was disintegrating."

"Whoa, whoa, whoa," Diego said as he put his cue stick aside.

"C'mon, man, I never did that and I'm not doing it now. I'm just saying I'm not jealous. I'm happy with my girl, and I'm happy for you that you've found someone new, okay?"

Still wanting to celebrate, Asher decided to let it go. He sunk a striped ball into the side pocket. "It's about time things started going my way. First, I get this inheritance from my uncle, and now there's Violet. And the crazy part is one led to the other. The music brought us together."

"So are you going to tell her now that you're not really a metalhead, or are you going to keep going along with it?"

With a loud crack, Asher sunk another ball. "Who says I'm not a metalhead? Maybe I've grown to like Rex's records."

"Seriously? Is that why you're dressed in all black? You never did before and never really liked metal either. You always listened to pop and alternative—"

"Am I not permitted to grow as a human being? You used to love *Ninja Turtles*, but you don't anymore, right? Maybe I've moved on from all that commercial radio garbage and found myself some real music."

Diego shrugged. "If you say so."

"I *do* say so. Don't tell me what I like and don't like."

"I don't know why you're being so hostile, man. I don't give a shit if you want to listen to heavy metal, okay? Rock your brains out."

"You don't understand," Asher said, realizing how true that was. "You don't get it because you haven't heard it."

"I told you my cousin Ximena plays all that shit."

"She may like metal, but there's no way she has stuff like this. Rex's collection has rare records you just can't find anywhere, not even to stream. I've got this one you really need to check out, man, the same one I fucked Violet to. I don't even know how to describe it. It's just so ... *powerful*."

"If you say so. Now are we playing pool here or not?"

Asher bent over the table and sent another ball into the side pocket, playing better than he ever had before. Diego wasn't getting what he was saying, but Asher was confident he would soon enough, once *Music to Sacrifice Virgins To* entered his ear canals.

"My luck is finally turning around," Asher said as he sunk a ball into the corner pocket. "And it's all thanks to my dead uncle's devil music." Diego started to say something to the contrary but was cut off by the sound of the cue ball sending another striped one home.

"I'm gonna make a fortune off some of these records, but I'm keeping a lot of them, along with the stereo. I don't give a fuck if my mom likes it or not. I'm tired of that bitch."

Asher had already explained to Diego about Mom's aversion to anything her brother had owned but hadn't disclosed what she'd said about the man being evil. It sounded too ludicrous, especially with her not going into details or giving any examples of Rex's evil deeds. Having known her for so long, Diego cared for Mom. Asher knew that, so he hadn't been surprised when Diego told him to take her feelings into account, despite them making no sense. He was starting to wonder if Diego always cowed to whatever women wanted. Asher had been like that with Rebecca. He'd be damned if he'd let any woman beat him down like that again.

Finally, Asher missed a shot, and Diego got a chance to play. He sank two before it was Asher's turn again. Normally, Diego won more often than Asher did, but today, Asher beat him three games in a row. To celebrate his victory, he went to the jukebox, looking for some heavy metal. It'd been hours since he'd heard any and felt the craving rising. Of course, the poolhall didn't have the selection Rex did, so Asher had to settle for AC/DC's "Highway to Hell." It was hard rock rather than metal, but at least it had the right attitude.

"How about one more game?" Diego asked.

"No way. Violet gets home from class soon, and I'm picking her up. You'll just have to live with your bitter defeat."

"He wins one time and suddenly thinks he's Tom Brady."

"Tom Brady played football, not billiards," Asher said as he started toward the door. "But like him, I am a winner, and I plan to stay one."

His friend didn't reply to this, but Asher didn't care for the look on Diego's face. Something about his expression implied mockery, as if he thought Asher was being conceited, that his newfound confidence was unwarranted or undeserved. He almost said something but didn't want to waste time on Diego when Violet awaited. Just knowing he was going to pick her up made his scrotum tighten. Asher curled his fingers, imagining the girl's throat in his grip. He was going to make her do dirty things for him tonight.

Diego stayed behind to play pool against himself. Once in his car, Asher streamed a death metal playlist he'd found online, bobbing his head to the fierce music. He really was beginning to dig it—a lot. He didn't just like it because of Violet either, though it made things easier now that he wouldn't have to fake being into metal. Having already dominated the girl sexually, Asher no longer felt the need to like what she liked to win her over. Sometimes, a new obsession just came to him, and he had no choice but to ride on through until it eased off or left him completely. He'd been that way before with hockey, World War II movies, craft beers, and—when he was very young—fire. Asher had grown up insisting he'd become a fireman one day and collected pictures from newspapers of burning buildings and automobiles. The sound of a passing firetruck's siren still got his fur up. A newfound appreciation for heavy metal was becoming another obsession, his next fire, and like the flames he'd once collected in photos, Rex's records weren't going to lose their glow anytime soon.

On the way to Violet's house, he stopped at the package store for a bottle of whiskey to go with the bag of weed in the glovebox. Located on a slow street, the old store was a standalone building in a small lot of crumbling gravel. The only other car was parked on the far side of the store, suggesting it belonged to the old man working the counter. Getting back in his Honda, Asher unscrewed the cap on the whiskey and took a swig. A deep chill had moved in, the sun hidden behind a thick veil of grayness, but the booze would warm his blood. Putting the car in reverse, the death metal came screaming back through the speakers, the rapid percussion encouraging him to peel out. He mashed the gas pedal to the floorboard, and the car swung wide. Popping it into drive, he hit the gas again—*hard*—and the Honda lunged over the curb and into the street, where something came into view too late.

It happened so quickly Asher hadn't even seen what whizzed past the dead bushes flanking the lot's entrance. He'd been too busy headbanging and turning up the volume. If not for the sudden thud, he might not have noticed it at all. The car shuddered slightly from the impact. Having always loved dogs, Asher hoped he'd hit a possum instead or even a cat—anything to not have to relive the death of Daisy, the family dog buried in his mother's backyard. Whatever he'd hit had fallen off the driver's side of the vehicle, so Asher rode the brake and rolled down the window for a look.

The child wasn't dead.

Though the front wheel of his bicycle was bent from the collision, it seemed the boy had been catapulted by the impact rather than struck by the bumper. He was on his hands and knees. Loose gravel was peppered into the wounds on his palms, and his jeans were torn around the kneecaps. He was looking straight down at the ground, his helmet askew, one sneaker halfway off. Instead of crying, the boy was breathing heavy, as if on the verge of hyperventilating. Asher guessed him to be anywhere between seven and ten years old.

"Fucking Christ," Asher hissed.

He peered up and down the vacant street, hearing nothing. The kid's parents weren't coming around the corner. No other kids pedaled behind him. The shopkeeper hadn't come out of the liquor store. They were alone.

"Mommy ..." the little boy whimpered, the first tears falling. "I want my mommy."

"Yeah?" Asher said. "Then stay home."

He hit the gas again, and pebbles launched from his tires, decorating the child as he shivered in the street. The boy was sobbing with his eyes closed now, so Asher didn't worry about the little shit getting his license plate as he sped off. Any kid who rides out in front of a car probably wasn't smart enough to think to get the number to begin with.

If Asher had accidentally struck this child two days ago, he would have stopped, but too much had changed in less than forty-eight hours. He'd decided to take and do what he wanted from now on. He took Violet's body. He kept his inheritance despite his mother's objections. For once, he was putting his own needs first and wasn't about to let some dumb little shit ruin his day just because he didn't know how to look both ways when he rode his fucking bike. That Asher had been distracted was irrelevant. He was through apologizing to people, finished being the nice guy who finished last. No more would he put the needs of others before his own. Such behavior had never sat right with him, but now, he was finally bold enough to not conform to society's rules and standards.

This was Asher Benton's time. There was weed to smoke, booze to drink, a hot girl to fuck, and a lot of music to listen to. He wasn't going to put any of that off to help some rugrat with skinned knees. It wasn't his fault the boy got hit, and he didn't want to stick around just so someone could tell him it was. Let the kid walk his busted bike home. Maybe he'd learn a lesson, something his parents obviously failed at teaching.

Asher doubted the old store had security cameras, but even if they did, the tall hedges would have blocked the view of the accident. The man running the counter was elderly, wearing glasses on a chain around his neck. He'd not put them on during their transaction, so it was doubtful he could give the cops a good description of Asher, and the kid had been half blinded by his own tears. Asher wondered if he should be more concerned, but he simply wasn't. Not about getting caught for the hit and run. Not for the safety of the child either. All he was concerned about was getting to Violet as soon as possible. The quicker he picked her up, the quicker his cock would be jack-hammering her guts and his hands would be around that pretty white throat.

He took another swig of whiskey and cranked up the volume.

SIX

A MIDDLE-AGED WOMAN ANSWERED the door.

Like Violet, she was a natural blonde, her eyebrows so white they were almost translucent. She was slender yet small, and though she had at least twenty years on Asher, he found her attractive.

"You must be Elizabeth's boy," she said, greeting him with a polite smile, though her eyes seemed to study him. "Asher?"

"That's right. You must be Violet's sister."

She smiled at his corny compliment. "Her mother, thank you. My name's Melissa. Violet's just upstairs getting changed. Why don't you come inside?"

As she stepped aside to allow him entry, Asher snuck a glance down her V-neck sweater at the woman's small breasts. She wore a silver cross necklace. Was that why Violet had chosen Wicca, as a rebellion against her parents' Christianity? Was she one of those teenage girls who was always doing whatever she could to be contrary to her parents? Was that why Asher was here?

"You seem like a young man past his college years," Melissa said as they entered the den. "How old are you?"

He didn't appreciate how direct she was being but let it slide for now. "I'm twenty-five."

"You know my daughter's nineteen, right?"

"I do. Is that a problem?"

"Not for her, apparently. You know, when you're my age, six years difference doesn't mean much either way, but when you're a teenage girl, an older man can steer you in a whole new direction. They have more experience, making them seem wiser even if they aren't."

Asher didn't know how to take that. "Okay."

She narrowed her eyes. "What I'm saying is, Violet is grown-up enough to date who she chooses, but I'm still her mother and want to look out for her."

"You sound like my mom."

"Well, Elizabeth has always been a good neighbor. My husband and I both like her. That's why I'm going to give her son the benefit of the doubt."

"Okay."

Melissa seemed dissatisfied with his monosyllabic replies. "Do you have anything you'd like to say? Anything to ask me?"

He shrugged. "No."

"Fine."

She walked toward the stairwell and called up to her daughter. There was another voice then, female but younger, coming from the upper landing. "She's in the bathroom!" Her words were followed by electronic beeps.

"Callie," Melissa said, "you'd better be working on your homework and not playing that video game again."

Callie didn't reply, but the beeps continued. Melissa headed up the stairs, leaving Asher alone on the bottom floor. The minivan wasn't in the driveway, so he figured the man of the house was at work. Good. Asher didn't need to go through the same rigmarole with him. He was too old to play the respectful young man meeting the parents. Passive niceties were a waste of time. He was only here to fuck their daughter.

Violet came bounding down the stairs with a wide smile. She wore tight black jeans with a worn, dark-gray sweater with a pattern of bats. A heavy scarf surrounded her neck like a 16th century ruff. Looking up at him, her eyes grew starry and adoring.

"Hey," she said, seeming almost bashful.

"Hey, baby."

He put his hands on her hips and brought her in for a kiss, sliding his tongue into her mouth. Then his hands moved around to cup her buttocks.

A throat cleared. Still kissing Violet, Asher opened his eyes to see her mother halfway down the stairs, glowering with her arms crossed.

"Excuse me," she said, agitated. "I'll thank you to not grope my daughter, especially not right in front of me."

Asher tried to pull back, but Violet only kissed him deeper. She was proving a point.

"Violet!" her mother said. "I won't have you disrespecting me. Not in this house."

Violet backed off and rolled her eyes. "Okay, fine, whatever." She placed her palms on Asher's chest. "You ready to go, babe?"

"You know it," he said.

They went to the door without saying goodbye to Melissa. The woman's face was taut with insult, but she said no more. Violet grabbed her coat and followed behind Asher like a puppy, practically skipping down to his Honda. Once they were in the car, she unfurled her scarf.

"You've got to be more careful," she told him, revealing the handprint on her neck. "I bruise easy, being so pale."

There was a time he would have apologized for leaving marks on a woman, but that part of his life was behind him.

"If I want to choke you, then I will," he said. "Besides, you loved it."

She blushed. "Yeah, but you don't know my parents."

"And I don't wish to."

"I kept it hidden by wearing my turtleneck."

"That's my good girl."

He reached for her breast, and when he found the nipple, he pinched it. Violet bit her bottom lip, making a squeaky Minnie Mouse sound. As he applied more pressure, she took shallow breaths to handle the pain. It reminded him of the boy he'd left crying in the street. Somehow, that only made him more excited to fuck.

As they drove out of the neighborhood, Asher put the music back on and offered Violet the whiskey bottle. She took a sip, grinning up at him from the passenger seat like a fangirl in the front row of a concert.

"Last night was amazing," she said. "At first, I didn't think I was ready for … I mean, I've never slept with a guy that soon. Actually, you're only my second lover. The only other guy I've slept with is my ex, Bryce. We lost our virginity to each other in high school and had plenty of sex during our eleven months together, but it was nothing like the sex I had with you last night."

"That's 'cause you're fucking a real man now."

She giggled. "I guess so. I mean … I never really *came* before. Not like I did with you."

Hearing this, Asher felt not just pride but power. He put his arm around the girl and played with her hair.

"Did you ever suck Bryce's cock?" he asked.

Caught off guard, Violet stammered. "Um … I mean, yeah … sometimes, as foreplay."

"But never a complete blowjob?"

"Well, like, for his birthday."

"So it was only for special occasions?"

"I just never really liked doing it. I always felt like I was choking."

"But you like it when a man chokes you."

"Not *like that*. It was more of a gagging thing. I felt like I was going to puke sometimes."

Asher slowed for a red light and turned to look her in the eye. "You're going to suck my cock."

Violet looked away. "Okay. I mean, sure. You went down on me, so later, I'll—"

"You're going to do it right now."

Her face flushed. "You mean …"

"You're going to suck my cock whenever and wherever I tell you to."

"But we're in public." She smiled at him out of nervousness. "Can't it wait until we're somewhere more comfortable."

He applied pressure to the back of her neck, pulling her closer to him, guiding her downward. "Violet, unzip my fly, take my dick out, and start sucking."

She did as she was told. Asher drove on, instructing her when to twirl her tongue and when to take him in deeper. The sludge metal of Belzebong ended to be followed by the thrash metal of Megadeth, and the fast tempo made him accelerate as he took them down the old state road. He gripped the back of Violet's skull and started fucking her mouth, and though she struggled and gagged, she kept his dick between her lips until she finally had to come up for air. Asher gave her time for just one inhale before pushing her down again.

"Don't cum in my mouth, okay?" she asked, her meekness making him harder.

They drove deeper through the wooded area, and when Asher started cumming, he held Violet's head down, unloading into her small, hot mouth. She whimpered but did not resist him, even as she gagged on semen.

"Don't spit it out," he told her, calm yet firm. "Swallow it. All of it."

As she gulped down his seed, Asher patted the girl's head gently, a warm rush of power filling his chest. He'd never been so demanding with a woman before, never gone against their wishes sexually or pushed the boundaries of consent. Now, he realized just how much time he'd wasted being so kind to the opposite sex. No matter what women said, *this* was what they wanted—a man to dominate them. As much as they claimed men were pigs and badmouthed them for behaving like assholes, that was exactly what women wanted men to be, even if they couldn't face it. Nice guys didn't fuck them hard enough, and deep down, women knew it, which was why the men who treated them good got ignored, rejected, taken advantage of, and cheated on. Every woman was either broken or waiting to be broken. Asher wasn't sure how exactly this revelation had come to him, but he accepted it as absolute truth.

Some semen remained on his stomach when Violet finally took his dick out of her mouth. He had her lick that up too. She grimaced a little but obeyed. When he finally let her sit upright, a drop of cum was dangling from her nostril. Oblivious, she sniffed it up before he could say anything.

The nature preserve was located on protected land, a scenic stretch of New England wilderness right out of a postcard. A month ago, the trees were the color of flames, but now the leaves had fallen to be carried off by indifferent winds. The afternoon was too cold for hikers, so when Asher pulled up to the trailways, they found the lot deserted, just as he'd anticipated.

Violet was still flushed in the face. Chewing a stick of gum drawn from her purse, she seemed to be regaining her composure after the shock of the rough oral sex. Asher almost asked if she were okay but caught himself before falling back into the bad habit of passivity. Though the girl seemed rattled, she did not seem afraid or even angry with him. Instead, she appeared thunderstruck. Perhaps Asher had moved too fast, but he just didn't care. He knew he had her.

Putting the car in park, Asher reached across Violet to pop open the glovebox and retrieved the Ziplock bag.

"You smoke weed?" he asked.

She looked at the green buds. "Yeah, sometimes."

He fetched the pocket pipe and had her pack a bowl with bud. As they smoked and drank, they listened to Blood Incantation, Witchfinder General, and the early work of Monster Magnet. Asher was surprised by how easily he was remembering all the band names. It was as if he'd already heard them in some distant past he couldn't quite remember.

"I want to listen to that one record again," Violet said. "The one we had sex to. Can we stream it anywhere?"

"No. I'll have to figure out how to convert the album to MP3 or something."

Once intoxicated, they got out of the car at Asher's insistence. Violet zipped up her black parka against the biting breeze, and Asher took her by the hand. Already, it was a block of ice.

"Where're we going?" she asked as they started on the trail.

Asher wasn't really sure. He just felt compelled to venture into the woods now that they were dead. There was a grim beauty to decay. But while he had no set destination for this hike, he did have plans for what they were going to do here, which was why he'd taken Violet to this secluded area.

"It's a nice day for a walk in the woods," he told her.

"Asher, I'm cold."

"Walking will warm you up." He grinned. "Amongst other things."

The materials he'd brought along weighed down his jacket pocket. As with the red bulb, he'd bought them with Violet in mind. The girl walked close to him, holding his arm. Her nose and cheeks had already gone pink from the cold, so she wrapped her scarf around half of her face. With her hood up too, she looked like a goth sherpa. Amused, Asher smacked her ass, and she stumbled slightly. Asher chuckled. Violet regained her balance without him offering any help.

"Maybe some whiskey will make me warmer," she said.

He handed her the bottle. As they journeyed deeper into the wilderness, they passed it back and forth, getting drunker to fight off winter's touch. But after half an hour of hiking, Violet had had enough.

"Asher, I'm really cold, babe. I can't feel my feet."

"Oh, all right. This spot over here will do."

Holding her hand, he led her off the trail into a dense thicket. Browned leaves crunched beneath their boots, muddy spots sucking at their feet. The brush gave way to a small clearing encompassed by towering maple trees, providing plenty of cover if someone else decided to hike the trail, though Asher was confident no one would.

"Why're we out here?" Violet asked, a little too whiny for his liking.

"Close your eyes and hold out your left arm."

"What?"

"You heard me. I have a surprise for you. Now close your eyes and hold out your left arm."

Though an obedient girl, Violet's eyes darted, revealing her anxiety. Her apprehension excited yet angered him.

Asher spoke more firmly. "Do as I tell you, Violet."

She slowly extended her left arm. Inhaling deep, she closed her eyes.

"Do you like bracelets?" he asked.

This seemed to relax her a little. "Um, sure."

Drawing them from his pocket, Asher opened one of the cuffs and slapped it on her wrist, closing it tight. She opened her eyes without permission, but Asher was too amused by the look on her face to demand she close them again. Looking at the handcuffs, Violet's face went slack, her eyes like two dead planets.

"Asher?" she whimpered. "What's going on? What're you doing?"

Clutching the other handcuff, he guided her toward a tree. "I'm opening a world for you."

He situated her like she was his own personal doll, putting her back to the tree. She did not resist him, but her limbs were shaking, maybe from the cold, maybe from fear—probably both.

"What're you going to do to me?" she asked.

"Don't spoil the fun by asking questions."

"But, Asher, I—"

"C'mon, damn it! Don't ruin it by talking!"

The girl fell silent, unable to look him in the eye when he raised his voice. Stepping behind her, Asher held her arms back on either side of the tree. The trunk was just the right size to cuff her arms around it backwards so her spine was pressed against the tree. As he came around to face her, he detected a range of conflicting emotions in the girl's face—dread, confusion, arousal, anticipation. The handcuffs had done their job.

Violet quivered as Asher undid her jeans. He slid his belt free, then had her bite down on the leather as he used it to strap her head against the tree. Yanking her jeans down, he unzipped her boots and stripped her of all the clothes she wore below the waist, except for her *The Nightmare Before Christmas* socks. Clutching her buttocks, he lifted Violet off the ground and entered her dry. She gasped, her legs tightening around him as he fucked her.

"You know," he said, pounding deeper. "Fucking is a form of possession. I enter you. I take control of you. I make you shudder and scream."

And she did.

Asher had his way with her for almost an hour before climaxing inside her again. Their movements had stripped pieces of bark from the tree, and they decorated Violet like drab confetti. Her bare ass bore scratches from rubbing up and down against the trunk. She was shivering in the aftermath of multiple orgasms, but Asher did not put her jeans and boots back on for her. Noticing his semen running down the inside of her leg, he scooped a glob with his fingers and brought it to her face, decorating her cheeks with it like war paint. He pulled the belt out of her mouth.

"Who is your master?" he demanded.

She replied without hesitation. "You are."

"Say it."

"You are my master."

"You live for me and only me."

"Yes, Master," she said with bated breath.

"I rule you now. You'll fuck for me, little girl, and you'll bleed for me."

Violet swallowed so hard he could hear it, and Asher knew it was time for the other item he'd brought along. He drew the straight razor from his pocket, held it up before her, and opened it to reveal the sharp, new blade. Her lower lip trembled. Before she could say anything, he put the belt back in her mouth and tightened it. Then he got down on one knee as if he were about to propose.

Eyes level with her crotch, Asher gently ran the blade over her trim, blond bush, teasing her. Though the sex had warmed her body, her skin returned to gooseflesh. Asher deftly planted the razor's edge just above her pubic hair in the supple flesh between her naval and vagina. He didn't go too deep as he made the first cut, using just enough pressure to break the skin. Violet tensed, and he almost thought she was about to kick him, but while she wiggled her legs, her feet stayed in place.

"That's it," he whispered. "Take it like a woman."

He carved the letter A into her, the blood stark red against her pale skin. Seeing it dribble, Asher was flooded with the sudden urge to lap it up, and in that instant, he seemed to pull out of a trance, shocked by his own behavior. He shook his head to toss the doubt away. So what if he'd never done anything like this before? That was then, and this was now. Like he'd told Diego, people change, and Asher saw no reason why he shouldn't. His transformation had already brought him great rewards, and somehow, he sensed he was just getting started.

He ran his tongue upward between the girl's labia, then higher to the weeping cuts, where he feasted like a vampire. As he suckled, he heard Violet whisper "oh, my god" repeatedly with that same combination of fear and desire.

"There is no god," he told her. "There is only darkness. Darkness and *me*."

Her next words pleased him. "Yes, Master."

Asher undid her bindings and allowed her to put her jeans and boots back on. Dusk had come, and the ashen sky was corroding with blackness, the silence of the woodland as peaceful as a grave. He breathed deep of the night air.

"Asher?"

"Master," he corrected.

"Master, I'd like to go back now. It's freezing out here."

He kissed her ear, whispering into it. "You don't mind pain."

She opened her mouth to say something but quickly closed it. Asher was cold too, but he was proving a point here. He was conditioning Violet. These grooming techniques came to him in sudden revelations, as if he were pulling them out of the ether. What surprised him most was how sure of himself he'd become. Though he'd had a moment of shock, stunned by his own actions, he did not doubt them no matter how sadistic they became. Folding his belt in half, he slapped the leather against his open palm. The snap made Violet flinch.

"It would be so easy, wouldn't it?" he said, more statement than question.

"What?"

"For me to kill you out here."

Violet went still and silent.

Asher went on. "I mean, there's no one around to hear your screams. You came all the way out here with me and let me cuff you to a tree. You made no objections when I fucked you hard and cut you and drank your blood. Most people would have fought back, but you didn't. Instead, you put yourself at my mercy. What do you think that says about you?"

She took her time answering. "I … I don't know."

"I do."

"Okay … what does it say about me?"

Asher smirked. "I'm going to let you discover that for yourself."

He smacked the belt in his hand once more just to see her jump, then looped it back around his waist. He brushed her cheek with the back of his hand.

"I'm not going to kill you, Violet. Do you know why?"

"Because you care about me?"

Asher resisted the urge to laugh. "Because I have big plans for you. For both of us, my sweet."

He kissed her forehead, and the girl cuddled into him. His words had calmed her, endearing her to him even more. It was amazing how the female mind worked. Now that Asher knew this truth, everything had become so easy.

Violet hugged his arm all the way back to the car.

SEVEN

FOLLOWING A VIDEO TUTORIAL, ASHER managed to connect the turntable to his laptop to convert *Music to Sacrifice Virgins To* into audio files. This way, he could play it anywhere using his phone via Bluetooth or AUX. As side A played, Asher could have sworn the music had gotten even heavier and crunchier. When it finished, he flipped the record over, suddenly realizing he hadn't even listened to side B yet. He'd been too focused on the hypnotic music of the first side, how it seemed to transform into something more sinister with every listen. He wondered if he should save side B to listen to with Violet—not because she would appreciate that, though she would, but because he had a strange suspicion the record's B-side would endow him with some sort of new wisdom, that it would further empower him. He wanted his sex slave to be there when the muse christened him so he could take her immediately if the mood struck.

After their tryst in the woods, the lovers had gotten high in the car again, listening to Cough while finishing off the bottle of booze. Violet cleaned the cum from her face with a napkin from the glovebox, and Asher took her to dinner at Denny's. He was burning through what little money he had but was confident it wouldn't be a concern much longer, though he wasn't sure why. For the first time in his life, he was blessed with the mindset that everything would work out. It was as if some dark guardian angel was watching over him.

He'd brought Violet home just before midnight. She wanted to come to his room with him and listen to records but needed to be up early for classes in the morning. Asher didn't walk her to the door. It wouldn't do for her to think he cared about her that much. A man had to keep a woman guessing, to lock her in a constant state of earning him. Once a woman knew you loved her, she quickly lost all respect. They stopped *trying*. This was when they ceased wearing makeup when you were just going to stay in. It was when they started wearing dumpy clothes, sometimes even when you went out somewhere. That's what Rebecca had done. Violet would not be permitted such insolence. Asher didn't care if they were staying in all day or just going out to grab something from a convenience store, he'd be damned if Violet wasn't going to look like a million bucks whenever they were together. She was young, pretty, and had a tight body. No excuse not to always be his trophy.

Though she'd not asked him to, Asher told Violet he would drive her to school in the morning, so he could dominate her again before she could have any doubts or reservations after what he'd done to her in the woods. Knowing he'd branded her lower abdomen with the first initial of his name brought a smile to his face.

Holding up the album, he decided he couldn't wait to listen to it tomorrow. Perhaps it would be better to take in its majesty alone before permitting Violet to hear it. It was passed down to him specifically, after all. He put the needle down, and the record spun beneath the Baphomet topper. He'd been recording with earbuds in, but Rex's speakers provided far better sound, and side B of *Music to Sacrifice Virgins To* deserved the best possible listening experience. Asher unplugged his headphones, allowing a gravelly male voice to rise from his dead uncle's sound system.

"We call on the Prince of Devils, the black god of the Philistine city of Ekron—Beelzebub—the Lord of the Flies, brother to the Hesperus star. And we call on the foul angel Astaroth, the Great Duke of Hell, eater of souls, scribe

of our grimoires, commander of the vipers from beyond the veil. " As the voice went on, screeching electric guitars rose in volume, accompanied by banshee screams, creating a hellish wall of noise. *"Now, we call upon The Fallen One, Lucifer, our unholy master, The Morning Star—the great, exalted one, Lord Satan. For he is the king of all evil. He is the great scourge of man, of all the creatures of the Earth.* "

Though similar to the chants on side A, this seemed more like an invocation, like it was building to something, unleashing something without name. It gave Asher chills. He did not just hear these words—he *felt* them. An uncomfortable warmth spread through his chest. His lungs felt filled with hot water. Sweat sizzled in his hair. There was pain but also pleasure. Now, he understood why Violet had not resisted him. His cock and nipples hardened, though his hands began to shake. The music grew heavier with doom that tested his eardrums. The choir of screams seemed to circle around the room, hellish and tornadic. Some of those voices were crying in pain unlike anything he'd ever heard before. Others were cackling with sadistic laughter. There were growls, snarls, and shouted blasphemies. Many of the voices sounded far from human.

"The demon must be called," the man's gravelly voice said. *"The demon shall come but first must be summoned."*

Some of the other voices joined him in this mantra while others howled with suffering.

"The demon must be called!"

Asher understood now. These weren't lyrics. These were instructions.

He stared at the title on the spine of the record's cover: *Music to Sacrifice Virgins To.*

"Endless power," the voice went on. *"Constant Victory. All the pleasures of the flesh, the blood, the soul. The demon comes only when summoned."*

There was a pounding Asher first took for drums. Then he realized it was coming from his bedroom door. It was locked, and the knob was shaking back and forth. In that instant, Asher was certain someone—*something*—had come to take his soul. A lifetime of agnostic disbelief was cast aside as terror pounded in his heart.

Then he realized one of the screaming voices wasn't coming from the speakers.

"Asher!" Mom yelled, knocking harder.

Standing, he lifted the needle from the record. The room fell silent but for the sound of her demanding he open the door. Asher exhaled with relief, chuckling at himself for getting so rattled. The music had just pulled him in. He wanted to learn more but couldn't until he got his mother to shut up.

He swung the door open. "What? What do you want?"

Mom stood there in her satin bathrobe. He couldn't help but notice the perfect shape of her breasts beneath the shiny fabric. It irked him how she always seemed to be thrusting those big, fake tits in everyone's face—even her son's. She seemed to feel his eyes on her and covered her chest by folding her arms. A myriad of emotions showed in her eyes—fear, disgust, bewilderment. It reminded him of how Violet had looked in the woods, only in place of desire, there was anger.

"Asher Benton!" she said. "What on Earth are you doing? It's three in the goddamn morning!"

"Too loud."

"Yes, it's too damned loud!"

"No, I mean *you're* being too loud, Mother. Don't scream at me."

Her eyebrows met. "*I'm* too loud? *Really?* You told me I wouldn't have to hear that evil crap. You swore you wouldn't play it while I was home. Now, you've got it blasting in the middle of the night, waking me up. I was banging on your door for a good five minutes."

Asher only sucked his teeth.

Mom's face hardened. "Asher ... what was that music you were playing?"

He shrugged. "Just some old heavy metal record."

"Let me see it."

"What for?"

"I want to see it, Asher!"

He stepped into his mother so suddenly she flinched. "I told you not to yell at me!"

But she refused to back down. "Show me the record—now."

"Jesus fucking Christ. Haven't we been over this already? I'm not a little boy anymore. You can't just order me arou—"

"I am your *mother,* and this is *my house!*"

In one swift movement, Asher backed his mom against the wall and pointed a finger right in her face. His words came out in a hiss. "This is the third fucking time I've told you not to fucking yell at me! *Don't* make me tell you again."

The rage she'd shown seemed to trickle out of her, replaced by a sudden fear. Seeing her that way gave him a rush that sharpened his senses. Asher could smell her sweat, even taste its salt in the air. He heard her pulse quicken, the gurgle of blood rushing through veins.

"Do you understand me, Mother?"

She gulped. "Okay … it's okay, honey. I understand. Please, just calm down."

He'd never spoken to her like this before. They'd had their share of arguments over the years, as any mother and child would, but he'd never moved in on her like this, never used his size as a threat. She may have been his mother, but she was also a woman, and he'd learned how they had to be handled—every last one of them.

"From now on," he said, "you don't come knocking on my door like that. You don't tell me when I can play my music or how loud it can be. If you come to my door, it should be with a hot meal or a beer, not your nagging bullshit. You chased Dad out of here with that. I'm the man of this house now. I'll do whatever I want to do, and you will show me respect."

She stared at him with her mouth open, face white as snow.

"Do I make myself clear?" he asked.

She nodded. "Yes, Rex. I understand."

Asher heard her call him by her brother's name, but she didn't seem to realize her error. Mom tried to scoot past, and he allowed it so she would go back to her room. She shut the door slowly, quietly, obediently.

Rex, he thought as he returned to his bedroom. *She called me Rex.*

Mom had looked like she'd seen a ghost.

Perhaps she had.

EIGHT

HE PICKED VIOLET UP EARLY so there'd be time for her to obey him before class. They parked behind a farmstand that had closed for the winter, and Asher smoked a joint as Violet fellated him. When he came, she swallowed without having to be told to—a quick learner.

Dawn was breaking. As the eastern sky relented to a dark blue, a star appeared, shining brighter than the others.

Violet pointed it out. "See that? It's not actually a star. That's Venus."

"Oh yeah?"

"You know, it can't be seen in the night sky and it's hard to find by day. It's most visible at dawn and dusk, but only briefly." She smiled at him in her adoring way. "That's why it's called The Morning Star."

Asher recalled something from the record's invocation. *We call upon The Fallen One, Lucifer, our unholy master, The Morning Star.*

Violet confirmed it before he could ask. "The Romans called the planet Lucifer. In images, they personified it as a male figure carrying fire, sometimes with a torch, sometimes in his bare hand. Usually, it was the left hand."

"I'm left-handed."

"I know. You're *really* good with that hand." She wiggled her eyebrows. "They say the left-hand path is one of evil. That's why nuns used to smack kids on the knuckles with a ruler when they wrote with their left hands. It was considered a sign of The Devil."

"Interesting. How do you know all this?"

"Oh, lots of ways. I grew up going to church. My parents made us. I heard all about The Devil and how I'd go to Hell forever if I was bad. Our pastor, Reverend Bower, was really into all that fire and brimstone shit, trying to scare people into having faith. That's Christianity for you—you're bullied by the God who insists he loves you. It's sick." She took another hit from the joint. "When I got into Wicca and Paganism, I did a lot of reading on different faiths. I wasn't looking for a new religion as much as I was looking to prove Christianity was only one of thousands of religions and therefore had very slim odds of being the correct one. I liked that it wasn't the earliest religion. I'd been raised to believe it was the only one, but there were all these other ancient faiths, so many different gods and devils."

Asher considered this. "Did you come to any finite conclusion?"

"Just to be Wiccan."

It wasn't the sort of answer Asher was hoping for, but he also wasn't sure what would be. Over the past week, thoughts of The Devil had dominated his mind, thanks to his new records and girlfriend. It seemed too coincidental that these messengers would come into his life at the same time, making him ponder the dark side of religion in a way he'd never bothered to before. Previously, thoughts of demons and fallen angels had been foreign to him. They were the stuff of horror movies and holy rollers. Now, he could not rid them from his brainpan. They called for further exploration.

"You should come hang out with me and my Wiccan friends sometime," Violet said. "Some of them know a lot more about this stuff than I do. Besides, I'd like for you to meet them. That is, if you want."

Asher had no interest in meeting the people Violet cared about, but he was curious about the roots of paganism and wanted more information about these gods and devils Violet spoke of—

particularly the devils. *Music to Sacrifice Virgins To* chanted the names of many demons other than Satan. He wanted to learn about who they were from more than just the internet.

"Okay," he said, much to Violet's delight. Clearly, she was excited to show off her new boyfriend to her stupid group of tree worshippers.

Dropping Violet off at the community college, Asher leered at the young bodies of female students as they walked toward the entrance. All those firm backsides. All those perky breasts. All those empty holes, uncut bellies, and unchoked throats. If Violet noticed him staring at these girls, she didn't say anything about it—a wise move.

With Carnage blasting through the Honda's speakers, Asher headed home. His buzz was already wearing off, and he didn't have enough cash to go to the weed dispensary. He'd been getting stoned more than usual but hadn't given it much thought. Hedonism was his new directive. Thinking back to the few times he'd tried cocaine in high school, he wondered if Diego might be able to hook him up with some. After a brief stint in rehab, Diego had gone off the stuff years ago, but that didn't mean he didn't still have connections. Asher wanted to play with a variety of drugs. He was open to experimenting with LSD and psychedelic mushrooms. He wouldn't have even said no to some heroin or fentanyl. Smoking weed enhanced the experience of listening to Rex's music, so Asher could only imagine what other drugs would do for it.

That he was broke was only a temporary concern. He still had this unexplainable certainty he was going to come into money very soon, even though he knew not where it would come from. It'd been almost a week since he'd searched for a job. Asher no longer planned to look for one. Maybe he would make money selling some of those rare records as he'd planned, but the more he listened to them, the less he wanted to part with any of them. Rex's music made Asher happy in ways he'd thought were impossible. He'd enjoyed other kinds of music before but had never made listening to music a central part of his everyday life. No other genre of music could be credited with changing his entire viewpoint the way heavy metal had, especially *Music to Sacrifice Virgins To*. Asher was excited to get home and listen to the album again, knowing there was more to unlock from it, more lessons to be learned. The record was slowly imparting great wisdom. The best way to accelerate that was to play it more often and listen more closely.

He stopped at a drugstore and shoplifted a box of black hair dye, a bottle of sex lube, and the audio cord he needed for his computer, not even bothering to conceal them. Only the self-checkout sign was lit, and there was no one manning the front desk's register, so Asher simply walked out with what he wanted. The thrill was minor because he felt no fear. The desire to turn his hair black had been nagging at him since yesterday, and he knew he'd have to do it if he was ever going to stop obsessing about it. He just wished he could grow his hair out faster. He wanted something to whip about while banging his head.

It was sleeting when he arrived home. Asher pulled into the driveway, pleased his mother's car wasn't there. Distractions wouldn't do. He had more important things to do than argue with her, though he hoped their last talk had set her straight.

Rex, Asher thought. *She called you Rex.*

A simple mix-up. If Asher's new attitude reminded Mom of her late brother, Rex must have been a badass dude. Asher wished he could have gotten to know him better before his death, especially as he'd been so gracious with his belongings.

Grabbing a beer from the fridge, he paired it with some walnuts for breakfast, using the holiday nutcracker Mom had purchased despite Christmas being over a month away. At least the nutcracker wasn't in the shape of a man. It was just striped like a candy cane. He crushed his empty beer can and left it on the counter, then carried a fresh one into his room.

His skin tingled as he turned on the stereo, the miniature Baphomet seeming to look up at him in silent invitation. *Music to Sacrifice Virgins To* was still on the turntable. Dropping the needle, the church bell chimed, and those fierce guitars rose with crunchier distortion than before. Again, the music sounded different, darker, heavier. Asher had finished recording the album to digital files but had yet to transfer them to his phone because the airdrop option hadn't worked. Using the cord he'd stolen from the drugstore, he connected his devices and began the process of downloading the album.

The sudden male voice on the record startled him. It was louder and clearer than ever.

"Behold the return of Astaroth ... the resurrection of Beelzebub, the dark one ... the rise of The Morning Star, herald of the dawn."

Since he was already sitting at his laptop, he searched the first name, Astaroth. He spelled it wrong, but the internet corrected him, offering multiple results. It seemed Astaroth was The Great Duke of Hell, a demon in the form of a nude man with wings. In illustrations from the 1800s, Astaroth was adorned with a crown and held a serpent in his left hand while riding atop a beast that resembled a hybrid of a dragon and a wolf. It was said that the name was first seen in *The Book of the Sacred Magic of Abra-Melin the Mage* in 1485, an occult grimoire in the guise of a novel, and continued to appear in books on demonology to this day. An "Ashtoreth" appeared in The Old Testament as a false goddess but, from what Asher gathered, was unrelated to the male demon Astaroth. There was a staggering amount of information out there that varied depending on the source, but what interested Asher most was the demon's inclusion in what was called The Evil Trinity.

Like The Holy Trinity of The Father, The Son, and The Holy Ghost, the forces of darkness also had a special threesome in Western occult traditions. As The Great Duke of Hell, Astaroth was linked with power, wealth, and divination—the ancient art of using supernatural powers to gain insight. The next member of the group was Beelzebub, also known as The Lord of the Flies. This demon was associated with corruption, gluttony, sloth, and lust. Completing this demonic trifecta was Lucifer himself, the grand leader of all fallen angels, representing pride, envy, and rebellion against God.

The record played on, the man's voice deepening. *"From the ninth circle ... from the pit of sulfur ... from the blood pool of the virgin ..."*

Asher liked the sound of that last part. *The blood pool of the virgin.* There was a touch of erotica to the phrase that tickled him.

With the files transferred to his phone, Asher opened the music app. *Music to Sacrifice Virgins To* had loaded successfully, but all his other music had vanished. Something had deleted every album he'd ever downloaded prior to his newfound love of heavy metal. He opened his music streaming service, where he'd been listening to all his other heavy metal lately, and it appeared to be fine, but his personal music collection was gone.

Asher's face pinched. "What the hell?"

He plugged the phone in again, and on the screen of his laptop, the menu showed all the deleted albums as still being on his phone, but when he tried to access them on it, they didn't appear at all. *Music to Sacrifice Virgins To* had erased them somehow. Having never been the most computer literate, Asher figured he'd messed something up but couldn't understand how he'd trashed all those files.

A smile came to his face when he realized it didn't matter anymore. Asher didn't need the garbage he used to listen to. All that hip-hop, soft rock, and pop music was behind him now.

Now, the voice spoke with no distortion, making its message clear. *"You belong to your father, The Devil, and you want to carry out your father's desires."*

Asher's smiled widened. "You're goddamned right I do."

"The demon comes but must be summoned," the record reminded him.

Asher wasn't sure what he expected to happen, but a feeling of elation had been snowballing in him, and now every fine hair on his body was standing on end, his stomach shuddering like an attacked hive. It was more than a high, more than a rush, more than an arousal. It was different from any sensation he'd ever experienced. Asher did not feel intoxicated; in fact, he felt more levelheaded than ever before. Finally, his life had direction, his idle hands a purpose. The words danced on the edge of his lips, waiting for him to arrange them correctly. The air in the room had a savoriness that was somehow electric.

The room was already lit red by the party bulb, but now the light began to flicker like a crimson bonfire. The walls rippled. The floor flowed like lava. Though the room was cool, clear waves warped the air like heat on a desert highway.

Could the marijuana he'd smoked earlier have been spiked with something? Surely, he would have felt it earlier than this. Could Mom have put something in the beer? That wouldn't be like her at all, and besides, Asher couldn't see how she could have with the cans still sealed.

Another surge of euphoria assured him this was something different.

"The demon must be called," the voice chanted.

Tilting his head back, Asher closed his eyes and extended his arms, palms up.

Though he'd heard them only once before, he recited the incantations almost perfectly, as if someone were coaching him like his own personal Cyrano. "I call on the Prince of Devils, the black god of the Philistine city of Ekron—Beelzebub—Lord of the Flies. I call on the foul angel Astaroth, The Great Duke of Hell, eater of souls, commander of the vipers from beyond the veil."

The stereo woofers throbbed as the music transformed into an electric drone. Though he heard crackling embers and the whoosh of flames, Asher did not open his eyes. The bedroom windows vibrated, jangling like a hundred rattlesnake tails, and just beyond the glass, thunder joined the album's percussion. A choir of static screams circled Asher's head. Cries of suffering—both human and animal—mixed with the mocking laughter of the album's narrator. But Asher knew no fear in this moment.

"Now," he shouted in unison with the voice, "I call upon The Fallen One, Lucifer, The Morning Star—*Lord Satan!*"

The room roared as it filled with light. Squinting, Asher opened his eyes to look for the source, but it was omnipresent. Crimson sunbeams split before him as if passing through a crystal prism. A pink, oval-shaped glow dilated and expanded until it matched him in size. It pulsed. Asher was forced to close his eyes again, putting his hands over them. Despite all the suggestions of fire, the temperature in the room seemed to have dropped twenty degrees. His nostrils flared at the perfume of rot. When the glow eased, Asher managed to open his eyes but did so cautiously, peeking through his fingers like a child watching a scary movie.

What he saw was more sinister than any horror film could have prepared him for.

The floor was coated in several inches of blood that bubbled up as it boiled. Dozens of black snakes slithered through the steaming gore. Others dangled from the ceiling in scaly festoons. They writhed on the walls, defying gravity, and covered the windows so no natural light could pass. A huge wreath of snakes was entwined on his mattress in a black orgy. Their sizes varied. Some had rattle tails. Others had gleaming flaps of skin attached to their ribs and neck that expanded like a cobra's hood. The unified hissing was loud enough to be heard even over the roar of the music.

From out the oval vortex, a humanoid figure appeared. The face was ageless and genderless, inhumanly human, like a composite of every face Asher had ever seen plastered onto a single misshapen skull. The features seemed in a constant state of change—all but the eyes, which were blood red with black, rectangular pupils like a goat's. They were impossible to read. The creature was adorned with skeletal wings—cardinal feathers on smoke-blackened bones. Asher expected demons to have huge horns, but this monstrosity only had giraffe-like ossicones—boney protrusions of cartilage covered by greasy flesh. Its nude body looked as if it had been dipped in used cooking oil, but it did resemble a man's, including the larger than usual genitalia. The end of the penis was a serpent's head, the forked tongue darting out of the urethra, dribbling blood.

As the creature parted its lips, Asher leaned in, thinking it was about to speak. Instead, more snakes emerged from its mouth, rising out of the beast's throat to spill over its chin in a black river. A thin serpent climbed the face and vanished into a nostril. Others coiled around the skull, while the rest joined the army below, splashing into the boiling blood at the creature's feet.

When Asher looked down, he realized dozens of snakes had coiled around his legs and were climbing up his body. He felt the weight of a heavy one against his spine just before the black boa constrictor draped itself around his neck like a scarf. Holding out his hands, he found snakes no bigger than worms wrapping around all ten of his digits.

Asher stood frozen, and yet he felt no fear. The demon had filled him with silent awe. He understood that this encounter was a gift. How few people had seen behind the curtain like this? How few people—even those with religion—had stood before a literal deity, good or evil? Even if the beast had only come to drag him down into the abyss, Asher was still grateful, for he understood he had been blessed with this visitation, and his uncle Rex was who he had to thank for it.

Asher had inherited much more than music. He'd inherited keys to the most forbidden of doors.

"*Sacrifice,*" the voice on the record chanted. "*Sacrifice. Sacrifice. Sacrifice.*"

NINE

IT WASN'T LUCIFER.

Asher had called upon The Evil Trinity, but only one demon had appeared, and he knew which one it was based on the descriptions from his research.

Astaroth.

The Great Duke of Hell had visited him from the beyond, and Asher thought he understood why. This was the demon of wealth and power—the two things Asher was seeking most. His own desire had conjured Astaroth just as much as the chants had. Asher was sure of it. Looking back at it now, it amused him that he'd thought Satan himself would appear. At first glance, he'd even mistaken the demon for Lucifer. But Asher was not worthy of a visit from the Prince of Darkness—at least, not yet. He was lucky enough to have been given a brief vision of Astaroth.

And it had been a vision, hadn't it?

His room hadn't caught fire. The floor wasn't covered in blood, and the snakes had disappeared. But Asher had no doubt it all had been real.

He sat on his bed for a long time, contemplating his next move, listening to the low hiss of the speakers now that the album had ended.

Asher's phone rang, giving him a start. Picking it up, he half expected a demon on the line to give him instructions. Instead, it was Diego.

"Hey, man," his friend said. "Got your call. What's up?"

"Call?"

"Yeah, you called but didn't leave a message. Was it a butt dial?"

Somehow, Asher knew it hadn't been. Someone had deliberately called Diego from Asher's phone, even if it hadn't been him. "Oh, right. No, it wasn't a butt call. Sorry, I've been stoned most of the morning and just spaced out a second."

"Hitting the weed pretty heavy these days, huh?" Diego chuckled. "You're becoming a regular stoner."

"Just trying to have a good time."

"Partying with that hot girlfriend you've been telling me about, huh? Good for you."

Asher started pacing. "Yeah, so, Diego … I was wondering if you still had any connections."

Silence on the line.

"Diego?"

"I'm here," he said flatly.

"I said I was wondering if—"

"Yeah, I heard you. I'm just surprised you would ask me that. You know what I went through, how hard it was for me to quit."

Asher knew then he couldn't ask for cocaine. It was too sensitive a topic. "Listen, I'm not looking for blow. I wouldn't do that to you, man. My girl and I were just hoping to get some hallucinogens. See, she's Wiccan, and she thinks we could have a deep spiritual experience if we trip together, one that'll strengthen our relationship. I was hoping you could hook me up with somebody who has acid."

"Acid? Seriously?"

"Or shrooms. Whatever."

Diego sighed. "I can't help but feel like …"

"Like what?"

"Like you're headed in the wrong direction, man. I mean, aren't you trying to find a job and move out of your mom's? Drugs are only going to slow you down. They might even stop you for good."

Asher's grip on the phone tightened. He didn't like being lectured by Diego or anyone else. "It's my life. I'll live it how I want to, okay? After all I went through with Rebecca, I just want to have some fun right now. Is that so wrong?"

"No, but you can't keep using your breakup as an excuse to—"

"Don't do that. Don't pretend to know what the breakup was like for me. You've got everything with Fernanda—I've got shit. Now, I finally have a chance at something special with a great girl. As my friend, you should want to help me."

"I do want to help you. I just think you're asking for the wrong kind of help."

Asher shifted his jaw. "Diego, are you going to help me or not?"

Diego didn't reply, but he didn't hang up either.

"You must have somebody from your past that you still keep in contact with," Asher said. "All I want is some hallucinogens. No big deal. I just want to make this girl happy."

Finally, Diego relented. "Let me make a call."

+

Diego's cousin wore a motorcycle jacket covered in pinback buttons of metal bands and horror films. Asher spotted some of the bands he'd just gotten into, including Dopelord, The Electric Hellfire Club, and Dying Fetus, as well as images from the movies *The Exorcist III* and *Hellraiser*. He took these buttons as good omens. They assured him the dark forces were guiding him to the right person.

Ximena Falco was clad in dark clothing, but unlike most goth-metal girls, she had tan skin and hair that was naturally black. Half Mexican and half Caucasian, she was twenty-six with an athletic body and the darkest eyes Asher had ever seen, the pupils and irises indistinguishable from one another. Though a good foot shorter than he was, Asher could sense the woman wasn't gregarious. Even after he complimented her taste in music, she remained socially frigid.

The three of them had met on neutral ground at a pizzeria. Asher had just enough money left to pay for a Dr. Pepper and the four hits of acid Ximena had brought in a folded piece of tinfoil. Now, he was truly broke.

"Powerful stuff?" he asked.

"It'll take you there," Ximena said, her eyes never wavering. "You'll only need one hit each trip, but Diego said you wanted four doses, so here you go."

69

Diego looked at Asher. "You ever drop acid before?"

"Once, in junior high, but I didn't feel much. Frankly, I think I got scammed by the older kid who sold it to me. It was probably just a piece of a Post-it note."

"Just make sure to do it somewhere where you both feel safe and comfortable."

"That doesn't sound like much fun at all."

Ximena glowered at her cousin. "He'll be fine, Diego. I was dropping tabs when I was eleven. I think a grown-ass man can handle it."

"Hey," Diego said to Asher, "didn't you say your girlfriend was nineteen?"

"What has that to do with anything?" Asher asked.

"I mean she's not old enough to drink. You could get into even more trouble giving someone her age acid, right?"

Again, Ximena scolded him. "Diego, would you shut the fuck up?"

"Yeah," Asher added. "No one is ever going to know we took it. I'm not a fool."

Outnumbered, Diego just shook his head. Excusing himself, he rose from the booth and started toward the restroom. Alone with Ximena, Asher leaned across the table toward her.

"Your cousin can be a stick in the mud sometimes," he said with a smile.

"He didn't used to be, though, am I right?"

Asher had to agreed.

"That's the fault of his fiancée," Ximena said. "She's practically neutered him."

"You don't like Fernanda?"

"How can I like someone who doesn't even try to get along with me? Diego is my family, but she tries to keep him from seeing me. She says I'm a bad influence."

"Well, I like bad influences."

Ximena smirked. "Oh, yeah?"

"How about harder stuff?" he asked. "I'll bet a bad influence can get it."

She narrowed her eyes. "My cousin said you only wanted some acid."

"But now that I have you here, I figured I'd ask what else you could get."

She continued to eye him suspiciously. "I'm not some big-time drug dealer, okay? I just do small-time stuff like this, here and there."

"C'mon. You don't have to hide from me."

"Who the fuck said I was hiding?" She leaned toward him, eyes like black ice. "I don't hide from nobody, you got that?"

"If that's true, then you won't have any need for bullshit. I've got money, and I want to make a large purchase. You could seriously benefit. If you don't have the goods, I'm sure you know somebody who does, and I'll offer a finder's fee."

She took her time replying. "Why didn't you tell this to Diego, then?"

"You know how he's been since rehab. Drugs make him nervous. That's why I want to work with you directly. You and your supplier. Diego doesn't need to know."

"The only reason you're even sitting here with me is because my cousin vouched for you. Now you want to meet with my supplier? You must be out of your mind."

A mean heat bloomed within Asher, but he stifled the urge to snap at the bitch. He needed her. There was an energy to Ximena, a dark aura that assured she was part of Astaroth's plan for him.

"Maybe I am insane," he said with a smile. "But I'm gonna get rich. I promise you that. Now, I'm offering you a chance to be a part of it. All you have to do is take a chance on me, and like you said, Diego has already vouched for me."

She stirred her straw in her soda. "Just for the sake of argument, why don't you tell me what you're looking for."

Now, Asher had her. "My friends and I are putting together a rave in an old factory, a party that'll put Caligula to shame. I'm in charge of *refreshments*. Coke, molly, pills. Whatever you've got."

"*This* is your plan to get rich?"

"No, it's just the beginning." As he leaned in, a warm tingle moved through his extremities. It was more than excitement. There was an energy behind the sensation, something foreign. "With the money I make selling dope at the rave, I'll be able to buy a much larger bundle from you and your supplier. That's when I really start wheelin' and dealin'."

To his surprise, Ximena suppressed a laugh. But it wasn't a sardonic laugh; it was good humored, laughing with him, not at him.

"You sound like a used car salesman when you say that," she told him. "All right, let me see what I can do."

They exchanged numbers before Diego returned to the table.

When they left the restaurant, Ximena gave Asher an unexpected smile before getting in the car with her cousin. "I don't know what it is, but you seem cool, Asher. Call you later, okay?"

The cold stoicism she'd come to the pizzeria with had completely evaporated. Maybe she didn't know why, but Asher did, and in his mind, he gave a silent hail to The Great Duke of Hell.

"See you soon," he assured her.

Her smile didn't waver even as they drove away.

Though not as pretty as Violet, Ximena was attractive in a darker way, and there was an edge to her Asher appreciated. If he could bend the woman to his will, she would make a fine minion and sex slave. Anything was possible with the power of Astaroth behind him.

There was still a couple of hours before Violet got out of school, so Asher returned home to listen to records. He wanted to play *Music to Sacrifice Virgins To* but felt it was too soon to call upon the demonic forces again, so he sampled some of the bands he hadn't heard yet, enjoying them all. It was strange how every album in Rex's collection appealed to him now. Not one of them turned him off.

Thinking over what he planned to do, Asher went to the garage to search through Mom's new tools. Finding something he liked, he brought it to his bedroom and hid it under his pillow. He was going to the fridge when he saw Mom pull into the driveway. Having left his bedroom door open, heavy metal filled the house in a glorious roar. Asher stood in the kitchen, waiting for her as he sipped his beer.

The instant Mom walked in, Asher could see how exhausted she was. She'd worn little makeup, and the crow's feet at her eyes were more pronounced, a purple sheen on her eyelids. Shaking her head at the music, she frowned at Asher as she threw her purse on the counter.

"Home early today, Mother?" he asked.

"I went home sick, but I'm just tired. Didn't sleep too well last night." She finally looked him in the eyes. "Will you please turn that music down? It's splitting my head."

Asher went into his bedroom and turned off the stereo, but only because he had questions only his mother could answer. When he returned to the kitchen, he saw her throwing the empty beer cans, walnut shells, and other trash he'd left out into the garbage. She did not complain about the mess, though. Asher noted the compliance. Mom was avoiding confrontation.

"So tell me about Uncle Rex," Asher said.

Her shoulders rose up her neck. "Honey, I just want to go lie down."

"In a minute. I want to know more about the man who left me all these records."

"I'm not in the mood to talk right now, especially not about him."

"Tell me why you hate him so much."

"Asher—"

He stepped closer to his mother, towering over her. "Tell me."

Mom sighed and put her hands flat on the countertop. "I'm not alone in hating my brother. Even all these years later, the family still wants nothing to do with him. That much was clarified when I started calling people to tell them Rex had died—or supposedly died. I've been unable to find any further information about it. No lawyer has contacted anyone. There's no obituary listing or anything. No funeral services listed. But then again, I have no idea where he's been living all these years or if he changed his name. Alive or not, my brother's a ghost."

"But I want to know why."

Mom pursed her lips. She asked if they could sit down, and Asher followed her into the living room. The room was gray, the daylight muted by curtains, but neither of them turned on a light. Finally, Mom opened up.

"My older brother was always different. Even as a child, he was withdrawn. He didn't play well with other kids—not even me. I don't really remember him playing at all. I mean, what kind of kid doesn't like toys? Rex always had to have everything his way. If you didn't go along with him, he would get angry. Sometimes, he would hurt you. He'd punch, kick, slap. When you'd cry, he'd start laughing. Then he'd hit harder.

"One time—and this is my earliest memory of him—when I was three and Rex was five, we were at the park, and I was on a swing. There were two others free, but Rex wanted the one I was using. When I told him no, he shoved me off. I landed hard on my face and got a bloody nose. Rex didn't even take the swing from me, though. He just walked away. He'd only wanted it because I'd been enjoying it, see? Of course, our parents punished him for it, but like always, Rex showed no remorse whatsoever. He seemed sad he'd been caught but only gave me a weak apology Mom and Dad forced him to say. It was like he just had no empathy at all. Never did.

"He was violent with his classmates too, from kindergarten on up.

He stole things from them, tricked them, beat them up. They didn't even have to do anything to anger him. Rex would just go up to another kid and bite them. Years later, Mom confided in me that he'd started biting her as soon as his baby teeth had come in. When he threw a chair at a girl in the second grade, the school finally forced him out. That's when my brother went away for a while. I was too young to understand at the time, but that was Rex's first stint in a behavior health center."

"You mean an insane asylum?" Asher asked.

Mom nodded. "I remember your grandmother crying every night he was away. But weeks became months, and she slowly stopped. She didn't seem to accept it as much as she just went dead whenever someone brought Rex up. Most of the time, my parents visited him when I was at my aunt's house, playing with my cousins. But on special occasions, we all went to see him. I remember the first Christmas he was in the sanitarium. He'd drawn pictures for us. Rex was a great artist even as a little kid, and we were all overjoyed he'd thought to give us these gifts.

"He gave me mine first. I think he did this to make sure I got to see it before Mom and Dad realized what he was up to. In the drawing, there was a blond little girl wearing the exact same outfit I'd worn that day. I still don't know how he knew what I was going to wear." Her eyes grew wet as she went on. "In the drawing, the girl was hanging with a noose around her neck. There were all these knives in her, and she was covered in blood. My parents were too shocked to even get angry until I started crying. Since he was already in the psych ward, they didn't really scold him, only told him he shouldn't show his little sister art like that. He just said, 'But it's a portrait.' Then he gave my parents the other pictures he'd made. They all showed the family in different stages of violent death. In some of them, Rex had drawn himself doing the killing. I didn't get to go along on any visits after that.

"As time went on, Rex was put on different medications. Sometimes, he seemed okay—or at least okay for him. He came home when he was ten, and for a while, things were fine. But it didn't last. Our parents enrolled him in a special school for troubled boys. Rex hated it because he said he was smart while the other kids were learning disabled, but while he hated slow kids, he found them easier to take advantage of. He started stealing again, but while he did get in trouble, this school was much more patient than public schools had been. They kept trying to work on his behavior, just like Mom and Dad. Rex wasn't being violent with anyone at school, as far as they knew, so he got to stay no matter how much he misbehaved. I think he'd just learned what would get him sent back to the asylum and what he could get away with even if he got caught.

"At home, I was the one to take most of his abuse, but most of it was psychological. I woke up one morning, and the first thing I saw was my favorite doll hanging from the ceiling by a cord. It had bloodstains on it. Rex was in my room, standing over me as I slept. When I awoke and started crying, he laughed and told me he'd murdered my dollie. And he just kept laughing. I found out later he'd cut himself on purpose just so he could get the doll all bloodied up. When my dad confronted him about it, Rex said it was just a joke. That's what he always said when he was caught being cruel—*it's just a joke.*

"But he got worse. I had this kiddie pool shaped like a turtle. One day I was playing in it, and when my mom went inside to answer the phone, Rex came over and held me down, face-first in the water. I couldn't do anything because he was so much stronger than me. He just laughed and laughed as I struggled. Luckily, Mom saw us through the window and came rushing out to stop him. If she hadn't, I might not be here. Again, he said it was all just a joke, but no one was laughing."

Asher knew how his mother was around bodies of water. She never went swimming when they went to the beach, and when Dad had talked about putting in a swimming pool, she'd vehemently rejected the idea until he let it go. She didn't even take relaxing baths, only showers.

"As bad as those childhood years were," Mom said, "the teen years were far worse. That's when Rex got into Satanism."

Asher leaned forward, excited to hear more.

"It started with heavy metal," she went on. "First, it was the glam rock stuff like Mötley Crüe's *Shout at the Devil,* but then he got into darker music. My parents had enrolled him in a public junior high school. He must have discovered these bands through older boys. Almost overnight, his room was like a shrine to heavy metal. He had all these posters torn from the pages of *Metal Edge* magazines he'd stolen from the Circle K. He also got really into serial killers. He would check out true crime books from the library and cut out the photos of Charles Manson and Richard Ramirez and put them up right alongside the rock stars. When the news about Jeffery Dahmer hit, Rex followed the story obsessively, saving all the headlines to put on his walls. And he had all these disturbing drawings he'd done tacked up too. Skulls, mutilated bodies, and demons. So many demons. His skills as an artist had really developed, and the images were so graphic and detailed. God, I hated them. But he was doing well in school, so Mom and Dad let it slide, saying—*hoping*—it was just a phase. Rex wasn't getting in trouble outside of the house, but later, we found out he'd just gotten good about not getting caught."

Asher had to stifle a smile. He knew Mom expected him to sympathize with her, to confirm her opinion that Rex was in the wrong, but that just wasn't how he felt. In some instances, he could predict what his mother would say next when she was telling a story about her brother, as if he'd heard it before although he hadn't.

"He was only fifteen when the police first came to the house," Mom said. "Rex had been peeping, for God's sake. Somehow, he'd found out where one of his female classmates lived and started watching her through her bedroom window. I think he just got off with a warning that first time. Our parents tried to keep me out of those things and rarely told me what was going on with my brother. Then two other girls complained to the principal that Rex was stalking them, but justified it by explaining that they rode the same bus to school and shared some of the same classes, so they were bound to bump into each other all the time. Again, I don't think he faced any real consequences. Even as he got older and his crimes worsened, he somehow always managed to dodge punishment. It was like he was bulletproof. What's worse is he started believing that. He said he'd sold his soul and Satan was protecting him."

Now, Asher couldn't help the smirk that curled the corner of his mouth. Dewy-eyed, Mom was staring into space and didn't notice.

"Rex did so many bad things," she said, "including to his friends and family. He only cared about himself and would get what he wanted by any means necessary. I was glad when he started sneaking out late and disappearing for days. I *hated* when he was home. My parents always punished him for the awful things he did, but he just kept doing them." She took a deep breath. "My brother was only fifteen when he was first investigated for sexual assault. A twelve-year-old girl in our neighborhood had been knocked off her bike, dragged behind an empty house, and molested before she was able to kick her attacker in the groin and get away. The assaulter wore a bandana over the lower part of his face, but the girl's description still matched Rex.

The police investigated but never gathered enough evidence to arrest him. Six months later, he was questioned about the rapes of two teenage girls, but nothing came of that either. When he was seventeen, he was finally arrested for raping and beating a waitress he'd been harassing at the local diner. He stayed in jail all of twelve hours before she suddenly dropped the charges without explanation.

"There were so many fights and thefts. Rex got into brawls with boys and even some grown men. He was good at fighting because he never relented. Even if the other guy was bigger or a better fighter, Rex was always meaner and crazier, always took things to the next level. One day, Dad had had enough and grabbed Rex by the collar during an argument. They wrestled, and Rex ended up breaking Dad's arm. Even when he was down, Rex kicked him, breaking a couple of ribs. Mom called the cops, and when they arrived, Rex cried and told them Dad had been beating him all his life and he'd finally fought back. Given Rex's history, the cops were skeptical, but Child Protective Services had to be called in anyway. He really put Dad through it. In the end, they worked something out with Rex returning to the sanitarium, but after a couple of weeks, the doctors told Mom and Dad there was nothing more they could do with him because he refused to talk to the shrinks. Their only answer was more medications, but now Rex was refusing to take them.

"He finally moved out on his eighteenth birthday. My parents had been threatening to kick him out once he was an adult, but he took the initiative and made his own arrangements. I didn't know where he was going and didn't care. I hated Rex and was relieved he wouldn't be there to torture us anymore. He got a place with his girlfriend. Even though he didn't have a job, he always had money because he was a thief and a drug dealer."

Asher thought of his recent shoplifting and his discussion with Ximena. He took another gulp of beer.

Mom went on. "I can't even begin to tell you how many times Rex was in and out of jail over the years. He never stayed in there long, though. He was always able to post bail and somehow found a great lawyer that kept him out of prison. It seemed there was never enough evidence to convict Rex, or people dropped charges, or he managed to make a plea deal involving no jail time. Mostly, he ended up with probation. For a long while, we didn't see or hear from him. It suited me fine but bothered my parents, especially Mom. So when he finally came back into our lives, we all tried to make it work. He was with a new woman—his relationships never lasted long—and said he'd turned over a new leaf after going to rehab. He swore there'd be no more drugs or crime, that he'd landed a job as a truck driver. And for a while there, things seemed okay with Rex. I mean, years went by. Everyone hoped this change in him would stick. It wasn't until later that we realized he'd just gotten good at hiding the evil within him. I think he always had the desire to commit worse crimes but had to put on a good face for a while first so no one would suspect him anymore.

"About eighteen years ago, two detectives came to the door," she pointed to the front door of their house. "They said they needed to talk to me about my brother, so your father let them in, thinking Rex had been in an accident on the road or something like that. But they wanted to ask me questions about Rex's life, his job, his relationships, his behavior. It just went on and on. At this point, I only saw Rex a few times a year for holidays at my parents' house. We'd never been close and didn't talk much. If not for Mom, I doubt I would've had any contact with him at all. But these detectives asked questions going all the way back to the stalking of his classmates in junior high. Finally, they informed me of the murders."

Asher raised an eyebrow. "Murders? Like, more than one?"

"A few weeks earlier, a couple of hunters discovered the body of a teenage girl deep in the woods of Black Mountain—so it happened many miles away from here in a different county, but it'd been on the local news. Everyone was talking about it because it'd been such a brutal crime. The victim had been strung up by her ankles and gutted like a deer. What the police didn't tell the press, though, was that there were signs this was a ritualistic killing. They'd found occult symbols carved into the woman, and a pentagram had been etched into the ground below her.

"At this point, one of the detectives explained he was with the FBI and was investigating a series of similar murders across the country—seven total. Two of the victims were teenage boys, but most were females in their teens and early twenties. One was only eleven years old. All the females had been brutally raped. The killings were horrific, the bodies mutilated, but the killer wasn't hacking them up to hide the body parts. These mutilations were done while the victims were still alive. It was all part of their torture. Some of the crime scenes had occult symbols painted in blood and other signs of ritual murder. The detectives wouldn't say why my brother was a person of interest in the case, but for me, they didn't have to. I'd always known he was heading down a dark path. So I told them everything I could, and they talked to my parents and others who knew Rex too.

"The investigation went on for months. Rex was taken in for questioning many times, and so was his girlfriend, Luna. His semi-truck was seized to be searched for evidence because the bodies had been found in towns along his driving route. They discovered all kinds of Satanic stuff in he and Luna's apartment—books on witchcraft and demonology; chalices and candles and daggers; Rex's artwork on the walls; and, of course, all his records. He also had ski masks, duct tape, handcuffs, and other things that raised suspicion, but the FBI still couldn't find any concrete evidence linking him to the crimes. It was all circumstantial, and Rex hadn't been in trouble with the law in over a decade. But they kept pressing. Initially, he refused to give them a DNA sample, saying he didn't trust law enforcement, that they'd rather pin an innocent man than admit they couldn't solve a crime. But then one day, for no apparent reason, he agrees to have his cheek swabbed. So they run the DNA test, and Rex's doesn't match any of the samples collected at the crime scenes. After that, their whole case seemed to fall apart."

"So he was innocent," Asher said.

His mother's gaze was pained. "I think it's more accurate to say he wasn't caught."

"What?" Asher said, suddenly agitated. "If the DNA cleared him, why would you still think he was guilty?"

"Because I'd seen the evil in him growing since he was just a child."

"You really believed he was doing The Devil's work?"

"I don't believe in The Devil, but I do believe in evil because I've seen it with my own eyes. I *always* felt in my heart that Rex's crimes would escalate. Even when he supposedly got his life together, I wanted to believe he'd put his demons behind him, but I had serious doubts. When the FBI described the murders to me, I knew—I just *knew*—my brother was behind them."

"What, so you're psychic now?" Asher said, nostrils flaring. "You can tell if someone's guilty just by looking at them? Is that it?"

Mom paled. "You didn't know him like I did. I've only given you the broad strokes here. Rex did increasingly worse things all his life. He was incapable of empathy and compassion, incapable of mercy or remorse."

"You sound like you're talking about the fucking Terminator here.

Just because someone listens to heavy metal doesn't make them a killer."

"Asher, you are not listening. His Satanic music was only a small part of a bigger picture. Most people—including the bands who make that music—are only enjoying it the way people enjoy horror movies. They like The Devil the same way they would Dracula or Freddy Krueger. But Rex took all those song lyrics to heart. He was—"

"A Satanist? Big deal. Far more people have been tortured and killed in the name of God than in the name of Satan. The holy wars, the crusades, the witch burnings and inquisitions. Throughout history, across the globe, God has always been the leading cause of violent death."

"Asher—"

"Lucifer had the good sense to rebel against a vain, capricious God. He chose to live by his own rules. Satanists do the same thing. There's nothing wrong with that."

"Unless it leads to violence and murder."

"Rex was exonerated by DNA evidence. What more proof of his innocence do you need?"

Mom made a fist and pressed it to her mouth, her eyes shut against the rise of tears.

"Did the cops ever find the real killer?" Asher asked.

She sniffed but wouldn't speak or open her eyes.

"Mom?"

"No! Okay? The murders remain unsolved. But everyone—and I mean *everyone*—suspected Rex. Your grandfather even admitted to me he thought Rex may have been involved in some of the killings if not all. Mom wouldn't admit it, but it was obvious she believed it too."

"Again with the fucking mindreading."

Mom snarled. "Don't talk to me like that! You don't understand anything! You don't know what a nightmare it was having Rex as a brother. If you did, you'd be more grateful he wasn't part of your life. He was only around you a handful of times at your grandmother's, before the murder accusations, and even then, I wouldn't leave him alone with you. You ought to be thanking me for that, not ridiculing me. Why on Earth would you defend him when you never even knew him?"

Asher ignored the question. "So what happened then? Regardless of what you believed, Rex was cleared by the DNA evidence. Did he move away from here? Hell, I know I would. Is that when you all lost contact with him?"

"Not exactly. Your father and I agreed we couldn't allow my brother in our lives anymore. Rex didn't want anything to do with me either. He never said it, but I think he knew I'd told the FBI about all the evil things he'd done when he was younger, and thought I'd betrayed him. He felt that way about everyone, even poor Mom, who'd always defended him no matter what. After the FBI backed off, they were forced to lift the ban on him leaving town, and Rex fled almost immediately. To everyone's surprise, his girlfriend, Luna, went with him instead of breaking things off with a suspected serial killer. The family heard from him less and less after that. He just sort of disappeared."

As she rose from the couch, Asher watched his mother. Despite all she'd told him, he believed there was more to the story—much more. Not just Rex's story but the story of Mom's relationship with him. She was withholding something dark, something delicious.

"You wanted to know about your uncle," she said. "Now you know. I'm tired, honey. Tired of talking about Rex and tired of hearing his old records coming from your room."

"It's not heavy metal's fault that—"

"Damn it, Asher, I know it's not the music's fault, okay? But it reminds me of him, and I don't want to be reminded at all."

Asher almost mentioned how she'd called him by her brother's name last night but decided not to.

Mom entered the adjacent kitchen and prepared a cup of herb tea in the microwave. Asher could see her from his seat in the living room—the way her shoulders had hunched up as if she were expecting someone to hit her. Just talking about Rex had put her on edge. When her tea was ready, she carried it toward her bedroom.

"I'm gonna lie down and watch my shows for a while," she told him.

When Asher's grandmother said she was going to watch her shows, she meant soap operas, but with Mom, that always meant true crime programs.

Asher stood. "Funny how you always watch those real murder shows to unwind."

She stopped. "Excuse me?"

"I'm just saying it's interesting how people will sit down after a long day's work and watch true crime to relax. I mean, those shows are just interview after interview of people reliving the most horrific moments of their lives. When did victims sharing their trauma become so fucking entertaining?"

Mom didn't seem to know what to say to that.

"Do you relate to those people because of what happened with Rex?" Asher asked. "Is that it?"

Mom just stood there, not even looking at Asher, as if she were a child waiting to be excused. He could have pressed her, but he'd gotten all he needed from Mom for now. It was time to pick up his girlfriend and carry out the new plan.

"Never mind," Asher said as he headed to the coat rack. "Just don't play your TV too loud."

TEN

XIMENA CALLED WHILE HE WAS driving to the college.

"My dealer, Terry, usually works out of his place," she told him. "But with you being a new client, he wants to talk on neutral ground."

Asher gripped the wheel harder. He would have preferred to go to the drug dealer's house to save time, but if he had to be patient, he could. The plan would still be followed through.

"Where at?" he asked.

"There's a coffee shop on Emerson Avenue. Can you be there in two hours?"

"Absolutely."

"Cool," Ximena said. Asher could hear distorted heavy metal music playing in the background. That she was so into it stirred something in his loins. "Looking forward to seeing you again, handsome."

"You know it, babe."

He sucked his teeth as he hung up, cocky in his certainty he'd be fucking Ximena soon. He imagined she'd be better in the sack than

83

Violet. Before this week, he never would have been ballsy enough to call a woman babe the second time they ever spoke. But Asher felt unstoppable now, unhindered and uninhibited. Pulling up in front of the college, he kept the engine running as he parked by the curb in the fire zone and played some Ozzy at high volume, cracking the windows so passersby would have to hear it too. He spotted a redhead with generous curves walking toward the lot, textbooks pressed to the large tits she hid under a green sweater. Her jeans were tight as pantyhose. When she walked past, Asher rolled his window down all the way and lowered the music as he called out to her.

"Hey, Red!"

The girl paused and looked at him, apprehension in her eyes. She said nothing.

"I like your hair," he told her. "I'll bet you've got a nice burning bush down there, huh? Hope you don't shave it all off."

She started walking again. "Fuck you, creep."

"My sentiments exactly. Just saying there's no need for you to skin the cat on my account."

The redhead kept walking. Her back was to him now, and her heeled boots put her big ass on display.

"Watch your step now," Asher told her. "They say redheads are wild in bed, but they also feel pain more intensely than normal people. Did you know that?"

He wasn't even sure how he knew that.

The young woman picked up her pace now as she headed to her car. Asher had put fear in her, and knowing that made his dick hard. He considered ditching Violet to follow the redhead at a distance. She would be going home. He just knew it. Asher could monitor her, making sure she was alone before he snuck in through a window. Once inside, he'd find Red in the shower because she liked to warm up that way on cold days like this. Asher was sure of that, just as he was sure she always kept the bathroom door open a crack to let the steam out so it would be easier to see herself in the mirror. Asher would strip nude and sneak in silently, then rip the curtain back and pounce on the busty bitch. She seemed like the type who folded in the face of true danger. She'd let him do it to her out of fear for her life, and that would make the rape that much more savory. He'd find out for sure if her pussy hair looked like hellfire. He would knock her up, and she'd be forced to consider if she wanted to keep her rapist's child or exterminate the kid like the rodent it was. Asher was fiercely pro-abortion. Not pro-choice, but *pro-abortion.*

The passenger side door opened, breaking Asher's violent daydream. His girlfriend got in the car and kissed him on the cheek.

"Hi, baby," Violet said.

"Feel how hard my cock is right now."

She touched her parted lips. Asher gave her a commanding glare, and her hand went to his crotch.

She squeezed his erection. "Another blowjob, Master?"

"Not right now. I'd rather wait and fuck you later—hard and nasty." He could see her blush beneath the pale powder she wore on her face. "Besides, we've got places to be."

"We do? I thought we might hang out with my friends like—"

"Maybe later. If I feel like it. Right now, we've got badder fish to fry. How much money have you got?"

She seemed confused. "You mean on me?"

"No, I mean in stocks and bonds. Yes, of course I mean on you."

"Let me check," she said, opening her purse as Asher drove out of the parking lot. "I have a few bucks from when I helped out at my aunt's shop." She dug out several bills and shuffled through them. "Fifty-three dollars."

He held out his hand. Violet hesitated, but only briefly. Asher slid the money into his pocket and turned the music back up as he drove them to Cyber City, an electronics store on the way to the coffee shop. Violet went inside with him but wisely didn't pry into his business by asking why he was buying the tracking device.

As they headed toward the coffee shop, Asher gave Violet her instructions as she picked at her cuticles.

"Are you sure about this?" she asked.

"Don't question me, Violet. I won't have it. Just do what I command. Got it?"

She nodded, looking at the floorboards. She reminded him of a nun bowing her head in prayer, but Violet was bowing not to Christ but to the demon. Astaroth had endowed Asher with power, and he'd been using it on Violet even before Asher knew that's what he was doing. The girl wanted to be with him and appease him—she was a submissive in need of a truly dominant male—but Asher had taken control of their relationship so quickly and completely, and now that he'd met with The Great Duke of Hell, he had a somewhat better understanding of his Satanic blessings. Violet's obedience was about to be tested. Asher was confident she'd do his bidding despite any personal risk.

They arrived at The Lazy Bean coffee shop, a quaint little spot with a Vermont hippie vibe. They were ten minutes early. Leaving Violet in the car, Asher went inside and grabbed a table by the front windows that offered a view of the entire parking lot. When an older model Dodge Charger pulled in, Asher recognized Ximena behind the wheel. She had no passengers, which was what Asher had been hoping for. A newer model BMW pulled up beside her car. Ximena hadn't been exaggerating. Terry the drug dealer wasn't just selling quarter bags of weed out of some one-bedroom apartment. He was serious. When they got out of their cars and started toward the entrance, Asher shot Violet a text.

The white BMW parked beside the black Charger. Wait until I say go.

She hearted his text.

Stepping inside, Ximena smiled when she saw Asher. There was a hint of mischief behind it. Terry walked just behind her, a middle-aged man with shaggy hair and large eyes. Judging by his style, Asher guessed him to be one of those granola hippies who'd turned into a materialistic businessman once he had money, a conservative who still went to Phish concerts. His handshake was like a bag of shucked oysters. Asher had deliberately taken the seat facing the window, and pulled out the side chair for Ximena, playing the gentleman, though he was only trying to control the seating arrangements. Terry sat with his back to the window—exactly where Asher wanted him.

The waiter came over, and Asher told him he wanted a black coffee. As the others ordered, Asher texted Violet under the table.

Now.

The waiter left, and Asher tried to get down to business, but Terry held up one hand like a crossing guard. "Not yet. For one thing, I don't want our server overhearing anything upon his return. For another, I want to learn about you, Asher, before I'll even consider anything."

The man's arrogance tightened Asher's eyes, but he forced them to relax and put on a false smile. There would be time to humble Terry, but this wasn't it.

He used his friendliest tone. "What do you want to know?"

"For starters, do you have any affiliation with any form of law enforcement—a cop or DEA agent or anything like that?"

"Hell no," Asher said, adding a chuckle for Terry's benefit. "The only good pig is a slaughtered one."

"You're not some criminal turned snitch or working with law enforcement in any way at all?"

"Of course not. I mean, do I look like I—"

"Lift your shirt."

"What?"

Terry's large eyes grew larger. "Lift. Your. Shirt."

Asher bit his bottom lip to avoid cursing at the man. Whatever passivity he'd displayed in the past would never be repeated. He wanted to grab Terry's skull, shove his thumbs into his eye sockets, and bash the back of his head into the window until it burst. He'd rarely resulted to violence since schoolyard fights as a kid, but he wasn't a little boy anymore. The desire to attack Terry was almost as strong as his desire to bend Ximena over the table right then and there and fuck her until she screamed.

Asher glanced at her, and she gave him a small nod, encouraging him to comply. Asher sat up in his chair and raised his shirt.

"See?" he said, putting it down again. "No wires, man."

"Good," Terry said.

The waiter returned with their beverages in paper cups. Terry's coffee had whipped cream and shavings of dark chocolate. Asher could have smacked him for it. But this did show a softness in the man. His armor would be easy to chip.

When the waiter went away, Terry said, "Ximena tells me you're hosting a rave."

"That's right. I'm looking for party favors."

"Mmhmm. And how're you going about this?"

"I'll make my profit from distributing at the rave at a higher cost."

Terry shook his head as if Asher was a moron. "That's not what I'm asking. I don't care what you do with the product once it's in your hands. What I'm asking is: what're you looking for and what's your budget?"

As Terry spoke, Asher watched through the window as Violet walked between Terry and Ximena's cars. She had her purse on her shoulder and was fiddling with it, but her eyes were scanning her surroundings. The girl was making sure no one was watching her. She pretended to drop something and squatted close to Terry's BMW.

"Coke, I guess," Asher said. "And whatever else you've got."

Terry only stared at him. He crossed his arms and gave Ximena the side-eye before returning his gaze to Asher. "You realizing we're discussing business right now, don't you, kid?"

Again, Asher was forced to plaster on a smile to keep from growling. "Of course I do."

"Then why're you being so fucking vague? I'm asking you direct questions, and I want direct answers. Now tell me what you want—including the quantity—and what you're willing to spend."

Asher wasn't sure what the going rates were for narcotics. "An ounce of cocaine and—"

"An ounce?" Terry said with a mocking grin.

Asher looked at Ximena. She wore an expression of stunned surprise.

"You realize you're talking about six or seven grand worth of coke?" Terry asked.

The dealer's snide tone caused Asher to make fists beneath the table. He breathed deep through his nostrils, reminding himself that the plan offered him plenty of opportunity to set this hippy prick straight, but only later. Spotting Violet heading back to his Honda, Asher decided to wrap this up.

"Money's not a problem," he told Terry. "You front me the drugs, and I'll pay you once I sell them. Everybody wins."

Terry's smug grin dropped. He gave Ximena more than the side-eye now—he glowered at her. "I can't believe you'd waste my time with this idiot novice."

Before Ximena could reply, Asher cut in. "I thought you hippies were supposed to be friendly."

Terry leaned over the table, locking eyes with Asher with what he probably thought was an intimidating stare. Perhaps it would have been to someone else. "There's a difference between friendly and being a fucking imbecile. I suggest you learn that before talking business with another supplier."

"You saying you don't want in on this?"

Terry stood, taking his pussy drink with him. "If you think I'm going to front some little punk thousands of dollars' worth of product, you're even stupider than you look." He glanced at Ximena as he turned to leave. "The next time you come to me with a potential client, make sure he has cash and a lick of common sense. Otherwise, you're out too."

Ximena offered a weak apology but didn't get to finish because Terry was already leaving. Asher never liked a man who turned his back on someone when they were speaking to him. The bells on the door jangled as Terry exited the shop.

"What the fuck, Asher?" Ximena asked. "You made both of us look like fools. Why didn't you tell me you didn't have any—"

"He's a fucking asshole."

"That may be, but he's my dealer. Not just for my own supply but for my sale product. I can't afford for him to be pissed off at me."

"Relax. Once I get my stuff, you won't have to work with that prick anymore. I'll be your supplier."

"What? How're you gonna get an ounce of anything with no cash? No dealer on Earth is gonna give you that kind of credit."

Asher leaned forward and put his hand over hers. "Let me worry about that." Their eyes locked, and Asher saw Ximena's breath catch. She wet her lips, not seeming to realize it. Asher smiled. "Just leave everything to me, baby."

A hot pulse rippled through his gripping hand, and Ximena's mouth opened, showing him she'd felt it too. He touched her thigh, closer to the crotch than the knee, rubbing her beneath the table. Her legs drew closer together at first, then relaxed as she wet her lips again. Asher doubted they were her only pair of lips that had moistened.

"I can see it all as clear as spring water," he told her. "All the dope and money and success we can stomach is within our grasp. I'll be on a throne with you at my side, drinking champagne from Terry's skull." Ximena's eyes went wide, unblinking as Asher slid his hand higher. "All you have to do is believe … believe and follow me."

He rubbed her vulva. If she'd been wearing a skirt instead of jeans, he would have slid a finger inside of her right there at the table.

Ximena sighed, an erotic sound. "I don't know what it is about you …"

"You'll find out soon enough."

He stood abruptly. Ximena looked at him as if she'd just woken up, then rose from her seat.

"When will I see you again?" she asked.

Asher kissed her cheek. "When The Devil gets his due."

ELEVEN

VIOLET'S PUPILS HAD DILATED, THE LSD in her system making her look manic and cartoonish. Asher was tripping too. His bedroom walls seemed to ripple like an ocean. He turned the girl over. Nude and on her belly, Violet made short, huffing breaths as Asher carved thin cuts on her backside with a new razor blade. He lapped at droplets of blood as they rose from her buttocks, the pale flesh gone pink. It tasted of salt and sex and rusty pennies.

The sound of *Music to Sacrifice Virgins To* swirled around his head. Violet was entranced by it too.

"Why does this record sound different every time you play it?" she asked between cuts. "It's like it just keeps getting better."

"It does."

"But, like ... how?"

Asher gently dragged the tip of the blade across her ass, making her wince before she shuddered with pleasure. He trailed the blade with his tongue, absorbing Violet's essence sublingually.

"You like it when I hurt you a little," Asher said.

"Yes, Master."

"You love it when I spill blood. Say it."

"I love it when you make me bleed."

Asher dug the blade a little deeper, delighting in seeing Violet clench her fists. Though feeling the pain now, the girl did not resist him.

He smiled. "You'd like to spill some blood too, wouldn't you, Violet?"

She did not hesitate. "Yes, Master."

"Say it."

"I want to spill blood."

"How much?"

"Lots of it. Buckets."

He ran his finger through the blood rising from her wound, then painted her labia with it. "You love me, don't you?"

"I ... oh, yes, Master. I love you."

"Swear it."

"I swear, I love you. I swear to God."

Her drove his finger into her—hard and sudden. "Swear to Satan."

"I swear," she said in a whimper of sexual submission. "I swear to Satan. I love you, my master. I swear it to Satan!"

The floor beneath them grew warmer. The album chanted, and Asher could no longer tell if the hiss of serpents was on the recording or coming from somewhere in the room. Again, the voice on the record was chanting for a sacrifice. The red light flickered and dimmed, telling Asher the time had come.

"Get dressed," he told Violet. "We're going out."

"But ... we're trippin' balls."

All he had to do was shoot her a look.

"I'm so sorry, Master," Violet said. "I won't question you again. Swear to Satan."

She stood and dabbed at the single stream of blood running down the back of her thigh. Asher helped her apply bandages to her ass before she slipped back into her lacy panties. As his girlfriend dressed, Asher turned off the music, reached under his pillow, and retrieved the small hatchet he'd taken from the garage. Her back to him, Violet didn't see it.

"Be right back," he said, leaving her to get ready as he made his way to the coat rack by the door. He snagged his parka and stuffed the hatchet into the deep pocket, leaving only part of the handle sticking out.

Mom was still in her room. She hadn't come out for hours, not even to say hello to Violet. That suited Asher just fine. He entered the kitchen and grabbed two beers from the fridge, then opened a drawer and withdrew a butcher knife. It wasn't the fancy new one from the block on the counter. Mom would notice if that one went missing. Instead, he'd chosen one of the older ones from the drawer of random utensils. He checked the thick blade—still sharp. The knife went into his other coat pocket, and he zipped them both. Drawing his phone, he opened the app that came with the tracking device Violet had attached to Terry's BMW.

The blip on the screen had remained at the same location for the past four hours. Night had fallen. The rich hippie must have settled in for the evening.

Violet stumbled down the hall in a psychedelic haze. "I don't know if I can do this."

Asher chuckled at what he knew but Violet didn't. He took her hand, guiding her down the darkened hall, toward darkness itself.

He did not tell her where they were going or why. Asher just streamed Paul Chain Violet Theater on the radio and attached his phone to the dashboard mount, using the GPS to lead him to the drug dealer's house. The acid was harder to handle when he was behind the wheel of a car, so he sipped his beer, hoping it would take the edge off the hallucinogen. He wasn't sure if that's how it worked or not, but it didn't matter, not with the power of Astaroth coursing through his veins. The LSD had been for Violet's benefit. Though obedient to him so far, Asher wasn't sure the girl would go as far as he needed her to tonight, so he'd added mind-altering drugs to the spell he'd cast over her like a black dream. If acid was good enough for Charles Manson's girls, it was good enough for Asher's.

Enveloped in thick cloud coverage, the night was starless, and the new moon offered no light. Outside the car, a freeze was setting in, but inside the vehicle, Asher retained the heat that had been rising about them on his bedroom floor. Violet swearing to Lord Satan had increased the hellfire, imbuing Asher with demonic power from beyond the void.

Astaroth would not guide Asher's hand tonight. Things didn't work that way. Asher understood he was touched by the demon's infernal light, but his choices would remain his own. It was the only way.

He glanced at himself in the rearview mirror. His eyes were huge and dark and bloodshot, and not just from the drugs. The mirror reflected someone other than the self he'd always known. Asher was being altered to the point of reinvention. It was a welcome change, but jarring nonetheless. He felt as if he'd been guided—not by Astaroth or Satan but by an inner voice that influenced him without words. The strange feeling he was not alone in his body sent a tingle up Asher's spine.

He whispered to his reflection. "You in there, Rex?"

Violet looked at him. "What, Master?"

"Nothing." He shook the thought from his head, figuring it was just the acid pulling tricks. "We're almost there."

She opened her mouth but quickly closed it, deciding not to ask questions.

Following the signal, Asher drove through a lush wooded area on the wealthy side of town. Large houses on sparse plots of land. Plenty of tree coverage. Lots of privacy. Reaching the location of the pulsing red dot on the screen, Asher stopped the car before a long driveway. If the trees hadn't been bare, he might not have seen Terry's BMW parked at the front of a two-story manor house which stood like a historic landmark. There was no fence to close off the four acres. Amber security lights cast the front of the home in a warm glow, but the windows were dim but for one on the second floor. Perhaps Terry was watching TV in bed or was loaded with Viagra and fucking a hippie hag to some horrible Grateful Dead album.

Ximena had told Asher that Terry usually did his deals out of his house. That meant he kept a stash here, and probably a sizeable one at that.

Asher drove on slowly, passing Terry's house, scouting for a dark place to park. He turned off his headlights. Violet had her forehead pressed to the passenger side window and was staring into the night in a drugged trance. At the back of the property lay a thin patch of woods. Asher went off road, guiding the Honda up a small slope, getting far enough away from the street for the car not to be seen but still far enough from the house not to be spotted by its inhabitants. He killed the engine, and when Violet turned to him for explanations, he drew the butcher knife from his pocket and placed it in her lap.

She stared down at it with dilated pupils, then picked it up, turning the blade back and forth, admiring it as she hallucinated. Though she seemed confused—even a little scared—she did not ask questions and followed Asher as he got out of the car. A cruel breeze bit at their faces and tossed dried leaves over their boots. In the passenger side window, Asher caught their reflections. Black-clad with their hoods up, they looked like they were wearing cloaks.

How appropriate, he thought.

They started toward the house, creeping through the brush like nocturnal predators. Asher drew the hatchet from his coat, liking the weight of it and how the padded grip would keep it from slipping out of his hand. He breathed through his nostrils, flooding his lungs with the cold night air. Despite all he'd learned and all he'd been blessed with, there remained a tremor of doubt now that he was at this stage of the Satanic plan. He did not doubt he would succeed—that's what gave him apprehension. There would be no coming back from something like this, criminally or spiritually. It would cement his union with Astaroth and the other kings of Hell, including Lucifer himself. And what did people always say about making a deal with The Devil?

Deep in the shadows of the thicket, a crackly voice chattered. "It's not too late to turn around."

Violet hadn't heard the voice. Asher was sure of it. This message was for him alone, and though it was benign, it was spoken on a demon's tongue. Asher peered into the blackness, finding nothing.

"You could end this right now," the demon whispered, "before anyone gets hurt."

Asher found it odd that such a chilling voice would be working like an angel on his shoulder. But then a fresh devil on his shoulder chimed in.

"C'mon, Asher," this other voice said, sounding more human, like a man's. "You've made it so far. You're *this close* to all that you desire."

Violet looked at him. "Huh? Did you say something?"

Asher's blood went cold as he realized he'd been speaking. The human voice had been his own, despite not sounding like him, despite him not forming the thought before putting it into words. The feeling he was not alone within himself was growing stronger.

"Master," Violet said. "Are you all right? Because I don't think I am."

"Everything's fine, sweetheart." He touched her chin, running one finger down to her choker necklace. "Listen to me now. I know you're scared and confused, but you shouldn't be—not with my power. You feel my power, don't you?"

She nodded. "Yes. I feel it. I've felt it getting stronger like … like I don't know what. It scares me, but it also excites me, you know?"

"I do. I understand completely. That's because I understand you better than anyone ever has or ever could. We connect on this deeper level. It's why I make you cum harder than you ever imagined. It's why you love me so much. Only I know what's best for you—*for us.* All you have to do is submit, baby, fully and completely. Trust me tonight and the world will be ours in the morning."

She nodded again. "Yes, Master."

"You do love me, don't you, sweetheart?"

"With all my heart and soul."

He kissed her cheek. "You couldn't have said that better."

Any praise made her smile. "I'm with you. Just tell me what to do."

"Just keep moving. And when we get there, follow my lead."

"Um … okay …"

Suddenly, the demonic voice gurgled from the blackness. "Asher, you must remember you have free will."

The words made him sneer. Asher knew what he was, what he was doing, and what he was after. He was calling the shots here. Of course he remembered he had free will. He was dripping in the stuff.

They stuck to the shadows until they couldn't any longer, then darted across the backyard to a circular patio with a table and chairs. On the table was an empty wine bottle and a full ashtray. Someone had been out here tonight before the temperature dropped. Asher crept to the sliding door at the back of the house. Seeing Violet trembling—from the cold or stress or both—Asher put a finger to her lips to keep her hushed. Pressing his ear to the glass, he listened for any noise on the bottom floor. All was silent. Though he was prepared to break in, he gave the handle a tug just to see if it was unlocked, and the door slid open a few inches.

The luck of The Devil, he thought.

"Are we really doing this?" Violet asked.

He hushed her again and whispered in her ear. "We have to, sweetheart. Don't worry. This man is a drug dealer and a violent criminal, a pimp and an abuser of women and children. He does not deserve what we'll take from him. Now just stay silent and follow my lead like I told you to."

Widening the gap, Asher slipped into the house as silently as a garter snake. Violet followed without another word, both hands gripping the butcher knife like she was wielding a sword. She looked even more petite than usual—a small creature lost in a too-big world. Her eyes were wild, the gaze of a madwoman within the soft face of a girl. It was innocence en route to hopelessness, the sort of transition evil feasted upon.

Asher didn't snoop through the house. He wasn't hoping to find drugs and money without Terry even noticing they were there. That was not the plan. The Great Duke of Hell had not endowed Asher with such gifts only to not be repaid.

He remembered what the voice on the album had chanted in the presence of Astaroth.

Sacrifice. Sacrifice. Sacrifice.

Heading directly to the staircase, Asher tiptoed with Violet close behind him until they reached the second floor. The smell of marijuana was rich, and a television could be heard, its light flickering through the ajar door to the master bedroom. They walked with their backs to the wall, inching closer. Adrenaline dried Asher's mouth. The hatchet shuddered in his grip. Beside him, Violet radiated anxiety.

Asher placed his eye to the crack in the door.

Terry was sitting up in bed, resting a bong on his belly as he watched *The Tonight Show*. He was alone, which came as a relief. It was all meant to be. After the attitude Terry had given Asher at The Lazy Bean, the desire to rush in and send the hatchet into the center of the man's face was a powerful urge, but vengeance was not the primary goal. Payback could wait just a little bit longer. Asher just had to hope Terry wasn't a gun owner. Though the man had a hippie vibe, he was also a coke dealer. He'd be a fool not to protect himself, especially if he was forgetful enough to leave his back door unlocked, unless someone—or more likely *something*—had opened it for Asher.

His pulse raced while everything else seemed to slow down. Asher was eager to do this, but at the same time, there remained an ounce of humanity in him. His conscience tried to nag him about what was about to happen, but with every doubt came a swift reassurance that this was the one true path—*the left-hand path*. Life was a cruel sport survived solely by the strong, those rare souls who could break through the suffocating barricade of morality to take what they wanted from this mean old world. From the abyss, a personalized directive had been forged by ancient demons. Asher knew better than to resist the greatest power he'd ever held, so in a psychedelic, Satanic delirium, he raised the hatchet and rushed into the bedroom, screaming.

Terry jumped, bongwater spilling everywhere, but as he tried to get out of bed, Asher swung the hatchet down on the man's thigh. Terry cried out in pain. Blood rose from beneath his sweatpants in a crimson bloom. Bracing for another blow, Terry put up his hands defensively, but Asher had only delivered what he considered a warning shot. He jumped into bed with the drug dealer, and when Terry tried to kick at him, Asher sat on his legs, the pressure making Terry's wound gush. Asher wrapped his free hand around Terry's neck and squeezed, wielding the bloody hatchet overhead. Terry's eyes went wide as he stared up at his attacker.

"You …" he croaked.

Asher grinned. "In the flesh, sweetheart."

"What do you … How'd you get in here?"

"You invited me."

Terry's eyebrows pinched together. "What the hell are you talking about?"

"You didn't want to do things the easy way. You asked for this. Now where's the stuff?"

The question made Terry run red. If not for Asher's hatchet attack proving how serious he was, the dealer probably would have told him to go fuck himself. But the man's fear was outweighing his outrage. Terry glanced to the right, noticing the young girl who'd stepped inside. Violet still held the knife with both hands, but it did nothing to steady her trembling. She just stood there, staring, unblinking, mouth agape.

"If it's dope you're after," Terry said, "you're shit outta luck. I don't keep product in the house."

"Bullshit."

"It's true. All I've got is my personal weed. Only a fool would keep his supply in his home."

"You're lying. Tell me where the safe is."

"I don't have a—"

Asher tightened his grip around Terry's throat, and the man grabbed his wrist, trying to wrench free. Asher came down again with the hatchet, cutting into Terry's forearm. A jet of blood spurted as the flesh was split. Asher felt the vibration of the steel hitting bone.

Terry screamed. "Fuck!"

97

Asher swung again. Terry raised a hand to block the blow, and the blade went between his middle and ring finger, severing the web of flesh and entering the meat. Asher let Terry writhe in pain, allowing his point to sink in. The man needed to understand Asher was serious.

"Okay, okay," Terry whimpered. "Whatever you want. Just don't hurt me again."

"The safe, old man. The safe."

Wincing, Terry gestured to a canvas print on the wall—a tacky portrait of Jim Morrison in a tie-dye spiral. Asher nodded to Violet. She came out of her dread trance and went to the painting, knocking it off the wall to reveal the door to the wall safe. It was a large door, suggesting multiple shelves inside.

Asher pressed Terry. "Tell her the code."

He spouted off the numbers, and Violet punched them into the keypad. The door came open on the first try, revealing far more goodies than Asher had anticipated. Bricks of narcotics were stacked beside bundles of cash, all wrapped in cellophane.

"Holy crow," Asher chuckled.

Violet looked back at him for instruction.

"Come get these pillowcases off," he said, tearing the pillows from under Terry's head, causing it to whack against the headboard.

Violet did as she was told and scampered back to the vault to load the emptied pillowcases.

Terry seethed. "You'll never get away with—"

Asher swung the hatchet, and Terry frantically tried to block the blows. His arms paid a severe penalty. Ribbons of skin left his body, blood misting the air between the two men as one of them dominated the struggle. The warm spray on Asher's cheeks sent a shiver of delight through his soul. Though this violence was on a much higher level than any he'd inflicted before, it felt somehow familiar, like he was returning to an old art form after a long sabbatical.

"Asher!" someone shouted.

But he had no mind to answer. He was focused solely on the task at hand—*the offering*. A hunk of human tissue shot up to his neck, sliding down slowly on his sweat. He licked the blood from his lips and snarled, eyes wide and black and merciless. The words came to him as if unearthed from the cobwebs of some suppressed memory.

"Rise up, powers that be," Asher said in a voice not entirely his own. "In the glorious name of Astaroth, I offer this blood sacrifice!"

Everyone screamed.

Asher swung and swung, finally connecting the blade with Terry's head. The dealer's cheek opened. He lost the end of his nose. He batted at Asher with what remained of his arms, but his efforts proved futile. The hatchet just kept coming. An evil heat had climbed up from Asher's belly to wrap around his heart, charring it. Though he kept mauling the man, whatever anger he'd felt toward Terry had vanished to be replaced by a sense of Satanic divinity. A morbid peace overcame him. He was imbued with the forces of darkness, a triumphant awakening that transcended any other spiritual endeavor.

"All hail Lord Satan!" he shouted in two voices at once.

Terry's face was becoming red pulp. Only shreds of skin remained, the cheekbones exposed, lips shredded to reveal a horrible rictus. Asher began bashing the bastard's teeth out. He swung over and over, the sound of the hatchet becoming a heavy, rhythmic percussion. Asher could almost hear the crunching guitars of his new favorite album. He was excited to get back to it and discover what the next messages would be.

He suddenly realized Terry was no longer moving.

Blood was everywhere. Still, it didn't feel like enough.

Looking back for Violet, Asher almost expected her to be crying in a corner, but the girl just stood there watching him with those dilated eyes. She was impossibly pale. The stuffed pillowcases were at her sides, the butcher knife in her hand. Asher didn't say anything. He didn't have to. He merely curled his finger in a *come-hither* motion, and his girl drew closer to the bed. Violet was still trembling, so he gently stroked her cheek, leaving a smear of the dead man's blood. Asher's hands were covered with it. Putting down the hatchet, he cupped Violet's chin in one hand and put the other to her mouth, running a gore-slicked fingertip over her bottom lip.

They locked eyes.

"Lick the blood from my fingers," he told her.

Violet hesitated, but as Asher pushed his thumb into her mouth, her eyelids closed in sweet delight, and she puckered her lips around the bloody digit. Placing his other hand around her neck, Asher forced her head back and pushed his index and middle finger down her throat, jabbing them in and out as if they were his cock. Violet sucked the blood away with total obedience. Releasing her, Asher put both hands over the hand she held the knife with and urged her toward Terry's splayed body. Guiding her hand, the blade went to

Terry's pajama top, cutting away the buttons to open the shirt. His chest was nearly hairless—a perfect canvas.

"It's your turn to spill the blood," Asher whispered in the girl's ear.

Violet appeared dazed, but she was not hypnotized or otherwise controlled by Asher or narcotics or any malevolent entity. They'd shown her the path, but it was up to her to proceed. It had to be this way. She had to succumb to the evil, not be forced by it. That's why Asher released her hand, using only his words to guide her now.

"Mark him," Asher said.

Violet angled the blade so the tip just barely broke the skin of Terry's chest. Seeing the first drops of blood rise must have excited her, because she moved quickly after that, forming the inverted star with five quick slashes. She then carved a circle around the star, engraving a large pentagram in the corpse's torso. Asher leaned in and kissed her, pinching her nipple as their tongues entwined. He could still taste Terry's blood on her lips. It gave him an erection. Being a good girl, Violet noticed and immediately cupped his crotch. He spun her around and pushed her onto the mattress—onto Terry. She was draped over him with her stomach on his, and Asher yanked her vinyl pants down to her knees, tearing the panties. He ran his hand over the remnants of Terry's face, slicking it with blood, then spat into his palm, lubricating his cock with the mixture before shoving himself deep into Violet's tight teenage pussy.

What she said next made the hairs on his arms stand up.

"Fuck me, Master. Fuck me in the name of Satan."

He hammered her insides, hard and fast and deep, Violet's fingernails ripping the bedsheets. The rhythm of their bodies caused Terry's corpse to shake back and forth beneath Violet. She moaned when her boyfriend thrust deeper and giggled as he smacked her ass, leaving a bloody handprint.

Asher was just about to cum when they heard the front door close downstairs.

TWELVE

PULLING UP THEIR PANTS, ASHER and Violet grabbed their weapons.

"Oh fuck," Violet said in a hush. "You don't think it's the cops, do you?"

Asher shushed her. The television's volume was low, so they could hear someone shuffling around on the bottom floor. The cops wouldn't dillydally like that. Whoever was down there lived here, probably Terry's wife or girlfriend, or maybe boyfriend for that matter.

Violet watched Asher, waiting for instruction. Whatever ecstasy had possessed her moments ago had fled, returning her to the same fear that had throttled her when they'd first arrived. It was as if she'd been transported through two alternate, monstrous worlds.

The creak of the staircase made Asher's neck muscles go tight. Whoever it was, they were coming up.

A female voice came from the hall. "Dad? You still awake?"

Though it was not a child's voice, she still sounded young, maybe Violet's age. Hearing this, what Asher had thought was a problem now presented itself as another gift from Astaroth, another opportunity for he and Violet to prove their allegiance to Satan.

He whispered to his girlfriend. "Don't be afraid. What's one more?"

Violet stared at nothing, her expression blank, body relaxed. The fear was receding again, replaced by a grim determination.

He kissed her ear. "You know what to do."

Taking her hand, he led her to the wall behind the door so they could hide.

"Dad?" the girl said just beyond it. "You up?"

She would never speak in this carefree manner again.

As she entered the room, the door covered Asher and Violet from the young woman's view. But she wouldn't have looked back anyway. The nightmare in front of her demanded her full attention.

She screamed in a way Asher had never heard someone scream before—terror, revulsion, and anguish infused. It was horror in its rawest form.

"Daddy!" she shrieked. "Daddy!"

That she'd reverted to this childlike term tickled Asher. He wanted to give her more time to absorb grief and fear, but he didn't want Violet to lose the advantage of surprise, so he kicked the door closed. Spinning around, the daughter cried out. She was a chubby brunette with a spattering of freckles across the bridge of her nose, reminding Asher of the plump redhead he'd catcalled at the college, but by the look of this one, she had to be a high schooler. When she jumped, her heavy tits jiggled under her dress, further enticing him. Seeing the blood-soaked strangers, the girl screamed even louder, and this seemed to trigger something in Violet. She lunged at Terry's daughter with the butcher knife. Like her father, the girl raised her hands to protect herself, but Violet must have expected this because she went low, using both hands to drive the blade into the girl's belly.

"No!" she groaned. "Please, no!"

But she was begging for mercy Violet wouldn't give. She must have realized that quickly, because she fought against Violet, kicking and thrashing until she got free of her, the knife still stuck through her naval. She limped toward the door, but Asher tackled her from behind, and when they hit the floor, the impact drove the knife deeper into her gut. The daughter made a sound like a mewling animal and rolled onto her back, clutching the knife handle, babbling desperate pleas for her life.

"Please ... don't kill me ..."

The skirt of her dress had ridden up, exposing pink panties. Asher got between her thick thighs and pinned her to the carpet. Her injury made it difficult for her to scream. Only wet croaks came out. The knife was buried in her gut up to the handle. Something must have ruptured, but she was still struggling.

While tackling the daughter, Asher had dropped his hatchet. He looked to Violet and nodded toward it, and she quickly snatched it up, then got on her knees beside the woman's head. As their victim started screaming again, Violet brought the hatchet down upon her mouth, the blade hacking between the woman's jaws. Violet gasped at her own violence, as if she'd been watching someone else do it. Her grip weakened, but the hatchet was stuck in the daughter's face. She gargled blood, still alive, her head split like Ms. Pac-Man.

Asher pulled the knife out of her doughy belly, breaking the dam that had been holding back her blood. It flowed freely, the deep redness exciting him further. This pudgy bitch had interrupted him fucking his girlfriend. Now, he was harder than ever. He slid the knife beneath her panties and tugged, ripping them open and cutting her groin in the process. Watching with a dead stare, Violet slid her bloody hand down the front of her pants, playing with herself, cheering her master on without a word.

Asher raped the girl as she lay dying.

When he was finished, he pocketed her panties and handed the knife to Violet. She understood immediately. The tip of the blade went to the daughter's forehead, where Violet etched an inverted cross. Asher smiled. He was proud of her.

Using some of the terms he'd heard on *Music to Sacrifice Virgins To*, Asher constructed his own unholy prayer. He chanted slowly so Violet could repeat every line.

"Behold, we offer these sacrifices to the foul angel Astaroth, The Great Duke of Hell, eater of souls, commander of the vipers from beyond the veil."

Taking the knife from Violet, Asher cut a sideways figure eight into the daughter's left breast to symbolize infinity. Now it was *his hand* that seemed to be guided—by what, he did not know. He etched a cross rising from the center of the eight, then carved a horizontal bar between the two.

A single word escaped him. "Leviathan …"

But he didn't know what it meant.

Over the stench of raw gore came the distinct odor of sulfur. The floor grew warm, just as the floor of his bedroom had. Beside him, the little Wiccan girl who'd read tarot cards and played with crystals—never experiencing any *real* magic—now paid witness to the darkest magic of all. Her eyes and mouth refused to close.

Asher went on. "We offer these slain souls to Lucifer, our unholy master, The Morning Star. For he is the king of all evil and the gateway to all power. He is the great scourge of man, of all the creatures of the Earth. And in his name, we spill the blood of our enemies and all those who might stand between us and his bidding."

They stared down at the dead girl's face, and just as Asher finished the prayer, the tears in her eyes began to boil. The eyeballs exploded in seconds, oozing down the sides of her face as flames burst from the sockets. The inverted cross on her forehead smoldered, releasing thick, black smoke, ironically reminding Asher of when a new pope is selected. Fire as red as blood rapidly engulfed the skull, and when Asher stood, he saw the pentagram Violet had etched into Terry's chest was also producing crimson flames.

"Hail Satan," Asher said.

As they gathered the loaded pillowcases, Asher noticed a small, black box Violet had thrown in with the bundles. As they exited the room, Terry's bed was engulfed by fire, and his daughter's body began to char. Noxious smoke followed, so Asher closed the door behind them as Violet headed for the staircase.

There was no need to wipe away their fingerprints. No DNA would remain.

Hellfire would cleanse all.

THIRTEEN

ASHER HAD COME PREPARED. BEFORE they got back into the car, he drew the wet wipes and spare sets of clothes from the trunk. The ones he gave Violet belonged to his mother. While they were too big on his girlfriend, they fit better than his would have. They wiped the red streaks off each other. As Asher put their bloodied clothes and weapons into a plastic bag, he had Violet run to Terry's BMW and remove the tracking device. They hopped into Asher's Honda, and the stereo he'd left on awakened, the roar of Paul Chain's guitars startling Violet. In the rearview mirror, the second story of Terry's house glowed like a rupturing volcano. All the way home, Violet kept babbling, shocked by what they had done but titillated by it too. Asher had her open one of the bundles of cash just to keep her busy. She counted out five thousand dollars in fifties. Then she tallied the bundles—seventeen in all.

"Eighty-five grand," Asher said. "And that's not even taking the dope into consideration. Not bad for one night's work."

Violet lit a joint. "Sure beats working at my aunt's shop."

"Beats working at a fucking bookstore too."

"I just hope we're, you know—safe. I was caught up in the moment, but now that it's over, I'm starting to worry. I mean, what if we—"

He shushed her. "Relax. The way we left them, it'll look like a simple housefire. There won't be enough left of Terry and his daughter to suggest otherwise. So cheer up, sweetheart. We'll never have to work again. The lords of Hell provide—*I* provide. Stick with me and all your wishes will come true."

Passing the joint, she nuzzled him. "I still can't believe it. It's like a dream … a nightmare followed by bliss. Fuck, I feel so *fucking alive!*"

Violet wanted to go home with him to have sex and listen to records, but Asher insisted on dropping her off around the corner from her parents' house.

"Tomorrow, get up when your folks do, to make sure they know you were home tonight," he said. "It will establish an alibi, though I doubt you'll need one. That house will soon be rubble and ash."

He was in a good mood, so before Violet got out of the car, he told her to peel off three grand from the cash bundle for herself.

"Whoa," she said, "I've never had this much money in my hands before."

Her gratefulness pleased Asher. Though she'd taken the same risks tonight, she didn't suggest they split the money or ask for any drugs. She hadn't shown jealousy when he'd raped the girl or tried to stop him when the violence began. On top of Violet understanding who was in charge, she'd also realized she'd become Asher's little princess of darkness. If she stayed loyal and useful, he would reward her.

"I'm gonna take the longest, hottest shower," she said as she got out of the car.

"Think of me while you're in there. Remember what we did tonight while you finger yourself and put your thumb in your asshole."

Violet giggled. "I've never done any butt stuff before."

"That's going to change. I suggest you break yourself in before I do."

She smiled, nervous but aroused. "Yes, sir."

When he got home, Asher carried the pillowcases into his room, then went to the fruit bowl in the kitchen for an apple. He bit into it, and nothing had ever tasted so sweet. Perhaps it was the profundity of this being the first food he ate in the afterglow of his first murder.

A note in Mom's handwriting was on the counter.

Asher—call your father. He misses you and wants to talk. Also, a man named Lenny called the house phone looking for you. She included the man's number. *He said it was important that he speak with you.*

Lenny? Asher thought. He didn't know anyone by that name. If he did decide to return the call, it would have to wait.

"Badder fish to fry," he said.

Going to his mother's bedroom, Asher put his ear to the door. He didn't hear the television. She was asleep. He retrieved the shovel from the garage, then returned to his car and opened the trunk. Once the clothes were buried in the backyard, he covered the spot with a large rock and went back inside with the murder weapons. He washed them, doused them in bleach, and washed them again. The knife was returned to the drawer. He placed the hatchet under his pillow before taking a shower, washing every last bit of blood away before diligently clipping his fingernails and digging out any human tissue from beneath them.

Returning to his bedroom, Asher admired the night's haul. Using the pen knife on his keychain, he poked a hole in one of the dope bundles, scooping out a touch of white powder. He sniffed it up, the medicine taste at the back of his throat assuring him it was pure cocaine. Not wanting to deal with his mother if he woke her up, Asher put on his headphones to play his favorite album and snorted a fat line.

This time, he put on side B.

Thunderous bass made fuzz of the speakers strapped to his head. Then came the howl of guitars, like a hundred bats screeching from a bottomless pit. Slow drumming confirmed the record's second side was even heavier than the first—no easy feat. A voice rose through the distortion, low at first, then growing stronger.

It was a woman crying. "Please … don't kill me …"

Asher went cold. It was the second time he'd heard these words tonight, and they'd been said with the same inflection, the same voice.

"Please … no …"

Asher sat up, listening closely as Terry's daughter begged for her life all over again. Then she cried out in a new form of agony.

"I'm burning!" she screamed as the music crunched and droned. "Oh God, the pain … the *pain!* Don't let me burn!"

Asher couldn't breathe. What he was hearing was impossible—

but was anything really impossible if Satan commanded it? Was he really hearing Terry's daughter burning inside her house? No, she was dead before the fire started. So was she toiling in Hell?

As if in reply, another voice filled his headphones—Terry's. Like his daughter, he was calling out to an unresponsive God. His wails told of excruciating pain, a brand of suffering unknown to the living. Asher could hardly believe his ears. Terry and his daughter were in Hell because he'd sent them there, and they would remain there for eternity. Any time he wanted to revel in the endless suffering of his victims, all he had to do was put on his favorite record. What a just reward for servitude to Satan.

Another voice chimed in then—the narrator Asher had first heard on the album, the same one who'd recited the invocations. "You've done well."

Asher smiled proudly. "Hail Satan."

"Hail. But there is more to do, Asher. The Great Duke of Hell is not yet appeased."

Asher was insulted. "But I have killed for Astaroth. And what's more is I made Violet kill with me. I sacrificed two souls and converted a third to the left-hand path."

"A good start, but just a drop in the bucket."

The voice was phlegmy, and the pitch altered with every word. It sounded like the man from the record but also sounded like the demon he'd heard in the woods outside Terry's house, the one who'd reminded him the slayings were his choice, that he had free will.

"Who are you?" Asher asked.

The voice chuckled, a horrible sound. "Who I was, or what I now am?"

"Both."

Another laugh, void of humor. "In good time, Asher."

"No." Asher stood. "How can I serve Satan to the best of my ability if I don't know everything that's going on?"

"The fool talks, while the wise man listens," the voice said sternly. "You can't expect all the answers right away any more than you can expect full power after just two human sacrifices. One of them was a seventeen-year-old girl, but she was *not* a virgin. There is more to know, but first, there is more to do."

To stop himself from pacing, Asher leaned on the dresser and caught his reflection in the mirror. Dark rings surrounded his bloodshot eyes. His hair was bushier than he'd realized, and sideburns were growing in. Somehow, he looked greasier, more disheveled.

When the man's voice returned, Asher saw his own lips moving in the mirror. A chill froze him in place. He was not thinking of the words as they came out of his mouth, and the voice was not his own.

"All that you desire, Asher, remember? You must be a man of pure lawlessness—a Caligula, a Nero. Endless power, total control, infinite bliss. The album holds the keys! God gave man five senses to distract him from the spiritual realm. The real world is too noisy and colorful and busy for most people to achieve a connection to the universe beyond the one they live in. But by practicing sensory deprivation with this album, in a darkened room, you are transported—you're fucking *transformed*."

Asher nodded at his reflection.

"The answers you seek are right there. Follow the record, Asher. Your task is written all over it."

Clearing his throat, Asher regained control of his speech as he searched his own eyes in the mirror. "It really is you ... isn't it, Rex?"

But he received no reply. The tightness in his throat faded, his vocal cords his own again. Still, the music thrummed, channeling dark thoughts into his brain with cyclonic aggression. The wails of tortured souls swam through his ears—not just Terry's and his daughter's but legions of Hell's prisoners serving sentences without end.

So she wasn't a virgin, Asher thought.

He picked up the album cover—*Music to Sacrifice Virgins To.*

Asher nodded. *The task is written all over it.*

Unpacking the rest of a pillowcase, he found the black box Violet had swiped from Terry's safe. Asher had forgotten all about it. It resembled an old lunchbox and had the same simple locking mechanism, requiring no code or key.

Asher opened it, a wide smile spreading across his face when he saw the gun.

FOURTEEN

"HOW ARE YA, CHAMP?"

Asher cringed at his father's corny nickname for him. Perhaps it'd been cute when he was young, but he was a man now.

"Doing good," Asher told him. "Mom said you'd asked for me."

"Well, yeah. You haven't responded to my texts lately, so when I called her about some of the divorce paperwork, I asked if you were around, but I guess you were out."

"Been busy."

"It's good to stay busy. Your mother tells me you've got a new girlfriend."

"Yeah."

"That's real good, son. Real good. Glad to hear you're moving on from Rebecca. How's the job hunt going?"

It was always like this with his father. Dad was a notorious work-aholic. It was half the reason his marriage fell apart. No wife wanted to be alone. Dad valued his family, but he'd valued the corporation he worked for even more, a company that wouldn't shed a tear if he dropped dead tomorrow. He'd just be quickly replaced by some other dupe willing to sacrifice his personal life for his corporate masters. It was the kind of life that made Asher sick.

"I'm not really looking for a regular job anymore," he told his dad.

"What does that mean?"

"It means I'm on a new path. I'm making my own success."

Dad sighed. "Jesus, you're not selling steak knives, are you?"

Asher flashed back to what he and Violet had done with a butcher knife the night before. "I'm not in a pyramid scheme. I'm doing things my own way. I'm self-employed."

"Okay. Doing what?" Dad asked, his tone doubtful.

"Look, I'm not a teenager, I'm a grown adult. I don't have to answer to you for everything I do."

"Asher, I'm still your father. You have no reason to talk to me like that."

"You have no reason to cross-examine me either. What I do is my business."

"I'm just showing an interest in your life. Is that so wrong?"

"Yeah, well, maybe you should've shown that interest in your family a long time ago. If you had, you might still be living here."

"Hey!" his father said. "Don't you talk to me like that!"

"You don't like it, don't call me."

"Jesus, Asher, what's the hell's gotten into you? Your mother told me you weren't acting like yourself. Clearly, she wasn't exaggerating."

"What do you care what Mom thinks?"

His father sighed again, as if trying to maintain his calm. "I want to see you, son. Can we do that? Can we talk face-to-face, man-to-man?"

Asher had no interest in visiting with his old man, but he also didn't want to come off as afraid to do so. "Maybe. Like I said, I've been real busy."

"It's only a forty-five-minute drive. You could come by and see my new place. Or I could come to you if you're really *that* busy."

"Yeah, all right. Let me get back to you on that. Right now, I've gotta fly."

Asher hung up without saying goodbye, and on his way out, he grabbed an apple from the bowl on the counter. It tasted even better than the one he'd wolfed down last night. He looked at it, wondering if it was some new breed of the fruit he'd never had before. They looked like the regular red delicious apples Mom always bought. He munched on it as he grabbed his coat and headed out to his car.

He'd slept little but felt completely refreshed. A line of cocaine in the morning certainly perked things up, but even aside from the stimulant, he was energized by his recent victories. The power was snowballing. Asher could feel black magic coursing through him, tingling in his fingertips like a static shock.

It was just past nine as he came down the driveway. The day was overcast, but even a trace of natural light now hurt his eyes, so Asher fetched his extra-dark sunglasses from his pocket. Putting them on, he noticed what he thought was Violet in the front yard of her house, spinning a baton. Looking closer, he realized it must be her younger sister, Callie. The girl was even more petite than Violet but had the same fallow hair, only longer and without the black streaks. Unlike her sister, she wore brightly colored clothes and no makeup. Spotting Asher, she waved and smiled, flashing braces.

He started toward her. "Hey, there. You must be Callie."

"That's me. Hi, Asher."

"Oh," he said, giving her a playful smile. "So *you* know who *I* am."

She shrugged. "I've seen you with my sister."

"Spying on us, are you?"

"No!" she said, grinning her metal grin.

"Sure you were," he teased, stepping onto the property. "You're a little peeper, ain't cha?"

Blushing, Callie came closer. "I am not. Maybe *you* are."

Asher glanced at the house, checking for any faces in the windows. He peered up and down the street. They were alone. He was close enough to smell the lingering aroma of the girl's body wash, a strawberry perfume that stirred something within him, something that could deliver pleasure through pain.

"Why aren't you in school?" he asked.

"It's Saturday. Duh."

"What's with the baton?"

She looked down at it and glowered. "Marching band."

"Something tells me that wasn't your idea, now was it, Callie?"

"No way. My parents are making me do after-school stuff, to help with my grades. But I don't get how twirling this stupid thing is helping me learn anything other than how to be a dork."

"Don't you mean a *bigger* dork?" he said, arching one eyebrow.

She giggled at the roasting. "You would know—*dork!*"

"You're cute when you laugh."

Callie blushed and looked away.

"I'm serious," he told her. "Seems like all the Vincent women are pretty—your mom, your sister, you—*especially* you."

She shook her head, still smiling. "No way. Violet's *way* prettier than me."

"Nah, she's just a little more … *developed* than you are. Once your body catches up to hers, you'll be the hottest girl in the house. Probably the hottest in your school too."

"Whatever. But you're dating Violet."

He came closer—much closer—but the girl did not take a step back or display any defensive body language.

"Yeah, I'm dating your sister," he said. "What're you saying? That I should be dating you instead?"

Her jaw dropped. "Asher! Oh, my God …"

Though she was shocked, Asher could tell he hadn't offended her. She blushed deeper, never losing her smile.

"How old are you, Callie?"

She seemed hesitant but told him. "Almost sixteen."

"Sweet sixteen. Well, how about that."

"I mean, my birthday's still four months away, but hey, I'm closer to sixteen than fifteen."

"But still fifteen."

She looked away, embarrassed by her youth.

"That's okay," he told her. "I don't mind that you're fifteen. In fact, I think that's wonderful."

She looked at him quizzically. "You do? Why?"

The breeze whipped a lock of blond hair across her cherub face, and Asher brushed it back behind her ear for her. He could sense a vibration in the girl, her pulse quickening at being touched by an older male, or perhaps by *any* male other than her father.

"It's wonderful because you're pure," he said.

"Pure? What do you mean?"

Before he could answer, the front door to the house came open, and they turned to see Melissa Vincent in the doorway, grimacing at her daughter, at Asher, at everything. "Callie. Shouldn't you be practicing?"

Callie deflated. "Okay, Mom."

"Take your baton to the backyard." Melissa eyed Asher. "There'll be fewer distractions back there."

113

Callie started toward the fence leading to the rear of the house. She gave Asher a small wave. "Bye, Asher. Talk to ya later."

"You sure will," he told the girl, still locking eyes with her mother.

Once Callie had closed the gate behind her, Melissa came down the driveway and stood toe-to-toe with Asher. Her face was pinched and bitter.

"Can I help you with something, Asher?"

He sniffed, running the back of his hand across his nostrils to clear the cocaine dribbles. "How are you today, Melissa?"

"Mrs. Vincent will do just fine."

She was in her house clothes—pajama pants and an old Boston Red Sox t-shirt. Asher noticed she wasn't wearing a bra. She must have seen him looking because she crossed her arms to cover herself. Though she wore no makeup and had her hair up in a bun, there was a still a sincere beauty to his girlfriend's mother.

"How are you today, Mrs. Vincent?" he asked again.

"Fine," she said sharply. "What're you doing here at eight-forty-five in the damn morning? Violet has a life outside of you, you know. You can't be taking her away at all hours."

He shrugged. "Hey, I was just getting ready to drive off when Callie waved to me. It would've been rude not to say hello. I mean, I want my girlfriend's family to like me, don't I?"

Melissa huffed and shook her head. "You have a weird way of going about it."

Observing her, Asher knew she would be harder to win over than her daughters. He hadn't cared about her opinion of him before, but now he believed it would be beneficial to change it. Everything was easier when someone let you in, when they submitted and succumbed.

Free will, he thought, remembering the demon's message. Had it really been in the woods last night, or had it been communicating with him—*through him*—in some cosmic manner he did not yet grasp?

It would take more than charm and manners to get on Melissa's good side. It was too late to pull that act. And if she were anything like her daughter Violet, she wouldn't respect him if he were too nice. Was it possible submission ran in some women's bloodlines? Testing Melissa would have to be a delicate exercise. Luckily, Asher wouldn't have to do it on his own.

"I'm gonna change your mind about me, Mrs. Vincent," he said. "You'll see."

She huffed, but beneath her bitchy exterior, Asher detected something softer, something malleable. Though she didn't seem pleased to be speaking with him, she also hadn't tried to wrap it up right away, as if she were glad to have someone to talk with at all. Having witnessed this brand of loneliness in his own mother, Asher was better able to spot it in Violet's. Melissa was married, but that didn't mean she had a husband in the romantic sense of the word. It didn't mean she was happy. Sometimes, a ring on the finger means exactly the opposite.

"Yeah," Melissa said, still standoffish. "I guess we'll see."

When Asher turned to leave, he saw the hint of disappointment on her face that he'd been looking for. Had she wanted him to elaborate on how he was going to win her over, or had she just been desiring any form of male attention, even from a man she didn't like? Maybe she just needed someone—anyone—to make the slightest effort to please her.

"See ya later," he said as he headed back to his car.

As he drove off, Melissa remained in her yard, watching him go with strained eyes.

Arriving at the shopping mall, Asher went clothes shopping first. Black jeans, including a pair made of leather. A motorcycle jacket with studs on the shoulders and matching spiked leather armbands. Black t-shirts featuring some of his favorite bands. He bought a sterling silver necklace with a cross that could be manipulated to invert it. At the lingerie shop, he picked out some vinyl outfits for Violet. He also grabbed a silk teddy that would look good on Ximena, confident he'd be fucking her very soon. Then Asher headed to the Army-Navy store and purchased several hunting knives, pocketknives, and two pairs of handcuffs, joking with the shocked clerk that his girlfriend liked her feet to be restrained as well as her hands. While there, he also grabbed two revolver holsters, not sure which one would fit Terry's pistol. He then purchased a Bluetooth boombox. Finally, he stopped at the home improvement depot for supplies. It felt good to buy everything with cash. It made him feel like a big shot, and there were no credit cards to leave a digital trail.

On the way home, he used the audio file on his phone to play *Music to Sacrifice Virgins To* and decided to take a sudden detour. There was a strange, heavy energy tremoring from his chest to his fingertips as he tapped them on the steering wheel. The pulsations were in rhythm with the fuzzy bass guitar. Screams of pain echoed on the track, followed by diabolical laughter that sounded closer to cackling hyenas than human beings. It wasn't long before Asher could smell the sulfur and feel the waves of heat closing in on him in the confines of the Honda. He drove on, banging his head to the music, feeling the groove in every bone. Reaching the old state road, he headed uphill, returning to the dense woodland where he'd strapped Violet to a tree and fucked her.

By the time he parked in the dirt lot, the inside of the car felt like a furnace and stank like a fish market. There were no other vehicles, nobody around. Asher got out and breathed deep of the cold, wet air. The skies had turned white as the afternoon went on. He turned the engine off and transferred the streaming album to the new boombox, *Music to Sacrifice Virgins To* blasting as he ventured into the woods as if pulled by some cosmic compass. The trails were deserted. The woodland was gray and withering. As he reached the clearing where he'd fucked Violet, gentle flurries whirled.

Asher wasn't sure what it was about this spot. He simply felt drawn to it like a nocturnal creature to moonlight. He put the boombox down on a stump but kept the music playing. The album's voice had returned with a familiar chant, one Asher recited in unison.

"We call on the Prince of Devils, the black god of the Philistine city of Ekron—Beelzebub—the Lord of the Flies, brother to the Hesperus star."

The music boomed with distortion. Then came the voices of the tormented, howling in agony, screaming in fear, weeping in endless horror.

Out of the ether, new words came to Asher lips, as if he were speaking in tongues. "Rise up, Beelzebub, and grant me the Satanic power I seek, so that I may coerce, seduce, and destroy. I have spilled blood in your unholy name, and with your dark blessings, I shall kill again. Anoint me, and bestow your sorcery upon me, so that I may be your most loyal warlock, a black knight in Lucifer's army—evil incarnate."

As he chanted this invocation, the flurries intensified to snow, and the dead trees swayed though there was no breeze, their clawed tips dancing across an alabaster sky. Dust devils spun the forest debris at Asher's feet, and a murder of crows launched from the treetops, escaping while they still could.

"Rise, Beelzebub. Rise!"

Small cyclones of air whisked leaves away until a perfect circle of dirt lay before Asher. He drew his new hunting knife from the sheath on his hip and squatted to carve a pentagram. Wiping the blade on his jeans, Asher brought the tip to the inside of his forearm and cut a sideways figure eight into his flesh.

"Leviathan," he said with three voices at once—his own, that of the man on the record, and that of the woodland demon.

Just as he'd done with Terry's daughter's breast, he etched a cross rising from the center of the eight, then carved a horizontal bar between the two.

"The Leviathan Cross ..." the trio of Asher said. "The symbol of sulfur, fire, and brimstone. With this icon, we mock Yahweh's crucifix, for the divine plan is no plan at all. God's rules are unjust, and man's prayers go unanswered. And so we have no need for his guidance, for man is his own center of balance."

Asher turned his arm over so drops of blood fell into the pentagram.

His next words were garbled by the vocal trio coming out of his mouth—a bizarre mixture of English, Latin, Aramaic, and Italian, combined with phonetic gibberish and guttural roars. The blood he'd spilt traveled through the lines of the pentagram with precision until the star was burgundy. Then the hellfire kindled, small flames of pure crimson rising from Asher's sacrificial gesture. Fire had always excited Asher, but he was forced to step back when the black smoke choked him. The stench was atrocious—a mixture of rot, offal, and feces. Asher's mouth grew dry. His gums tasted like rusted metal. His irises ran red. Though it was snowing, he was drenched in sweat.

Dead branches stretched off the surrounding trees, growing longer, the limbs giving birth to smaller, knotted branches. They curled closed and unfurled again, releasing bloats of charred dust that poisoned the air like fallout. Above the music came the buzz of insects that should have been gone this time of year, and clouds of flies appeared suddenly, surrounding the clearing and circling around Asher, putting him in the center of a tornado of insects. Their buzz became almost musical. It reminded Asher of throat-singing, only more demonic and otherworldly, and though he could not name each type, the flies ranged in size from fungus gnats to giant horseflies.

Some of the snowflakes writhed when they landed on Asher, and when he looked down at the ones stuck to his coat sleeves, he saw they were not snowflakes but maggots. He put up the hood of his parka to keep them off his head but was otherwise unfazed. Still, the organic stench grew more pungent—a vile bouquet of rotting yams, dumpster metal, and raw excrement. Asher expected the evil entity to rise from the burning earth. Instead, it emerged from the woods in shadow, a fairytale beast coming out of the black forest.

Asher saw the horns first. They were long and high like buck antlers but came to singular points like that of a steer. Instead of being bone-white, they were black and shiny like the surface of a vinyl record, branching from a head of dead flesh resembling clay. The demon had no mouth. Instead, its chin ended in a whiskered shoot like the trunk of an anteater. Mammoth horns jutted from its cheeks in huge, obsidian spirals. The being's anthropomorphic body was adorned in flies—so many it was hard for Asher to tell if they covered its body or if they *were* its body. As Beelzebub pushed through the thicket, bare branches reached for the beast like the pawing fingers of the dead, and the demon left smears of feces on everything it grazed. Globs of it dripped from its arms and ran down its legs, the hooves leaving a greenish-brown trail where maggots swam in the bubbling filth.

Asher choked back the bile at the back of his throat.

When the demon spoke, it did so with its hollow eye sockets, the lids moving like little mouths. They were lined with crooked, yellow baby teeth.

"Asher Benton," Beelzebub croaked. "Thou hast summoned thy forces of darkness."

"Yes. I have called for you, Lord of the Flies, for you are the fiend of gluttony and corruption, of coveting and lust."

The demon cooed, a disturbing, infantile sound. A heavy froth had formed at the end of its snout, resembling semen clinging to the head of a penis.

"I come seeking more power," Asher said. "I ask for Satan's blessings."

"Lucifer, I am not."

Asher had read it was a common misconception for people to think Beelzebub was just another name for Satan, when it was actually a demon underling, a second-in-command to Hell's throne. He'd researched demonology enough to understand the incantations on the album and grasp what he was dealing with.

"Yes," Asher said. "You are an alastor, part of The Evil Trinity."

This concept was primarily seen in Western occult traditions, with interpretations varying across alternating texts and belief systems. But deep in his gut, Asher knew it to be true. The Evil Trinity was the royal dynasty of Hell—Astaroth, Beelzebub, and Lucifer. Through Satanic worship and murderous acts, Asher had managed to draw two of the three out of the abyss. He was proving himself worthy to the devils he conjured as well as himself.

"You are a demon of the highest order," Asher said. "I serve you just as I serve Astaroth and Lucifer. Let me be your vessel for the blackest magic. Let me do your will."

"There is only thou wilt."

"All right," Asher said, surprised the demon was disinterested in the concept of its own bidding. Instead, Beelzebub was telling Asher the only will he served was his own. "Then let me do my will with your power, for I am dedicated to glory of The Evil Trinity."

"Of what does thou offer?"

"Blood, Your Greatness. I've killed two already and will kill more." From his coat pocket, Asher drew the panties he'd taken from his female victim. He presented them to the beast, also showing the Leviathan cross he'd cut into himself. "I shall spill the blood of anything that walks or crawls, anything that breathes."

Beelzebub bent over and slowly reached for Asher's arm. The demon's hand was more of a claw, the fingertips ending in hard points that resembled its horns. The flesh was gray with rigor mortis and moist with liquid feces, maggots writhing in the pit of its palm while others fell like rain. Taking Asher by the wrist, Beelzebub lowered its eye sockets to Asher's wound, the lids attaching to his limb like leech suckers. The demon's eye holes slurped up the blood, and though the sight of it was ghastly, Asher tingled with elation, as if it were a pretty girl sucking on his neck instead of vampiric ghoul feasting on his sacrificial blood. He felt the tiny veins in the demon's eye sockets burrow into his flesh like inch worms, connecting to a vein in his arm to siphon more blood from the source. Asher offered himself to Beelzebub, never backing away from the demon's revolting presence. Wanting to prove his devotion, he showed no fear or disgust, only bowed to the demon.

Beelzebub raised its head again, Asher's blood glistening on the infant teeth in its eye holes. The demon took Asher by the chin and grazed its anteater trunk across his cheek. Whiskers like the legs of houseflies twitched against the softness of his skin, the snout dribbling an off-white slime from what looked like a puckering anus. The trunk wormed into Asher's mouth. At first, he froze, but then he forced his body to relax, stifling the urge to vomit as he wrapped his lips around it. Using only his mouth, he milked the demon's hairy trunk, the snout driving deeper until Asher had to bend his head back to allow the trunk down his throat. The foul mucus pumped into Asher's belly, warming his stomach acid as a halo of flies formed around his skull. Beelzebub chanted as its trunk ejaculated, sounding like the backwards English Asher had heard on *Music to Sacrifice Virgins To*. When the trunk left his gullet, Asher clutched his pained gut, struggling not to puke. He hacked up maggots, some shooting from his nostrils. His eyes went full crimson, matching the flames that had come to surround the clearing.

Beelzebub continued to chant in reverse. Asher was unable to understand what was being said but understood he was graduating. The demon put the tip of one finger to Asher's forehead, christening him with filth as it made the sign of an inverted cross, just like the one Asher wore around his neck. Its final word was the only one Asher could decipher.

"Incubus," Beelzebub said.

FIFTEEN

ASHER HAD SHOWN THE PRINCES of Hell he could be persuasive. Ever since he'd inherited Rex's collection, he'd developed a skill for seduction that would shame the most lascivious of Lotharios. Initially, he'd utilized this newfound ability to obtain sex from Violet and desire from Ximena. Now, he realized there was much more he could do with this power, especially with Beelzebub having increased it. Asher had suckled the teat of black magic—a reward for his bloodshed. Diligence made him proud, and he aimed to make The Evil Trinity just as proud, a son out to impress his many fathers. He'd invoked the forces of darkness until he'd become a force of darkness himself.

Though he'd brushed all the maggots off, the stench of Beelzebub clung to Asher as he returned to his Honda. He had new clothes in shopping bags on the back seat but didn't want to change until he'd washed. By the time he got home, the car smelled like a septic tank. At least Mom wasn't home. Asher took everything out and went inside for a shower, grabbing an apple to wash the taste of demon mucus from his mouth. At the sink, the inverted cross of filth on his forehead was washed away, but somehow, Asher knew he had absorbed its dark energy. As he showered, he noticed the wound on his arm had scabbed, the crust as black as midnight, making the Leviathan cross look like a tattoo. He'd been branded, just as he'd branded Violet. He served Satan; she served Asher. His world was in perfect balance, and his reign was just beginning.

The house phone was ringing when he got out of the shower. Asher ignored it as he groomed himself. He'd washed his entire body three times and sprayed himself down with cologne, gagging at the mere memory of Beelzebub's stench. Brushing his hair back, he saw the roots, realizing how long it was getting. His hair was growing at an accelerated rate, and his sideburns were thick and whirly. It made him look feral, something Asher enjoyed, but he still wanted it to be jet black, so he applied more coloring, laughing at himself in the mirror once he'd put on the protective shower cap. The phone was still ringing when he came out of the bathroom. It had been for several minutes now.

Annoyed, Asher picked up. "What the fuck is so important?"

A man cleared his throat. "Hello. Is this Asher?"

"Who the fuck is this? Why did you let the phone ring on and on?"

"Oh. Sorry about that. My name is Lenny Casella. I've been trying to reach you for a few days now."

Though he'd forgotten it, Asher suddenly remember his mother leaving a note about the man calling. He would have told Lenny to go fuck himself, but curiosity got the better of him. Any stranger who came into his life, especially now, had to be investigated.

"Well, you've got me," Asher said. "What can I do for you, Lenny?"

But now that he had Asher, Lenny seemed to trip over his words. "I, uh … I'm calling because … well, I … I knew your uncle, Rex Von Spades."

Asher's shoulders tightened. "How did you know him?"

"Rex was my friend. In a sense, he was like a mentor to me."

"In what way, exactly?"

"Oh, just in a general way."

But Asher suspected it was more specific than that. "So are you calling to offer your condolences?"

122

"No. Or, I mean, yes—I am sorry for your loss. But I'm also calling about what Rex left behind. You see, he sort of owed me something and—"

"How did you get this number?"

"I hired a private investigator to help me track down Rex's belongings, and he gave me information on his surviving relatives."

"Well, if you're looking for inheritance money, you've called the wrong place."

But Asher sensed that wasn't what interested Lenny. He'd figured out what the son of a bitch wanted before he could even say it.

"It's not that," Lenny said. "I'm not looking to collect anything other than what's rightfully mine."

"And just what do you dare to consider rightfully yours?" Asher snapped, wanting to hear Lenny say it.

"Well, you see, I'm a big vinyl collector, just like Rex was. Before he died, he'd borrowed some of my records. Most of them I can replace easily, so I'm not worried about those, but there's one I really need to get back."

His suspicions confirmed, Asher gripped the phone harder. "What makes you think I have it?"

At first, Lenny didn't seem to have an answer to this question, at least not one he was willing to admit to. He took a deep breath. "He, um … he told me he was leaving his collection to his nephew. My record must still be in there with the others."

"Did he say why he was leaving them to me?"

"He just said he loved you and wanted you to have them."

"Bullshit. We barely knew each other. This might go more smoothly if you don't lie to me."

Lenny cleared his throat again, a nervous tic. "I don't mean no disrespect to you or your family."

"Oh, yeah? Then why are you trying to steal from us?"

"Steal? I'm not trying to steal anything from anybody. That record is rightfully mine."

"So you keep saying. Let me ask you this, though. How did you find out Rex was dead?"

Lenny was silent.

"My mother and I have tried to find an obituary or funeral announcement—hell, even a police report—but we can't find a trace of him."

"*Police?*" Lenny asked, sounding nervous.

"Answer the question, Lenny. How do you know my uncle died when he barely seems to have existed the past ten years?"

"He was my friend."

"Rex wasn't anybody's friend. I think you know something we ought to know."

"We?"

"My mother and me," Asher said, though that wasn't who he'd meant. "Tell me what you know. Make it the truth if you ever want to see your precious record again."

"So you do have it?" Lenny asked, more statement than question.

"Maybe. You haven't even told me the name of it yet."

"You know which record I'm talking about, kid."

The change in Lenny's tone made Asher tense. The masks were off now. Strangely enough, he could perfectly picture Lenny, a middle-aged man with dark hair and a thick moustache, beady eyes and pockmarked cheeks.

Asher stood firm. "If you've got something to say, then say it."

"He was a murderer from the beginning," Lenny said, *"not holding to the truth, for there is no truth in him. When he lies, he speaks his native language …"*

"What're you talking about?"

"Read your bible."

"Fuck your bible. What're you? Some kind of holy roller?"

"Far from it, kid. Your uncle directed you to a storage unit and told you to ask for John, only there wasn't any John there. That's 'cause Rex wasn't leading you to a man but a book. Remember the code for the lock? Look it up."

"Blow it out your ass," Asher said, though he sensed Lenny was finally telling him some truth. "You don't know what you're talking about. The record doesn't belong to you. Nothing of Rex's does."

"Listen, Asher. You're playing with fire here—serious fire. I trust you know what I mean by that. You're dealing with forces you're not prepared to handle."

"And what? You're here to save me from them? Please. I know *exactly* what I'm doing. Preach that horseshit somewhere else, sweetheart."

Lenny fell hush. "What did you just call me?"

"Sweetheart! You like that, sweetheart?"

"Nah … it's just that I've heard that before. We need to talk. That's all I want to do, kid—talk."

Asher considered this. Clearly, the man wasn't going to just go away. Not without being forced to. Asher knew how to make someone disappear, and Lenny seemed determined to become his next unwitting victim, but before he could sacrifice him, Asher had to hear the man out. There were too many secrets surrounding Rex. Lenny knew something, and Asher aimed to find out what it was.

"I've got your number on the caller ID," Asher said. "Is this the best line to reach you at?"

"Yeah. It's my cell."

"Where are you calling from?"

"Never mind that now."

"For fuck's sake, I'm just curious how long it would take you to meet me somewhere. Are you close by?"

"Close enough. I can be in town by tomorrow afternoon."

That Lenny knew his number and location made Asher's blood grow hot. What was stopping the bastard from breaking in and stealing *Music to Sacrifice Virgins To*?

"I'll call you," Asher said.

"I'll start the drive tonight."

"No, damn it. I said I'll call you when I'm ready to."

"Yeah, well, I'm coming anyhow. This can't wait. Trust me."

Asher seethed. "I told you I don't need saving!"

"I ain't interested in that, kid."

"Damn it, I'm not a kid, I'm—"

"See you tomorrow. Don't forget to call me first thing."

Asher started to say something, but Lenny had already hung up.

Leaning against the counter, Asher thought about everything the man had said, retracing every line for clues. He went to the small bookshelf in the living room, pawing through the unorganized magazines and paperbacks, his mother's collection of *Chicken Soup for the Soul*, Martha Stewart, and *Complete Idiot's* guides. His father's Robert Ludlum and Clive Cussler paperbacks were gone, but Grandma's old Holy Bible was still there. Just picking it up made Asher wince in disgust, but he opened it to the book of John. He scrolled until he found the numbers that matched the code for the storage unit—0-8-44.

John 8:44: *You belong to your father, the devil, and you want to carry out your father's desires. He was a murderer from the beginning, not holding to the truth, for there is no truth in him. When he lies, he speaks his native language, for he is a liar and the father of lies.*

Asher read the verse over and over. Lenny had only quoted part of it, but Asher had heard the first line before too, back when he'd first started listening to *Music to Sacrifice Virgins To*. The narrator had chanted those very words before stating the demon must be called.

Back in his room, Asher took the coveted record from the turntable and returned it to its sleeve. He drew the black box from under his bed and grabbed the revolver he and Violet had stolen from the drug dealer. It was loaded, and a plastic case of ammunition was tucked into the box. Asher vowed to keep both treasures close from now on. He tried out the holsters he'd purchased at the Army-Navy store. One fit the .38 perfectly, so he ran his belt through it and secured the pistol to his hip, covering it with his Bongripper t-shirt.

Now, he needed to figure out what to do with the album. He wanted to carry it with him everywhere, but it simply wasn't practical. Even if he kept it in his car, someone could break in and snatch it while he was away. Speaking with Lenny made Asher realize he wasn't the only one who knew of the record's existence and great power. Some would want to destroy it. Others would want it for themselves. Asher wasn't going to let any of that happen.

He considered switching out the record sleeve with another album but did not want even that small of a change. *Music to Sacrifice Virgins To* had to remain the perfect masterpiece he now held in his hands. It was so flawless, so pure—evil concentrate. He could buy a safe, but where would he put it? He could have Violet take the record for safekeeping, but he couldn't risk her parents finding it and possibly destroying it. He could ask Diego to hold on to it, but the record was too special to trust even his closet friend with.

Asher paced through the house, contemplating. His stomach rumbled and he belched, tasting the apple he'd eaten and the faint aftertaste of Beelzebub's ooze. Suddenly, it came to him. Though he did not yet possess a complete understanding of the Lord of the Flies' sorcery, it had been bestowed upon him. Returning to his bedroom, he held the record out with both hands, staring at it. There was no incantation, no words to initiate this spell. There was only his desire to protect the album. To Asher, this was the slabs the ten commandments were carved into. *Music to Sacrifice Virgins To* was the Holy Grail of Satanism—he was sure of it. The sacred music had to be protected and preserved at any cost.

Admiring it—*loving* it—caused Asher's irises to turn the color of spring roses. His jaw dropped, and a black fog escaped his mouth, hissing like cobras. Sweat rolled down his spine as his brain twitched in the confines of his skull. Heat coursed through him, making his muscles spasm before he went completely serene.

Suddenly, there was nothing to worry about.

Asher cradled the album to his chest with his right hand and reached out with his left. Dragging one long fingernail down the wall above his bed, he etched the Leviathan cross into the paint, and the drywall began to ripple like gentle waves on a lake. Asher pushed the album into the wall with the same ease as a spoon through pudding. In the concavity, a pit of black snakes coiled around the record for safekeeping, their eyes glowing red like their new master's. Asher stepped back, watching in awe as the wall fused together again without leaving so much as a crack or spilling any drywall crumbs.

He knew then the record would be safe. The house could burn down or be swept away in a flood, but *Music to Sacrifice Virgins To* would survive unscathed. Such was the glory of Satanic black magic—*his* black magic.

The doorbell rang, pulling him out of his reverie. Asher's every muscle flexed. He drew the pistol from its holster and moved down the hall slowly. Was it possible Lenny had come already? And if he had come, was he alone?

Asher cocked the gun's hammer back before reaching for the doorknob. He waited, listening, holding his breath. Someone knocked.

"Asher?" Violet called from the other side.

He swung the door open, still holding the pistol out in case someone was with her. Violet gasped when she saw the barrel of the .38 pointed in her face. Seeing she was alone, Asher ushed her inside and locked the door behind them.

Violet trembled in his grip. "What's going on?"

"Let's go to my room."

"Is everything okay?"

"Fucking excellent, now move."

Once in his sanctuary, Violet gazed up at him with watery eyes. "Asher—er, I mean, Master ... we're okay, right?"

He looked at her quizzically. "Why wouldn't we be?"

"Well ... I mean ... after what happened last night. What we did ..."

"Relax."

"It was on the local news, you know. About that drug dealer's house."

"And?"

She shrugged. "They just said it was a bad housefire. Everything was burned to cinders."

"No mention of foul play?"

"Nah. They're saying it was an unfortunate accident."

He touched her beneath her chin. "Then what're you so worried about?"

"I dunno," Violet said, blushing a little. "It's just that ... well, last night—when we were doing the ... the *crime*—I was, like, lost in the moment, you know? I'm not really sure what came over me—over both of us. It definitely felt right at the time. It was exciting. Thrilling, really. It was fucking *orgasmic*. But now that it's all over ... it's like the reality of it is crashing down." She nuzzled into him like the pet she was. "I guess I'm just scared."

"Oh, baby girl." Asher kissed the crown of her head. "You worry too much."

"You're not worried? Not even a little?"

"Course not."

She whispered. "But ... but we *murdered* two people."

"We only did what had to be done, and we've been rewarded nicely." He opened his dresser drawer and tossed her a brick of cash. "I know what will cheer you up. Let's go buy a new car."

Violet's eyes went wide. "Whoa ... are you serious?"

"Yeah. Fuck the Honda. That car *stinks*. Literally." He chuckled. "Afterward, I'll take you out for a nice steak dinner. Just you and me. Sound good?"

"Um—"

"Of course it sounds good. Let's get our coats."

"But ... I mean, shouldn't we be careful with the money? Shouldn't we, like—I dunno—*hide it* for a while, so nobody notices we've suddenly got all this cash? People will get suspicious, right?"

Asher crossed his arms. "Are you asking me or telling me?"

The blood left Violet's face. "Asking, Master. *Always* asking. Forgive me. I just care about you so much. I don't want anything bad to ever happen to you."

"That's my good girl," he said. "I know you love and worship me—"

"I do. I so do."

"—but you must understand that I know best. If spending the

money was a bad idea, it wouldn't have even occurred to me to spend it. The act of me doing something is all the assurance you need that it's the right thing to do."

Violet looked at the floor, nodding. "You're right. I don't know what I was thinking. I just love you to death."

"I can forgive the occasional transgression," he said, patting the back of her head. "After all, you're just a woman."

He chuckled as he squeezed her, causing Violet to chuckle too, laughing at herself in a spellbound acceptance of her inferiority. The control he wielded over her gave Asher an incredible rush. It was better than any drug he could name. This was the beauty of his powers, the dazzling afterglow of service to Satan.

"I just couldn't stand to lose you," Violet said, cuddling into his chest. "You're the best thing that's ever happened to me—*ever*. I want us to be together for all time. A happy marriage, not like the stupid one my stupid parents have."

Asher raised an eyebrow. "Your parents have a bad marriage?"

"The worst. I don't know if they stay together for me and Callie, or because of the house and their money, or what, but they haven't been happy together for a long time. And what's worse is they pretend like everything's just fine. But they can't hide the truth from me. I live there. I see how they really are together. Callie does too."

"Do they fight?"

"Yeah. When Dad's home, anyway. Seems he's always away on business these days, just like he is right now. Sometimes, I think he doesn't even care."

"Does your old man smack your mom around?"

"My dad? Oh, God, no. He would never lay a hand on any of us."

"Does he cheat on her?"

"I doubt it. I mean, no—no way."

Asher smirked. "You're looking at him through a daughter's eyes. You think he'd never cheat on your mom or hurt any of you, but you don't know."

"But I do know. Dad can't cheat on Mom. That's the problem. He's … he's impotent."

"What?" Asher laughed. "You're his daughter. How would you know something like that?"

"I've heard them arguing about sex when they thought I was asleep. Our rooms are adjacent, and I can hear them through my bedroom wall. It's the worst."

"You're sure that's what they were arguing about?"

"I'm positive! I've only heard them fight about it a hundred times."

Her tone was a little too pissy for Asher's liking, but she was feeding him information he could weaponize, so he let it slide.

"I even know they've tried medication," Violet said, "but nothing seems to help my dad get ... you know ..."

"Get hard?"

Violet winced. "Ugh! It's so gross to think about. But yeah, they've had this problem for a while now. At least a year. And it's driven a wedge between them in everything they do. My dad sleeps on the couch a lot. They never sit at the table to eat at the same time. They're like two strangers sharing a roof and a pair of daughters."

Mrs. Vincent was starting to make more sense to Asher. She was a cunt because her cunt wasn't receiving any attention, and now that her oldest daughter was dating, it must have stung Melissa even more to be forced into celibacy. It was her husband who had sexual dysfunction, not her, and yet she, too, was being deprived of all the pleasures of the flesh. It was unfair, unreasonable. Asher almost pitied her—almost.

The Honda was too foul-smelling to trade in, but Asher had enough money for it not to matter. He decided to keep the old car. The shitbox might come in handy. Taking an Uber, he and Violet arrived at a car dealership where he picked out a black Dodge Challenger, having been inspired by Ximena's black Dodge Charger. This was a huge step up. The salesman looked at Asher a little funny when he paid the twenty-eight grand in cash but made no objections. As they left the lot, Asher told Violet they needed to christen the new ride, so he bent her over and fucked her mouth, grabbing her hair and thrusting as heavy metal blared. She swallowed his cum without even needing to be told to, and he rewarded her obedience with the steak dinner he'd promised. At the restaurant, Violet once again pitched the idea of Asher meeting her friends.

"There's a party going on tonight," she said. "More of a get-together, really. I thought maybe we could stop by for a while?"

Asher drank his beer, eyeing the hostess with the big tits. He had the strange desire to hack them off and use them as bed pillows.

"What do you think?" Violet asked when he didn't respond.

Though he had no interest in entering Violet's social circle, Asher had acquired new abilities he was eager to test out on others. "Are these your Wiccan friends?"

"Wiccans and pagans, yeah. But there's a couple that identify as Satanists. They're card-carrying members of The Temple of Satan."

While researching, Asher had learned about this organization. At first, he'd been excited by the prospect of a Satanic community, but the group was openly atheistic and only used the name and aesthetic of Satan to troll Christians who overstepped the separation of church and state. When the Jesus freaks put up the ten commandments at government buildings, The Temple of Satan showed up to erect a statue of The Devil to challenge them. They counter-protested against God's hate groups and raised money for Planned Parenthood clinics. While the Catholic Church protected pedophile priests and evangelists stole money from the elderly, these so-called Satanists were out there actually trying to do good in this world. It made Asher sick. What a disappointment. What an insulting way to use Satan's name.

"Gee, I can't wait to meet them," he said.

SIXTEEN

THEY WERE A BUNCH OF fucking nerds.

Standing in the corner of the living room, Asher scowled as he scanned Violet's friends. They seemed less like pagans and more like renaissance fair geeks, the kind of people who got very serious about live-action role playing games. There was a blue-haired lesbian with a shirt that read "you are enough." One ugly couple in tie-dye shirts had matching ankh necklaces, the man having huge plug earrings that stretched out his lobes, while his girlfriend sported a septum piercing and no eyebrows. There was a woman who was obviously transgender, pairing a long skirt with a five-o'-clock shadow. The others were equally insipid, the kind of people who saw themselves as unique while conforming to the norms of nonconformists. Asher loathed them instantly, but it was the self-proclaimed Satanists he despised most. They represented The Temple of Satan, therefore not representing the Prince of Darkness at all. Their black hoodies and pentagram pendants seemed like mockery. They were posers. They were fucking clowns.

It wasn't much of a party either. There were only eleven people in the house. The music was lame folk crap playing at a low volume, some Bob Dylan knockoff wheezing about his feelings. Though there was beer and hard seltzer, no one was passing a bong around or laying down any rails of cocaine. Not that Asher needed anyone to offer him narcotics—he'd brought plenty along with him—but the lack of such party favors further lowered his opinion of his girlfriend's friend circle.

Violet clung to his arm. "Having fun?"

"I've had more fun at the dentist."

"Hey now, these guys are cool. Just give them a chance, please."

"I'm just glad you're a Satanist now and not one of these lame Wiccans anymore. I mean, look at these people. Look at these girls with their hippie tattoos and circus freak piercings. If a woman wants to modify her body, it should be with collagen injections or implants for bigger tits. And the guys are even lamer with their man-buns and waxed, hipster moustaches. They look like the type of losers who call themselves male feminists. What a disgrace."

"They're not all like that." She pointed out the members of The Temple of Satan. "C'mon. Let's chat with Deanna, Paul, and Barney."

"Barney?" Asher laughed. "His name is fucking *Barney?*"

"Yeah, he's tried to get people to use nicknames he came up with, but none of them have stuck."

"Not even 'douchebag'?"

Violet sighed but didn't dare talk back.

"Oh, all right," Asher said. "Don't fucking pout. Let's go. I want to have a word with them anyway."

When she introduced him, the one called Paul did a double take, as if he were rattled by Asher's presence. Paul was a spindly, buck-toothed blond in his twenties, smaller and weaker than Asher in every sense. Though he remained polite, Paul was clearly intimidated. Deanna held Paul's hand, which Asher found disgraceful, seeing as she was an attractive girl—black hair with a purple stripe, full lips and firm tits, and none of the piercings that ruined the faces of the other females there. When Asher shook her other hand, Deanna's breath caught. She trembled in his grip, but not from fear like her boyfriend. Asher looked into her eyes longer than he did the other two.

Barney was the overweight one. Not morbidly fat but much larger than anyone else in the house. His shirt was wrinkled, the shoulders speckled with dandruff, and the pentagram on his necklace was off center. When Asher shook his hand, he got a whiff of Barney's body odor.

"So you're the Temple of Satan crowd, huh?" Asher asked.

"We're part of the local chapter," Deanna said, bashfully putting her hair behind her ear. "There are chapters in almost every state now."

"What a blessing."

Barney glanced at the inverted cross around Asher's neck. "So you're a Satanist too?"

"Not *too*. That would imply you three are also Satanists."

The trio lowered their brows.

"But we are Satanists," Barney said.

Asher shook his head. "Your cult is atheistic. What kind of a Satanist is an atheist?"

Paul spoke up but with an apologetic tone. "Well, LaVeyan Satanism believes—"

"LaVeyan?" Asher laughed. "You mean Anton LaVey? That corny fuck who wrote *The Satanic Bible*? What a joke. One glance at that book is more than enough to tell you what a waste of paper it is. I mean, fuck, with a name like *The Satanic Bible*, you'd think it'd be the Necronomicon you see in horror movies. Instead, it's just a bunch of dipshit chants written by some keyboard player who didn't even like heavy metal."

"Well, I mean, it's not supposed to be a truly evil book."

"Yeah," Deanna added. "It's more of a lifestyle guide."

Asher scoffed. "No real Satanist would even deign to wipe their ass with its pages."

The group was stunned by his bluntness. Violet gripped Asher's hand, but he ignored it.

"You call yourselves Satanists, but it's only a trolling. How can you serve Satan if you don't believe in him?" he asked the group.

"There are different kinds of Satanists," Paul said. "The Temple believes that—"

"I know what your stupid cult believes."

"It's not a cult," Deanna said. "We're an organization. It's more political than religious."

"Pretenders to the throne is what you are. There's only two Satanists standing here, and neither of them are you three posers."

Barney looked at Violet. "You're a Satanist now?"

"Yes," Asher answered for her. "She's done more in the name of Satan than all of you combined."

The group looked away. No matter how rude Asher was, they refused to stand up for themselves. Asher was drawn to that. All three would prove malleable.

"When did you become a Satanist, Violet?" Deanna asked her.

"The moment I introduced her to his infernal light," Asher said.

Paul looked at him blankly. "Excuse me, but she was talking to Violet."

Asher stepped into him. "Are you telling me to shut up?"

"No, no, no." Paul stepped back, his palms up in apology. "No, I didn't mean that at all."

"That's what I thought. You really do believe in nothing—not even yourself."

Violet squeezed his arm. "Asher …"

"Master!" he corrected, causing Violet's friends to flinch.

"Sorry, Master," she said quietly.

"She calls you *master?*" Barney asked, more surprised than disgusted.

"You all should," Asher said with a grin. "And perhaps you will."

Deanna's face soured. "Violet, can I talk to you in private?"

Asher knew exactly what it was about but allowed Violet to walk off with her anyway. He had no fear that anyone could pry his girl away from him, least of all some cheap LaVeyan Satanists. When the girls went off together, Asher stared at the boys. Paul had paled and was playing with the tab of his can of hard seltzer. Barney, however, seemed intrigued by Asher's machismo. His eyes were lit, a nervous smile dimpling his cheeks.

"What kind of Satan worship do you do?" Barney asked Asher.

"The kind that holds meaning."

"So, like … you do rituals and stuff?"

"And stuff, yeah."

Barney looked to Paul, then back at Asher, as if trying to choose between the two. Asher could sense the man's interest. Barney had seen Asher's control over Violet, and it excited him. Overweight and far from handsome, Barney had "involuntarily celibate" written all over him. All Asher had to do was show him what a real man acted like, and Barney would probably follow him into a burning toilet.

"If you guys want to prove you're serious about Satanism," he said, "you should join me in a real ritual tonight."

The dorks looked at each other.

"What about the party?" Barney asked.

"You call *this* a party? Any second now, the host is gonna pull out his Dungeons and Dragons guidebook and twenty-sided dice, and the only single chicks I see are either dykes or have a penis. You're not into that, are you, Barney?"

"Hell no."

"Good. There may be hope for you yet."

Barney smiled, already proud to be recognized by Asher. Paul remained ghost-white and flavorless. He would be more difficult to sway, and Asher doubted he was worth the effort, but he could think of a few things the nerd might be good for.

"What about you, slim?" Asher asked Paul. "You down for real ritual tonight?"

Paul hesitated as he tried to come up with an excuse. "I'll have to talk to Deanna."

"Christ," Asher said, shaking his head. "Asking your woman for permission? What the fuck is wrong with you? Did your testicles never drop?"

Paul wouldn't look at Asher. Barney stifled a laugh. The girls returned, Violet bringing Asher another beer. He crushed his empty one and tossed it on the floor, then patted his girlfriend on the ass. Deanna saw this, but though she wore a bitchy face, she said nothing.

"Everything okay, sugar buns?" Asher asked Violet.

She kissed his cheek. "Yes, sir. Yes, Master."

"How about you, Deanna? Everything okay?"

Deanna shrugged, defeated. "Fine, I guess."

"That's just super. Glad you and Violet sorted things out. The boys and I have decided to have a Satanic ritual tonight."

Deanna looked to Paul, who said nothing, too intimidated by Asher to oppose him.

"Sounds great," Violet said, wrapping her arms around her lover's waist.

"I'm down," Barney added, making no effort to hide his enthusiasm. "Maybe we could use the basement?"

"Fuck that," Asher said. "We're gonna do this right. Proper devil worship involves connecting with nature. A bonfire in the woods is the way to go, and I know just the spot."

Nudging her boyfriend, Deanna made a motion like she was going to leave. "I think we're going to stay here at the party. You guys have fun."

"We're gonna have the most fun," Asher said as he stood in her way.

Reaching into his motorcycle jacket, Asher bypassed the hidden pistol, drew two plastic bags from his inside pocket, and showed them to the others. One was packed with green buds, the other with fine powder.

"This here is Godfather OG," he said of the marijuana. "Widely considered the strongest weed on the market. The THC levels are above thirty percent." He gestured to the other bag. "Or if you prefer to ski the snowy peaks, I've got some uncut coco right here. Straight from Columbia, pure as snake venom."

"Holy shit," Barney said, staring at the drugs.

Even Paul was impressed. "That's a lot of dope."

"Violet and I could use a hand with it," Asher said. "Let me show you how much better of a party I throw."

Deanna's jaw dropped when she saw the cocaine, assuring Asher she was a sniffer, but still she resisted, even teased. "Why do you remind me of a creep trying to lure kids into a van with free candy?"

Asher locked eyes with her. Of the three, Deanna was the one he was most interested in. "Maybe I am a creep. Somebody's got to be. Somebody's got to make other people feel normal by comparison. I've never put any value in normal. I can tell you feel the same way, Deanna. Always have."

As Asher stared into them, something changed in Deanna's eyes. They softened, seeming to grow larger, like a child's. Her wariness gave way to a silent awe as she was pulled into Asher's subtle spell.

"You're going to come with us," he told her, "and it's gonna be fire."

✝

With Violet riding shotgun, Asher led the way, the others following in Deanna's Hyundai as the Challenger whipped through the dark, splitting the fog that crept along the asphalt.

Asher asked Violet a question he already knew the answer to. "So what did you and Deanna talk about?"

"She only pulled me aside to ask if I was okay." Violet rolled her eyes. "She seemed to think I was in some sort of trouble being with you, like I was being beaten or some shit."

"What did you tell her?"

"I told her to mind her own fucking business. I mean, she acts all

137

liberal and open-minded but then has a problem when my boyfriend and I have a consensual relationship as dominate and submissive. When I pointed out her hypocrisy, she dropped it, but didn't seem happy about it."

Asher turned onto the old country road. "How do you know Deanna?"

"She's just a friend I made back in high school."

"Is she a good friend? A close one?"

"Not really. That's why it pissed me off so much that she tried to play the concerned sister, like she was going to rescue me from an abuser or something."

"What about the other two?"

"I only know Paul because Deanna's been dating him for a while. He's never left much of an impression. Kind of a wallflower, I guess—nice but uninteresting. And everybody knows Barney. He's one of those guys that invites himself to everything. I think we all just tolerate him out of pity. Some girls think he's creepy, and he is a little desperate, but he's never done anything out of line."

"Have you ever fucked any of them?"

Violet gaped at him. "Are you serious?"

"You know I am. Now tell me."

"Jeez, no, of course I haven't. Paul's a pussy, and Barney's a fat pig who smells like a Burger King dumpster."

"And Deanna?"

Violet gave him an exaggerated look of shock that quickly became a smile. "No. I'm not gay. You know that better than anyone."

"Homosexuality is different for women than it is for men. You're all more bisexual than you care to admit."

"Yeah, well, maybe, but I never fucked Deanna. Although …"

"Here it comes," Asher said with a grin.

"It's no big deal, but she and I made out a few times. Nothing serious. The first time, we were on molly at the club, dancing together. It just felt so good to touch someone so soft, and one thing led to another. We made out while we danced, but it didn't go any further than that. But there've been a couple of times we made out at parties, mostly to tease the guys and get them all excited for nothing. It's fun to mess with guys' minds sometimes. They make it so easy."

"So you haven't fucked her, but it sounds like you want to."

"No … or, I mean, I dunno."

"You don't think she's hot?"

"That's not it. She's totally hot."

"I think so too. And I'll bet she's smoked more meat than Hickory Farms."

"Asher!"

"We should fuck her tonight."

Violet held back the giggles. "You're so bad."

"And you love it."

"You know I do."

Her grabbed her thigh and squeezed. "So it's settled, then. Tonight, we fuck Deanna."

"What about Paul?"

"Nobody wants to fuck Paul. Not even Deanna. I can see it in her eyes."

"What I mean is, won't Paul be mad if we try to fuck his girl-friend?"

"So what if he is?"

It always excited Violet when Asher talked with such unapologetic testosterone. She scooted closer and ran her fingernails through one of his sideburns. "What will you do if he tries to intervene? Will you beat him up?"

"No. I'll kill him."

She purred in his ear. "Tell me more."

Taking her hand, he moved it to the holster, letting her feel the cold steel of the firearm. "I wouldn't even have to use it. All I'd have to do is show it to him, and Paul would crumple like a napkin."

"No doubt." Violet moved her hand away from the pistol, gliding up his chest with her fingernails, a kitten eager to play. "I've never had sex with a girl before."

"You'll love it. I know I do."

"I dunno. Maybe. I mean, if you really want me to do it … and if you'll do it with me …"

"I'll tell you this. I don't want to do what The Temple of Satan does. I want to do what Norwegian black metal did in the nineties."

Violet nodded. As a metalhead, she completely understood what Asher meant. He was referencing the horrific crimes committed by bands like Mayhem and Burzum, black metal artists who'd taken their obsessions with evil to shocking extremes. Some were in prison for what they'd done. Others were in graves. Asher admired their devotion. *That* was the sort of devil worship he respected, not the thoughtful rebellion of modern Satanism. Violet's friends were about to learn a painful lesson.

When they arrived at his favorite spot in the woods, Asher grabbed his boombox as he got out of the car. Deanna parked alongside him, and Paul exited the Hyundai carrying a glass bong with a base shaped like a human skull. Liking the look of it, Asher snatched the bong out of Paul's hand and began packing it with dense weed. Climbing out of the back seat, Barney looked all around, marveling at the scenery as if he'd never been in the woods before. The group passed the bong around, everyone taking long puffs, with Asher generously replenishing the bowl when it got low. The weed was just as intense as he'd described. The effect was almost instant—not just a deep, stoned feeling but a dreamy, hallucinogenic dementia. Asher was their DJ, playing stoner doom metal to intensify the psychedelic effect—Alastor, Orange Goblin, and Ufomammut breaking the woodland silence with thick riffs.

Whipping out the cocaine, Asher used his pocketknife to lay rails on the hood of his new muscle car. Violet hesitated, having never done cocaine before, but a little nudge got her to put the tiny straw in her nostril. Paul passed, claiming he stuck with just weed and alcohol, and Barney claimed to be too high already to add coke on top of it. He was enthusiastic about doing some later, but Asher assumed Barney was only being agreeable, wanting Asher to like him. Deanna was the only one to immediately take Asher up on his offer. This cemented his suspicion she had a habit.

"Whew!" she said after a snort. "This shit really is pure. God damn."

Asher joined in their inane conversations only when he had to, preferring to study the others, but he didn't show aggression the way he had at the party. He'd already asserted dominance. Now, it was time to seduce and conquer. Asher's chest swelled with confidence. He openly adjusted his crotch, watching Deanna watch him. Her eyes lingered on his groin a little longer than the others' did.

"C'mon," he said to the group while still staring at Deanna. "Let's get that bonfire going."

The long walk began, Asher leading them into the black thicket, a Pied Piper with his stolen children. Minds pummeled by an excess of potent drugs, the others stumbled their way through the deep woods, the red glow of the boombox's speakers their sole guiding light.

"Where're we going?" Deanna asked.

"The Devil's psychedelic wasteland," Asher said. "A place God forgot."

She giggled, high and happy. "You're strange, Asher."

"Should we gather some kindling?" Barney asked.

"No need," Asher told him.

"Is there a metal trash can out here or something? Does anyone have any lighter fluid?"

"I told you—there is no need. Satan provides."

Eyes half-closed, Barney smiled. "That's awesome."

When they reached the clearing, Violet giggled the way she always did when she got horny, clearly reminiscing of her last time here. Asher was thinking about his last visit too, when he'd been graced with Beelzebub's rancid presence. It seemed only right for this same spot to be where Asher utilized the gifts the demon had given him. There was no lingering odor, no maggots writhing in the dirt, but the bloody pentagram he'd etched into the earth remained, a moonbeam breaking through the trees to spotlight it.

A familiar voice made Asher's ears perk up. It came from the woods in a haunting melody, like the hoot of a barnyard owl, but Asher recognized it as the same demon that had whispered to him outside of Terry's house on the night he'd taken his first victims.

"Let's see what you can do on your own," the demon cooed.

No one else seemed to have heard the voice, not even Violet.

Asher placed the boombox on a stump and queued *Music to Sacrifice Virgins To*. The newcomers didn't seem to notice the difference between this music and the other metal he'd been playing, but Asher saw recognition in Violet's zoned-out stare. A darkness moved across her pretty face, tongue gliding over her teeth, eyes wide open. She did not know exactly what was coming, but by now, Asher had warped her enough that even the anticipation of evil made the girl shiver.

"Everybody, form a circle," Asher said.

He put himself between Violet and Deanna, and everyone encircled the pentagram at their feet.

"What about the bonfire?" Barney asked. "I can gather some kin—"

Barney stopped short as Asher made a swiping motion over the pentagram with his left hand—the hand of the wicked. The symbol erupted with crimson flames nearly four feet tall. Asher watched the others, savoring the looks on their faces—surprise, fear, delight, wonder. Barney cackled as if he'd seen a parlor trick, but Paul stared at the unnatural flames with dread. On either side of him, the girls jumped back, and Asher took their hands in his, pulling them back into the circle.

Deanna was trembling. "Holy shit. Is this real?"

"It's very real," Violet assured her.

Deanna looked up at Asher, but the only confirmation he offered was a sly grin.

"How'd you do that?" she asked.

Asher shook his head. "How sad for a self-proclaimed Satanist to doubt their master's power."

"Master?" she said in a hush.

Violet smirked knowingly. "That's right—*master.*"

Asher couldn't have been more pleased with his girlfriend. He pulled her in close, then did the same with Deanna. Paul didn't even notice. Everyone but Asher was staring into the flames, hypnotized by their impossible redness. Asher's attention stayed on Deanna. He stared down at the perfect mounds of her breasts beneath her black hoodie, and the alluring curve where her back ended and her buttocks began. He admired the fullness of her lips and the way her jaw moved back and forth as she stared nervously into the hellfire. He wanted to wrap his hand in Deanna's hair and tear it from her scalp, to scoop out one of those big, beautiful eyes and devour it while he fucked the socket.

The music swelled, a cold breeze causing the treetops to crack in rhythmic percussion. Beyond the fire's blood-red glow, the woods sunk deeper into the emptiness, their shadows intensifying as the moon vanished behind a sudden rush of clouds. They churned and undulated, their dark underbellies twinkling with sporadic, silent webs of lightning.

Asher concocted a new chant, melding words he'd heard on the record with ones straight from his blackened heart. He was a pastor in The Devil's church, composing a sermon to lead his congregation.

"We gather here in worship of the light-bearer, Lord Lucifer. From the bottomless pit, he rises evermore, leading us away from all forms of authority, freeing us from the chains of a sheepish society of cowards and fools. We bow not to the threats of God! We spit in the face of his vain demands for eternal servitude. He promises reward in the afterlife but offers us nothing on this Earth, whereas service to Satan is its own reward! Lord Lucifer leads us into temptation, never scolding us, always assuring us our urges are natural and should be carried through. His rewards are instantaneous. He does not guide us, only encourages us to make our own choices without fear of judgment or divine repercussions."

Eyes closed, Barney let out a moan. "Hail Satan."

Asher let the interruption slide. Barney had no concept of what was really happening here, but he would find out soon enough. They all would.

"Lucifer," Asher continued, "I bring you these so-called Satanists who have dared to do good in your unholy name. Tonight, I shall show them the error of their ways and lead them into the abyss for you, Master, for *I am your most loyal warlock!*"

Heat tore through Asher's body like an electric shock. He titled his head back. The pain was pleasurable, causing his mouth to water and lifting a drop of pre-cum from his cock.

"*Burn, baby, burn!*" he shouted.

The circle of worshippers was suddenly surrounded by a ring of fire too high to jump over. The girls on either side of him clung to Asher's arms. Barney opened his eyes and gasped. Paul screamed, spinning in every direction for a way out that did not exist. Only Asher could free them now, but there was nothing they could do that would convince him to.

Paul whimpered. "Please ... please, no ..."

"Holy fucking shit," Barney said.

Beside Asher, Deanna quivered. "Oh my god ..."

"God's not here, sweetheart," Asher said, "and he's not taking any messages. You want to pray to someone? Pray to me." He paraphrased an old poem. "I am the master of your fates. I am the captain of your souls."

Deanna turned to Violet for help, but one look at her dead stare told Deanna she would find no support there.

"Take off your clothes," Asher told Deanna.

Again, she tried to pull away, so Asher backhanded her across the face. Paul cried out for him to stop but made no effort to intervene. He was visibly shaking. Asher almost expected him to piss his pants. Stunned by the violence, Deanna went pale, making the blood dribbling from her nose shine even redder. The sight of it fueled Asher's desire, and he shouted at her to disrobe again.

Music to Sacrifice Virgins To was no longer music. It was an otherworldly wall of noise completely foreign to human ears. When the others screamed for help, the album's demons screamed back, mocking them. Asher twisted Deanna's arm up behind her back. She cried out in pain, then made one desperate attempt to hit him in the groin, but Asher was too quick. He knocked her legs out from under her, and Deanna fell, her head just inches from the burning pentagram. This time when she was told to undress, she was scared enough to obey. As Deanna took her clothes off, Asher looked to the other two.

"You," he said, pointing at Barney.

The fat man stammered. "Y-y-yeah?"

"Bring Paul to me."

Barney turned to his friend, hesitating. He told Paul he was sorry, then tried to grab him. Paul dropped the bong. Deciding to take his chances with the fire, he bolted toward the towering flames only to be forced back by the searing heat. Barney came up behind Paul, put him in a headlock, and dragged him to Asher.

"Here," Barney said, submissive in his terror. "I got him for you! I got him for you, Asher!"

"Master," Asher corrected.

Barney nodded. "Master! Yes, Master."

Asher unfolded his pocketknife, holding the blade up before the men's faces. Then he offered it to Barney, handle-first. Asher wasn't worried about giving any of them a weapon. The forces of darkness would protect him—not that he needed it. What was a pocketknife when he was carrying a gun? Barney only stared at it, sweat wetting his forehead.

"Now kill him," Asher said. "Kill for me. *Kill for Satan!*"

Still Barney didn't reach for the knife. Asher had never seen a man look so lost.

"Murder him now," Asher said, "or I'll murder you both. But hey, to show you I'm a good sport, if you make his death painful, I might let you have Deanna when I'm done with her."

Barney glanced at Deanna in her mismatched bra and panties. She had the tender form only girls in their twenties can achieve, a succulent dish of human flesh asking to be devoured.

"You'll let me live?" Barney asked Asher.

"If you convince me you're worth keeping around. This is your chance, Barney-boy. There will not be another."

Barney seemed to mull this. Paul was sobbing now. He struggled against Barney, but the heavyset man was stronger, and when Barney finally took the knife, Paul froze as the blade was pressed just below his ribs.

"Barney," Paul whimpered. "You don't have to—"

The knife silenced him. Barney jabbed the blade under Paul's ribs, driving it up to the handle. Paul gasped deep. Whimpering one final apology, Barney tore the blade free only to drive it into his friend's navel. Deanna screamed and screamed. Applauding, Violet bounced on her toes. Paul bent over, vomiting blood, and Barney's face grew slick with tears, but he continued stabbing.

"*Now,* Barney," Asher said. "*Now* is the time for you to hail Satan."

Barney complied. "Hail Satan."

"Say it like you mean it, fat boy!"

"*Hail Satan!*" As Paul crumbled, Barney started stabbing him in the back. With every thrust of the blade, he shouted out again. "Hail Satan! Hail Satan! *Hail Satan!*"

Paul became a mess of blood. Barney dropped him in the dirt, where he convulsed at his girlfriend's feet. Shrieking, Deanna threw her hands over her face and kicked her legs to scoot away from him.

"I told you to strip!" Asher barked at her.

Violet rushed Deanna and grabbed her by the hair. "You heard the master!"

But Deanna was too hysterical to think straight. Violet unhooked her friend's bra, freeing two perfect tits. To Asher's delight, Violet went right for Deanna's nipple, biting into her and shaking her head back and forth like a puppy with a chew toy until the nipple split open. Deanna fought back. When she punched Violet in the face, Asher drew the pistol and pointed it in Deanna's face. She froze. Standing, Violet repeatedly kicked Deanna in her side until Asher told her to back off. He leaned over Deanna.

"Panties," was all he had to say.

Deanna slid them off, revealing a shaved vulva. Asher snatched her panties and shoved them into his pocket. The heat of Hell warmed his skull, eyes going red, wisps of black smoke channeling out of his nostrils. When he undid his fly, Deanna parted her legs for him.

"Please," she said. "I'll do it. Just don't hurt me."

Asher blew her a kiss, then lowered his left hand to the soft skin of Deanna's belly. She shuddered at his touch. Pressing his index finger into her, he used his longest fingernail like a scalpel, breaking the skin with an ease that surprised even him. Deanna cried but tried not to move as he cut her, knowing resistance would only bring her more suffering. Branding her with the letter A, Asher made the ends of it into inverted crosses, then etched a pentagram in the center of the A.

When Deanna's blood trickled to the dirt below, darker blood rose out of the earth. First, it formed little puddles around them, but then the blood pushed out of the ground with greater urgency until Deanna lay in a burgundy deluge the size of a kiddie pool. Horror paralyzed her. Asher dipped his finger in the blood, then brought it to Deanna's lips.

"Suck it," he said.

Deanna put the finger in her mouth. Asher shoved in two more and took her by the neck, jabbing his bloody fingers against the back of her throat. She squirmed and gagged. Violet laughed. Releasing Deanna, Asher got on his knees and lowered his head to suckle at her bleeding tit. Once his lips were covered in blood, he kissed her lips.

"I want you to know something," he said, his forehead pressed to hers. "I'm gonna fuck your dead body."

Deanna screamed, but there was no help to cry out for. Violet got on her knees behind Deanna's head, grabbed her wrists, and pinned down her arms. Barney just stood there, his eyes refusing to blink. Asher moved his coat to show him the holstered pistol, a clear warning not to intervene.

Asher shouted at the flaming pentagram. "I offer this soul in the name of Lucifer!"

In the palm of his left hand, another pentagram appeared. It rose from his flesh in pink blisters, the symbol perfectly drawn and centered. He used this hand to strangle his victim as he raped her, only releasing her throat so she could beg him to keep raping her as he'd told her to. He made her praise him and hail Satan, hurting her when she so much as stammered. These sadistic acts must have pleased the dark forces, for demonic voices made a chorus on *Music to Sacrifice Virgins To,* and yellow fingers with black talons for nails pushed out of the earth like zombies clawing out of graves. The deformed hands emerged, revealing jaundiced flesh covered in weeping sores. They rubbed against Deanna, caressing her, groping her, all while Asher continued to violate her, stripping her of her humanity.

The arms of the demons tore their way out of the ground, but they did not emerge beyond that. Violet watched them with a look of amazement, and when Asher told her to take off her jeans and panties, she obeyed, and he ordered her to straddle Deanna's face.

"Don't let her breathe," Asher told his girlfriend. "Cover her mouth with your pussy and close her nose off with your ass."

Doing what she was told, Violet gripped Deanna's head with her thighs so she couldn't move it. Their victim made a few desperate gasps before Violet got the position just right to smother her. Asher grinned wide as his girlfriend shuddered in a pre-orgasmic state. The claws of the demons began tearing into Deanna, peeling away little kites of skin and burrowing into the muscle. One of them fingered her nipple wound. Her screams were silenced, body pinned, her soul up for the taking. Violet came hard, bouncing on Deanna's skull like it was a carnival ride.

So not to break his word to his victim, Asher waited until Violet had smothered Deanna to death before allowing himself to ejaculate. He came with volume, flooding her corpse with his evil seed, and the demons stabbed at Deanna's body, driving their fingers all the way into her wounds. Hands crawled up her sides and met at her bleeding navel, then opened her midsection like a book. Recognizing this as an invitation, Asher plunged his left hand into the guts, twisting the innards and holding them up before Barney.

"The knife!" Asher demanded.

Barney seemed to have forgotten he was even holding it.

Asher held out a length of intestine. "Cut it!"

Tears in his eyes, Barney came forward with the blade, but the stench of human offal caused him to turn away and vomit. Asher snatched the knife from him, severed the intestine, and starting unspooling the rest from the corpse's cavity until he had enough to form part of a Leviathan Cross with them. Then he turned to Paul's carcass to get the rest he needed. As he disemboweled the man, Asher surprised himself with his butchering skills. Somehow, he knew exactly where every organ was in the human body and how to handle the gutting as easily as possible. He draped Paul's intestines across Deanna's—a final embrace for the lovers—and completed the Leviathan Cross.

From the boombox, babies cried over the crunching guitars and bass drum. Snakes rattled and hissed. Flies buzzed and animals mewled. The narrator chanted in a foreign tongue Asher could not identify. Some of the sounds hardly seemed possible for a human being to make, but Asher understood he wasn't listening to a normal man or even a single entity. Each time he listened to the record, he had a better understanding of it. Soon, he would unlock all its mysteries and achieve complete power.

Shafts of hard muscle pushed up from the earth—from out of Hell. They were like stiff forearms, but instead of ending in fists, there were knots of bulbous flesh, mustard colored with black studs of bone jutting out. At the tops of the fleshy knots were lipless mouths. Crooked teeth stuck out of dark, diseased gums as they bit into the splayed intestines, tugging them until the guts snapped in mists of blood. The mouths chewed the innards as they sank back into the ground.

The demons were satiated. They were appeased, and for now, so was Asher. As he and Violet got their feet, he noticed Paul's skull bong had shattered when he'd dropped it. It pissed Asher off. He'd intended to take it home with him.

An evil thought wormed into his brain.

Asher returned to Paul's corpse with the knife.

SEVENTEEN

BARNEY MURMURED TO HIMSELF ALL the way back to the cars. He was panicked but knew better than to run or fight. Asher tried to reassure him, but only so he could maintain control over his new minion's mind. Though he'd offered Barney free use of Deanna, all that remained of her by then was a grotesque, mutilated corpse. Barney declined, but probably fearing Asher would take him for an ingrate, he expressed his gratitude.

As they'd left the crime scene, all the blood on them dried and flaked away, the hellfire cleansing the trio of killers. Though Barney was shaking, Violet didn't seem remotely upset by anything that had happened. Unlike when they'd murdered the drug dealer and his daughter, these kills left her glowing rather than flooding her with anxiety. Asher's hold on his girlfriend was just that firm. She'd been the first person he'd wielded Satanic power over, and now, Asher had her in a willing stronghold. She'd killed and tortured not just to appease her master but to satiate her own hunger for the diabolical, a hunger that was only intensifying.

"You both did well tonight," Asher said. He patted Violet on the ass. "Especially you."

She grabbed his right arm with both of hers, looking up at him with starry eyes as they made their way back to the cars. Asher carried the boombox in that hand. Deanna's car keys were now in Asher's pocket, and hanging from his left hand was her hoodie. He'd wrapped it in a ball and was using it as a bag for the thing he'd taken from her boyfriend—one memento carrying another. Asher had also pocketed the dead girl's panties, just as he had done with those of Terry's daughter. The blood had not come off Deanna's the way it had with the trio's clothes, which pleased him. Asher wanted them bloody.

"Okay," he said to Barney once they'd returned to the parking lot. "Here's where we stand. You wanted to be a Satanist. Tonight, I made you one—a *real* one. None of that faggy shit you all were into before. You've seen my power. You know what I'm capable of. Isn't that right, Barney?"

He nodded. "Yeah …"

"You did as I commanded. You committed murder in the glorious name of Satan."

"Yeah …"

"How does it feel?"

Barney shook his head. "I dunno … I … oh, man, I can't believe this happened. I just can't believe it."

"Believe it, Barney-boy. And believe this too—you are now one of my children, a soldier in The Devil's army. You will be my servant, but I'll use you more as a henchman. You're to do whatever I tell you to. Understand?"

Barney briefly hesitated, then took a deep breath. "Yes."

"Yes what?"

"Yes, sir. I mean Master."

Asher patted Barney's cheek. "Atta boy. Now remember, every-one at the party saw *you* leave with Paul and Deanna in her car. *You* murdered Paul. Keep that in mind in case you get the stupid idea to turn on me and go to the police. If you squeal, you'll get a life sentence at best. You realize that, don't you?"

Barney nodded, tears rolling down his face.

"It'll also be your word against mine and Violet's. Satan won't protect you, but he will protect me, and I'll protect her with black magic. Now, if you're a good boy and a loyal minion, I'll protect you too from now on."

Looking up, Barney sighed—not with despair but with relief. "Okay, Master."

"Swear to Satan."

"I swear to Satan."

"Good. Remember what I said, Barn. Serving Satan is its own reward. So is serving me. Here." Asher reached into his coat for the remaining narcotics. There was plenty of cocaine and weed left, which he gave to Barney. He then peeled off a thousand dollars in hundreds from the wad he'd brought along to buy the car with. "This is all for you, but it's the least of my gifts. The next woman I offer you will still be alive, but you must earn her from me. Know that I am your new god."

Barney nodded emphatically. "Yes, Master. I am at your command. I serve only you and Satan."

"You serve Satan *through* me."

"Yes, Master. As you wish."

Asher stared into Barney's eyes. Beneath the horror, there was a deep earnestness. Barney wasn't lying to him. He wouldn't fucking dare.

"Good boy," Asher said, patting his cheek again. He handed him Deanna's keys. "Take Deanna's car to a parking lot, the biggest one you can find. Be mindful of any security cameras and keep your hood up. Abandon the car there and walk home. Do not call for an Uber or any other taxi because that'll leave a record. Don't call on any friends to pick you up either. I'm the only person you can trust now."

"Okay …"

Asher pressed the palm of his left hand flat on top of Barney's head. The evil heat snaked through Asher, and as he clutched Barney by the skull, black vapor emanated from the pores of his fingertips.

"I cast thee in shadow," Asher said as the smoke funneled into Barney's ear canals and nostrils. "You'll have a long walk home, but now no one will notice you. You won't be stopped by police. Not with the shroud of Satan to conceal you."

Barney vibrated as the spell was cast, and when Asher released him, the minion seemed to slink back into shadows without moving. It was as if a cloud moved over Barney only, blocking out any light.

"Run along now," Asher said. "I'll be in touch."

Barney left, and Asher put his mementos in the Dodge's trunk, wrapping the hoodie tight around Paul's flensed skull so any remaining blood wouldn't stain the interior.

He was in such a good mood he allowed Violet to choose the music for their ride home.

She chose wisely.

Music to Sacrifice Virgins To never got old. It only got better.

EIGHTEEN

THEY'D BEEN SO EASY TO lure into his spell. Even though they'd been intimidated by him, Paul, Deanna, and Barney still followed him into the woods. Deanna had been eyeing him with desire. He could have easily fucked her instead of raping her, but he'd gotten carried away, lost in the moment. Barney had started idolizing Asher almost the moment they met. Paul had been afraid of Asher but still went along with things until his blood began to flow.

Asher remembered what Beelzebub had said. *Incubus,* the demon had dubbed him, granting Asher new powers. Now, he had the ability to lure and seduce while still being a total bastard, weaving a web of black magic around anyone foolish enough to get too close.

After dropping Violet off, he'd gone home too, planning to get some shut-eye. Getting in late, only the light over the stove was lit. Mom was asleep. Asher was glad to not have to deal with her. Even remembering her voice made him grind his teeth. Something would have to be done about her, but he wasn't sure what yet and had more important things to tend to.

Asher couldn't rest. He hadn't been able to sleep for days now. The odd thing was he didn't feel tired. He tried to sleep because he thought he needed it, especially because he was meeting with this Lenny person in the morning, the man who said he'd known Uncle Rex, the one who wanted to steal *Music to Sacrifice Virgins To* from Asher. It was best to get some rest so he would be sharp for that, but Asher only tossed and turned before giving up. He would just have to rely on cocaine to keep him sharp, if he even needed anything. Lately, he'd felt as focused as a laser. He was fearless now, and that made him unstoppable.

Unwrapping Deanna's hoodie, Asher removed Paul's skull. He'd skinned it before leaving the woods, but small bits of tissue and cartilage still clung to it. If he wanted it clean, he could soak it in bleach and other chemicals, but he couldn't leave a severed head in a bucket in the garage for Mom to find (though picturing it gave Asher a laugh) and didn't want the skull completely stripped of gore. The sight and smell of it were sweet reminders of the horror he had wrought. Raising the skull so he was face-to-face with it, Asher nibbled at the spongy bits of flesh, devouring Paul's physical body after he'd devoured his soul.

Following the ritual sacrifice, the demons had feasted on Paul and Deanna, then dragged their mangled remains down through the soil, taking leftovers back to Hell with them. All that remained was a huge puddle of blood encircled by burnt cinders. Deanna's hoodie would be disposed of, but Asher put her panties into the same shoebox he kept Terry's daughter's panties in. These were not just mementos. They were charms now, as potent as voodoo bones, animal feet, and other juju tokens. Asher had come to understand that all power came from cruelty. The sorcery improved with each atrocity. He was eager to fill that shoebox until it overflowed with the panties of his innocent victims.

Asher had other plans for Paul's head.

Getting a wrench socket and the power drill out of the garage, he returned to his room and used it on the skull, drilling a hole through the crown the size of a quarter. He then drilled a smaller hole on one temple. Asher went to the bathroom, unscrewed the head of the faucet, and removed the nickel-sized screen. Back in his room, he pushed the screen down through the socket until it lay flat at the bottom. With a little force, the wrench socket fit perfectly in the concavity of

Paul's nose hole, creating a makeshift bowl for him to stuff weed into. He lifted the crown of the skull to his lips and puckered them around the hole he'd carved, then lit the bowl, using the other hole at the skull's temple as a carburetor.

Paul had broken the glass skull bong before Asher could steal it from him. Asher had been angry over it, but now he saw it as one of Satan's blessings in disguise. Paul's actual skull made for an even better pipe.

Incredibly stoned, Asher unwound in the living room in front of the TV. When he turned it on, it was already set to one of Mom's true crime channels. He let the show play while researching black magic on his phone, trying to get an even better understanding of what a warlock could do, but the true crime show pulled him in. It was a story about a reverend who was a loving husband, father, and son— a real pillar of the community who was secretly a serial rapist who, over the course of nineteen years, raped at least thirty women and girls, ranging in ages from eight to seventy-nine. And that was just the victims they could confirm. If he hadn't "accidentally" killed his final victim (a preteen member of his flock he'd been secretly molesting for years), he might never have been caught. The docuseries interviewed multiple victims, and their PTSD blubbering turned Asher on. It almost tempted him to let some of his own victims survive, for the aftermath of such violence continued to torture people for the rest of their lives, whereas murder ended their suffering. But his killings were not just self-serving. He served another—a demon lord who had to be appeased with human sacrifice.

By the time the show was over, the sun was coming up. Stepping outside, Asher's breath made fog in the crisp air of morning, and gazing at the pink horizon, he was flooded by feelings of accomplishment and pride, but more than anything, he had a sense of duty. Satanic intuition told him it was going to be a big day.

Asher made the call. Lenny picked up instantly.

"First thing in the morning," Asher said.

"I appreciate that. I'm at a McDonald's off the highway. I'll be there soon."

"I've decided on a place to meet."

A pause before Lenny replied. "What's wrong with meeting at your house?"

"Everything. Don't come here. If you do, there will be dire consequences."

Lenny scoffed. "Okay."

"Look—if you want to do this, we're gonna do it my way. Got that?"

"Just tell me where we're goin', kid."

Holding the phone to his ear with his shoulder freed Asher's hands to slide the pistol into its holster. "There's a spot near this nature preserve that's very private. Head up state road—"

"Fuck that. I'm not going in the woods with you."

Asher tensed. "And why is that?"

"I ain't interested in getting murdered."

A coldness slithered through Asher. What exactly did Lenny know? He had to find out, even if he had to cave to get the meeting.

"That's ridiculous," Asher lied. "Nobody's killing anybody. But if you're that paranoid—I mean, if you're that *afraid of me*—why don't we meet somewhere public?"

"Name it."

"Kirby's Place. Wait, no, they won't be open at this hour. How about a cup of coffee at The Lazy Bean?"

Another pause. "*Coffee?* Are you serious?"

"Look, they open at seven-thirty."

"All right, then. I guess that works for me."

"See you soon, sweetheart," Asher said and hung up.

He had text messages from the day before—his father and Ximena. She wanted to see him, and Asher could guess why. He finally texted back now, telling her to keep her schedule open for the night, that he'd be in touch. Asher didn't bother reading the texts from his old man yet. Once dressed, he grabbed an apple for breakfast, and as he bit into it, he suddenly realized the symbolism.

An apple—*the forbidden fruit*. This was what Eve had eaten in the garden, casting the whole of humanity out of paradise. All she'd wanted was forbidden knowledge, to discover all that God denied us and better understand the worlds beyond her own. Asher was after the same thing. No wonder apples tasted so good to him now. Nothing was more delicious than blasphemy.

He heard his mother. "Heading out again already?"

Asher turned to see Mom in her pajamas and bathrobe.

"Don't question me," he said.

Her face hardened. "I am *your mother*, Asher."

"Then make me some breakfast."

"You know I have to get ready for work."

"What kind of mother sends her son off to school on an empty stomach?"

"I wish you were in school. I wish you were on some sort of path."

He smirked. "I'm on the left-hand path."

She frowned with concern. "Asher, you've got me so worried."

"Chill out, would ya? You want some weed? Maybe something stronger?"

"No, Asher. Jesus, stronger drugs? What have you gotten yourself into?"

"Mind your own business."

"My child *is* my business."

"I'm not a child."

"You're sure acting like one!"

Asher moved on her quickly, snatching the hair at the back of her head and pulling her into him. To his surprise, Mom slapped him, so he slapped her back—*hard*. Her eyes went wide as her cheek turned pink, and Asher slapped her again.

"This is your last warning," he told her. "Stay out of my business and off my ass!"

Mom sniffed back tears. "My God, Asher … you're just like him now."

"Am I getting through to you, bitch?" he asked, shaking her.

She shut her eyes tight. "Yes! Okay, okay … please …"

Asher shoved her away. "Bacon, eggs, and hashbrowns. Toast with butter and jelly. And put a pot of coffee on. Act like a woman, for fuck's sake."

Mom looked at the floor. She could tell Asher to get out of her house. She could change the locks while he was gone, send his father after him, or even call the police. But Asher knew she wouldn't. There is no love as unconditional as that of a mother's, and Mom didn't want them to become estranged. She'd already lost a husband and a brother. Losing a son on top of that would be too devastating. So she might squawk at him, but she'd never make good on any threat. Perhaps she would try to reason with him or coax him or make him feel guilty, but never retaliate, and that made her his most loyal minion, even though she would never know she was one.

Without another word, Mom turned on the stovetop and started pulling pans and spatulas from the drawers.

"Know what I love about eggs?" Asher said as she took them out of the fridge. "It's essentially a chicken abortion. You're eating a fetus.

You're eating *the unborn*."

Asher laughed, but his mother didn't. It annoyed him how some people could have no sense of humor. She put the eggs, some cheese, and the gallon of milk on the counter. She always used milk for the protein shake breakfasts she took with her to work. Popping the cap, she turned her head away in disgust.

"Ugh," she said, covering her nose and mouth as she poured some milk into the sink. It came out in runny, yellowed clumps. "Spoiled already? It was fine yesterday." She checked the carton's sell-by date. "This should be good for another twelve days at the very least. I don't get it. That's the second time this week."

"They don't make 'em like they used to, huh? Christ, you're really starting to sound like an old crone."

She ignored his comment and dumped the milk down the garbage disposal, then started cooking.

"Hey," Asher said. "I watched one of your true crime shows this morning. It was really good. You know, until now, I've never understood your obsession with that shit, but now I get it." He chuckled. "Watching people bawl their eyes out over the horrible things that happened to them is very entertaining. Hell, it's like porn."

Mom grimaced. "*Porn?* My God, Asher, how could you say that?"

"Don't act so innocent. You hardly watch anything but those shows."

"Yeah, but they're not like porn. Not to me."

"Then what are they?"

She didn't have an answer to that—or at least not one she cared to share.

"C'mon, Mom. Tell me why you love the suffering of others so much."

"I *don't* enjoy the suffering of others."

"Sure you do." Asher put his feet up on the kitchen table, something she'd scolded him for when he was a kid. Now, she didn't say a word. "You're just as sadistic as anyone, Mommy. Just look at what you did to me."

She turned away from the stove to face him, looking more hurt than outraged. "What are you talking about? I've always been a good mother to you!"

"Then why did I turn out like this?" he said, gesturing to himself. "You raised me to be what I am. You and Dad. But you divorced him, taking my father away from me, just like you took my uncle away from me."

"That's *not* what happened!"

"Sure it is. You destroyed our family. Now, you're trying to destroy me."

Crying now, Mom threw the spatula against the wall, smearing it with melted cheese. "No! There are two sides to every story, Asher. I didn't take your father away. We had a good marriage, and you know it! We just drifted apart as we got older. You can see him any time you want, but instead, you ignore him. And as for your precious uncle—the one you're so enamored with now—he was a fucking *monster*. I thought I explained that very clearly."

"He seems like a pretty awesome dude to me."

Mom put both hands on the counter, leaning on it for support as the tears fell upon its surface. She took a deep breath. Asher waited, sensing she was about to confess something he would want to hear. Taking his feet off the table, he leaned forward like an eager student, and his mother finally faced him. She looked tired, wounded.

Mom crossed her arms in a self-hug. "When I was twelve, your uncle Rex raped me."

A tingle went through Asher's extremities.

"It was the day after his fifteenth birthday," Mom said, choking a little on her words. "We were alone in the house, and he said he wanted a present from me ... and then he ... he *forced* himself on me. He didn't leave any bruises, but he did punch me in the stomach when I tried to resist, and me being a virgin, he also wounded my ... my *insides*. Rex pinned me down, and when he was finished, he said that if I told anyone, we'd both be in trouble because it was illegal for a sister to have sex with her brother. He convinced me we would both go to jail and never see our parents again ... and I believed him. So I kept our secret.

"Rex never touched me after that. He basically ignored me. I actually remember him always telling his buddies there was no reason to keep dating a girl once you'd had sex with her. I shouldn't have been hurt by that, but I was anyway. I felt like my brother hated me, and even though he'd been the one to hurt me, I wanted him to love me again, as weird as that may sound. But he blew me off every time I tried to talk to him. As I got older, I tried to just forget what had happened so I could have a normal relationship with him again. I justified his sexual assault as him having been a mixed-up kid who'd had a moment of insanity, like he'd been confused about what sex should be and had made a terrible mistake. But Rex never even apologized or showed any remorse for what he'd done to me. Later, I learned more about sexual assault, but it wasn't until I was in my forties that I really realized the full scope of what he'd done to me, but by then, so many years had gone by, and I didn't want the shame of telling anyone what had happened. I kept that secret for decades. Other than your father, you're the only person I've ever told."

Not knowing how to react to this, Asher only stared at her. Her story was shocking, but at the same time, Asher felt a grotesque arousal, and as dark as her confession was, somehow it didn't surprise him. Not because of everything else she'd told him about Rex, but because he had a sense of *déjà vu*, as if he'd witnessed the rape in a dream he'd forgotten.

"Your uncle *raped me*, Asher. Now do you understand why I forced him out of my life? Do you understand why I hate seeing you copy and idolize him?"

Asher mulled this. He was tempted to defend his uncle but couldn't. Looking at Mom, he knew she was telling the truth. In another time, he would have pitied his mother, but that time had passed. Though it had only been weeks since he'd received his inheritance, that defining moment seemed like a lifetime ago. He was a completely different man now.

"Do you see what *I* mean, Mommy dearest?" he said. "When someone you love does anything you don't like, you push them out of your life rather than forgiving and forgetting—just like with Dad."

The hurt that befell his mother's face amazed him. She sobbed like he'd never seen her sob before. Making anyone cry gave Asher a sadistic thrill, but making his own mother sob uncontrollably was the top tier.

"Don't forget the eggs, Mom," he said, pointing at the sizzling pan. "I don't want them burned."

But she was useless. She ran out down the hall, wailing and slamming her bedroom door behind her. Asher shrugged. Most of the food was ready now anyway. Finishing cooking, he served it up and poured a cup of coffee. He chased it with a line of cocaine to start the day, but even these stimulants paled in comparison to the energy gained from hurting his mother.

It was a good breakfast, almost as tasty as the morsels of flesh on Paul's skull.

Before heading out, Asher went to Mom's door. It was locked.

Asher knocked but didn't get a reply. Pressing his ear to the door, he heard her crying softly.

"I think I know why you like those true crime shows, Mom," he said to the door, loud enough for her to hear. "It gives you comfort, doesn't it? It helps to know there are other people out there who suffered the way you did at the hands of an evil person. I mean, that's what you consider Uncle Rex to be, right? An evil person—a fucking demon?"

She did not reply.

"I think its cathartic for you to watch those shows, even if they make you reflect on your own trauma. I find that shit fascinating." He chuckled. "The show I just watched was also about rape. Every time they showed a picture of one of the victims, I asked myself the same question—was she hot enough to risk getting caught for rape? Was she hot enough to risk going to prison for murder? The reverend who committed these acts seemed to think so. Now that I think about it, I can't imagine a higher compliment a man could give a woman than to rape her. He's telling her she's so beautiful that he is willing to risk his life and his freedom just to have her for one brief moment. Maybe you should take that into consideration, huh? Maybe you should appreciate Rex more than you do."

Still, he received no answer, but her sobbing grew louder, more hysterical.

Asher burped the taste of bacon, then headed out the front door with a wide smile on his face.

It was going to be a good day.

✝

Driving out of the neighborhood, he spotted Violet's little sister walking down the street, carrying a backpack on her way to school, her ponytail bobbing. Callie was alone, so Asher pulled up alongside her and leaned out the window.

"Hey, beautiful."

The teen smiled bashfully. "Hey, Asher."

"Need a ride? I'm meeting a friend right now, but the school is on the way."

Callie didn't even hesitate. Once she was in the car, Asher patted her thigh, not lingering too long, just enough to express physical intimacy.

"How've you been?" he asked.

"Pretty good."

"Yeah?" he asked, as if he didn't believe her.

"Yeah. I'm good. Why?"

"Okay, don't tell your sister I said anything, but she says your folks are having difficulties."

Callie looked down at her scuffed sneakers. They'd once been white but now were gray from frequent use and infrequent cleaning.

"Want some new shoes?" he asked. "We can take a detour and get you some. Maybe a cute pink pair."

"No," she said, frowning. "I *hate* pink."

"Okay. No pink shoes. Judging by your mood, I'm guessing you already knew your folks were having trouble, huh?"

Callie nodded reluctantly. "They fight sometimes."

"Just sometimes?"

"Seems like more than usual, actually."

"Do you know why they've been arguing?"

She looked at him now, her eyes narrowing. "Just grownup stuff, I guess. I try not to listen when they yell at each other. I usually go outside."

"That's why you were on the front lawn yesterday, isn't it? You didn't want to practice that stupid fucking baton. You were just trying to get out of the house so you wouldn't have to hear them bicker. That's why your mom was in such a foul mood when she came outside."

Her eyes misted, and she looked out her window. "Dad's in Reno for work. They were arguing over the phone."

"Uh huh. And I'll bet you could hear every word, right? They were yelling that loud."

"Yeah. They were fighting about stupid things like groceries and the thermostat being too high."

"Those things are not the source of their anger, though. I know what they were really fighting about, Callie. Would you like to know?"

Callie sniffed. "How ... how do you know? Did Violet tell you something? God, she's always—"

He shushed her gently. "Remember, you can't say anything to her about this little talk. I'm trusting you because I want to help. Now do you want to know why your parents are fighting or don't you?"

She nodded again. "Okay."

Asher turned down a side road with fewer houses, taking a longer, more secluded route on purpose. "Your mother is mad at your father because he can't make love to her anymore. You see, your dad can't get an erection."

Callie sadness turned to shock, her face flushing in an instant. She looked so young then—young and lost, profoundly innocent.

"You know what an erection is, don't you?" Asher asked.

Callie nodded again. "Of course I do. I'm not a kid."

"Well, Callie, your mom needs a man who can get an erection. A strong penis is important to women. They need one to make them whole."

She was either too embarrassed or uncomfortable to reply—perhaps both.

"Have you ever seen an erect penis?" he asked. "Not online, I mean in person."

"*What?* No. I never ..."

"Like you said, you're not a kid anymore. You're fifteen now. You must have been intimate with a boy by now."

"No!" she said, growing more upset. "Did my sister put you up to this? Did my mom?"

"Of course not. Why would they ask me to ask you these things?"

"I don't want to get in trouble. I shouldn't anyway. I've kissed boys, but that's it. I've been good."

Asher smiled to himself. "So you *are* a virgin."

She neither denied nor confirmed, but Asher believed Callie had confessed her virginity without exactly meaning to.

"So you've never even seen an erection," he said. "Not even in a dirty movie?"

"Eww, no! I don't watch those."

"C'mon. You've never been curious?"

She shook her head. "No way. That's gross."

"The human body isn't automatically gross. A hard penis is natural, Callie. Without erections, there would be no sex, and that means the end of the human race."

"Duh. I know that."

"You need to learn how not to be afraid of them, then, don't you?"

"I'm not afraid!"

"Yes, you are."

"Am not."

"Am too," he said, teasing her now.

The childishness of their back-and-forth made Callie smile a little, Asher's good ribbing cheering her up.

"Listen," he said. "Would it help you to see what one looks like?"

The girl flushed again, eyes going wide, mouth agape.

"I think it would help you," he said. "You'll be less intimidated by boys' sexuality—by *your own* sexuality. When you decide to lose your virginity, you'll have a better idea of what to expect. But the immediate benefit is you'll understand what your mother is going through right now because she's gone without one for so long."

Still, Callie didn't answer, but Asher noticed she was gripping her kneecaps. She didn't seem scared of him, exactly, but uncomfortable. Perhaps she was intimidated by the possibility of seeing a hard cock, but she also didn't say no.

Asher slowed down and pulled up at the end of a cul-de-sac, leaving the car running as he parked in front of a house that was under construction and currently empty.

"What're you doing?" Callie asked.

"Real quick. It won't take but a second."

Callie started to say something but shut her mouth when Asher unzipped his fly. He'd grown hard just talking to her, and his bulge looked big even to him, as if his cock had suddenly gained an extra inch. Looking down at it, Callie's eyes went impossibly wide. He exposed himself, expecting her to turn away, but she didn't. It was almost like she couldn't, as if his erection were a magic snake hypnotizing her with a dance.

Incubus, he thought with a smile.

"You'd like to touch it, wouldn't you?" he said, deliberately arranging the question to suggest he knew what she wanted better than she did. "Go ahead. Just touch it. Get a feel for it."

Now, he couldn't tell if Callie was curious or terrified. Her eyes never left his crotch, but she also didn't move her hands off her knees.

Reaching over, he gently lifted her arm by the wrist and guided her hand where it belonged. Hand over hers, he closed her hand around the shaft and squeezed. Then he put her hand back on her knee, stuffed himself back in his jeans, and started driving again. Not only was it important for him not to push things too fast, but he also wanted to leave the girl wanting more now that he'd tickled her budding sexuality. More than anything else, he wanted to keep her pure despite how badly he wanted to fuck her.

Callie didn't say much as they drove the rest of the way to her school. She didn't seem frightened, and her eyes had dried. She looked nervous, but it was a bashful kind of nervous, underlined by an excitement she struggled to contain. Asher turned on the radio and tried to talk to her about music, but she wasn't into heavy metal like her sister was. He kept things light, never returning to the subject of sex or even mentioning what they'd just done. When he dropped her off, she gave him an awkward smile before getting out of the car.

"Bye, beautiful," he said. "See you real soon."

She blushed. "Bye, Asher."

He drove away confident, knowing the girl would never talk. He'd given her a secret to share with a man instead of a boy, a molestation she mistook for a moment of intimacy. She was budding into a woman, and he was an older boy who'd acknowledged that in a physical manner. That he'd had her touch him instead of groping her seemed to reassure Callie, giving her the false idea that he was letting her control how far they would go. That Asher was the one to stop them before things could go any further would only cement that thought deeper into her mind.

Asher was getting better at understanding people—especially females. He'd developed an unnatural ability to tell what others were feeling and know where their head was in the moment. He couldn't read minds, exactly, but he could read emotions and predict actions, just as he had with Barney last night and Mom this morning.

His powers were multiplying.

He aimed to use them on Lenny.

When Asher arrived at The Lazy Bean, he noticed a middle-aged man in the corner booth wearing a motorcycle jacket with a faded Slayer t-shirt underneath. Though his hairline was receding, his hair was long, greasy, and black, with a horseshoe mustache. Leather boots and ripped jeans, a chain running from his belt to his wallet. A spider tattoo on his neck had greened with age. He spotted Asher immediately, but while his eyes showed recognition, the man offered no expression.

Asher came to his table and sat down across from him. "Hello, Lenny."

"Hey, kid."

The backs of Lenny's hands were tattooed too, but the old ink made them even more blurry than the tattoo on his neck. Asher could make out what was on Lenny's fingers, though. The tattoos on his right hand spelled out "Hail." The first three fingers on his left hand said "666," and an inverted cross was on the pinky.

"Still scared I'm going to kill you?" Asher teased.

Lenny only stared at him with hard eyes. There was a time Asher would have been intimidated by this man who looked like a Hell's Angel fresh out of prison, but he didn't fear anyone anymore.

"Spare me the thousand-yard stare," Asher told him. "It's not going to work."

"I'm just lookin' at ya."

"What're you, a fag?"

"Hell no. I just wanna get a good look at you … Asher."

Lenny didn't seem to be looking at him but *through* him, like he was trying to find something that didn't show on the surface.

"Look," Asher said. "I ain't got all day. I'm doing you a kindness even being here."

Lenny smirked. "Guys like us aren't known for our kindness."

"What do you mean by that?"

"Come off it, kid. You know exactly what I mean."

The young waiter interrupted them. They both ordered black coffee, but Lenny asked for cream on the side. The waiter scurried away.

"I'm surprised you picked this place," Lenny said. "Couldn't you find somewhere with a hot waitress instead of that blond boy?"

"Hooters doesn't do breakfast, old man. Now why don't you cut the bullshit and tell me why the fuck you've come into my life."

"You know why I'm here."

"Yeah, you keep saying that. Why don't you just humor me and spit it out?"

Lenny leaned forward. "I'm here because I know what you are— *who* you are."

"You don't know shit. You just met me."

Lenny's smile was stained by a lifetime of nicotine. "Nah, man. I know you, I know you've got the record, and I know why you don't want to part with it."

"I *won't* part with it. Believe that, sweetheart."

"There!" Lenny said, pointing at Asher. "Right there!"

"Right what?"

"You called me sweetheart again. Just like before."

"So fucking what?" Asher laughed.

"I know you, man. I fucking *know you.*"

The waiter returned, placing full mugs and a small pitcher of cream on the table. He tried to ask if they needed anything else, but Asher cut him off, telling him to just leave them alone already. The waiter frowned but slinked away silently. Lenny took the pitcher of cream, but as he poured it into his mug, the coffee filled with crusty flakes. Seeing curdled dairy twice in one morning was an odd coincidence, but Asher didn't think much of it. He expected Lenny to yell for the waiter. Instead, he shot Asher a knowing look.

"Just as I thought," Lenny said. "You've not only been listening to the record—you've been worshipping. You've already gained power."

Asher made fists under the table, resisting the urge to grab his gun and blast that smug look off Lenny's face. "I don't know what you're talking about, old man."

"You think I don't know the signs?" Lenny asked, pointing at the pitcher. "There was nothing wrong with this cream when it was placed on the table. It only spoiled when it got close to you."

Asher huffed. "You're out of your mind."

"*You're* a *warlock*. Dairy spoils in your presence, and there's a slight red tint to your eyes most people wouldn't notice, but I know what to look for. These are clear signs of witchcraft. Based on them, I'd say you've killed at least two people in the name of Satan."

Asher went cold. There was no reason to deny it any longer. Lenny knew so much. Now, Asher had to figure out what to do with him, but first, he wanted answers.

"You really believe in that stuff?" Asher asked. "Witches and ghosts and goblins?"

"I believe in what I see, and right now, I'm looking at a devil worshipper." Lenny showed Asher his hands, as if he hadn't already noticed the Satanic tattoos. He pulled down the collar of his shirt and drew out a necklace with a Leviathan Cross pendant. "You starting to get the picture? I ain't the enemy, kid. I was your uncle's best buddy. We used to raise hell together—literally. He was a warlock, like you, only much more powerful. I'd say he was the most powerful servant of Satan I've ever met. You should be proud to share blood with Rex Von Spades."

"Maybe I am."

Lenny smiled. "Hell yeah, you are. Shit, you even look like him."

"What is it you want from me, Lenny? And don't give me that story about Rex having borrowed the record from you before he died because we both know that's a load of horseshit. You want it for the black magic it offers. You want power that is rightfully mine. I'm not giving you *Music to Sacrifice Virgins To*—not for *any* reason—and if you try to steal it from me, I'll show you just how powerful of a warlock I really am."

The look on Lenny's face assured Asher the man knew he was serious.

"Do I make myself clear?" Asher asked. "Do you get me, sweetheart?"

Staring at Asher, Lenny leaned over the table and whispered. "Rex ... you're in there, aren't you? I know you are. I can *see* you! Talk to me, dude."

Asher tried to laugh it off. "You're one crazy old man."

"Talk to me, Rex," he said, a little louder this time. "Talk to me!"

"Keep your voice down."

"Rex, c'mon. Can't you talk to me?"

"What're you talking about? I'm not Rex. I'm Asher."

Lenny shook his head, his expression grave. "No. You're both."

Asher was enveloped by a deep chill. "What ... what are you telling me?"

"Rex, man, the spell worked but it didn't work. If you talk to me, I can help you fix this. I know you're in there. Say something!"

"What spell? What worked but didn't work?"

Lenny sat back, and this time, he spoke to Asher rather than into him. "Your uncle ain't dead, kid. I mean, he is dead, but he ain't gone. All that stuff he left you ... those weren't gifts. Your inheritance was all part of his plan. See, he needed tokens for his black magic, same as any witch. *Music to Sacrifice Virgins To* isn't just a record, but of course you know that by now. But what you don't realize is your uncle is the one who made that album, and he recorded it in Hell."

The chill that had overtook Asher went colder, hollowing his stomach. He would have gulped, but his mouth was too dry to swallow.

"Kid," Lenny said. "Your uncle needed someone from his own bloodline to let him in."

"Let him in what?"

"What else? *Your soul.* Rex wanted a young, healthy male body to take dominion over. The voice you hear on that record is his. Those chants were supposed to let him possess you and transfer his Satanic power into you."

Suddenly, so much made sense, but Asher didn't want it to make sense, didn't want it to be true. But it made sense. This was how he'd done so many evil things with ease. His uncle had enough experience for both of them.

"It worked but it didn't work," Lenny said again. "He got in you, but you're not out. He doesn't have total control. See, the reason demons tend to possess children is 'cause they're not mature enough yet to resist it. Since their brains aren't fully formed, they're easier to control. You're young, but you're still an adult. Obviously, he's influencing you, but you're still there—still here in *this* world instead of in the limbo souls are supposed to go to when they're possessed by a demon."

"Demon …" Asher muttered, staring at nothing.

"You can bet your ass he's a demon now."

"If this is all true—"

"You know it is."

"Then why didn't the possession work? Why doesn't Rex have total control over my body? Just because I'm not a kid?"

Lenny shook his head. "I don't know for certain. Maybe it's just how Lucifer wants it. I never had the power Rex had, so I don't understand Satanic sorcery to the same degree he did."

"You were a minion."

"Well, not exactly."

"Yes, you were. But if you're still trying to help Rex, then why did you want to take the record from me?"

"It's been weeks since he left this world. I'd expected Rex to contact me once he had dominion over you so we could continue what we'd started. When he didn't, I figured the plan hadn't worked. I thought if I got the record back, I might be able to resurrect him somehow, or maybe I could even gain the power Rex had and continue his work for him."

"What work? What did you two start that you wanted to continue?"

"Same shit you're doing now, kid. We are the sons of Satan. Our father is The Devil, and we're here to do his will. Murder, rape, arson—every fuckin' sin in the bible. Worship, black magic, and summoning demons. We walk the left-hand path." He released a long breath. "Do you really think you're ready to join us?"

Asher crossed his arms and leaned back. "Lenny, I think a better question is are *you* ready to join *me?*"

Lenny's eyes fell. "Now that I've met you, I see you've got a better understanding of the power you're dealing with than I originally thought. But you don't know what I know. Shit, how could you? I've been at this over thirty years. I can teach you things."

"Rex teaches me. But you may prove useful too. I just need to know I can trust you."

"Hey, now that I see what's going on, I don't want to take the record away from you. I just want to help."

"Your word isn't worth anything to me yet. Only time will tell if you're trustworthy."

"I always served Rex well. That's why I was the only one he told his possession plan to."

"How do I know you won't try to help him take me over completely?"

"Like I said, I'm no warlock. I wouldn't know how to help him with that. But he's still in there, in you. I knew it when you called me sweetheart. That's what Rex used to call everybody in his sarcastic way. What if he wants things as they are now? Maybe the possession didn't go according to plan but worked out for the better because of it. Like you said, Rex is teaching you. Maybe he's come to like having a pupil, almost like a son of his own. Either way, by working with you, I can continue to do his bidding."

Asher considered this. Intuition told him Lenny was being earnest, that he was desperate to continue serving Rex in whatever way he could, as if his soul depended on it. Perhaps it did. But what would happen if Rex managed to communicate with Lenny without Asher realizing it? What if Rex gave Lenny instructions on how to complete the possession?

No matter what he decided to do with Lenny, Asher knew he had to keep him close.

"You weren't wrong about going to the woods," Asher told him. "I was prepared to kill you if it came to that. I'm carrying a gun right now."

"Me too. But I'm always strapped. Just like Rex was."

"I want you to tell me more about Rex."

"Sure. What do you wanna know?"

Asher finished his coffee in one gulp, the heat not bothering him. "Let's start with everything."

NINETEEN

LENNY AGREED WITH EVERYTHING MOM had said about Rex, except for her rape, which Asher didn't bring up. But where Mom had suspicions about Rex's other heinous crimes, Lenny offered confirmation. Rex *was* a sadistic serial killer. He'd been a rapist, a thief, and an arsonist, amongst other things. No crime was too cruel for him, for he had no respect for human life other than his own. No punishment was enough of a deterrent, and as he got older, Rex became a master of not getting caught, using black magic and the assistance of demons to avoid detection. The only people that caught him ended up dead. Lenny had not only witnessed these killings, but he'd also assisted with them, even assassinating people at Rex's command. They'd been at it for decades. Speaking of these terrible crimes brought a smile to Lenny's face. Rape made him sentimental. Murder made him nostalgic.

They spoke for a long time in Asher's car, having left the café to avoid being overheard. They smoked a fat joint as Twisted Sister played on the radio, Lenny telling Asher how he'd seen the band live in their heyday. He'd grown up on rock 'n roll and developed an obsession with heavy metal as a teenager in the 1980s. As he'd entered his twenties, he'd worked as a roadie in the Florida death metal scene, only leaving the state after being busted several times for dealing drugs and soliciting prostitutes. Wanting to go someplace where nobody knew him, Lenny came all the way to New Hampshire and met Rex in the underground music scene. They became fast friends, and Rex hired Lenny to be a roadie for his band, but Rex couldn't seem to get along with any band members long enough to even put together a show. He'd been too controlling over every aspect of their songs. He had a vision for how they should sound, and it proved too experimental and disturbing for the tastes of others. But while he was unable to keep a band together, Rex developed a small following of other Satanists, which he appointed himself the leader of.

"So what happened?" Asher asked.

"We became a death cult. Rex was our unholy messiah, leading us into the arms of Satan."

"I get that. I mean what happened to Rex? How did he die?"

Lenny sighed, saddened to even talk about the loss. "One of Rex's favorite sins was gluttony. Drugs, booze, loose women, junk food—he gorged on it all. Fifty-some-odd years of not taking care of himself just caught up with the guy. He got the cancer. Knowing he was gonna die, he arranged a final black mass. We all gathered in the woods. Rex had this girl with him—some nine-year-old he'd kidnapped from a playground or some shit. He needed a virgin sacrifice. Nothing gets you in better with the big man than that. Satan loves a virgin soul. So Rex cuts her from her neck to her pussy and drinks the blood straight from her jugular. What a showman he was!

"See, Rex had gotten to be such a high-ranking, skilled warlock he could communicate directly with Lucifer. Like, he had full-on conversations with him. And after years of service, Rex had worked out a deal. He didn't want immortality 'cause his body was fucked by that point. He wanted a fresh, new body, but like I said, Satan required the possession to be of someone within Rex's family. Of course, he had no wife or any children he cared to claim, so he'd turned to his extended family, choosing you. With everything set into place, the next part of the ritual was Rex committing suicide."

Asher hadn't expected that. "He killed himself?"

"Sure did. I know 'cause I was there. All his followers were."

"Where are the rest of these followers now?"

"Shit, man. Without Rex's black magic to protect us, we were suddenly exposed. The murders and everything else we'd done so carelessly came back to haunt us in the form of police and FBI investigations leading to our doors. Most of us got busted. Many are in prison or killed themselves to be with our dark lord in Hell. I was one of the lucky ones who got questioned but wasn't charged with anything. I think that was Rex protecting me from beyond the grave 'cause I was his right-hand man. He still needed me."

"What about Luna?"

Lenny gave him a quizzical look. "You know about Luna?"

Asher only knew of Rex's girlfriend because his mother had mentioned her. He wasn't sure if they'd stayed together all these years or not. "Yeah. Is she still around?"

"Nah, kid. She went away years ago when she took the fall for Rex, confessing to a murder he committed to keep him from going back to prison. That's how devoted she was to him."

"What a gal."

"Actually, she was. Luna was the high priestess in our cult. I was Rex's right-hand man, but Luna was his true sidekick. She outranked me by a mile. We all looked up to her. Called her the Princess of Darkness."

"Rex couldn't use his power to keep her from going to jail?"

Lenny shrugged. "Just like God, Satan moves in mysterious ways. Rex did make sure she had everything she needed in prison. From what I heard, she's still doing Satan's work behind bars, which is good, seeing as she's serving life without parole."

"Back to Rex—how'd he commit suicide?"

"After he sacrificed the little girl, he sacrificed himself in the name of Lucifer, offering his soul and his complete servitude for all of eternity. He only asked for two things in return. One was to possess *you*. The other was to finally get to record the album he'd always dreamed of. As a token of his dedication to the dark forces, he made his death extra gruesome and blasphemous. He stripped nude and carved a pentagram into his forehead, then slit his forearms open and drank his own blood before cutting his throat. Then he had us crucify him upside-down like fuckin' St. Peter. Once he was gone, we were supposed to set the cross on fire, but before we could, Rex spontaneously combusted. Craziest thing I ever saw, and I've seen my share of crazy shit, lemme tell ya. Rex went up so quick and left nothing but ash, but

173

you shoulda seen it. His ashes were like black smoke. They just drifted into the air and vanished into the night sky, every last bit of him."

Asher was impressed. "So he recorded the record *after* killing himself?"

Lenny nodded.

"Then how did it get in the storage unit?"

"Satan has his ways, kid."

"And you're saying it was recorded in Hell?"

"That's right, for the sole purpose of bringing Rex's demonic power back to the realm of the living. Real evil never dies."

Asher smirked, liking the sound of that, but he still had one more question. "You said you were into heavy metal as a teen. Is that what first got you interested in Satanism, or was it Rex?"

"Sure, I liked the 'devil music' aspect of metal 'cause it was rebellious and pissed off the squares. But being a metalhead didn't automatically make me a Satanist. It was anger toward God that led me down the left-hand path."

"Why were you mad at God?"

Lenny sighed. "I guess I can tell you, considering. When I was seven years old, I was repeatedly molested by my cousin over one summer. He was about nineteen at the time. But as terrible as the rape was, what made it even worse was my parents—and my extended family—were Christian fundamentalists, and the church we went to stressed that homosexuality was one of the deadliest sins. So here I was, a victim of child abuse, but I was too afraid to speak up 'cause my attacks were homosexual in nature. See, I thought *I* would be in trouble. Not just with my parents but with everyone in my church. I was fuckin' terrified that God was angry with me, and every time my cousin molested me, I had the added trauma of thinking I was gonna burn in Hell for it."

"Fuck, man. That is brutal."

"Shit, yeah. I even started praying my cousin would die. I asked God to kill him, then felt guilty 'cause the ten commandments forbid killing, and in my church, thinking of a sin was nearly as bad as doing it. My cousin eventually joined the Navy, and even when I saw him again years later, he acted like nothing had ever happened and so did I. But by then, I'd already turned my back on God. He'd ignored my pain. I was a good, Christian child, and he allowed me to be raped by a member of my own family, again and again. For that, I'll always hate him. So I turned to Satan 'cause the enemy of my enemy is my friend."

After their conversation, Asher told Lenny he had things to do but he'd be in touch, so he shouldn't leave town. Lenny seemed eager to stay with Asher—to stay with Rex—but knowing they were one in the same now, he obeyed his master and went back to his old Firebird. They drove off in opposite directions.

Music blasting, Asher sped down the road, ignoring traffic signs and running a red light. A few angry honks were directed at him, but no sirens. He kept glancing in the mirror, looking into himself, silently asking his uncle to communicate with him. Rex had talked with Asher's mouth before, reciting invocations and such, but there'd been no direct dialogue, not even internally. Now that Asher knew Rex was sharing his body, he hoped he could coax him into a conversation, but so far, his uncle remained mute.

"We both want the same thing," Asher said to his reflection. "But I guess you'll talk to me when you're ready." A thought occurred to him. What if Rex wanted to speak directly to him but couldn't? "If you're *able* to talk to me, I'm sure you will eventually. I'm not angry with you for possessing me. If anything, I owe you a debt of gratitude. You've changed my life for the better, Uncle Rex."

The house was empty when he got home. Mom had pulled herself together and gone off to work. *A slave like every American,* Asher thought. *Well, not me.*

Drawing a beer from the fridge, he checked his text messages.

First, there were Dad's. Another plea to see him. Asher deleted them without replying.

There was also one from Diego, just asking how he was doing. It seemed like ages since Asher had talked to his best friend. Maybe it was time to bring him into the Satanic fold. Rex had Lenny. Asher wanted a right-hand man too. He'd made Barney a henchman, but Asher needed someone smarter to serve as his sidekick, someone he'd known longer and could trust easier. Asher called him, but it went to voicemail.

"Hey, man," he said to the recording. "We should hang out and catch up. I've got some great news. Things have been hectic, but my life has really turned around for the better. Call me back when you get a chance."

Asher left it at that. Right now, he was more interested in Diego's cousin anyway. He called Ximena, and she picked up on the first ring.

"Where have you been?" she asked.

"Busy. What's up with you, sweetheart?"

"Shit's gotten crazy since we last saw each other."

"You're telling me."

"So you heard about Terry and Maxine?"

"Maxine?"

"That's Terry's daughter. I figured you must've seen it on the news."

Asher sipped his beer. "I don't watch the news. What do I care what the rest of the world is up to?"

"Oh. Well, Terry died in a house fire the other night. He and his daughter both burned up. They say the heat was so intense the bodies were completely cremated."

"Yeah, well, these things happen. What's one less drug dealer?"

Ximena huffed. "It matters to me. He was my main source. Now I'm shit outta luck."

"Don't worry. Your luck is about to change, Ximena."

"What do you mean by that?"

"I told you I'd take care of you, didn't I, sweetheart?"

Her tone changed, becoming more pleasant and playful. "I kinda like it when you call me that."

"I'm sure you do—*sweetheart*. And I mean the things I say. You don't have to worry about losing your source of income. I managed to get that big score I was looking for with another dealer. I can hook you up with the best snow your brain has ever skied."

"Asher ... jeez, not over the phone," she said, giggling, though she was serious.

"Don't worry about that either. I'm invincible. As long as you're with me, you're protected under my demon wings."

"You're a trip, you know that?"

"A trip straight to Hell, first class. Now give me your address. I'm coming over tonight."

She breathed into the phone, warm and inviting. "Asher, I sort of have a boyfriend."

"He can't come."

Ximena laughed. "You're a very naughty boy, aren't you?"

"You have no idea." He crushed the empty beer can and threw it on the floor for Mom to clean up. "So what's the problem? Does this douchebag live with you?"

"No. We've only been dating for a month or so. And he's not a douchebag, okay? He's a nice guy."

"Boring, you mean."

"He's not boring."

"Nice guys are weak. They're afraid of women and their rejections. A man like that can't excite you the way I do. He's not Mr. Right. He's just Mr. Right Now."

"Oh, stop," Ximena said, though she didn't deny it. "Okay. I've got my own little house. The money I made working for Terry was the only way I could afford the rent. That's why I've been freaking out. But you're saying you've got product?"

"If I said it, you should take it as an absolute truth."

"Mmhmm. Okay."

She was being playful, so Asher allowed the jab. Besides, what good was truth when you served the Father of Lies? Ximena gave him her address, and he told her to stay home after sundown. He said he'd be bringing her product, so she didn't pester him for a specific time. Ximena would wait like a good girl. She had a new master and didn't even know it yet.

Thinking about what he was going to do to Ximena's tight body caused Asher's loins to stir. He was still horny from having little Callie squeeze his cock. Asher hadn't had an orgasm since he'd raped Deanna last night. His first thought was to go across the street and get Violet, to use her mouth like a whore's pussy like he always did, but it was still early, and she would be in class for several more hours.

Knowing this gave Asher an idea.

✝

"I told you that you can't just drop in unannounced," Melissa said. "Besides, Violet is at school."

"Yeah, I know," Asher said, standing on the Vincent family's front porch. He looked up and down the street. Empty.

Melissa squinted, the door only half open to greet her daughter's boyfriend. "If you know Violet's not home, then what're you doing here?"

Asher smiled, raising one eyebrow. "Thought you could use some company, what with your husband out of town and your girls in school."

Her expression hardened. "Is this some sort of joke?"

"I don't hear anyone laughing," Asher said as he pulled the gun from its holster.

Melissa paled. She made a desperate, foolish attempt to slam the door shut, but Asher put his boot in the jam and shoved the door inward, knocking into Melissa. She fell on her butt, and Asher forced his way into the house and bolted the door behind him as Melissa scrambled to her feet, screaming. Before she could get away, Asher snatched her by her long, blond hair and pressed the barrel of the revolver to her temple.

"Don't scream," he told her. "If you scream again, the last thing you'll feel is the cold kiss of a bullet passing through your skull."

Melissa began to cry, whimpering "oh my god" over and over.

"God ain't gonna to help you, sweetheart."

Though her hair looked nice and she had a little makeup on, Melissa was in her house clothes, as if she'd gone out in the morning but was now home for the day. She was barefoot and wore pajama pants and a t-shirt, and as he wrapped his other arm around her, he could feel the lack of a bra strap. Melissa squirmed when he grabbed her breast, Asher twisting the nipple until she shrieked, but she quickly closed her mouth, remembering his threat.

"That's my good girl," he whispered in her ear. "Now move."

Keeping her pressed close to him, he ushered her into the kitchen, stopping her at the island block.

"Please," she said. "What do you want?"

"It's not what I want, Melissa. It's what you want—what you *need*."

"I don't know what you're talking a—"

She gasped as Asher yanked down her pajama pants with one hand. She kicked, so he yanked her head back by the hair, and when she opened her mouth to cry, Asher shoved the pistol into it. He didn't have to say anything. Melissa went still, silent but for her uncontrollable whimpering.

"Beige panties?" he said, looking at her butt. "No wonder you're not getting any. Men hate beige underwear."

She said nothing, but he felt her breath catch when he mentioned her not getting any.

"A blond MILF like you would be better off wearing all black. Get a thong for that juicy ass."

He gave her butt a slap, enjoying how it jiggled and how this older woman trembled at his touch. Taking the gun out of her mouth, Asher bent Melissa over the island block and slid her panties down too. Frozen by terror, she'd finally stopped resisting him. Squatting behind her, Asher spread her legs wider, then dove his face between her buttocks and started eating her pussy from behind. Her whole body tensed, and Asher pressed the pistol into her side as a reminder

178

to obey.

But he wouldn't need to threaten her for long.

The mean heat kindled in Asher's lungs, filling them with black smoke, which he blew into Melissa's vaginal canal. It climbed up into her insides, twisting her body into the thrall of his Satanic sorcery. She gasped as he sucked on her clitoris, and when he slid a finger inside her at the same time, her legs shuddered as she let out a moan. There was still fear in her voice, but it wasn't as strong now.

"Please," she said with a heavy breath, but it wasn't clear if she was begging him to stop or if she was asking for more. "Please ... I ... I ..."

Asher put the gun on the floor, spun Melissa around, and lifted her up onto the block island. She did not resist him. Her eyes were glazed, lips wet. In this position, Asher was able to get his tongue deeper into her. His girlfriend's mother rocked her hips, lost to him now, and Asher lapped at her while using three fingers, driving them hard and fast and deep.

Melissa came, and this time, he allowed her to scream. Her orgasm was so intense her legs became a vice grip around Asher's head, her gyrations nearly sliding her off the counter. But Asher wasn't finished with her yet. He kept eating, kept thrusting, kept making her squirm until she shuddered with multiple orgasms. She was still shivering from them when he leaned over Melissa and kissed her. She kissed him back with hunger, sucking the flavor of her pussy from his tongue. When her hands fumbled for his belt buckle, Asher pulled back, smiling down at the mess he'd made of her. Her face was flushed from sex, eyes wide with confusion and desire. She reached for his crotch again, but Asher pushed her hand away.

"No," he said. "You haven't earned that yet."

She stared in disbelief. "You don't want to ... I mean ... what's happening here?"

"Baby steps, sweetheart. You're all hot and bothered now, but when it's over and reality sets in, that bitchy attitude of yours might come back. You'll remember how I forced my way in here with a gun, and you won't be so friendly then."

She sat up on the island block. "No ... I mean ..."

"Women like you love to cry rape. But who's gonna believe a rapist only wanted to eat you out?"

Her brow lowered, eyes darting in befuddlement. She kept moving her lips but couldn't seem to find the words.

"I gave you what your husband couldn't," Asher said, brushing his hand beneath her chin to make her look up at him. "I bet you haven't cum like that in years."

She stared right into his eyes. "I haven't cum like that *ever.*"

"Now you see why your daughter likes me so much, huh?"

Mentioning Violet made Melissa grimace with shame, as Asher knew it would. But he wanted to keep her aroused, so he slid his hand under her shirt and caressed her breast. It was larger than Violet's, and though it wasn't as perky, it made up for it with fullness.

Asher grinned. "You want to fuck me so bad right now, don't you?"

She hesitated but confessed. "Yes."

"Tell me."

"I want ... I want to have sex with you."

"No, no. Say 'fuck me.'"

The word seemed to make her uncomfortable, and her lower lip trembled when she said it, soft and sweet. "Fuck me. Fuck me, Asher."

"Call me Master."

Melissa gulped, shocked but turned on.

"Fuck me, Master," she said.

Asher's cock was hard as granite. He wanted to split Melissa in half with it, but he'd meant it when he'd said she hadn't earned it yet. Better to let the spell of his incubus smoke permeate her completely.

He kissed her cheek. "Next time, sweetheart. Next time."

When she looked into his eyes now, Melissa went pale. "Look at you ... look at your eyes."

Asher didn't need a mirror to know his irises were red, the pupils pinpoints, the whites of his eyes completely bloodshot.

Melissa trembled. "What ... what are you?"

He ran the thumb of his left hand across her bottom lip, and despite her fear of Asher, Melissa's lust was beyond her control. There would be no resisting him, because deep down, she didn't want to. His spell hadn't controlled her. It had set her free. So when he touched her lips, she took his thumb into her mouth and sucked, twirling her tongue.

"I'm your darkest wet dream come true," he said with a grin.

Picking up his pistol and pocketing Melissa's panties, Asher turned and walked out, ignoring Melissa as she called his name, begging him not to go.

TWENTY

DRIVING BY OUR LADY OF Mercy—the local Catholic church—Asher had to laugh.

What kind of idiot would seek religious advice from an adult male virgin in a dress? he thought. *That is, unless the priest is fucking the choir boys, as they seem to enjoy doing.*

This got him back to thinking about virgins. With each murder, he was gaining new powers and strengthening the ones he'd already been granted. As a rising warlock in Satan's army, he had to continue his progression by appeasing the dark lords. More than anything, he wanted to communicate with Lucifer directly, just as his uncle had. Asher's task had been spelled out for him all this time, right there on the title of Rex's record.

Music to Sacrifice Virgins To.

Without intending to, Asher had been working his way up to an even more horrific crime than anything he'd done in Satan's name so far. He realized that now and knew he had to act, but if he was going to make a grand gesture to Lucifer, he had to do it right. The act had to be pitch-black and glorious, a ritual that would swing the gates of Hell wide open for him. So before continuing with his plan, he had to contemplate, but didn't want to wait too long. There was a hunger in him only fresh blood could satiate.

Stopping at a bookstore, Asher was amazed he'd wasted so much time working in one. He was beyond "honest work" now, convinced he'd always been destined for greater things. Grabbing a few titles, he returned to the electronics store and bought audio software for his computer with *Music to Sacrifice Virgins To* in mind.

He spent the afternoon with the books he'd picked up, studying witchcraft, including the history of witches. Much of it was New Age nonsense, but the works of English occultist Aleister Crowley and other writings that had come before him were rooted deeper in authentic sorcery, even if they weren't all Satanic. Researching the grand history of human sacrifice—from medieval torturers to enthusiastic Aztecs to the young maidens who were buried alive in ancient Japan—Asher took notes of the different aspects that excited him, developing a rough draft ritual of his own ... or at least his and Rex's. He also installed the audio software, which enabled him to itemize the individual audio tracks on the *Music to Sacrifice Virgins To* file he'd uploaded. Asher separated the guitars from the drums, adjusting the distortion and lowering the hiss. This made it possible for him to isolate the multiple vocal tracks.

What he heard stunned him.

There was a track of Rex's chants and another of the backup howls of demons speaking phonetic gibberish. A third vocal track consisted of human voices crying out in agony. Now that they were isolated, Asher realized he recognized them.

Terry and his daughter screamed just as they had when Asher murdered them. The sobs Deanna made when he'd raped her were clear, and Paul's desperate screams for his life echoed out of the recent past. The voices of Asher's victims became one great cry out of the abyss as their souls burned eternally, trapped in the pit of fire as a direct result of Asher's deliverance through slaughter.

Lenny had been right. This record really had been recorded in Hell.

Since the album changed a little every time he played it, Asher isolated Rex's vocals and let it play out, hoping for a message beyond the usual invocations. Somehow, Rex was both inside Asher, guiding him instinctually, and saying different things on the album at the same time, as omnipresent as he was omnipotent. Though his vocal track didn't address Asher directly, there was a chant Asher had not heard before.

"Our sigil is that of Lucifer—the inflamed Seal of Satan—born of the great monolith of black sorcery. Its X shows us metaphysical power in the physical realm. The inverted triangle is the sign of water, the key of life itself, and the V is duality, for the demon is legion. Drink from its deep well, for The Seal of Satan is the chalice of all creation."

Asher opened one of the witchcraft books to a section on symbols and found The Seal of Satan, better known as The Sigil of Lucifer. Acting on instinct, he grabbed a marker and recreated the symbol on his bedroom wall, forming the X, V, and triangle into the overall shape of a goblet.

"We drink from this Unholy Grail," Rex's vocal track instructed. *"And refill the chalice with the blood of the innocent."*

Placing the palm of his left hand against the sigil on the wall, Asher closed his eyes, hoping to open a portal the way he had with Astaroth, only this time, he was hoping to summon Lucifer himself. The sigil grew warm against his flesh, but that was the extent of any demonic presence. Asher understood. Just as Melissa had to earn his cock, he had to earn a visit from The Prince of Darkness. Such a reward came with a hefty price tag. There was more work to be done—much more.

His phone rang with a call from Violet. Asher picked up.

"I'm off from school now, Master," she said. "I know it hasn't even been a full day, but I miss you so much. You're all I can think about. Can I come over?"

"No. I've got plans tonight."

He could hear the hurt in her voice. "Oh. Okay. Maybe tomorrow then?"

"Maybe. We'll see."

"Did … did I do something wrong?"

He paused just to give her time to worry. "You'll probably see me tomorrow. I just need to take care of a few things first."

"Okay. If I can assist you with them in any way—"

"When it's time for you to do something, I'll tell you to do it. Master knows best."

"Right. I mean, of course. How silly of me."

Asher changed the subject. "Have you talked to your sister to-day?"

"Um, a little. She just got home too. Why?"

"What about your mother?"

"I mean, we said hello when I got home, but …"

Her lack of interest confirmed Violet's family had kept their mouths shut. Asher smiled to himself. Everything was moving along the way it should.

"I was thinking about Callie," Asher said. "Next time we get together, you should bring her along."

At first, Violet didn't say anything. Then she dared to ask a question. "What for, Master?"

"Just because I like her."

"You do?"

"I just said I did."

"Sorry, Master. I didn't mean to—"

"You'll do anything for me, won't you, Violet?"

"Of course. Absolutely. I serve you. I swear it to Satan."

"Excellent. So if I want to see your sister, you'll make it happen."

"Sure. As you wish."

"Are you close with Callie?"

"I mean, she's my sister, but she's a lot younger, so we don't have much in common."

"Spend time with her tonight. I want her to see you as her best friend. You're her big sister, so she looks up to you. Use that to mold her."

"Into what?"

Asher sighed. "Don't be stupid. I'm saying you can turn her into putty in your hands, and from there, she'll graduate to being putty in *my* hands."

"Yeah, okay. I can do that."

"That's my good girl."

Violet giggled with delight, sounding almost as young as her sister. "I love to make you happy, Master. I live for it. You know that, right?"

"Without a shadow of a doubt."

Ending the call, Asher opened a new bundle of cocaine and did a quick bump off the blade of his pocketknife. He noticed something else in the package and reached in for it, drawing out a letter envelope. Opening it, he discovered several sheets of acid.

"Perfect," he said.

TWENTY-ONE

ON HER STOMACH, XIMENA WAS stretched out naked on the bed, giving Asher a view of her soft, brown curves and the tattoo that went all the way down her spine. It was many small tattoos to make one large one, the images of ribbon ties looping into holes and crossing over, like the ties at the back of a corset. Around one leg was a tattoo of an anaconda, slithering up her calf, coiling behind the knee, then remerging on her thigh. The tattoos were an improved form of self-mutilation over the cutter scars on her upper arms. Her black hair was up, a tendril hanging down on each side of her face, framing it along with her bangs. Asher was on his knees beside her, leaning over to snort a line of coke off the girl's perfect caramel ass. It was but a small sample of the brick of cocaine he'd given her.

Ximena's place was decorated with framed horror movie posters, with heavy metal album covers pinned above her queen-sized bed. She also had two pet snakes in a glass case. Her furniture was black as well as cheap, with goth girl trinkets scattered about, including a

185

coffin-shaped box for her jewelry, a fake skull to put her reading glasses on, and real animal skulls arranged atop her dresser. Hanging from the corner of the mirror were a variety of necklaces, each with a different pewter pendant—an ankh, a skull with bat wings, snakes, a bull's skull, and a pentagram. Her place wasn't filthy, but it was cluttered and disorganized, her bathroom looking like a tornado had ripped through it. A small television had been propped up on the box it had come in, covered in a thin film of dust.

But at least she had a decent stereo. The *Rocktober Blood* soundtrack played softly from the speakers. Retro metal had made for the perfect soundtrack to their second round of lovemaking.

Ximena took a hit off her pipe, filling the room with the earthy smell of marijuana, and passed it to Asher.

"You're a really good lay, you know that?" she said.

They'd fucked twice since he'd arrived, Asher moving on her the moment he walked through the front door, and Ximena returning his advances by jumping into his arms and wrapping her legs around his waist. She'd been ready for him, wearing nothing but a black kimono and matching thong panties, which he stuffed in his back pocket after peeling them off her hips with his teeth.

Asher took a toke, then gently put one of her buttocks between his teeth, applying slight pressure. Ximena purred. He bit down harder. She gripped the bedsheets as his teeth sank in, groaning as pleasure and pain became one. Asher bit harder still, nearly drawing blood before she begged him to stop. He released her and admired the mark he'd left on her backside like a branding iron. It was already beginning to purple.

Ximena smiled. "You really are bad, aren't you?"

"The fucking worst."

She sat up so they were face-to-face, presenting her pillowy breasts with their pierced nipples, the silver studs matching the one in her clit.

"Wanna see something cool?" she asked.

"Nothing could be cooler than the way you deepthroated me."

She wiggled her eyebrows with pride. Asher wasn't just flattering her. Ximena had taken him all the way into her mouth, twirling her tongue with the expertise of a porn star and never breaking her stride when he came down her throat.

"There's plenty more head where that came from," she said, running her acrylic nails across his bare thigh. "But check this out."

Opening the drawer of the nightstand, Ximena drew a dagger with a foot-long black blade curved like a slithering serpent. It was an antiquated weapon, a style more for collecting than practical use, but it was just right for her hands.

"Looks like a metal snake," he said. "You're really into snakes, huh?"

She nodded. "I love them. Some believe they represent transformation because they shed their skin and their beauty is reborn. Others see them as temptation, like the serpent in the Garden of Eden that tempted Adam and Eve."

"And what do they represent to you?"

"Both. Medusa had a head full of snakes she used to turn men to stone. I'm kind of obsessed with the idea of that. To have that kind of power." She turned the blade in her hand.

"This type of dagger is called a kris. Feel."

Asher grazed the blade's edge with his fingertip. It broke the skin with the ease of margarine.

"Like a razor," he said.

Ximena took his wounded finger and put it in her mouth, sucking the drops of blood, never breaking eye contact, just like when she'd gone down on him.

"Are you into bloodplay?" she asked.

"That's an understatement."

"I used to be a cutter. I guess I just needed that release when I was a teenager. Now, I only shed blood for sensual reasons."

She took his arm toward her, lowered the blade, and dragged the sharp edge across the back of his forearm. It wasn't a deep cut, but significant enough to draw much more blood than his pricked finger. Lying on her belly again, Ximena slowly kicked her feet back and forth as she suckled his split flesh. She was deliberately messy, smearing the blood over her lips and chin, her drool turning pink.

Taking the dagger from her, Asher grazed the blade up and down her back and buttocks as if he were shaving her, teasing Ximena by not breaking the skin.

"C'mon, baby," she said. "Open me."

Instead, Asher made another cut on his forearm, slicing much deeper than Ximena had. His blood flowed, thick and dark, and he squeezed the muscle as he held his arm above her head. Ximena turned over and gore spilled onto her face, and she opened her mouth like a baby bird being fed. Her tongue twirled with Asher's blood, small bubbles of it forming on her full lips. It dribbled from the sides of her mouth as she feasted in vampiric delight. Asher grabbed the back of her head and pushed her face against his forearm, and Ximena darted her expert tongue into the wound, sucking the blood with the same insatiable hunger she'd shown while devouring his semen.

Ximena gasped with desire when he manhandled her. He wet his fingers with his blood and started drawing The Seal of Satan on her abdomen. Ximena rubbed her thighs together and played with her breasts, and when he leaned over her to finish the artwork, she licked his scrotum. Though he began growing hard again, Asher remained focused on completing Lucifer's sigil.

The sudden urge to kill Ximena overcame him, but Asher restrained himself. Murder was becoming a compulsion he had to learn to control. While slaughtering Ximena would give him sadistic pleasure, he saw too much value in her to go through with it. It would be a waste to end her life when she was already so close to the occult. He could mold her with minimal effort because she was already so willing, so dark, so diabolic. Even if he tried to kill her, Asher doubted the demons would allow it. There was the sense she had an important role in all of this.

"C'mon, baby," she said, caressing him. "Hurt me."

It was a request he was happy to grant, but instead of using the dagger on her, Asher slowly waved his left hand over the Seal of Satan he'd drawn on her torso. Ximena shrieked as the lines of Asher's blood boiled. She rushed to wipe it away, but the blood seeped into her pores like sweating in reverse, her skin blistering and peeling with third-degree burns. The smoldering sigil turned her flesh white, then singed it black, tattooing her with a lasting scar in the perfect goblet shape of Satan's seal. As she writhed and wailed, Asher waved his hand in the opposite direction, and the burning suddenly stopped, a black mist emanating from his fingernails to soothe her wounds.

He straddled her. "I love that look on a woman's face—that look of agony and terror. It's almost as sexy as total submission."

Ximena looked up at him with childlike eyes. The fear was fading into a shuddering awe, leaving her mesmerized despite the pain. They stared at each other as Asher began to masturbate. Again, he noticed the change in his genitals. His long, girthy cock seemed to be growing bigger all the time. When Ximena's eyes landed on it, she sucked in her bottom lip. Using the blood still weeping from his arm, Asher lubricated his erection and was soon shooting semen at the girl below him. The drops of sperm landed perfectly on her burn wounds and nowhere else. Ximena held her breath as the cum ran rivers through the Seal of Satan on her abdomen, and once it was full, she groaned and clutched her stomach in a new form of pain.

The flesh of her torso began to ripple. Lumps appeared, rolling and twisting below the singed epidermis, as if her intestines were trying to burst from her body. Sweat formed on her brow as she huffed like a woman in labor, and when Asher leaned back, he saw Ximena's vagina dilate.

A scaly, black nugget pushed out of her. The end of the mass had two rubies on it, and it wasn't until Asher saw the flittering tongue that he realized the rubies were eyes. The nugget pushed out further, revealing the serpent's body. It looked like a python, thick and black and slithering. When she opened her eyes, Ximena cried out in horror at the sight of it exiting her in a dark puddle of afterbirth. That horror strengthened as her anus opened and small snakes oozed out. When she screamed, she began to choke, her throat bulging the same way it had when she'd given Asher that expert blowjob. She breathed heavily through her nostrils so not to suffocate as another black python rose between her teeth, slithered down her face, and coiled around her neck like a noose. Her hips bucked, every inch of her trembling. She took in a deep breath once her throat was cleared, and smaller snakes escaped her nose, with even tinier ones rising from under her lower eyelids. Even Ximena's snake tattoo began to move, spiraling around her leg like stripes on a barber pole.

Her vagina dilated again, and this time, Ximena moaned with pleasure. As she gave birth to another serpent, the others formed a pit around her and Asher, and the room grew hotter and drier, the air filling with the odors of sulfur and decay. The walls pulsed like a dying heartbeat.

Ximena climaxed as the thick middle of the snake passed through her dripping canal. Her toes curled, eyes rolling over white, a drop of blood coming from the lip she'd bitten down on.

Though Astaroth did not appear, Asher could feel the beast's presence fill the room. He acknowledged it with the latest words Rex had chanted on the album, whispering them in Ximena's ear.

"Our sigil is that of Lucifer—the inflamed Seal of Satan—born of the great monolith of black sorcery. Drink from its deep well, for The Seal of Satan is the chalice of all creation."

Without hesitation, Ximena ran her fingers through the semen on her blistered belly, then licked them clean.

And then there were two, he thought, hearing Rex's voice in his head.

TWENTY-TWO

"I NEVER THOUGHT IT WAS real," Ximena admitted.

They were still in bed together, Asher on his back with her cuddling him with her head on his chest. The room had cooled, and the sulfurous stench was beginning to fade, but the demonic snakes remained in the bed with them, drifting slowly over their nude bodies.

"Black magic, witchcraft, The Devil," Ximena said. "I thought it was just the stuff of horror movies. I always liked the aesthetic of Satan, just like all things dark and spooky, but never really believed in the supernatural or life after death." She played with the hair on his chest in an adoring manner. "But then, I never thought I'd be fucking *an actual warlock.* There've been other guys who fancied themselves as pagan witches, and some stoner occultists who saw themselves as wizards, but none of them ever produced any *real* magic. It was all talk, all delusions. Just more bullshit guys did to try and impress the goth girl. But you? You're the real deal. I may be high, but that was no hallucination."

"You've only glimpsed my true power," Asher told her.

"If you can make snakes come out of me, I can only imagine what else you're capable of."

"So the snakes don't disturb you?"

"The whole thing disturbed me at the time. I was so scared. But then … I dunno … it just started to turn me on so quickly. It sounds crazy, but my fear disappeared, and I just became entranced, like a sleep state, a dream. I don't know how or why …"

"I do. It's because I am not just a warlock but an incubus."

"That's, like, some sort of sex demon, right?"

"Exactly—a seductive demon in human form. In medieval times, fucking an incubus was believed to result in the birth of lesser demons. In your case, it produced the snakes of Astaroth."

She cocked her head. "Astaroth?"

"The Great Duke of Hell. One of The Evil Trinity. He saw something in you, something he helped me to see."

"And what is that?"

"That your darkness is not just surface level. It's not a costume or a phase you're going through. It runs much deeper than that, and you need an outlet for it. That's why you cut and pierce and tattoo yourself—the desecration of your flesh releases some of the pressure of that bottled-up darkness, like steam from a kettle."

She slowly sat up in bed so they were facing each other. "So what happens now?"

"That depends on you. Do you want to continue suppressing the darkness that germinates within you, or do you want to use that evil to achieve victory and bliss?"

Ximena crawled on top of him, pressing her breasts to his chest, her lips inches from Asher's. "I'm a smalltime drug dealer in a dead-end town. My dad was an abusive drunk, and my mother was a lazy drug addict on welfare. Neither of them made much effort to raise me. The only real family I have is my cousin Diego, but Fernanda is keeping him on a short leash these days. The bitch doesn't even want me in his life. And you're right about that guy I've been dating. He's okay, but he's just too meek. It's strange being a girl sometimes. Society tells you to get a guy who treats you right, and in many ways, you want one, but you're just more turned on by dominant males other people think are bastards. This is why men complain about never knowing what the fuck women want. We don't know ourselves! But you didn't have that problem at all. It's like you tore into my mind and exposed all my needs and desires to read me like a book." She sighed. "Anyway, my point is, I don't have a whole lot going for me. Never have. Now that I've seen your power, I'd be lying if I said I didn't want some of it for myself."

She kissed him deeply.

"You must offer yourself to me," he told her. "Fully and completely."

"I do."

"I shall be your master, and your only god will be Satan."

Ximena kissed his cheeks softly. "Yes, daddy."

"Good girl, but call me Master."

Asher gave her butt a little pat, and Ximena moved off him so he could slide out from under her and the snakes. Getting out of bed, he began to dress, and Ximena watched him with puppy eyes.

"Where are you going?" she asked.

"Don't worry, sweetheart. You're coming with me."

✟

On the ride there, he called Lenny and told him where to meet them, then called Barney and did the same, telling his minions what they needed to bring. Asher and Ximena stopped at a gas station, and he filled up the five-gallon gas can he kept in the trunk of the Dodge, then bought a couple of twelve packs of beer.

Ximena had quickly fallen in love with the black ball python that had been her firstborn, and she wore it around her neck like a feather boa. The other snakes would get their own glass tanks with the money Asher had given her. The one around her neck complemented the tight black dress she wore with her knee-high leather boots. Despite all the sex he'd been having, Asher's loins churned looking at her, but he remained focused on his sinister plans.

Snow flurries whipped against the backdrop of a night sky without stars. The late hour and slippery roads left the streets vacant. Asher sipped his beer as they drove on, only lowering the volume of the blasting heavy metal as they drew closer to the parking lot. Lenny arrived first, and everyone got out of their vehicles, Asher introducing Ximena to him. Lenny gave Asher a knowing look, as if to say, "you're a lucky guy." Popping the trunk, Asher brought out the beers and the gas can.

"You bring yours?" he asked Lenny.

He nodded. "I've got two cans in my trunk."

"Get them."

Lenny returned to his car just as Barney pulled up in a jalopy. The Delta '88 Oldsmobile was so rusted the paint looked like a cheetah's coat, and the bald tires struggled in the slush. At least he'd been smart enough not to keep Deanna's Hyundai, even though it was in vastly better condition than this old hunk of junk. Barney parked beside Asher and came out of his car carrying a large gas can. He was dressed in black just like his master, including a new motorcycle jacket, with a t-shirt that read: *Mortician with Benefits.*

"Glad you could make it," Asher told him, looking Barney over for any signs of hesitation. "After the other night, I wasn't sure if you were fully with me or if you chickened out and headed for the border."

Barney shook his head. "No, Master. I would never do that. I serve you."

Asher believed him. There was a simplicity to Barney that made him easy to manipulate. He clearly wanted someone to show him the way, for he'd been incapable of forging a path for his life on his own. In a short amount of time, and despite the violence and horror Asher had brought into his life, Barney had made an idol out of him.

When Asher introduced him to the others, Ximena grimaced as she wiped her hand on her side to clear off the clamminess of Barney's handshake. Lenny gave Asher a troubled look, expressing disapproval of the newcomer, but knew better than to question Asher, for Lenny's master dwelled within him.

"Nice snake," Barney told Ximena.

"Nice shirt," she replied.

Barney looked to Asher. "Where's Violet? Isn't she coming?"

"Not on a school night," he joked. "Now quit asking questions. You have a job to do."

Ximena gave Asher a curious look, as if to ask who Violet was, but she said nothing.

Though they'd parked in the back of the lot, the church was easy to see even in the darkness and increasing snowfall. Our Lady of Mercy was an old cathedral, typical to New England churches, with a towering steeple and gold onions on its four towers. Atop the steeple was a large cross of black iron. Asher started toward the church, and his acolytes followed, each carrying a can full of gasoline. As they drew closer, the colorful images of saints appeared in the stained glass windows, watching them with dead eyes.

Asher addressed his followers. "I've gathered you here for our first act as a cult. Each of you has shown enthusiasm to serve me in my quest for Satanic power. Each of you has expressed your devotion to Lucifer. This is your chance to prove it together, as one."

The others nodded, and Barney gave the metalhead horns salute.

"Each of you take a side," Asher said. "And keep your eyes open for any passing cars, though I doubt there'll be any."

The flurries had become large snowflakes that whipped in every direction as the storm crept into town. The roads would be even more empty than they'd been on the ride over, lowering the odds of anyone passing by the church, which was further uphill with a long driveway, isolated from the road.

Ximena and Barney took either side of the church, and Lenny covered the rear. Asher wanted to stand on the front steps when they did this so he could watch the doors go up in smoke. The group doused the walls of the building from end to end while Asher soaked the entrance. Barney came around and asked if he should break a window so they could throw the gas cans inside, but Asher advised against it because it might set off alarms. Besides, the gas cans should be kept for future use. There was so much he wanted to burn.

Asher called the others to the front of the church so they could stand where newly married couples posed for wedding pictures, then drew his Zippo lighter from his jeans.

He'd always been thrilled by fire.

Choosing a Catholic church had been deliberate. It was the form of Christianity that seemed to fear The Devil the most, with their exorcisms and other pious voodoo. But at the same time, Catholics never acknowledged how much evil they'd put forth into the world with centuries of torture, fearmongering, and child abuse. The legacy of Catholic cruelty was almost admirable, but their hypocrisy and lies made them a worthy target for a Satanist's wrath.

As the church ignited, the rising flames turned the red of blood, swallowing Our Lady of Mercy in a squall of hellfire. It devoured the structure, the heat buckling the loadbearing walls and exploding the stained glass windows. Smoke alarms sounded. The face of St. Christopher flew out in one piece, only to shatter upon the asphalt. The towers ignited with ease, their gold onions becoming bright balls of crimson as the structures buckled. Even the snow did nothing to dimmish the fire's power. The church became a volcano, black smoke forming a mushroom cloud above the wreckage as Asher's Satanic cult stood back, admiring their work.

"From this moment on," he said, "we are a family."

Asher handed out beers.

"Hail Satan!" he shouted, raising a bottle in toast.

The others did the same. "Hail Satan!"

"The next time we destroy a holy place," Asher said, "it will not be empty."

The last thing Asher saw as they left the parking lot was the flaming cross at the top of the steeple as it broke free and fell to the ground, inverted.

TWENTY-THREE

HIS BODY WAS CHANGING.

Not only had Asher's dick gotten bigger, but his chest was fuller, shoulders higher, muscles harder. There was more hair on his chest and arms. His form was athletic, the small amount of fat around his midsection having gradually vanished, leaving him lean with popping abdominals. Without having to dye them, his sideburns were black and wiry, his hair shaggy and wild, and his eyebrows met in the middle. His fingernails were longer and came to fine points, with the ones on his left hand twice as thick as the ones on his right, almost like claws.

Admiring his transformation in the mirror, Asher washed his hands to get the stench of gasoline off them and scraped the dried blood from beneath his nails. It would have been easier to shower, but he was beginning to like the greasiness of his hair and his own body odor. The pheromones were part of his incubus spell, one of the many hooks he put into women to drag them in. Better to not bury that with soaps and deodorants.

Returning to his room, he noticed another odor, one that enticed him. It was the stench of rot. He drew Paul's skull out of its hiding place, confirming it was the source of the smell. The dead human tissue had a unique, pungent aroma, like a combination of spoiled pork and bad eggs mixed with undertones that were fecal yet flowery. While Asher had once been repulsed by the stench of Beelzebub, he was beginning to enjoy such pungency. Asher packed the bowl of this skull bong with weed and took a long toke, inhaling the dope smoke and the vapors of death.

He still hadn't slept and had no desire to, but the insomnia left dark rings under his eyes, reminding him of the photos he'd seen of his uncle. When he'd come home last night, Mom was in bed with her door closed. Now that he had so much money and influence, Asher considered getting a place of his own or even shacking up with Ximena, but he was attached to his childhood home and enjoyed dominating his mother with emotional abuse. He didn't hate her, exactly, but hurting her gave him a sadistic thrill, and her fear of Rex, even after his death, was amusing to witness.

Just before dawn, Asher brought a shovel to the yard and dug up the spot where he'd buried his and Violet's bloody clothes on the night they murdered Terry and his teenage daughter, Maxine. Asher didn't regret killing either of them, but he scolded himself for raping the girl—not because of the pain and horror it had caused her but because she'd been young enough to possibly be a virgin. He had no way of knowing if she'd ever spread her legs for a boy before Asher forced his way into her, but if she had been a virgin, sacrificing her would have granted him far more power. By taking her virginity by force, he may have spoiled an opportunity.

Asher couldn't beat himself up over it, though. The daughter of a drug dealer had a pretty good chance of being a teenage slut, but even if Maxine had been a virgin, it wasn't like she'd be his only chance to slaughter one. Perhaps he'd made a mistake, but he wouldn't repeat it. He was learning, maturing.

Digging up the clothes, Asher stripped right there in the yard and put on the bloody shirt and jeans. They were covered in earth and small insects, with a few worms that clung to him like leeches. Standing in the cold, pink dawn, Asher stretched his arms out in a T and made a silent prayer to all the demons of the abyss. The unearthed murder clothes were his shroud of death, an unholy uniform for a devout Satanic killer. The night he'd buried them, he'd done so to hide evidence, but now he realized Rex had urged him to bury them for the purpose of bringing Asher closer to the very essence of death. His was covered in earth, just like a coffin, and the blood and tissue on this clothing had begun to decay. It all gave Asher a strange sense of peace and belonging. He'd become a reaper in human form.

Returning to his room, he heard his mother in the kitchen but wasn't interested in messing with her this morning. He had other things on his mind—soft, girly things he hungered to bleed. Soon, the front door closed, and Mom drove off to the office, and when Asher got a breakfast beer from the fridge, he spotted a note from her on the counter.

Please, clean your room! It's starting to stink in there. I don't want ants and roaches.

Asher grinned. She could have told him this to his face but was now too intimidated to do so.

I'm going out with a friend tonight, Mom went on, *so I won't be home until late.* Asher knew what that meant. The slut was going on a date to shove her fake tits in some middleclass slob's face. *You're on your own for dinner,* Mom's note ended with. *I left some ground beef in the fridge for burgers.*

Asher crumpled the note and threw it on the floor.

He spent the morning in his room, experimenting with different forms of witchcraft, testing the authenticity of what he found in the spell books. The older the texts, the more accurate they were. Over the past two centuries, humankind had lost touch with the occult, outside of seeing it in entertainment, but Asher had found that most people who enjoyed scary movies and heavy metal were not evil people at all. They enjoyed horror only when it was safe, gravitating toward Stephen King books and slasher movies but avoiding real beheading videos, bestiality porn, and other true horrors. But Asher enjoyed it all, from *A Nightmare on Elm Street* to *1 Lunatic, 1 Ice Pick.*

It was around noon when Diego called.

"Hey, man," Diego said. "I got your message. Sounds like you're doing good."

"Better than good. Fucking fantastic."

"Cool, cool."

Asher detected something in Diego's voice. His friend wanted to talk to him about something but wasn't sure how to begin.

"What is it?" Asher asked.

"What's what?"

"You tell me."

"I just want to make sure you're doing okay."

Asher lowered his brow. "I just told you I was fantastic."

"I know."

"So are you losing your hearing?"

Diego sighed. "No."

"Just because I've been busy doesn't mean I'm not okay. It means I'm becoming a success."

"At what, though? Did you find a job?"

"Nah, man," Asher laughed. "I'm past all that now."

"Then I guess I just don't understand."

"That's all right. You will soon."

"Okay …" Diego said, sounding lost. "Listen, if you're not busy tonight, I was thinking you could come over for dinner. Fernanda is one hell of a cook, and we'd both like to see you."

"Really? *Fernanda* wants to see me?"

Diego tried to laugh it off. "Well, you know what I mean."

"Your cousin tells me Fernanda won't even let you see her anymore."

"Not exactly, she just … wait … You're talking to Ximena?"

"Someone has to spend time with her now that your fiancée has banned her from your life."

"It's not *that* bad. Fernanda has just been a little moody lately because of the pregnancy."

"Is she okay to cook in her condition? I mean, how far along is she now?"

"Six and a half months. But she's still plenty mobile. I couldn't keep her on the couch if I tried, and besides, she lives to cook. It's her passion."

Asher considered this. He'd been wanting to convert his old friend to his new way of life. Why wait any longer?

"All right, then," he said.

"Great. Bring your new girlfriend too."

Agreeing to bring Violet along, Asher wrapped up the call, telling his friend they'd have plenty of time tonight to talk in person. He wanted to look Diego in the eyes and find out why he'd seemed so concerned. Had Ximena told her cousin something she shouldn't have? Asher doubted it. Having experienced his power firsthand, she'd be a fool to have it turned against her.

He only heard the doorbell ring because there was a pause in the music as one song ended and another began. Asher kicked Paul's skull under the bed and went to the front door, hoping it was Mormons or some other door-to-door salesman for Christ. It would be a pleasure to fill them with horror. He might even let them in to have some real fun.

He opened the door to find Melissa Vincent looking more beautiful than he'd ever seen her before. She wore a clingy black dress that ended mid-thigh, with black stockings and pumps, having taken his fashion advice. Her blond hair was freshly blown-out, her makeup immaculate. She wasn't presenting herself today as the mother of his girlfriend or the housewife next door. She was here as the Melissa she'd been before the kids or had always wanted to be. Dark eyeshadow gave her an aura of haunted yearning, and her lips were moist with desire.

"I bought this dress just for you," she said. "I thought I'd come over so you could see it."

"Very nice. But it'll look even better on my floor."

She smiled bashfully, reminding Asher of Melissa's youngest daughter, Callie. He stepped aside to let her in. Melissa briefly hesitated, as if asking herself if she were really doing this, but then she came inside, just as Asher knew she would. After what he'd done to her in her kitchen, no amount of doubt or guilt would free Melissa from his clutches. Her need for him even outweighed her loyalty to her family.

She looked at his filthy clothes. "A little stinky, aren't we? I could wash those for you if you like."

He touched the underside of her chin. "Of course you would. Anything I like, you'll do it. Isn't that right, Melissa?"

"Y-y-yes." She trembled at his touch. "I'll do whatever you want. Just make love to me, please."

He gripped her chin. "I'm not going to *make love* to you." He relished seeing her face fall. "I'm going to *fuck the hell out of you.* If you think you came hard last time, just wait until you have my fat cock inside you. You're gonna be limping for a month."

Melissa instantly brightened with excitement. Still gripping her chin, Asher pulled her close, and she shuddered against him with frightened arousal. Though she was under his spell, part of her still feared him, and that was just the way Asher liked it. He nibbled on her bottom lip. She ran her hand down his chest and abdomen, then cupped his crotch over his jeans.

"Oh my god," she whispered when she felt the size of his bulge.

"On your knees," he commanded her.

Melissa obeyed, and he stepped closer, putting his crotch before her face.

"Take it out," he said.

Melissa undid his belt and fly, then tugged the waistband down. Asher wore no underwear, so his half-hard penis flopped out, brushing Melissa's nose. She coughed on the smell of his unwashed genitals, but the sight of his extra-large cock left her stunned. She stared as if mesmerized, seeming almost afraid to touch it. The look on her face made Asher grow harder, the head of his cock purpling with a rush of blood cells.

"Now worship it," he demanded.

Melissa gently gripped his erection, again reminding him of her youngest daughter. Then she wrapped her other hand around it too, needing both to squeeze the whole thing. She kissed the head, licked the shaft, and then put it in her mouth. She was barely able to take in half of it. Asher gripped both sides of her head and thrust deeper until she gagged.

"It's just ... it's just so *big*," she said with a cough.

Asher slapped her face with his erection, startling her. He wondered if she'd ever been smacked with cock like that. Melissa wasn't as orally skilled as Ximena, but she was just as submissive as Violet when he fucked her face. Even when her gag reflex caused her to retch, she didn't ask for mercy.

"That's right," he said, hammering her mouth. "Take it like a woman."

Finally, he pulled her up by the hair and yanked the plunging neckline of her dress down to expose the black, lacy bra. Having mothered two children, Melissa's breasts had some sag to them, but they were ample in size and beautifully pale, with a spattering of freckles across her cleavage. He began biting them, each nibble a little harder than the last. She winced in pain, then moaned in pleasure, her flesh rippling with goosebumps as he gnawed her nipples.

He couldn't take her to his bedroom. The stench of death was too repellant for normal human beings. Asher considered bending her over the back of the couch, but a better idea came to him. Taking her hand, he led Melissa to his mother's bedroom, then threw her on the unmade bed. Her skirt rode up her thighs, revealing a garter belt and crotchless panties. Melissa had come to him *ready*. Now, it was time to make her more careful about what she wished for.

Placing his hands on her kneecaps, Asher spread her legs with force, the pain in her pelvis making her hiss between her teeth. But that was nothing compared to the shock of his swollen cock entering her. Melissa gasped, convulsing beneath him as he drove in hard and deep, stretching her more than any man ever had.

"Does it hurt?" he asked.

She could barely speak. "Y-yes … it's been a while, and you're girthy."

"Suffer, Melissa."

He shoved all the way into her until he reached the tight end of her canal, making her whole body tense. Asher's energy was limitless, his thrusts brutal, tearing Melissa's vagina as she bucked in the throes of painful orgasms.

"Oh my God," she cried. "Oh my god, oh my god!"

Asher smacked her. "Keep his filthy name out of your mouth!"

A pink handprint glowed upon Melissa's face as she nodded obediently.

"Say you love Satan," he told her. She blinked in confusion, so he grabbed her by the throat. "Say 'fuck me, Satan'!"

"Fuck me, Satan," she whimpered.

He twisted her nipple. "Louder!"

"Fuck me, Satan!"

Asher leaned over her, and the inverted cross on his necklace fell into Melissa's mouth. Still choking her with his left hand, he jackhammered her into another orgasm, feeling the tackiness of her blood on his shaft, and when he was ready to climax, he pulled out, sat on her chest, and jerked off in her face. His semen came out black as tar. It ran down Melissa's forehead like used motor oil, a sludgy discharge that greased her face and stung her eyes, causing her to close them tight. Having not seen the color of the semen, she kept her mouth open wide to receive it. Her face pruned in disgust as the black slime hit her taste buds, but when she bent over to spit it out, Asher yanked her head back by her hair and stroked her neck like he was milking a cow.

"Swallow the filth of Satan," he demanded.

Melissa grimaced as she was forced to obey him, but the moment she swallowed, the semen came back up. Dark vomit flowed down her chin and onto her breasts. Small bits of it were moving. When

Asher looked to the head of his penis, he saw some sort of grub twitching out of his urethra. Upon Melissa's cum-drenched face, an orgy of black maggots and inchworms crawled.

A loud buzzing filled the room like distortion from an amplifier. As the temperature rose, flies flew out from under the bed in droves, their bodies lining the walls in a sickening wallpaper. The odor of decomposing flesh poisoned the air, and when Melissa blinked the cum from her eyes, she went pale at the horror unfolding all around her.

The ceiling swirled in a vortex of bloody sewage. Bone shards and teeth were trapped in its current. The hellish filth broke off into moist stalactites that dangled over Asher and Melissa, and the sound of babies crying emanated from the sludge. Melissa screamed, but Asher kept her pinned to the mattress.

"There is no escape," he told her with the tenderness of a groom. "Let the evil in."

Her eyes went crazed and bloodshot. She could not speak, only make stunted noises, the gibberish of the damned.

As the ends of the stalactites reached the floor, the insects clung to them like fly tape, and the filth converged, forming a putrid mound upon the carpet. Asher sensed what was coming—*who* was coming—so when the mound took shape, he praised the rising demon.

"Hail the Prince of Devils!" he said. "I beckon the black god of the Philistine city of Ekron—Beelzebub—the Lord of the Flies, brother to the Hesperus star."

Forged of insects and human waste, Beelzebub stood tall, his antlers smoldering as the end of his anteater snout puckered. Pink mucus dribbled from it. Melissa screamed uncontrollably until Asher pressed a finger to her lips. She hushed instantly, his sorcery giving him total dominion over her. Still, the fear was alive in Melissa, and her body convulsed beneath him, tears spilling over the rancid semen on her cheeks.

With Beelzebub watching on, Asher shoved his tireless erection inside Melissa again. She shuddered, her eyes rolling back as pleasure and pain became one. It began to rain within the bedroom, a revolting mixture of gore, pus, maggots, and liquid feces. Asher fucked the trembling mother in the nightmare of his own mother's bed. Beelzebub's hooves stomped closer, and when the demon's wet hands fell on Asher's shoulders, he tilted his head back and smiled. The beast's snout pressed against Asher's lips in a sloppy kiss, funneling the black magic of Hell itself into his soul. Flies covered Asher's head like a death mask. The wooden bedposts burst into flames.

Beelzebub moved back, speaking with a buzzing chorus of fly wings. Most of the words were incomprehensible, a mixture of dead languages and ones foreign to Asher. But one word stood out, clear as a witching hour bell.

"Leviathan," the demon said.

Using the nail of his left index finger, Asher cut into Melissa's breast, etching the Leviathan Cross into the fatty tissue, matching the one on his arm. He looked up into the vortex as a large shape emerged, and paid witness to the sea serpent swimming through the septic gore. Dozens of spider eyes covered its head, and its mouth was lined with crocodile teeth. Though its body was black, its fish scales glowed a rainbow of reds, blood oozing from its gills.

"Leviathan," Asher muttered in worship. "Hail the great demon serpent of the deep."

The monster spoke with the growl of a coyote. "Behold, I am the behemoth of chaos, for I have returned to this realm to devour the damned. Deliver them unto me."

"Thy will be done," Asher said, backed by Rex, their voices in unison.

His first thought was to murder Melissa as an offering, but he'd put too much work into her to toss her into the abyss. There was still so much he could use her for, so much left to be done to this pathetic housewife and her daughters. He just had to hope she would retain enough of her sanity to function.

"You will feast on many victims," Asher promised Leviathan.

The serpent writhed and sank beneath the murk, appeased for now. Returning his attention to Melissa, Asher realized she'd passed out. He continued fucking her unconscious body, further tearing her, and went as deep as he could when he ejaculated, flooding her insides with his evil seed, an incubus spell that would never let the poor woman go.

✝

Melissa awoke in the bathtub.

She came to with a start, and Asher spoke to her gently as he ran the soapy loofa over her naked body. Realizing she was no longer in a hellscape, the terror in her eyes settled to a stable dread.

"What is happening?" she asked, trying not to cry.

"Easy," Asher told her. "Just take it easy and let me wash you."

Asher sat nude on the edge of the tub. When they'd murdered Deanna and Paul, hellfire had burned the blood off him and his acolytes, eliminating all evidence of the slayings. This time, the nastiness remained, forcing Asher to finally bathe. He'd washed himself first, then carried Melissa off the soiled mattress and into the bathroom. His mother's bedroom was ruined. Though the vortex had closed and the insects vanished with the demons, blood and fecal matter remained on the walls, ceiling, and floor, with teeth and chips of bone driven into the drywall. It would take a crime scene cleanup crew to remove the mess, but even then, the room would remain uninhabitable. Asher doubted the stench would ever go away. Luckily, he'd come to enjoy it. He doubted Mom would, but he would deal with her reaction later. She was going straight from work to her hot date, so she wouldn't be home anytime soon, if the whore even came home tonight at all.

Melissa stared into the russet-colored water she was soaking in. Asher could see in her eyes that she remembered everything that happened up until she'd passed out, but did she believe it or think it was just a vivid nightmare? She looked at the engraving on her breast, and when she sat up, the pain in her groin made her wince.

"Just take it easy," he said. "Remember what the bible says—*be still and know that I am God.*"

She stared at him with haunted eyes. "You're not God. You're The Devil."

"Wow," he said with a laugh. "That's a huge compliment, but no, I'm not The Devil. I just do his bidding, just as you do mine."

"No …"

"Yes, Melissa. You and your daughter both. And soon, your youngest daughter too."

She sat up all the way despite the pain it caused her. "No! Please. Take me, but please leave my girls alone."

"Nah. Fuck that. I prefer to take all three of you."

She begged him until he silenced her with a simple raising of his hand. He'd never seen a woman more desperate. Even the ones he'd raped and murdered hadn't looked as crippled by hopelessness as Melissa did right now. It was enough to make him want to fuck her again—to force her to do the most degrading things he could imagine—but he had an evening to prepare for.

"I'm so scared," Melissa whimpered. "And I hurt."

"Yeah, your pussy is going to need a few stitches."

206

"Oh, no …"

"Hey, at least your husband's out of town. Not that he'd notice any changes to your pussy anyway, the limp-dicked loser." He smiled at her. "Despite everything that's happened, you still want me."

Melissa was unable to deny it, so she said nothing.

"You are under my spell, sweetheart," Asher told her. "There's no point in resisting, so you might as well enjoy yourself."

"I do enjoy myself with you. That's what makes me so afraid. That and … whatever those things were. *Fuck!* How is any of this even possible?"

Asher squeezed shampoo from the bottle into her hair. "Every horror is possible, no matter how fantastic, for if it can be dreamed, it can be born. Evil is as old as time—older than any life-form on Earth. It permeates every inch of our universe, for there is a never-ending supply of new horrors, cruelties, and abominations. Even before man gave a name to Satan, his presence filled their hearts with dread. Every religion has different names and origins for them, but demons have always been with us, tainting our lives with wickedness and death from the moment we crawled out of the primordial ooze."

Asher opened the drain, releasing the murky swill so he could refill the tub with clean water.

"What do these demons want?" Melissa asked.

"Oh, I think you know the answer to that. I believe Violet told me your family is Christian."

She nodded yet looked somehow ashamed.

"Something tells me you haven't been to church in a long time," Asher said. "These days, so many people who call themselves Christians have abandoned their churches, even though they still believe, or at least claim to. Religion is going out of style in the twenty-first century. It's antiquated."

"Is that why you've done all this to me? Because I stopped going to church?"

"No, stupid. I've done all of this to you because it's *what you wanted*."

"I … I didn't …"

"Admit it. Before me, your life was nothing but stress and disappointment. Despite having a family, you've been desperately lonely, a housewife forced into the life of a hermit. Sure, you love your kids and maybe even your husband, but you are unfulfilled. Fifty is inching closer every day, Melissa, and you've been left wondering where all those precious years went. You always thought there'd be time to pursue your dreams and do something with your little life, but motherhood ate up far more time than you anticipated. You were too busy to notice it when your girls were little, but now they're nearly grown, and you've found yourself alone in a big, empty house, wondering what happened, terrified this might be all there is."

Her bloodshot eyes looked at him quizzically. "How ... how do you know all this?"

"I knew it the moment I forced myself on you in your kitchen, because I didn't have to force you for long."

"But that's just sex. It'd been missing from my life. A woman has needs, same as a man."

"You don't have to tell me." He squeezed the soapy loofa over her shoulders. "You were calling for an incubus without even realizing it. When your wish was granted, you offered yourself to me completely."

"Incubus," she said. "So you really are a demon."

"What woman doesn't want a demon in the sack? Don't be afraid, Melissa. I'm here to encourage your urges and fulfill your desires. We make our own Heaven or Hell, right here on this Earth. I'm merely showing you the way out of the Hell you created for yourself. You've rotted in that house far too long. I have come to put the *living* back in your life."

Melissa stared into space. "Living?"

"Really living!"

Her expression was grave. "Asher ... are you going to kill me?"

"Not unless I have to."

This didn't seem to comfort her at all. "Are you going to hurt my girls?"

"I know what you're going to say. You'd rather die a thousand times than see your children die."

"Of course I would!"

"Nothing's more noble than a mother's love. That's how I know I can count on you."

"What do you mean?"

"If I wanted you or your girls dead, I would have killed you already. Hell, I could've offered you to the serpent Leviathan today. Instead, I spared you, because I'm confident you'll serve me well. Your reward for that servitude is more than just mind-shattering orgasms. If you want to keep your family safe, you'll have to earn it.

Understand?"

She nodded slowly.

"Don't look so fucking grief-stricken," he told her. "I'm giving you things your husband and your God failed to—passion, thrills, euphoria. I understand why you're scared, but you mustn't forget all the benefits of being with me."

She narrowed her eyes. "I'm *with* you?"

"You're mine now, sweetheart. You and your children. How I treat you all depends on how good of girls you are."

Taking a deep breath, Melissa hugged her knees, allowing Asher to wash her back. She was defeated and knew it.

"Just tell me what to do," she said.

TWENTY-FOUR

VIOLET ARRIVED WEARING JEANS AND a long-sleeved Fleetwood Mac t-shirt, so Asher scolded her and sent her home so she could change into something sexier for the dinner. He wasn't about to introduce her to Diego looking so plain. Asher believed any woman with him had better look like she'd just stepped out of the beauty parlor—full makeup when they were together, hair down, and nice clothes, particularly when they had plans with others. He didn't have to worry about Violet talking to her mother because Melissa had driven herself to an Urgent Care to have her vaginal wounds tended to. Asher had instructed her to go straight home afterward and stay there with Callie to await further instructions. When Violet returned in a formfitting minidress, he let her inside and she threw her hand over her nose and mouth.

"Holy shit!" she said. "What is that fucking smell? It's awful!"

"Some friends visited me today. Special friends."

"Oh. You mean …?"

"Yes. *Them*. Now c'mon."

He urged her toward the door with a pat on the butt.

"Your mom's gonna freak out when she smells that," Violet said.

"Freaking out is just what mothers do. I saw that very clearly this afternoon."

"Really? What happened?"

He nudged her outside. "Just get in the car."

As they drove to Diego's, Violet put her head on Asher's shoulder, cuddling up to him like the kitten she was. One night away from him had only increased her fondness. Knowing he could do anything to the girl and that she would do anything for him—including kill someone—filled Asher with light.

"How's your sister?" he asked.

"Good, I guess. I spent some time with her last night, just like you said. We watched a movie together and listened to some music. I'm trying to introduce her to metal gradually with mild stuff like Iron Maiden, but she's just not feeling it yet."

"That's all right. It's showing an interest in her that's important here. Think she'll be up for hanging out with us?"

"Oh, for sure. Callie's one of those girls who'd do anything to hang out with an older crowd, to make her feel cool. But my parents probably won't allow it. They don't even like *me* hanging out with you, let alone the baby of the family."

"Don't worry about your parents. Dad's away—physically and emotionally—and I think your mom is really coming around."

Violet gave him a silly look. "Why would you think that?"

"Trust me. I know women."

She shrugged it off, cuddling closer. "Whatever you say, Master."

"That's right. Callie comes out with us tomorrow night. Understand?"

"Yes, Master."

Diego and Fernanda lived in a split-level building, their apartment on the top floor and their neighbor's apartment on the bottom. The yard offered a fair amount of space and privacy from the other homes on the block. Asher parked on the side of the building. The sun was going down, and dead trees cast long shadows through the neighborhood. As they walked to the front door, Violet tried to hold Asher's hand, but he batted it away. She should know better than to get so lovey-dovey. Perhaps she needed a reminder of what this really was—what *he* really was.

A young boy was pushing an old man in a wheelchair through the front door. They were the downstairs neighbors, and once in the entryway, the boy rolled the crippled man to the door to their apartment.

"Can we watch *Pokémon*, Grandpa?" the kid asked.

The old man chuckled. "How many times can you watch the same show?"

"It's not always the same."

"Coulda fooled me," the old man said, still chuckling.

The boy knocked on the door, and a preteen girl opened it for them, her pigtails draped over a Supergirl t-shirt. When she caught Asher's eye, her smile disappeared and she looked away.

Asher and Violet ascended the staircase, and Diego opened his front door to greet them. He had a fresh haircut and was wearing a collared shirt and slacks, looking more mature than ever. Though Asher had ordered Violet to wear a dress, he'd put on his usual black jeans and a wrinkled band t-shirt, having changed out of the filthy death-clothes after bathing. So Diego's neatness curdled Asher's stomach bile. Family life was killing his friend even before his woman could pop the baby out. It was a sorry thing to see.

Diego closed the door behind them as they entered the warm, inviting apartment. The décor was a mix of modern American and classic Latino culture. It was a tidy place, with freshly vacuumed carpets and throw pillows covering the sofa. They even had live plants.

Fernanda appeared from out of a yellow kitchen, cradling her swollen belly like a football. Her eyes were bright behind her glasses, her smile reflecting the glow pregnant women are said to have. Despite her being six months along, Asher had to admit she still looked good, even with the small baby bump. Everyone was introduced, and Diego led them to their seats at the dining table, then poured Asher and Violet craft beers into highball glasses—the most yuppie behavior Asher had ever seen from Diego. Asher knew then just how neutered his best friend was becoming. He could only hope there was time to save Diego from himself, if he was still worth saving at all.

They made small talk as Fernanda prepared plates, Diego politely asking Violet about her life and interests, with Violet replying with the same inane pleasantries. It was the sort of tepid, pointless conversation that made Asher's blood burn. Humans always had to fill the air with chatter, speaking more than they listened. He expected them to get into the weather next, but Fernanda called everyone into the kitchen to collect steak fajitas with mixed vegetables.

The relief didn't last long. As soon as the four of them sat at the table, the small talk continued, with Fernanda asking Violet the same questions she'd missed out on while cooking. They talked about college courses, goals, family, the town. Violet explained how she'd met Asher, the story making Fernanda smile. Asher was grateful Violet was being social for the both of them. She asked all about the pregnancy, leading Diego and his fiancée to ramble on about their baby like all expecting parents do. Asher could almost feel his friend's manhood disintegrating. It was as if every masculine trait Diego had come into the relationship with had been absorbed by his "partner" and she'd shitted out this pathetic daddy.

When they went into a ten-minute conversation on the different kinds of cribs, Asher left the table and got another beer, drinking it straight from the bottle like a real man. He was getting restless. The food was quite good, but it wasn't what he'd come here for. He didn't want to hear about baby names or have Diego whip out the Uno deck. It was time to take care of business. Returning to the table, he reached under the collar of his shirt and pulled out the inverted cross necklace hidden underneath. Fernanda noticed, and Asher relished the change in her expression, that pregnant glow giving way to discomfort. Sitting down, Asher thudded the beer bottle on the table and belched.

Violet tried to make a joke of it. "His compliments to the chef!"

Diego and Fernanda smiled politely. Asher just sucked his teeth.

"So, Asher," Diego said, "you haven't said much this evening. Why don't you tell me the good news you'd mentioned on the phone?"

"I'd be happy to." He put his elbows on the table, getting closer to the young couple. "The good news is, I've got tens of thousands of dollars and enough drugs to make tens of thousands more."

Fernanda looked at Diego, but he couldn't take his eyes off Asher.

"What're you talking about?" Diego asked. He smirked as if Asher was playing a joke on him. "Are you Scarface now or something?"

"Tell him, Violet," Asher said, still looking at Diego.

Violet nodded. "He's not kidding."

"Why don't you look out the window?" Asher told Diego. "You can check out my brand-new Challenger."

"Okay," Diego said, remaining in his chair. "So where did all this money and stuff come from? Did you sell your uncle's records?"

"Fuck no. I wouldn't dream of doing that now. But Uncle Rex is how I got rich and successful."

"How's that? Did he leave you money?"

"Better. You know what they say about teaching a man to fish. Rex didn't just teach me—he gave me the biggest fishnet the world has ever seen." Asher clutched his inverted cross, extending it toward Diego as far as the chain would allow. "He gave me *power*."

Everyone fell silent. Diego shook his head. Rising, Fernanda started clearing the table, her eyes downcast.

"Don't bother with that now," Asher told her. "I'm telling you both something very important. It might just change your lives— yours and the baby's."

Fernanda's face dimmed. "Please don't mention my child in the same breath as that evil cross around your neck."

"Evil?" Asher raised his eyebrows. "Why, Fernanda, I didn't know you were a religious woman."

"I wouldn't say that, exactly."

"Then what would you say?"

She sighed. "I'd say you're being silly, Asher. Silly and rude."

"Oh, really?"

Diego cut in. "Dude, just—"

"Hold on a second," Asher said. "Let the woman speak for herself."

"I said all I needed to say," Fernanda told him.

"You're telling me I'm silly for having an unconventional religion? That I'm rude for even bringing it up?"

She said nothing, gathering the cloth napkins.

"Look, man," Diego said. "Believe whatever you want, we just don't want to get into it."

"How kind of you to allow me to have my own faith."

"C'mon, I didn't mean it that way."

"I've come here to help you, brother, and you're shutting me out?"

Fernanda stacked the dishes, clapping them loudly. "We don't need that kind of help. We're starting a family here. Diego doesn't want to be involved in drug deals and whatever witchcraft you've gotten into. I'm telling you the same thing I told his cousin, Ximena. Diego is a father now. He has responsibilities. He can't be fooling around with things that could get him in trouble."

Violet came to Asher's defense. "Hey, he's not trying to get you guys in trouble; he's trying to give you a gift."

"Well, he can keep it," Fernanda said. "I'm sorry, Asher, but if you're selling dope and worshipping Satan, maybe you're not mature enough to be part of Diego's life, and you're definitely not the kind of man I would want around my child."

Diego tried to calm her. "Honey, take it easy. Just let me handle it."

She replied to him in Spanish, and the couple argued in their private language until Fernanda vanished into the kitchen. Asher instructed Violet to join Fernanda to help her clean up, so she followed her in there, apologizing for the "misunderstanding" and complimenting the woman's cooking.

"How about you show me that new car?" Diego said.

The men went outside, but when they reached the Challenger, Diego barely even looked at it. His eyes were glued to Asher, his face slack with annoyance and a touch of sorrow.

"What the fuck is going on with you?" he asked.

Asher reached into his coat for a joint and lit it up. "I could ask you the same thing. You've changed, Diego."

"*Me?* Are you kidding? Look at yourself, man! You're barely recognizable."

"Dressing in black is hardly as big of a deal as becoming some soft, yuppie husband. I can't believe I used to envy what you had with Fernanda. Now, I see she's carrying your balls in her purse. It's pathetic. Your life is going right down the shitter, and you're the one doing the flushing."

Diego pointed at Asher's face. "Hey, fuck you, man. I'm not whipped. I've just grown up—something you seem incapable of. It's like you're living backwards."

Asher scoffed. "You just don't get it, do you?"

"No, I get it just fine. You and Rebecca broke up, you lost your job, and you moved back in with your mom. But instead of that putting a fire under you to step up and be a man, you start dating a teenager and wearing rock band t-shirts, getting high every day instead of looking for work. And then you've got the nerve to say *my life* is going down the shitter?"

"You don't know what you're talking about. I'm doing better than ever. I'm peaking."

"Jesus," Diego said, shaking his head. "I knew I shouldn't have introduced you to Ximena. She's the one who got you into this drug dealing crap, isn't she? How deep in are you?"

"Would you forget about the drugs, already?" Asher blew smoke from his joint. "Despite what Fernanda thinks, I'm not trying to get you into selling dope."

"So what, then? You're really trying to sell me on this stupid Satan crap?"

The disrespect caused Asher to clench his fists, but he had to keep trying. He couldn't let his best friend fall victim to a life of mediocrity. The path Diego was on had been walked a billion times by a billion other men—marriage, fatherhood, an unfulfilling job, and then it was off to the old folks' home to rot away, staring at game show reruns and wondering what the point of it all had been. Asher could prevent all of this. He'd unlocked the ancient secret. He had found the light, but it came not from God but from The Morning Star—Lucifer.

"Listen to me, man," Asher said. "Would you just *listen* to me? Don't be so closed-minded. I've stepped into something here that's bigger than hitting the fucking lottery."

Hands on his hips, Diego stared off into the dusk.

Asher went on. "I'm not just talking about money here either. I'm talking about women being your sex slaves. I'm talking about no one being able to fuck with you ever again. I'm talking about absolute power."

Diego shook his head. "I didn't want to believe it was this bad. Your mom told me you were like this, but I didn't want to believe it."

"What?" Asher's shoulders tensed. "You talked to my mom?"

"She called me, hoping I could help. She said you've been spiraling. Now, I see that was an understatement."

Asher bared his teeth. "That nosey bitch. Where does she get off?"

"She *loves you!* And so do I, damn it. That's what makes this so hard for us. Don't you see that?"

"I'll tell you what I see. I see a way to give you and your family everything you could possibly want. You'd never have to worry about anything ever again. But you can't accept a life that's unconventional. Fernanda won't allow you to."

"Stop blaming everything on her. This isn't about my relationship with my fiancée. It's about my relationship with you. We've been friends a long time, man, but if you insist on living a life of delusions and drugs and *fucking devil worship*, then yeah, you can bet your ass I'm gonna side with Fernanda and do what's best for our baby." He stared at Asher, long and hard. "You need to get your shit together, bro, before it's too late. You only get one life."

Asher smirked. "Speak for yourself."

"Where is all of this coming from? You don't even sound like you anymore."

"It comes from the abyss, just like any knowledge worth knowing."

It seemed all Diego could do was shake his head. "I don't believe this shit …"

"Just because you don't believe in The Devil doesn't mean he'll go away."

"Yeah, well, I'm going away—back inside. I'm hoping we can still have a nice visit, but you need to cool it with all this talk. I can't force you to change your mind on things any more than you can force me to change mine, but if you're gonna be a guest in my home, you're gonna respect my family's wishes. I won't stand for you upsetting Fernanda in her condition."

Considering this, Asher took another hit off the joint. "I'm gonna finish smoking this. I'll join you guys in a minute."

"Okay … no more talking about drugs and devil worship, right?"

"You won't hear a peep."

Diego went back inside, leaving Asher to think in peace. The only other voice was Rex's, and he was saying things Asher already agreed with. At least someone else saw what Asher was seeing in Diego. The poor guy had gotten caught in the bear trap of marriage and children, a trap all women set for their man eventually. Starting a family spells the death of a man's freedom and privacy. It neuters him around all other women while also giving the one woman he's allowed to fuck the option of using sex as a bargaining chip or weapon against him. It destroys his financial independence and devours all his free time, forcing him to abandon personal dreams to make the dreams of others possible, for he is no longer allowed to make his own choices. This is all particularly true when that man is marrying a controlling prude like Fernanda. Asher had never felt so negatively toward her before, but now that he saw Fernanda dominating his best friend, it was clear she'd been a snake in the grass all this time, just waiting for the chance to strike Diego with the double-barrel shotgun blast of matrimony and a baby.

If only Diego had been more careful, he wouldn't have knocked this bitch up in the first place, and without the pregnancy, Diego probably wouldn't have proposed to Fernanda at all. Even if he didn't realize it, Diego had been imprisoned by this woman, and he needed a way out before it was too late. If he wasn't going to help himself, Asher would have to rescue his friend without his consent and let Diego thank him later once Fernanda's grip on him had loosened.

Though his measures would seem drastic to most people, Asher was no longer confined by societal norms. The laws of others didn't scare him anymore. In recent weeks, he'd learned the best way to get results was to go at something with unrelenting force and let the losers clean up the mess left in his wake.

By helping Diego, Asher would also be helping himself.

He drew his phone from his pocket and made the call.

✝

Fernanda had put a pot of coffee on, and Violet sat with the couple in their living room, sipping from a mug. She looked up at Asher with serious eyes, as if she could tell what he'd been planning. Her blind obedience would come in handy.

Asher accepted a cup of coffee from the hostess. Diego must have reasoned with Fernanda after he'd come back inside, because she was being hospitable to Asher despite the anger she'd shown him earlier. Asher did not apologize for anything, though, and he sensed that irked her even more. But he was true to his word and did not bring up Satanism or drug dealing again. The couple's big opportunity to benefit from Asher's wisdom had passed.

There was forty minutes of small talk before Asher's phone vibrated with the first text in the group chat. He waited for the other two text messages, and when they arrived, he messaged the group with his orders, then asked Fernanda for a refill. He'd been behaving, so she fetched the pot.

Asher stood when she finished pouring. "Have you felt the baby kick yet?"

"Yes," she said, offering a small smile. "It only became noticeable in the past few weeks, but now it seems like they kick me all the time."

"*They?* You're having twins?"

"No. We just don't know the gender yet. We decided to keep it a surprise until the baby's born."

Diego nodded. "The old-fashioned way."

"Hoping for any particular outcome?" Asher asked.

"No," Fernanda answered before Diego could speak for himself. "We'll love them just the same, no matter what sex they're born as or what gender they identify with once they're old enough to."

Asher had to force the cringe off his face. Fernanda's liberal views regarding her unborn child just further assured Asher he'd come to the right decision.

"May I feel?" Asher asked, pointing to her swollen belly.

Fernanda's shoulders inched higher, and she looked at Diego. He gave her a look like a shrug.

"Well ..." she told Asher. "The baby's just not moving around right now."

"Maybe it will once it senses Uncle Asher's hand on its home."

He noticed Violet's eyes narrowing as she tried to figure out what her master was really trying to do here. Knowing she was at the ready gave Asher a thrill. He'd felt that same rush, only larger, while ordering his acolytes to burn down the church, and he was eager to feel it again. His death cult awaited his command. Asher now knew he'd been born—or at least possessed—to lead them into the fire. Unfortunately, the same could not be said for Diego while Fernanda was around.

She was obviously uncomfortable with Asher asking to touch her belly, but most people would submit to anything to avoid conflict, choosing to just get something over with rather than make someone mad at them. It was one of humankind's most embarrassing weaknesses. Asher gladly used it to his advantage, slowly reaching out to Fernanda to place the palm of his left hand on her baby bump.

"Oh," she said, surprised by his brazen assurance. "Okay ..."

Fernanda stood there holding the coffee pot as Asher felt the warmth of the creature within her. It did not stir, but Asher could sense the energy of the fetus and its unparalleled innocence. It was enough to bring a tear to the hardest of eyes, but Asher's eyes were more than hard. They were baneful—untouched by the so-called miracle of life—and though he could not see them, he felt his eyes tinting red beyond bloodshot.

Fernanda must have sensed something too, because she tried to step back from Asher's touch. He followed her, his palm never leaving her belly, and just as she started to say something about it, Asher showed everyone what a warlock could do.

"Your baby is now diseased," Asher said.

His left hand burst into crimson flame. Fernanda shrieked as the fire singed her blouse, and Asher used his other hand to grab her by the back of the neck. She swung the coffee pot, hitting Asher in the side of the head with it, but he only gripped her harder, even as glass shards entered his head and hot coffee poured down his neck. Fernanda screamed as the flames engulfed her belly, devouring the blouse and making the skin of her abdomen peel.

Diego shot up from the couch. "No!"

Violet rose but only looked at Asher for instruction. As Diego came at him, Asher drew the revolver hidden under his shirt and pistol-whipped his friend in the forehead, knocking him down. His left hand remained on Fernanda's cooking belly, the flames simmering but still eating her, filling the apartment with the stench of burning flesh, reminding Asher of home. Fernanda buckled. Asher cradled her and dragged her to the couch.

"By the power of Satan, I have cursed the life within you," he told her. "Your baby will be born blind, deaf, and dumb. It will sweat blood and be covered in boils that never heal. You can't decide on a gender, so it will be born with both sets of genitals, neither of which will function. It will be a freak, a monster."

Fernanda sobbed, her eyes closed tight so not to look at him.

"Still want the baby?" Asher asked.

"*Yes!*" she screamed.

There was a commotion from the floor below. The old man was yelling at someone to stay back. The preteen girl was crying hysterically. It all tickled Asher's ears, but it was the footfalls coming from the stairwell that really excited him.

"Let her in," Asher told Violet.

She started toward the entryway, and Diego began to rise from the floor, blood dribbling down the bridge of his nose. Violet kicked him in the stomach to keep him down. Shock caused his eyes to bulge as he begged his friend to stop what he was doing, even though he didn't know what that was. He crawled toward his fiancée, trying to tell her everything would be all right. Fernanda only bawled. Watching the couple, Asher savored their pain and confusion—the perfect cocktail for horror.

Violet opened the door, allowing Ximena to step inside. She was carrying the kit Asher had texted her about fetching from his car and wore the black python around her neck like a tie. Having not met yet, Asher's women shared a curious glance, but Ximena's jaw fell slack when she spotted her cousin with a gash in his forehead and Fernanda writhing with burn wounds.

"What the hell's going on here?" she asked.

Diego turned to see her. "Ximena? Oh my God … Ximena! Help us!"

With the door open, the sounds of a violent struggle on the bottom floor could be better heard. A young boy cried out in pain as something shattered. A series of thuds shook the walls. Asher recognized Lenny's voice and Barney's laughter.

Ximena stared at her cousin. "Diego … what—"

Asher cut her off. "Cuff them."

She hesitated, her dark eyes searching Asher's for a morsel of mercy. "What is happening?"

Asher raised his left hand as it glowed crimson again, tiny flames forming on his fingernails like candle wicks. There were no whites to his eyes now. They'd gone entirely red as if all the blood vessels had popped. His pupils were pinpoints, and the crimson tint of his irises gleamed beneath his unibrow.

He sneered at Ximena. "Question me again, and you'll find your mouth filled with the black vomit of yellow fever. Now do as I say and cuff your cousin and his bitch."

Though she was slow doing so, Ximena opened what Asher called his "rape kit" and removed two pairs of handcuffs. She started whispering to Diego, but Asher barked at her to shut her fucking mouth, so she did, and cuffed Diego's hands behind his back. Fernanda was on her back, so Ximena cuffed her hands in front of her as the expecting mother whimpered for rescue that would not come. Squatting, Violet put her hand over Fernanda's mouth to silence her.

"Asher!" Diego said. "What the fuck are you doing, man? Please, can we talk about this? I'm sorry if I insulted you … *please*, I'm your best friend. Don't do this."

"What is it you think I'm going to do?" Asher asked.

Diego's face pinched. "I don't know. But please. Please don't hurt my family."

Asher shook his head. "This is for your own good, brother."

"*What?*"

"It's because you're my best friend that I'm doing this for you."

Ximena dared to step closer to Asher. "Whatever you're thinking of doing, please just—"

Asher didn't let her finish. Channeling the blackest magic from his core to his fingertips, he waved his left hand before Ximena's mouth, and black vomit began to pour out of it—not a projectile like normal vomit, but a slow waterfall of chunky, brackish puke. She fell to her hands and knees as she continued to regurgitate, a black pool of up-chuck spreading on the hardwood like an oil spill. Asher waved his hand again, and the vomiting stopped.

He got down on one knee beside her. "Which family does your loyalty belong to?"

Ximena spat out a wad of congealed bile. "I'm sorry, Asher, I—"

"You will address me as Master," he reminded her.

"Yes, Master. I am loyal to you. I just wasn't prepared for this."

"You are part of my new family, Ximena. Don't you realize how lucky that makes you?"

"I do."

"I can give you anything you could ever ask for. What does your blood relative offer you? Diego is a slave to Fernanda now, and she already told me how she scolded you simply for being who you are. But I encourage you to be you, Ximena. I'm the only one who accepts you, the only person who will ever love you for who you really are. I am your guide. All I ask is for you to follow me."

She nodded, sniffling. "All right. What do you want me to do?"

Asher knew he couldn't push Ximena too far too fast. She'd helped him burn down Our Lady of Mercy, but torching a church was not the same as what was happening here. Violet and Barney had proven their devotion through bloodshed. Now, it was Ximena's turn, and what better way to prove her loyalty than to involve her in this attack on her cousin's family. But forcing her would defeat the purpose. Ximena had to be coaxed. She had to be romanced. Most of all, she needed a reminder of all Asher offered her and how little she had without him.

"I only want you to do what must be done," Asher told Ximena. "Fernanda doesn't want you to be a part of Diego's new family. She'll never welcome you the way I have. She manipulated your foolish cousin—*tricked him*—into getting her pregnant, just so she could take over his life. Now, she's trying to push everyone in his life out of it. His cousin, his best friend—everyone. I've tried to reason with Diego, but this cunt's hold on him is like a fucking vise grip. We must free him from her, Ximena. You see that, don't you?"

She nodded, but Asher could tell she wasn't getting it yet.

"Did you bring it?" Asher asked.

She nodded again, then reached into her leather trench coat and produced the kris. The dagger's serpent-like blade reflected the glow of Asher's left hand as he ran one finger down it. The python around

Ximena's neck flicked its tongue, its eyes the same hellish color as Asher's as it constricted a little tighter around her neck.

"There are only two ways to rescue Diego from the ruins he's made of his life," Asher said. "Both involve the spilling of blood."

Diego started shouting, so Asher closed and opened his left hand, several gashes appearing on his palm as a pentagram was etched into the flesh by an unseen artist. The image did not stop at that. More intricate cuts were made until a goat's head emerged from the center of the star, forming the Sigil of Baphomet. The moment it was completed, Asher thrust his arm out, pressing his bloody palm to Diego's mouth.

Asher spoke in Satanic tongues, Rex chanting through him to guide Asher's sorcery. The veins on his extended arm stood out, pulsing and glowing the color of strawberries as his fingers extended and wrapped completely around Diego's head. Asher chanted louder, hearing the names of lesser demons on his tongue, and when he finally released Diego, the man's mouth was stitched shut with miniature black snakes that sealed his bloody lips tight. Realizing he could no longer speak, Diego's eyes began to water.

"Now," Asher said, returning his attention to Ximena. "I've silenced Diego, but it's on you to save him."

Ximena looked at the dagger she held. Then her dark eyes fell on Fernanda, who was still gagged by Violet's clutching hand.

Asher addressed both of his girlfriends. "See Fernanda's belly? I didn't just singe it to make her squeal. I issued a very special curse. Now, it's time to deliver."

Violet screamed as Fernanda bit into her palm. She drew her hand away and lost her balance, falling on the floor, and her dress and high heels kept her from getting up quickly. Hands still cuffed in front of her, Fernanda made a dash for the door.

Asher aimed the revolver and fired a single round, hitting her in the stomach.

Diego screamed behind his sealed mouth, but Fernanda didn't scream at all. She only grunted before dropping to her knees, clutching the bullet wound in her baby bump. Blood flowed steadily. Diego tried to get up, but his head wound made him dizzy, and Asher easily shoved him back to the floor.

"You see how much I love you?" Asher asked him. "I swear … the things I do for my fucking friends."

Holding her injured hand, Violet reeled back and kicked Fernanda in the face, dropping her all the way to the floor.

"Get Diego's feet," Asher told Ximena, testing her loyalty. "There's rope in the rape kit."

She tied Diego's feet together, and this time, she didn't try to whisper anything to her cousin. Her face was expressionless, as if her soul had fled, leaving her body on autopilot.

"Bring the bitch over here," Asher said. "Both of you."

Ximena and Violet each grabbed one of Fernanda's hands and dragged her to Asher.

"Put her in the vomit," he said.

They slid Fernanda into the puddle of Ximena's black puke. Asher gently touched Fernanda's face with his left hand, the sigil trickling his blood upon her face in a Satanic baptism. She was sobbing uncontrollably, and drops of Asher's blood fell into her mouth and covered the lenses of her glasses. The vomit beneath her began to bubble, the excitement of the demons watching from the underworld bringing an evil heat to the apartment.

Asher prodded Fernanda's bullet wound with his thumb, then sent his thumb into her. She bucked from the pain, screaming, making Asher's loins churn.

"Hey, Diego," he said. "Maybe I should get a sample of this pussy so I can figure out how it whipped you so easily. Maybe see what all the fuss is about, huh?"

Diego couldn't even muster up the will to shout at him from behind his sealed lips. The man had resulted to weeping on the floor, incapable of saving the family he held so dear.

"Or maybe," Asher said, "I should kill two birds with one stone, so to speak."

Following his orders, Violet raised Fernanda's hands above her head and sat on her arms so she couldn't flail. Then he had Ximena get between Fernanda's legs. Though she kicked, her stretch pants came down with ease, and Ximena slipped the blade of the kris between her pelvis and panties, cutting them free.

Asher leaned over so his face was an inch from Fernanda's, savoring the terror in her eyes as he scooped up her panties. "Yeah, you feel that, don't you? It's more than the pain of the bullet wound. You've felt the harshness of my sorcery since I first laid my hand upon your belly. That's because I have poisoned your womb." He smiled as Fernanda wept. "Maybe you don't feel the baby moving anymore, but that's okay. We're gonna move it for you."

Ximena was holding the dagger with both hands, pointing it downward as she hovered over Fernanda.

"You know what to do," Asher told Ximena. "If it offends thee, pluck it out."

She slowly raised the kris above her head and whispered. "Hail Satan."

Asher grinned, his yellowed teeth more jagged than before, but as they braced to perform a brutal cesarean section, Fernanda bucked her hips again. She arched her back, and something small and metallic emerged from her vagina. It wasn't until she'd passed it that Asher realized it was the bullet. Fernanda's body had expelled it from her uterus.

"You can lower that blade," Asher told Ximena. "I'm sensing we won't be needing it."

She did. "What do you want me to do?"

"Stay between her legs and prepare to deliver."

Ximena gulped but did not object. Violet was snickering, amused by the birthing of the bullet. She put it in her pocket as a gruesome souvenir. Asher was proud of both women in different ways—even excited for them—but it was Fernanda who stole his attention.

"Are you ready, sweetheart?" he asked.

Her sobs became a scream as she thrust out her pelvis. Laughing, Violet encouraged her to push, and Ximena told her to breathe, as if they knew what they were doing. The women served as cruel midwives, entertained by Fernanda's suffering. Asher could see the change coming over Ximena. His influence was too powerful for her to resist—not that she wanted to. She was finding the same thrill in sadism Violet had. Asher was always introducing them to greater pleasures, be they sexual or of a violent nature. So when the underdeveloped fetus began to ooze out of its mother, Ximena cupped the fragile membrane of its skull and tugged. It didn't matter much that it tore. Asher's curse had been stronger than he'd realized, assuring a coffin birth. Even if he hadn't shot her, the witchcraft had already robbed Fernanda of her child, for only by terminating the pregnancy would Asher ever free Diego from the nightmare of being a husband and father. It wasn't what his friend wanted, but it was the best thing for him.

But Asher couldn't deny his ulterior motives. The abortion would also serve him and the family well. He had plans for this dead fetus.

"Get a trash bag," he told Violet.

TWENTY-FIVE

HIS MINIONS HAD TURNED THE neighbor's apartment into a slaughterhouse.

Barney was covered in blood. Lenny's motorcycle jacket was spattered with it, but he wasn't dripping with the stuff the way Barney was. It must have been a frenzy of violence.

The old man was still in his wheelchair, but it had been tipped on its side, leaving him crumpled on the floor. Blood trickled from his ears and slack mouth, his dentures shattered beside his head. It was difficult for Asher to tell if he were still alive, but even if he was dead, he had fared better than his grandson.

The little boy only had the bottom half of his head. His body was on its stomach on the floor, his brain matter and skull fragments spread out in a fan. The wall was pocked with bloody holes where his head had been repeatedly bashed into the drywall. One hole was bigger and bloodier than the others—the kid's killer had found the stud. Over the holes, a message had been written in blood.

"Who did this one?" Asher asked.

Barney grinned with pride. "It was me, Master! I murdered the kid for you."

"You wrote that?" Asher asked, pointing to the blood graffiti.

Barney nodded, still all smiles.

Asher pursed his lips. "I'm guessing it's supposed to say 'Hail Satan.' But you wrote 'Hail Satin,' you moron."

The smile vanished from Barney's face. "Sorry, Master. I've never been so good at spelling."

At least he'd drawn the pentagram correctly. It was just below the misspelled text, the ring dripping blood. Asher had instructed his men to leave frightening messages for whoever found the bodies. He looked at the graffiti on the other walls, guessing Lenny had done them, given that they weren't written with the grammar skills of a second-grader.

Lenny was the person Asher had called when Diego left him outside alone. He'd given him directives before sending the group text to him, Ximena, and Barney.

"The neighbors must be taken care of," he'd told Lenny on the call. "That way, they won't be able to call the cops when they hear the commotion upstairs. But as long as we're executing them, let's use this opportunity to strike fear into the heart of this town. Hell, maybe even the whole country. So don't just kill—*overkill.*"

Lenny and Barney had followed those orders.

All glory to The Morning Star was scrawled in blood above the couch, with inverted crosses in place of the letter T. Additional messages in black marker were equally Satanic and ominous.

Our death cult offers these souls to Lucifer.

Reap the souls of the human sheep!

We rise from the blood pool of the virgin.

Asher remembered those last words from the record's chants. He'd liked the sound of *"the blood pool of the virgin"* when he'd first heard it. Now, he appreciated it even more.

"Where's the girl?" he asked.

Lenny pointed with his head to a closed door. "In the bathroom."

Stepping over the grandfather, Asher realized he was dead after all. A kitchen knife was lodged so deep in his belly that only half of the handle stuck out. His eyes were open and already appeared to be flattening, as all corpses' do.

When the men entered the bathroom, the girl in the tub scooted back as best she could. Duct tape pinned her arms to her sides and wrapped her feet and knees together. Her head was a mask of duct tape with no holes for her eyes or mouth. Only a small hole for her nostrils made it possible for her to breathe. Now that he saw her up close, Asher estimated she was about thirteen years old.

"We saved her for you," Lenny told Asher.

Lenny's experience made him stand out from the other members of the family. Having served under Rex, he could anticipate not just what Asher would want but what the evil spirit inside him would want too. Regarding this little girl, they both wanted the same thing. It was time to take evil to the next level. Lenny understood that.

"Good work," Asher told his minions.

"Thank you, Master," Barney said. "Do you think I've finally earned my reward?"

Asher didn't know what he was talking about. "Reward?"

"I know serving Satan is its own reward, but you'd said if I proved myself to you that you would let me have one of our female victims." He leered at the child in the tub. "With your permission, I'd like to pop that little cunt's pussy."

Asher slugged him in his fat gut. Barney keeled over with a groan, and Asher grabbed him by the hair and whipped his head back on his neck. "You dumb motherfucker! Don't you realize her potential?"

Barney struggled to get enough air to speak. "I just ... wanted ... to get laid."

"Imbecile. You're not to touch her. You put so much as a finger inside her and I'll take both your hands."

"Okay, okay! I'm sorry, Master. I didn't know you wanted her for yourself."

Asher smacked him on the back of his head. "You don't know a fucking thing! I'm not gonna rape her. *Nobody* is going to rape her. At her age, she's almost guaranteed to be a virgin. I won't let anything ruin that, and you shouldn't either. Understood? Now wrap her in some blankets and toss her in the trunk of your car."

Barney's eyes darted. "Um ... my car?"

"You have a problem with that?"

"No, Master. I just don't want to get caught with a kid in my—"

"What makes you think you'll get caught? I've cloaked you before, and I can do it again. Unless you're questioning my power ..."

"No, Master! Never. I'll wrap her up now."

The girl whimpered behind her silver mask as Barney went to

gather bedsheets.

"How'd it go upstairs?" Lenny asked Asher.

"Swimmingly. Well, not totally. My friend couldn't be converted. I still managed to free him from the prison of family life, but he fails to see it as a good thing. Sadly, I doubt he ever will."

"So what's to be done with him?"

"The only thing we can do. Like I told the girls, there was only two ways to save Diego, and both involved bloodshed. One way was to slaughter his wife and their unborn child in the hope this would liberate him. It was a long shot, but I'd hoped this would open his eyes. Now, I see we'll have to go the other route."

"Kill him?"

"It's the best thing we can do for him now—the only thing, really. It's like putting a sick dog out of its misery."

Though Asher believed he was doing what was best for Diego at this point, he also benefited from his death. Killing strangers in the name of Satan earned him favor with the demons, but murdering his best friend took greater gumption, proving Asher's devotion to The Lords of Hell. The massacre had offered several souls, including that of an unborn child, but Asher wasn't through yet. Visions of fresh horrors danced through his mind. Tonight, his evil rise to power would progress, his spirit ever-darkening, imbued with a sorcery only ritual human sacrifice could grant.

"Want me to go up there and kill him for you?" Lenny asked.

"No."

"Taking your best friend's soul yourself, huh? I'm impressed. Satan will be too."

"I don't need you to tell me what will make Satan happy. Besides, I won't be the one killing him."

Barney returned with the bed clothes, and Lenny helped him get the girl out of the tub. She wiggled like a beached fish, but they managed to cloak her in the sheets, then wrapped her in it with more duct tape.

"That's enough," Asher said. "Any more and she'll look like a silver mummy."

Barney laughed like the sycophant he was, then tossed the girl over his shoulder in a fireman's carry. Before he and Lenny walked out, Asher dispensed a black mist from his palm to camouflage them from any potential witnesses, then gave them the location where to meet him.

"Remember what I said," Asher warned. "I don't want her soiled, and I don't want her dead before I get there."

The men carried her out. Asher took another look at the apartment. In the master bedroom, the nightstand was overturned, and a dresser had been pilfered, probably by Barney looking for cash or jewelry to pawn. There was no graffiti here, so Asher went to the carcass of the little boy, scooped a fistful of brains into his left hand, and returned to the bedroom to decorate.

"Let them know who we are," he said to himself in Rex's voice. "And let them know what's coming."

Smearing the child's bloody gray matter on the wall, Asher painted the Sigil of Lucifer.

When he returned to the top floor, Violet was stretched out on the couch drinking a beer. Ximena sat across from her, smoking a cigarette with unsteady hands. Diego was sprawled on the floor, still confined and muted, his eyes glossed by horror.

In the pool of gore and vomit was Fernanda. Asher's black semen was still dripping from the gaping wound in her side. She was also still breathing, though she'd clearly gone into shock.

Asher looked to Violet. "Kill her."

She bit her bottom lip, looking like a benched ballplayer finally being asked to go to bat. Asher had called upon her, which was a blessing all its own, but she seemed to understand the greater meaning behind what he was ordering her to do. This slaying wouldn't be just for Asher. It was an offering to Lucifer himself.

Violet did not hesitate. She grabbed the first thing she saw that could serve as a weapon, snatching a porcelain lamp from the end table and knocking off the shade. She yanked it so the plug popped out of the wall and carried it to Fernanda, standing over her, playing God. Violet tried to frighten her, but Fernanda was beyond fear now. There was nothing behind her eyes but dazed misery. It was Violet's job to extinguish it.

She slammed the bottom of the lamp down on Fernanda's face, and her nose shattered, followed by her glasses, but she barely moved. Though her body was alive, Fernanda no longer was. Violet swung the lamp sideways and broke it against her victim's skull, then wrapped the cord around Fernanda's neck and began to strangle her. At first, Fernanda did nothing, but despite her being dead inside, her body reacted to the lack of air. She jerked on her way to the grave with Violet staring her in the eyes as she sent her there.

Asher took one last look at Diego. It was such a loss, such a god-damned shame. He almost regretted what had happened, but better for Diego to die quickly than suffer the slow death of neutered manhood.

Asher sighed. "Well, old pal, all things must come to end. I take solace in knowing I tried to guide you into Satan's arms. At least I saved you from a rotten wife."

He patted Diego on the shoulder, getting no response.

Then Asher turned to Ximena. "Your turn."

She nearly dropped her cigarette. "What?"

"It's time for you to kill your cousin."

Ximena stared at nothing as she rocked back and forth in her seat. Asher had anticipated hesitation despite everything she'd done so far. She'd hated Fernanda, making it easier for her to attack the woman. The coffin birth of the fetus had been beyond Ximena's control, making it a little easier for her to go along with it, and once she had, her sinister urges had taken over, inspiring her to yank and tear the unborn from Fernanda's vaginal canal. Ximena had potential. She was loyal to Asher, and he nurtured her destructive side. She'd come to him with the ability to kill already in her heart. All he had to do was give her a nudge.

"What better way for you to show your dedication and earn your place by my side?" Asher told her. "Kill your cousin—*your own blood*—in the name of Satan."

She opened her mouth as if to speak, then closed it just as quickly.

Asher sat beside her and took her hand. "Everything worth having requires sacrifice. Don't just do it for me, Ximena. Do it for yourself. The rewards will be beyond your wildest, wettest dreams. Now grab the dagger and end his life."

Ximena took a deep breath. Asher removed the cigarette from between her fingers, took the kris off the coffee table, and placed it in her lap. She inched toward the handle, and Asher almost worried she might try to attack him with it instead, but he dismissed the idea as ludicrous. She knew well enough to fear him and was too obsessed with him to break the spell that easily.

"Do it, sweetheart," he whispered in her ear. "And do it *now*."

Gripping the knife, Ximena rose from her seat and put her pet snake around her neck again. Violet sat beside Asher, eager to take her place by his side, as if to show up Ximena. They watched as she approached her cousin on the floor. Much like his fiancée, Diego no longer showed fear or pain, but the shock could only protect him so much. Ximena seemed to understand this. On her knees, she leaned over Diego and kissed his cheek, and this time when she whispered to him, Asher allowed it. As long as she murdered him, she could say whatever sweet bullshit she wanted. The act would render the sentiments worthless, like all thoughts and prayers.

As Ximena prepared herself for what she was about to do, Asher decided to heighten his enjoyment. He guided Violet's head toward his lap. She eagerly undid his fly and pulled out his semi-hard cock. It was still tacky with Fernanda's blood, but that only seemed to make Violet more eager to put it in her mouth. Ximena watched them with no expression, but when Asher winked at her, one side of her mouth curled up in a smile. Her eyes went wide and crazed, limbs shaking as she raised the dagger overhead, drops of Fernanda's blood still dripping from the blade and raining down on Diego's face.

"I offer this sacrifice!" Ximena screamed. "Hail Satan!"

Asher cheered. "Hail Satan!"

Violet hailed with her mouth full.

Shrieking like a banshee, Ximena drove the blade down through Diego's right eye. He spasmed and grunted but could do little else. Ximena went into a frenzy, stabbing her cousin in the face again and again, pockmarking his cheeks and cutting off the tip of his nose. She didn't go for a quick, merciful kill but instead focused her attack on his head, mutilating his face as if to strip him of his identity. Perhaps not being able to recognize him made it easier for her to do what had to be done. Asher didn't care either way. Ximena was putting on a bloody good show, driving the dagger into Diego's ear canal and bouncing the blade off his skull. She kept on stabbing, kept on screaming, lost to the thrill of the kill and the promise of Satan's power.

With every thrust of the blade, Asher thrust his cock deeper into Violet's throat. He grabbed her head in both hands and pumped in and out of her mouth, his red eyes never leaving Ximena as she butchered Diego's face with monastic focus. She destroyed his other eye. The blade hit his mouth, and the tiny snakes that had stitched it shut wormed away from his lips to slither through the blood on the floor. Diego's throat made small clicking sounds as he struggled for his last breaths, but he did not plead for his life or curse his cousin's name. He simply accepted his fate, and in a way, Asher took this as Diego's parting gift, as if he were offering his life to his cousin now that it had so little value to him yet so much value to her. This was the sin that would get her into Lucifer's good graces. Perhaps, in some strange way, Diego sensed that. Perhaps he even forgave her in his final moments.

When Ximena's arms finally gave out, Diego's face was gone. All that remained was a mound of pulped meat. Some of his cheek bones was showing, and he'd lost his bottom lip, leaving him with a horrible rictus grin. Ximena must have stabbed him at least fifty times. He'd either bled to death or she'd hit brain.

She looked up at Asher, and he curled his finger in a *come-hither* gesture. Arms slick with blood, Ximena crawled across the floor, through her own black vomit and Fernanda's afterbirth. The python around her neck was spattered with Diego's blood. Its scales seemed to be *absorbing* it. Ximena stayed on her hands and knees even when she reached Asher, nuzzling her face into his crotch so she and Violet could worship him at the same time. Their tongues glided over his shaft and balls, the women taking turns fellating him and licking the blood from Ximena's hands. When he was close, Asher stood, positioned his girlfriends' heads together, and coated their faces with his black seed.

TWENTY-SIX

ASHER BELIEVED HE KNEW WHY the demon had taken Deanna and Paul's bodies to Hell but left his cult's other victims where they'd died. The clearing in the woods was some sort of gateway, because a sacrifice made outside, in nature, was simply more effective. On this Earth, demons lurked in the shadows of the wild, whispering to the vulnerable to manipulate their souls. Every black forest had a big, bad wolf. The most primitive of devil worshippers understood this, and witchcraft had remained intricately linked to nature throughout the ages. While Asher's creativity was celebrated by the demons of the abyss, traditions held value and offered rewards that could not be gained through other means.

His men were waiting in the clearing when they arrived. Barney had changed into the spare set of clothes Asher had told him to keep in his car, and Lenny had wiped the blood off his motorcycle jacket. It was a logical precaution to take when escorting a child hostage wrapped in duct tape through town, but they were only going to get bloody again. That's why Asher hadn't bothered to put on different clothes. He and the girls had washed up a little before leaving Diego's apartment, but they hadn't changed out of their filthy attire, which were crusted with blood, vomit, afterbirth, and Asher's tar-like semen. He liked seeing his ladies soused in the fluids of a murder orgy.

Setting down the boombox and trash bag he'd been carrying, Asher approached the human-shaped lump of blankets at Lenny's feet. He punted it in the side with his steel-toed boot, hearing the girl groan.

"Still alive," Asher said. "Good."

Lenny spoke low so only Asher could hear. "I don't mean to question you, but I just want you to know I've done this sort of thing before, so I know the steps and the words, just in case you're unsure."

Asher crossed his arms. "Oh, is that right?"

"No disrespect. I'm just saying I don't know just how much Rex influences you or what he's taught you so far. I only want to help you do this right. This is the next big step, and it's a doozy."

"I just orchestrated the murder of my oldest friend and his pregnant fiancée. Tore the fetus right out of her." He pointed to the trash bag. "Take a look if you don't believe me."

"Of course I believe you. You're Rex's descendant and host—the *chosen one*. I'm not saying this'll be difficult because it involves a child. Clearly, you're beyond being affected by that. By now, I think we all are. What makes this sort of ritual tricky is it really grabs the big guy's attention, so you want to make sure you do it right. Lucifer can be very particular."

"You say that like you know him. Have you met The Prince of Darkness?"

Lenny shrugged. "Well, not exactly, but Rex had, many times, and he relayed the messages. Satan demands absolute loyalty, and he tests that loyalty with particulars. It's kind of like how David Lee Roth put in all Van Halen's rider contracts that there should be a bowl of M&Ms in his hotel room with all the brown ones taken out. He wasn't being a prima donna. It was to be sure the hosts of the concert respected him and were professional enough to actually read the contract. If he walked into his room and saw brown M&Ms—or, worse yet, no M&Ms at all—then the band would know they were dealing with incompetent shysters, and they could bail out or at least confront the hosts before the show."

Asher considered this. "All right. So then we pay close attention to detail. You and I will handle the important stuff. Rex hasn't steered me wrong yet, and I know he wants this as much as I do. So I'll instruct the girls to make sure everything is done correctly. You can instruct Barney if you need him to lift anything heavy or something, but it's best to keep that shit-for-brains away from the action on this one."

"Amen to that—no pun intended. This is a big moment for you, for all of us. Hail Satan."

"Hail Satan."

Lenny was proving useful, but that didn't mean Asher trusted him. Not yet. He wasn't sure he would trust any human ever again, unless he'd taken dominion over them as he'd done with the girls. He only wanted to rule humans, to make everyone too scared of him to even consider betrayal. Lenny had been Rex's second in command (or so he said), but Asher wasn't ready to designate him as such, even though he had a huge edge over Barney. When it came to the family hierarchy, Asher's highest hopes were for Ximena. Violet was intensely obedient and eager to kill, but she lacked initiative and maturity. Ximena had the darker aura, and that she committed heinous acts by her own volition impressed Asher. He had only told her to kill Diego. It was her decision to turn his face into hamburger. He'd seen the capacity for evil in her from the start—the love of serpents and all things dark and spooky. Even before they'd met, Ximena's soul had been a twisted, broken thing. This made her the more worthy candidate to be his Satanic queen.

Asher turned on the boombox, filling the night with the roaring metal of *Music to Sacrifice Virgins To*. A more fitting soundtrack had never been paired. A bass drum thudded, guitars screeching, a chorus of demons singing in dead languages. When Rex's voice came to the foreground of the recording, Asher chanted along with him, the words coming to him though he'd not heard them before. He was tapping into Rex's memories, which had been implanted in his brain. It was getting easier to resurface them.

"I call to thee, King of All Evil," Asher chanted in unison with his uncle. "I come to praise your Satanic majesty with the blood of the innocent on my hands. I call upon thee, our father, The Devil, and all the fantastic pleasures of the dark."

The nip in the air caved to a sudden moistness. Though there was no breeze, the branches of the dead trees swayed and clacked against each other. A foul smell emanated from the thicket.

Asher had his family form a circle around the little girl on the ground. Having prior knowledge, Lenny drew a knife and carved a pentagram in the dirt with the hostage at the center. Each of the star's five points aimed directly at one of the cult members, with Asher at the bottom of the circle. Lenny cut open the bedsheets and rolled the girl out, then started cutting away the duct tape on her head, nicking her face and drawing a little blood. He left her arms and legs bound and her mouth sealed. The girl's eyes were alive with panic.

Asher and his uncle continued the invocation. "We gather here to offer you this virgin, Lord Lucifer, to feed her soul to you so it may satiate your hunger and thirst. May she forever burn in your cauldron. May she suffer beyond eternity. May the offering of her pure and chaste soul be the key that unlocks my greatest power."

The ground grew muddy as blood rose through the soil. It percolated, spreading crimson mist around the bound victim. Dozens of holes appeared in the earth. Asher expected the jaundiced claws of demons to return and snatch the girl the way they had Deanna's and Paul's bodies. Instead, the heads of large, black rodents popped out of the burrowed pits. The rats clawed their way to the surface, their buck teeth gnashing, their eyes the color of cherries as they scampered around the sacrificial girl. When they touch her, she recoiled, screaming behind her gag.

"Lord Lucifer," Asher said. "Give to me the power I have earned, so that I may do your unholy bidding and serve you in this world and the next. Hail Satan!"

The others hailed as one, raising their fists in the horns salute. Looking to each of them, Asher saw their eyes were wide with a combination of sadistic desire and spooked anticipation. Ximena was sucking her bottom lip, her snake from Hell coiled around one arm. Barney was bouncing from foot to foot. Violet was fidgeting with her dress. Lenny was the only stoic one, but even he refused to blink, not wanting to miss a single second.

Asher stepped through the school of rats to stand over the child. Though he could only see part of her face, he'd never seen anyone so afraid. It aroused part of him but soothed him as well, offering a certainty he'd not had until this point. This would be his most successful ritual yet, a virgin sacrifice just like the album had been calling for. Staring down at the little girl, Asher began to sweat, the heat of demonic sorcery spreading through his chest to funnel to his extremities. His fingers elongated and his toes tingled, his penis stirring in his jeans like a copperhead roused from its den. Extending his arms into a T with his palms down, the Baphomet sigil in his left hand glowed red, summoning hellfire that shot out of the earth with the force of busted hydrants, forming pillars of flame. They rose to meet his hands in small fire tornados, and the rats scurried away from the searing heat, climbing onto the girl as she squealed.

Turning his palms to face each other, a jet of crimson flames bounced between Asher's hands. He played with it like raw pizza dough, flipping and turning the ethereal magic. His long fingers danced as his hands turned burgundy. Dark claws split his nails as they emerged from his fingertips. The inverted cross around his neck shined a holographic crimson, a beckon to The Evil Trinity, a tribute to Lucifer's grandness.

Asher got down on one knee beside the terrified girl. A few rats trotted through the blood and onto his boots, and one climbed up his back to perch on his shoulder like a parrot. It hissed Satanic chants. Asher hovered his arms over the girl, palms facing her, and made a round motion like he was caressing a globe. Hellfire burst from his hands and made a ring of flames around the human sacrifice, which then rose over her to form a dome. The girl was not burning, but she was trapped beneath the half sphere of fire, and over a dozen rats were trapped in there with her. As the heat intensified, the rodents scurried about, searching for a way to escape, but the walls of fire contained them. When they tried to dig back into the ground, Asher used his powers to fill the holes with boiling blood, making them retreat to the surface. He started closing the dome around the girl. Her skin grew pink and began to peel.

As the half sphere of flames constricted, the rats panicked. They climbed on top of the girl to escape the walls of fire inching ever closer. With the heat intolerable, they tried to make a desperate escape by burrowing into the only surface left. Their claws tore into the girl's body, ripping at the soft belly. The rodents worked as a team, gnawing at the child with their buck teeth and digging into her stomach. She writhed in agony, her eyes gone huge with horror. A rat disappeared into her insides. The others flung bits of her flesh like dogs kicking up dirt. Another rat shoved its way into her, squeezing past a spongy tube of intestine, forcing it out of the girl's body. The remaining rats became a stampede as they tunneled into the guts. Blood trickled from the girl's nostrils. Her eyes rolled back. Fire singed her hair off and ate away her skin. The rats escaped out of her back to burrow into the earth beneath her, down toward the abyss they'd emerged from.

Asher breathed in the stench of burning child. It was more intoxicating than any drug. His sacrifice was now a crispy, blackened skeleton soaking in the bubbling blood of Hell. With a wave of his hand, the hellfire shrank to tiny candle wicks that extinguished themselves, but the pentagram in the dirt continued to glow like magma. His acolytes remained at each point of the star, some of them stunned pale, others beaming in triumph. Violet even clapped her hands and gave Asher a proud-of-you smile.

Lenny was the first to speak. "All glory to the warlock Asher Benton! Hail our exalted leader! *Hail the new son of Satan!*"

He threw up the horns salute, and the others complied.

"Hail!" they chanted, following Lenny's lead. "Hail! Hail! Hail!"

Soaking in their adulation, Asher felt a surge of sorcery go through him like an electrical current. It brought him the sweetest pain, and he smiled through clenched teeth. Killing the girl had served its purpose. He was getting stronger. Stepping to her skeletal remains, he gave her another kick with his steel-toed boot, and her bones crumbled like clumps of dirt. He put his foot on her skull and pressed. It burst into ash.

"Spread her," he told the group.

They closed in on the corpse and kicked at her remains until there was nothing left but dust. As they spread out her ashes, Asher retrieved the trash bag.

Reaching in for the slimy mass, he held it up in one hand. The dead fetus didn't even look real. It more resembled a doll made of plasma and brittle bones. The spell he'd cast on it had started to work but must have tapered off upon the baby's death. It was born with strange lumps and had both sets of genitals. The limbs were easy enough to snap off. Asher handed one to each member of his death cult, keeping the head and torso for himself.

Asher addressed his followers. "Tonight, we feast with the beasts."

Then he bit into the tiny skull.

Lenny immediately started on the leg like it had belonged to a chicken instead of an unborn child. As Asher sucked out the brain, he glared at Ximena holding the little arm until she took a hesitant bite out of it. Violet, for all her servitude, also seemed reluctant to engage in cannibalism, but one look from Asher and she put the fetus's hand into her mouth and started peeling the meat from the fingers like she was skinning carrots. Barney was the last to partake, which surprised Asher. The goon had destroyed a little boy's skull while he was still alive yet seemed to have reservations about ingesting human flesh. But he was too weak to go against the mob. Needing to fit in, he took a bite of the leg and nearly gagged forcing it down.

From the boombox, the guitar riffs dropped to a steady drone underlined by the whispered cackles of demons. Mothers cried out for their babies, and babies cried out for their mothers. Animals growled and mewled. Murder sounds were amplified—blades going into flesh, bones breaking, guns going off. Death rattles made a ghoulish percussion.

Asher dug his talon-like thumbnails into the chest of the fetus and cracked open the ribcage. Ripping out the heart, he swallowed it whole.

TWENTY-SEVEN

LENNY HAD PICKED UP XIMENA and Barney, but Asher sent the men away and took both women with him in his Dodge. He was tempted to make his girlfriends fight for the front seat but decided they'd handled enough violence tonight. It might be amusing to see them battle for his affection, but there were other ways to do that. Violet rode shotgun and Ximena sat in the back seat, using Violet's wet towelettes to clean themselves up. The trio barely spoke as he drove them out of the woods. Asher put on Slayer's *Show No Mercy* to kill the silence.

He thought about his decision to have his cult members devour the fetus. It had seemed like the natural progression, but now he wondered how he'd come to such a gruesome conclusion. In the moment, he'd reflected on his mother making eggs and how he'd teased her about eating the unborn. Was it Rex who hungered for human flesh, or had this been the guidance of other demons, like the one who often whispered to him from the dark? The one thing he was certain of was that feasting on the fetus had granted power not just to him but to his loyal acolytes. Though they did not know it—and wouldn't know how to handle it if they did—Asher had blessed them with the infernal light of Hell. Of course, he did this for his own benefit. By imbuing the others with the darkest magic, he could better protect them from potential enemies like police officers and the vengeful family members of their victims. Preserving his minions was vital to his mission. He didn't think he would always need them, but they served him well right now.

Asher was pleased with the way the ritual sacrifice had unfolded. He'd given the proper instructions, and Lenny had not corrected him in front of the others. Though Lucifer had not appeared, Asher was confident he'd been watching and listening, even admiring the work of such a dedicated warlock. Lenny had been right to lead the others in cheering for Asher. He was not just their leader but a Satanic savior. Everything was going so well. Lucifer be praised!

"You both impressed me tonight," he told his women. "You're good girls."

Violet smiled, wiggling in her seat, so young and beautiful. Asher looked at Ximena in the rearview mirror, and when their eyes met, she gave him a seductive leer.

It's incredible how many women have a praise kink, Asher thought. *You can do whatever you want to them as long as you follow it with a "good girl."*

"Our family has so much potential," Asher told them. "You can feel it too, can't you?" The girls nodded. "It makes me think about The Manson Family. Only nine murders could be attributed to them, though they may have killed as many as twenty-four. We've already killed ten."

"Ten?" Ximena asked. "We killed five people tonight. Six if you count the baby. Who're the others?"

He saw no reason to hide it. "Two were phony Satanists—your typical headbanging goth types. The others were Terry and his daughter."

"Wait … *you* killed Terry?"

"Violet and I did. It was a great time."

Violet confirmed as she packed a pipe full of marijuana.

Ximena leaned forward so her head was between the front seats. "Why didn't you tell me before?"

"You weren't ready to hear it," Asher told her. "You didn't need to know until you were a member of the family. I had to seduce you first. I had to fuck you hard and make you murder people, including your own cousin. Only then would I know for sure that you'd want to be mine at any cost."

"I guess you're right." Ximena stared into space. "Asher, am I going to die?"

"Eventually, yes."

"That's not what I mean …"

"Why would you be worried about that? I just said you've been a good girl. I'm proud of you. Violet too."

Ximena hesitated to say what she said next. "When you made me throw up that black stuff, you said it was the vomit of yellow fever. Do I have yellow fever now?"

"No. I rid your body of it once you'd barfed. I didn't want to hurt you, sweetheart, but you needed to be taught a lesson about obedience. Understand?"

"Yes."

"Yes what?"

"Yes, Master."

Taking a toke, Violet passed the pipe to Asher. The smoke was smooth as it traveled through his lungs.

"Like I was saying," Asher said, "we've already taken more lives than The Mason Family was confirmed to. We should all be proud of that. The Beasts of Satan—an Italian Satanic cult—only had four confirmed kills. Even the most notorious Satanic killer, Richard Ramirez, only had fourteen confirmed, though he claimed more than twenty. Our death cult is not so much following in the footsteps of notorious murderers—we're superseding them. We're on target to be the new champions of Satanic serial killers."

"That's fucking awesome," Violet said.

"Damn right it is. These days, most violent cults are rooted in Islam, but some Christian ones are out there too. Satanic cults are mostly myths—paranoid fantasies inspired by hoaxes like *Michelle Remembers* and the McMartin preschool trial. Far-right delusions of rich pedophiles running sex cults out of pizza places. Even the Toledo nun murder was arranged to look like Satanists had done it, but actually, it was a Catholic priest who killed the nun because she was threatening to expose his evil deeds. The truly dangerous cults always involve a messiah who claims to have a direct line to God—Jim Jones, David Koresh, that goony-looking dipshit from Heaven's Gate." He laughed. "Perhaps the most dangerous is The Pope! He's protected more evil people than any man on Earth."

"There's one problem with all those cults and serial killers," Ximena said. "They all got caught."

"Well, yes. They fucked up. But just imagine all the killers out there who never got caught. Not just the Zodiac Killer types we all know about but serial murderers nobody knew about at all. What gets me is how some killers will confess everything to the police once they're apprehended. I have a theory about why they do it. It's not remorse or guilt. It's that the murders have been the most exciting thing in their lives, but they've been unable to talk about them with anyone for fear of being turned in. So once the cops nab them, they spill all the beans because they're just so damn happy to be able to share their greatest accomplishments with someone else, even if it's a pig. But us being a family of killers, we get to celebrate our accomplishments together."

Violet cuddled into Asher. "You're so smart. I love listening to you."

"Do you think Manson or Ramirez had Satanic powers?" Ximena asked.

"It's possible," Asher said. "But if so, they didn't use them to their full potential. I won't make that mistake."

"So there will be more murders?"

"Of course. Not just to appease the demons but for our own pleasure. Have you ever tried not to scratch an itch? Have you ever wanted to buy something so badly it was all you could think about until you bought it? That's how killing people is for me."

"But why?"

"Because *I'm evil.*" He glared at her in the mirror. "And *so are you.*"

Ximena didn't have a comeback to that. Asher was beginning to wonder if she doubted him or was just overly curious. He supposed not everyone could be as easily led as Violet and Barney. That she had a stronger will was one of the things that made him favor Ximena, but he would have to watch her for signs of dissention.

Asher pulled over and put the car in park on the shoulder of the road. He turned in his seat to face Ximena.

"I have a question for you," he said. "What did you say to Diego just before you killed him?"

Ximena hung her head. "I told him I was sorry. That I could not help myself."

"Did you ask him to forgive you?"

She shook her head. "How can I ask someone for forgiveness when I cannot forgive myself?"

"You're too hard on yourself, Ximena. You had urges, and you acted upon them."

"That's just it," she said, looking into his eyes. "I can't control myself when I'm around you. I can't resist you."

He stroked her cheek, tucking a lose strand of hair behind her ear. She looked so small now, so helpless.

"You don't really want to resist me," he told her. "None of you do. Society has indoctrinated you into this delusion of civility. People condemn violence even though it's one of humankind's oldest and purest urges. The only thrill greater than the hunt is the kill itself. Now you know that firsthand."

"But why did it have to be Diego? He was the only family I've ever really had."

"That's exactly why it had to be him. I would've loved for him to join our cult, but he refused to acknowledge the glory of Satan. He thought it was all some immature make-believe. So we did what we had to do to set him free. More importantly, killing your only family was a way for you to show your dedication to your *new* family, to me, and to Satan." He pointed at both women. "Each of you came to me—at least in part—because your families were dysfunctional or nonexistent. I replaced them for you. You both already had an interest in the occult. I just brought you deeper into it. Before me, all you had was bullshit tarot cards and cheap, do-nothing crystals. I showed you *true sorcery*. Neither of you had a man—a *real* man. I gave you the attention you deserve. Are you not grateful?"

Violent replied without hesitation. "I'm super grateful." She looked at Ximena. "I mean, isn't it wonderful how he's taken all the uncertainty out of our lives? We don't have to agonize over our decisions anymore because the master makes them for us. He's taken charge, and I, for one, love it."

Ximena nodded. "Yes, Master. I am grateful to you. And I really am excited for us. It's just been a lot to take in, especially tonight. Things escalated so quickly."

Clearly, she needed a little tenderness. It was important for Asher to remember his incubus power and use it to keep the reins on his female stable. He leaned in and kissed Ximena sweetly, then ran his hands up the sides of her skull, his black nails gently scratching her. She returned his kiss with greater passion, moaning as their tongues entwined. When they parted, Asher leaned into Violet and kissed her too. She nibbled his bottom lip with carnivorous lust. When they finished, he put his hands on the backs of each of their heads, drawing them closer together.

"Now each other," he said.

Ximena leaned into Violet, which told Asher she'd been sexual with other girls before. Violet showed some reluctance but caved to her master's desires and allowed Ximena to slide her tongue into her mouth.

"A many splendored thing," Asher said with a smile.

Ximena took Violet's wrists and urged her into the back seat. Asher hit the road again, occasionally glancing in the rearview mirror to watch his girlfriends make out. He smoked and belched, tasting dead fetus in the back of his throat. He sang along to Slayer's "The Antichrist." It'd been a wonderful night, and it was not over yet.

When they arrived on Asher's street, his driveway was empty. Mom had not come home yet. The clock on the dashboard read 2:17 a.m.

Fucking whore, he thought. *Fucking fake-tit, bleached, and painted whore. Fuck you.*

He supposed it was good she hadn't come home to see the horror he'd made of her bedroom. She might have called the police, and Asher did not want to deal with that, though he was confident the black magic would protect him. He had an idea of how he was going to handle Mom seeing her bedroom covered in gore and feces, but he was glad to not have to address it just yet. He wanted to celebrate the night's smashing success.

Asher pulled the Dodge into the Vincent family's driveway.

"See you tomorrow?" Violet asked.

"Oh, I'm not dropping you off. We're all going in."

She gave him a confused look. "But ... my mom is ..."

"I told you not to worry about her."

"Well ... I guess I could sneak you guys in through my bedroom window."

"Fuck all that. We're going through the front door. I want to see your mother—and your little sister too."

Violet paled as Asher grabbed the rape kit from the back seat. They got out of the car, and Asher let Violet lead the way. She walked slowly, as if trying to delay the inevitable, then stopped at the front porch with tears in her eyes.

"Master ... please ... I can't ..."

"What is it?" he asked.

"You all are my new family—honest. But I can't kill my mom and Callie. Please don't make me. Please don't do this."

Asher put his hand on her shoulder. She was shaking.

"If I want them to die, then they'll die," he told her. "But relax. That's not what we're here for."

Violet sniffed. "You promise?"

"If I said it, it's true."

She eyed the rape kit in his hand.

"I don't wish your family dead," he assured her. "It's not necessary. At least not right now. I have other plans for them. This kit has many uses."

"Okay," she said, crossing her arms. "I doubt they'll want to join our cult, though, if that's what you're thinking. Mom's always been a Christian, even if we stopped going to church."

Remembering all he'd made Violet's mother do, Asher couldn't help but scoff. "You just let me worry about Mommy's beliefs. She just might surprise you. I know she has me."

"What do you mean?"

"Enough questions, sweetheart. Open the goddamn door."

With a deep breath, Violet unlocked the door as quietly as she could. As the three of them stepped in, Asher noticed the sour look on Ximena's face. Was she angry she'd been forced to kill her family when Violet didn't have to kill hers? If she was irritated by a lack of fairness, she would just have to get used to it. Asher knew what was best even when his minions didn't understand his decisions.

They headed upstairs. Violet started toward the master bedroom, but Asher stopped outside a different door. Though it was closed, he knew what awaited behind it. He could feel the warmth of the teen girl's body and smell her tiny cunt. Licking his lips, he turned the knob and poked his head inside.

Callie was on her bed on top of the covers, dead asleep. She wore only an oversized t-shirt and striped panties. Her long, skinny legs were pale beneath the moonlight coming through the part in the curtains. The urge to jump on her was incredibly strong. How easy it would be for Asher to jostle her awake by tearing those panties off. How easy it would be to cuff her to the bedposts spreadeagle and rob her of her virginity, her dignity, her humanity.

But that went against his plans. Asher had to control himself, even as the demonic urges grew more vicious. So when Callie stirred, he whispered a single-word spell.

"Sleep."

He closed the door, assured Callie wouldn't wake until sunrise.

"Okay," he told his girlfriends. "Let's go see Mommy."

Violet opened the door to her parents' bedroom. The room was dark, the only illumination coming from a night-light in the adjacent master bathroom. Melissa was sleeping on her side with her knees pulled up, reminding Asher of the fetus his cabal had devoured. He'd expected her to sleep in unflattering pajamas, but instead, she was in a lacy, black slip. She was continuing to take his fashion advice. He'd told her to stay home and await further instruction. Melissa had obeyed and went as far as to prepare herself for Asher should he choose to return. She'd even gone to bed wearing makeup. Melissa had been waiting for him like the smitten victim of a vampire, and just like a vampire, Asher planned to drain her—not of blood, but of her heart and soul and will to live.

Throwing off his coat, Asher started to undress. He nodded to Violet and Ximena, and they disrobed. Once naked, Asher crawled into bed with Melissa. She stirred but did not awaken. The girls stood on either side of the bed awaiting their master's orders. Ximena was expressionless. Violet looked nervous, which was understandable. Though he wasn't going to make her kill her mother, Asher had a greater sense of fairness than Ximena might think. She had proven her loyalty through total obedience, doing something she'd not wanted to because Asher demanded it. Now, it was Violet and her mother's turn to do the same.

Spooning Melissa, Asher pressed his erection against the cleft of her buttocks. He scooped a breast into his left hand. Melissa moaned. She startled awake, and Asher shushed her.

"Master?" she whispered.

Even in the darkness, Asher could see the confusion on Violet's face. She'd had no idea what had been going on between her boyfriend and her mother. Now, she was a part of it, even if she didn't fully realize that yet.

"I've come back for you," Asher told Melissa.

"Oh, I've missed you so much, Master." She kissed him repeatedly as she spoke. "Please don't stay away from me so long again. I want to be with you always."

Asher slid his hand between Melissa's thighs. She was instantly wet. She tilted her head back as he kissed her, and when she opened her eyes, Melissa gasped seeing her nude daughter standing at the edge of the bed, watching.

"Oh my God," Melissa said, sitting up. "Violet, I … it's not what it …"

"Stop," Asher told her. He put his arm around Melissa's waist and pulled her into him again. "Your daughter doesn't mind. Isn't that right, Violet?"

Violet spoke in a hush. "Yes, Master."

Melissa noticed the naked stranger at the other side of the bed. "Who're you? What's going on here?"

Asher snapped his fingers at Ximena. "The kit. Bring it to me."

She handed it to him, and he ordered Ximena and Violet to get into the bed. As he opened the kit to prepare the tools, Asher admired the sexy trio.

"Who am I?" he asked.

"You're our master," Ximena said.

"You are our master," Violet agreed.

Seeing her daughter under Asher's spell brought tears to Melissa's eyes, but even her grief over Violet succumbing to the man Melissa knew was a demon did not lessen his hold on her.

"You're our master," Melissa admitted.

"Fuckin' A right," he told his harem. "You exist to please me. My desire is your desire. My pleasure is your greatest pleasure."

His women spoke in unison. "Yes, Master."

"Now, Violet," he said, "why don't you give your mother a kiss?"

Violet didn't bother trying to get away with a simple peck on the cheek. She knew what Asher wanted, and so did Melissa.

As the mother and daughter engaged in the taboo, Asher had Ximena fellate him.

"See how deep she sucks that dick?" he said to Violet and Melissa. "You're both going to learn to do that too."

Laying out his tools on the mattress, Asher cuffed Melissa's hands behind her back. She did not resist him. Instead, she moaned with pleasure, the spell of the incubus too strong for her to think of anything but the dirtiest sex. Asher had Violet put the ball gag on her mother, then handed her the vibrating dildo to use on the same cunt she'd been born from. Melissa's fresh stitches ripped open. She winced from the sharp pain but didn't seem concerned about making her injury worse.

The orgy went on for forty minutes before Asher drew his pocketknife and started cutting up his sex slaves. He didn't hurt them badly, only opened their flesh to get blood flowing. The deepest wound was the one he gave to himself. Digging the tip of the blade into the crook of his arm above the Leviathan Cross, he opened a vein and squeezed, raining blood onto the faces of the women. They lapped it up like dogs. Pouring out, his blood grew blacker. The foursome writhed in a perverted tryst. Asher stacked the women on top of each other face down and took turns fucking them, going from one pussy down to the next, then working his way up again. He forced them into incestuous, lesbian acts and had Ximena coach the Vincent women on how to control their gag reflex as he shoved his enlarged cock down their throats. He sodomized them without asking for consent. He smacked them and twisted their limbs. The women groaned in the good kind of pain and shuddered with orgasms, but the noise didn't wake Callie in the other room. Asher's sleep spell had put the girl in a coma-like state. It was a shame she had to miss this.

A gravelly voice called to Asher, seeming to come from every corner of the room at once. It was the voice of the shadow demon, the one he heard at pivotal moments in his progression to Satanic glory, a voice only Asher could hear.

"The thief comes only to steal and kill and destroy. The warlock comes so others may have life and have it to the fullest."

Asher understood what the demon meant by the altered bible quote. Hedonism was as much a part of Satanism as sacrificial murder. Leading others into temptation was the signature work of The Devil. Asher had corrupted these women. He'd used their desires to manipulate them and capitalized on their empty hearts, lack of purpose, and the want to be wanted. He'd turned a lonely housewife into a whore who had sex with her daughter's boyfriend. He'd made a teenage girl into a serial killer. He'd coaxed a lost soul into murdering her beloved cousin. But in many ways, he had freed these women. They were no longer confined to the lives that had been thrust upon them, no longer restrained by polite society's moral principles. Though they were in his possession, they'd never been so liberated.

The warlock comes so others may have life and have it to the fullest.

The mattress began to tear from the inside out. From the puddles of blood came wiggling, yellow fingers over a foot long. The black talons cut through the fabric like the glide of scissors through wrapping paper, and the arms of several demons shot out. They'd been beckoned by the blood orgy, and as their deformed limbs broke out of Hell, their hands caressed the exposed humans. Eyes closed, Asher's women moaned as they were groped by leprous digits. The bulbous head of a ghoul without eyes emerged, blood trickling from the dozens of small horns jutting from all sides of its skull. Its mouth was that of a shark's. Unfurling through the rows of teeth came the beast's tongue—a thick, wart-covered hunk of black flesh that lapped at the nude women and coiled around the snake tattoo on Ximena's thigh. It entered her vagina, stretching her with its girth, digging deeper and deeper as if it had no end. She gripped a pillow so hard it tore and burst with feathers.

Red-fleshed goblins rose out of the soiled bed with hard cocks and engorged breasts that leaked blood from their nipples. These creatures stayed half-hidden in shadows even as they joined in the debauchery. A faceless yellow demon approached Melissa, holding its barbed cock. Before she could react, it was driven into her ass, and she screamed as the barbs latched to the walls of her colon. The demon sodomized her even more roughly than Asher had. The other goblins sucked and fondled the girls, but when they tried to have vaginal intercourse with his women, Asher objected.

"Their reproductive organs are mine alone," he told them. "You may pleasure Ximena and Violet with tongues and fingers only. They are not here to pleasure *you*. They're here to pleasure *me*. As for Melissa, you can tear her apart as you wish. She is my offering to you."

The creatures submitted to Asher's demands. It exhilarated him. He was growing so powerful he had authority over not just humans but also demons. These goblin creatures added to Ximena and Violet's sexual experience and ganged up on Melissa to fuck all three of her holes. Lucky for her, only one of them had a barbed penis, and once that demon came blood inside her anus, it lost interest in her.

One ghoul with feminine features joined Violet in fellating Asher. He stroked its lion's mane and grazed his fingertips along the gnarled, purple flesh of the creature's labia, but when he tried to insert a finger, it was pinched by an internal crab claw. He yanked it free before he could lose it. The bed became a moist sponge of gore, and the demons began to sweat maggots, the larval organisms oozing from their pores like pus. Soon, the Satanists were deluged with vermin.

When Asher ejaculated, his black seminal fluid was infested with C-shaped, gray grubs, and as he groaned, hundreds of red gnats flew out of his throat. He came with great volume, drenching his harem.

The stew of his Satanic seed and all that spilt blood formed a pool in the sagging center of the mattress, and the demons retreated into it, sinking below the bubbling surface. Lost to Asher the incubus, the women writhed in the filth, smearing fluids and vermin across each other's bodies, slurping up handfuls and slicking their swollen labia. They rolled their wounds in the filth to absorb it into their bloodstreams. Soon, they were laughing like little girls in a pillow fight.

Asher sat back against the headboard and admired his blood orgy sluts. They crawled toward him. Violet cuddled his left side, and Ximena cuddled his right. Melissa's anus and vagina wept a dark trail of blood as she moved between Asher's legs and rested her head on his lower belly. Then she put the head of his penis into her mouth to suck out the last drops.

There was no fight left in any of the women now. There was not even the desire to fight.

Asher was their undisputed master.

Asher was king.

TWENTY-EIGHT

MOM STILL WASN'T HOME WHEN Asher got there, but someone else was. Asher sensed the presence before seeing or hearing anyone. He drew his pistol.

Could it be police? No, not this soon and without a warrant. Had someone else come to steal *Music to Sacrifice Virgins To?* Lenny? It didn't seem plausible for Mom to have come home without her car, and if she had, she would be losing her mind over the den of horror her son had made of her bedroom.

That's where Asher sensed the presence of another—in Mom's bedroom. Had Beelzebub returned to that filthy place to grant Asher even more power? Was Leviathan swimming in the ceiling again, waiting to bestow Asher with its wisdom?

He was alone. He'd left all three of his women at the Vincent house so they could clean everything up before Callie might see the mess. It would be no easy feat. Melissa would have to take the mattress to the dump and buy a new one before her husband came home from his business trip, but right now, she was more concerned about her retorn vagina and gaping asshole. Asher told her she could seek medical attention only after the master bedroom was clean. For now, she would just have to plug herself with tampons and gauze. Melissa had taken the worst pounding because Asher refused to let lowly demons abuse Violet and Ximena. They were his cabal girls. Melissa was just a bonus piece of pussy to Asher, a woman to control and torture just for the fun of it—nothing more. He had no plans to radicalize her the way he had Violet and Ximena. That's why those two had to be preserved as his personal whores, whereas he didn't care who—or *what*—fucked Melissa. She would remain dedicated to him either way.

Creeping down the hall, Asher kept his eyes on the door to the master bedroom, the gun clutched in his left hand. There'd been so much killing tonight, but he was always ready to kill again. He'd not been exaggerating when he'd told the girls how strong his bloodlust was.

The stench preceded the room. Though it had grown worse, its foulness delighted Asher. As he took aim at the center of the door, it slowly came open on its own, revealing an ethereal crimson glow that permeated the space. Silhouetted against the backdrop of this light was a humanoid figure.

Asher took aim. It would be easy enough to shoot the intruder down, but first, he wanted answers.

"You!" he said. "Step into the light so I can see you."

A musical voice replied, and Asher could not tell if it was male or female. "Welcome home, my son."

The figure was too trim to be Asher's father.

"I said step into the light!" Asher demanded.

But the person didn't have to. The red glow intensified, revealing a beautiful man in a flowing burgundy robe. It was open just enough to reveal his hairless chest. He was not handsome; he was *beautiful*, his features soft and smooth like a woman's, though he donned a full beard and had wide shoulders. He reminded Asher of a young Ewan McGregor or even a young, cleaner version of Mötley Crüe's Vince Neil. He had the same platinum-blond hair hanging to his shoulders. Even his goat-like eyes could not detract from his loveliness.

Asher lowered the pistol. "Who are you?"

The man smirked. "Like the record says, *the demon must be called*, and you, my young friend, have been calling—and calling quiet loudly, I must say."

Every inch of Asher's skin rippled with goosebumps. He stuck the revolver back into its holster. There would be no need for it, and even if there was, it would prove useless in the face of such evil.

"I suppose you were expecting horns?" the robed man said with a smile. "Maybe a pointed tail or a fucking torch growing out of the top of my skull like Baphomet? No, the bible—*His* bible—is truthful some of the time. It says I'll always be attractive to humankind. And why wouldn't I be? How disadvantageous it must be to be ugly. What a needless hurdle."

Asher took a knee. He tried to speak but couldn't find the words. He was too starstruck.

"They'll be plenty of time to bow in Hell," the robed man said. "Come inside."

Asher did as he was told. Stepping into his mother's room, the red light was bright enough to reveal every bit of putrescence. There was not an inch of space here that wasn't coated in fetid slime. But there were no other demons here—only the great one.

"Lord Lucifer," Asher finally managed to say. "Is it really you?"

"Just Lucifer. The word 'lord' leaves a bad taste in my mouth. I associate it with Him."

Asher nodded. "As you wish, Lucifer."

"No need to proclaim your loyalty, Asher. Your actions speak volumes to your character … and your personality." Lucifer stepped closer, his square pupils dilating. "Though we both know there's more than one personality in this husk, now isn't there?"

Asher nodded. "My uncle, Rex."

"Correct. His soul stirs just beneath the surface of your own. Rex Von Spades was a champion of Satanists. He did great work while he was alive, so I rewarded him by letting him continue his work, with a catch of course. You know what they say about making a deal with me, but hey, what businessman isn't out for himself, first and foremost? Only a bankrupt one! I allowed Rex to record his album in Hell—we made beautiful music, don't you think? My love of heavy metal is well documented, but honestly, I love all kinds of music, provided they have an evil message. Heavy metal just does it better than any other genre." He chuckled. "Anyway, the only chance Rex had of returning to this plane of existence was to use that music to lure a blood relative to the left-hand path. Only then could he possess them, but as you can tell, Rex didn't gain full control of you. Do you want to know why?"

"Yes, my master," Asher said, wanting whatever Lucifer wanted. He remembered Lenny telling him that adult souls were more difficult to conquer, which was why demons so actively pursued children for possession. But he sensed there was more to it than that.

Smiling, Lucifer turned to the nightstand, and Asher noticed the bong made from Paul's skull was sitting atop it. The Prince of Darkness raised it to his mouth, and the weed inside the bowl ignited on its own. He breathed deep of the smoke, then passed the bong to Asher. That he was sharing dope with Lucifer gave Asher an indescribable thrill. He felt like an actor who'd finally landed a starring role in Hollywood. He'd been welcomed into the fold of the demon king's wings.

"What you're thinking is true," Lucifer said. "The souls of adults are better secured against possession than the souls of children. But Rex was a grand wizard of black magic. He could have taken over the bodies of most adults—particularly the weak-willed and feebleminded, or those who're lost in life as you were—but I had bigger plans for him … and *you*."

Asher's eyebrows raised. "Me, Master?"

"I saw potential in you, son. Still do. After all, you share the same blood as Rex, and he was one of my most successful modern warlocks. Think of it as having Satanic genes. Your uncle's evil acts gave him great power that was passed on to you when he possessed you. You inherited his sorcery just as you did the record. This is how you've managed to expedite your transformation into a warlock and incubus. That's why you were able to conjure Beelzebub and Astaroth for counsel so early in your career. You had the advantage of Rex's influence. Given that your personal life was such a shit show, we all trusted you'd take to this new way of living with a smile, and you did. You've excelled at it, Asher—beyond expectations."

"Thank you, Master. I live to spread your glory."

"Of course you do." Lucifer put his arm around Asher's shoulders. "Tonight was especially glorious! You had your best friend killed, murdered a pregnant woman and *fucking ate* her fetus, had an old man and his young grandson slaughtered, and made your first virgin sacrifice—all in one night! And then, to celebrate, you had a Satanic orgy so perverse it summoned sex ghouls—literal perverts who are spending an eternity in Hell for the sexual assaults they committed while they were human beings. It was a nice touch the way you made a mother toss the salad of her own daughter—I mean, just fucking *fantastic!* Your cabal worships you. What you've done—particularly to the women—is quite impressive, even for an incubus."

"You honor me, Lucifer. I do it all for you."

"Bullshit."

Asher shuddered seeing The Devil's eyes narrow.

"You honor me with the things you do," Lucifer said, "but you're really in this for your own gain. As soon as you tasted power, your hunger for it became insatiable. There's no need to deny it. You're not in the wrong. This is exactly as it should be."

"It is?"

"Absolutely. Think about it, son. Do I demand my followers to spend their lives on their knees thanking me the way God does? No. Do I force people to do what I want by threatening them with eternal damnation the way He does? Fuck no. Controlling people goes against my nature. You know who I really want you humans to worship? *Yourselves.* To get up off your praying knees and see God's cosmic scam for what it is. There's no fun without free will, Asher. Not for me or my underlings. I only encourage people to act on the desires you've had all along—the impulses to cheat on your spouses, kill your prick bosses, and take the things you want from this world without caring how it affects anyone else. Greed, sloth, gluttony, lust—acting on these natural urges is supposed to be a bad thing? Are instincts worthy of punishment? Fuck that. I'd say that's ludicrous. So when I see you out for yourself—no matter what it takes to get what you want or how much it hurts others—I see the potential for greatness. That's why you're a warlock. The best way to serve me is to serve yourself."

Lucifer's words made Asher stand tall. He felt courageous and lethal.

"Now," Lucifer said, "you and your uncle will achieve more as one than you ever could separately. You're on track to become more than just an incubus or warlock. I came here tonight to applaud you—I always acknowledge good work—but I've been watching you from the shadows since the night of your first murder, whispering to you all along."

Asher thought of the demon who'd spoken to him from the woods outside of Terry's house, the one who'd cheered him on and guided him during times of violence and debauchery.

"Well, it wasn't me, exactly," Lucifer said, as if reading Asher's mind. "Those shadow demons are my familiars, my all-seeing eyes.

Busy as I am, I can't always make appearances like this. But I do relay messages through shadow demons."

"Thank you, Master. For everything."

"You know, 'master' is so impersonal. Wouldn't it be better if you could call me Father?"

Asher tingled. "I would love nothing more."

"See, that is what I mean when I say you're destined to be more than a mere warlock or some lesser demon. I've had many children, but you're an honor student that stands out from the others in my brood of vipers. You truly could be the next son of Satan. But there's one catch."

"I'll do anything. Anything at all."

Lucifer smiled. "Oh, I don't doubt that one bit. But you can't be the son of everyone now, can you? I am a jealous parent, Asher. Very jealous indeed."

Asher was in a cold sweat. He could feel the heat on his shoulder radiating from The Devil's palm. Lucifer's expression was filled with tenderness. Even his breath was sweet.

"Just as you made Ximena prove her loyalty to you, now you must prove yours to me," The Devil told him. "It's the only way for you to truly be my son. You understand, don't you?"

Asher nodded slowly.

"That's a good lad." Lucifer tussled Asher's hair. "Listen, I've got my hands full with The Middle East right now, as usual, and I'm assisting this trio of Ohio teenagers who're planning to blow up their school. Dayton's water smells like manure and there's litter everywhere, but let me tell you, *the food* … it's also terrible!" He laughed. "But I'll be in touch. Keep up the nice work, okay? Make Papa proud."

"Yes, Father. I guarantee it."

With a snap of his fingers, a coffin of flame closed around Lucifer and imploded on itself, express carrying him into oblivion. The stench of sulfur lingered in his wake. Dazed by all that had happened, Asher went to the kitchen for a beer. He downed it quickly and opened another, then grabbed the nutcracker and started working on walnuts to nibble on, just to give his hands something to do. They were still shaking. Meeting Lucifer was a dream come to fruition, but even a warlock trembled when faced with such insurmountable evil. The Prince of Darkness was a stunning presence that left behind an eclipsing shadow.

Asher supposed it was natural for a son to fear his father. That had been the way boys were raised since man's inception. It wasn't until recent years that fathers had been forced to soften. Now, they had to rule with kindness even when their kids were terrors. They had to fear their children would be taken away from them if they so much as yelled at the little bastards. This was why the younger generations were such a bunch of whiny, spoiled brats who thought they had everything coming to them. Society had emasculated men. Without stern fathers to take charge, the boys of today had little chance to grow into men themselves. Masculinity was now considered a bad thing, passivity was applauded, and queerness was fashionable. No wonder testosterone levels in males had been dropping across the board. What hope could today's young males have in a country hijacked by women and weaklings?

Asher had never feared his birth father. Dad had been as passive of a parent as he had a husband. He wanted to be Asher's *friend*, going too easy on him because he never wanted his son to dislike him. And what happened to guys like that? The very thing that had happened to Dad. Their wives divorced them in pursuit of real men, and the sons they'd failed grew up wanting nothing to do with them.

Then there was Mom. To Asher, she was one of many women who had done everything they could to demonize men, blaming them for all their problems, just like she did with Dad, Rex, and now Asher too—her own son. Rather than take accountability, women preferred to be perpetual victims. Everything that was bad about their lives was always the fault of "the patriarchy," something that no longer existed in wealthy countries. No matter how many female CEOs and surgeons and judges and politicians and self-made millionaires there were, women still insisted on pretending misogyny was as bad as it had been a hundred years ago, and that they weren't where they wanted to be in life because men had somehow conspired to hold them back. In their narrow view, everything was a "boy's club," despite all the special treatment women received in the twenty-first century.

Women were shit.

Men were shit.

Even children were shit.

Human beings did not deserve mercy and were unworthy of pity. Besides, there were way too many of them for any individual death to really be considered a tragedy. Even mass graves didn't upset Asher.

What was a handful of murders when the global population was in the billions? The planet was overcrowded. Asher was doing this world a favor.

It was Uncle Rex who helped him see women for what they really were. Asher's ex-girlfriend, Rebecca, had nearly destroyed him. Now, he realized it was his own fault for giving her the power to do so. Women needed to be put back in their place, once and for all. It would make everyone happier. Just look at his relationship with Ximena and Violet. Even Melissa had benefited from submitting to Asher. Dominating a woman was the only way to assure they stayed respectful and loyal to you, just as being a stern, intimidating father was the only way to raise a boy into a man.

A father had to lead by example. All Asher had ever seen in his father was weakness. All he'd seen in his mother was selfishness (and now promiscuity). It was no wonder his life had been such a directionless disaster. He'd been raised by failures.

Now, Asher had a new father to learn from and was building his own family. Before discovering Satan, his life had been a hefty scoop of dog shit. He'd had nothing. He had everything now—money, respect, women, power. Asher was living the ultimate male fantasy. He'd thought he owed his good fortune to Satan, but Satan said Asher had earned these things on his own. Better still, Asher knew how to get even more and wasn't afraid to grab that brass ring for himself.

TWENTY-NINE

IT WAS A QUARTER TO eight when Mom finally walked in the front door. She was wearing the flashy minidress she'd gone on her date in, an outfit more suited to a younger woman. The plunging neckline showcased her ample cleavage. High heels took the middle-aged sag out of her ass. Sitting in shadow, Asher watched her from his seat at the kitchen table as she kicked out of her shoes and hung up her coat. She hadn't noticed him yet, but she'd clearly noticed the odor.

"Dear God …" she said with a cough.

Mom went to the living room window to let in some fresh air, but Asher interrupted her.

"Don't," he said, startling his mother. "And leave the curtains drawn."

"Asher? Honey, what on Earth is that stench?"

"What stench would that be?"

She glowered at him. "You know damn well what stench! Jesus, did something crawl under the house and die? It smells like absolute shit in here."

"That's because it is shit. Some of it, anyway."

Mom came closer, tossing her purse on the table. "What are you telling me?"

"They say a picture is worth a thousand words. Why don't you go in your bedroom and see for yourself?"

Mom's face pruned. "What did you do?"

"I could ask you the same question." He cracked open another walnut. "You leave for a hot date and don't come home until morning. There's only one thing you could have been doing." He raised his hand to his mouth and pantomimed fellatio.

"Asher! I am *your mother!* My personal life is none of your business!"

"What's the lucky guy's name, Mom? Or was it more than one? Did they run a train on you behind the Chili's dumpster?"

That Mom tried to slap him surprised Asher. She had more guts than he'd given her credit for. She was still scared of him, but outrage made her react without thinking. Asher was quicker than his mother and caught her arm in mid-swing. Standing, he twisted her arm up behind her back. His mother's cries of pain excited him.

"Let's go to your bedroom," Asher said, ushering her forward. "I've redecorated so it's more suiting to a whore."

She stumbled as he shoved her. "Let me go!"

He ignored her as they struggled toward the bedroom door, Asher taking the nutcracker with him.

"Asher, please! Why're you doing this to me? *I'm your mother!*"

She coughed as the smell worsened, and when they reached the door, Asher kicked it open, revealing the bodily fluids dried on the ceiling and the walls. Mom gagged, and he shoved her to the floor. It was still damp from blood and diarrhea. She instantly vomited, tears streaming down her face. It only made Asher more pumped.

"My God," she groaned. "What is happening?"

Looking up, Mom noticed the bong made of Paul's skull. She shrieked, and Asher kicked her in the stomach to silence her. Going to the boombox he'd placed on the nightstand, he turned on *Music to Sacrifice Virgins To*. The album was now little more than driving, grinding noise and a choir of demonic screams. The little girl he'd murdered last night screamed the loudest.

Asher took his shirt off. "I've got to hand it to you. You were right about Rex's music and what it would do to me. But I'm sure you've realized that. Still, I'm gonna show you just how right you are."

On her knees, Mom put up her hands in a passive manner. "Asher … please …"

"You don't even know what you're begging for."

"Why? *Why?* Why're you doing this?"

Asher spoke, but it was Rex's voice that replied to her. "C'mon, sis. We had so much fun when I did it to you the first time."

Asher saw the recognition in his mother's eyes. Her dead brother's presence was clear to her now. There was no longer any doubt, no rationalizing away the evil unfolding before her.

"Please, don't …" she whimpered.

"Don't what?" he asked, undoing his belt.

"Don't hurt me."

Asher smiled as he lowered his jeans. His mother's eyes went wide with horror as his penis fell out. Though flaccid, it was already eight inches long. The flesh had chafed from the amount of sex he'd been having. It peeled like a snake's skin as it started getting hard.

Mom couldn't even speak. She only made guttural sounds, her jaw dropped in terror, eyes frantic in search for an impossible escape.

"I can't lie to my mother," Asher said. "This *is* going to hurt."

She made a move to run, and Asher punched her in the face, knocking her back onto the floor. He raped his mother savagely, beating her and spitting on her, his monstrous erection making her entire body go tense.

"I've haven't stretched this pussy so good since I was born," he said, taunting her as she begged for mercy he would not give.

Asher reveled in her horror, and her pain only made him grow harder. He ripped her dress open, exposing her manufactured perfect tits. Biting down on her nipple, Asher began nursing, feasting on his mother's blood as he fucked her. Mom's hands flew, and she dragged her fingernails into his neck, just missing his face. The pain was exquisite. Asher returned the favor by snatching her hand and putting the middle knuckle of her index finger into the nutcracker. The joint broke so loudly he could hear it even over the music. Mom wailed. Asher did the next finger, then the next, crippling her one digit at a time. Though she kicked and bucked, she was no match for his strength. Asher did not stop until both hands were destroyed.

"I've decided to be born again," he told her. "I have a new father, one far better than the loser you allowed to knock you up."

He thrusted deeper, and Mom screamed as something tore within her.

"If you'd been smart, you would've let Rex impregnate you all those years ago," Asher said. "He's a great uncle but would have been an even better father to me. I could've gotten started earlier. Just think of the heights my sorcery could've reached by now."

Asher drew his pocketknife and flicked it open. He dug the tip into Mom's torn nipple just to watch her squirm. Then he raised the knife over his head and brought it down into Mom's breast. He slashed the skin and fatty tissue, then drove the knife in, impaling the implant. He ripped it off her ribs with a wet pop, laughing at how it jiggled. Then he did the same thing to her other tit.

"There," he said, "now you're natural again. See, nature plays a vital role in witchcraft, and I want everything to be just right for this."

Mom's pain was so immense Asher wasn't sure if she was even processing what he was saying. He supposed it didn't matter now. Though he was tempted to ejaculate inside of her just to make the violation that much more abominable, instead he pulled out and decorated her face with his black sperm. It took to her skin like sulfuric acid. Mom's face burned as the semen ate through it, eroding her lips and the tissue of her chin to expose the bloody, skeletal grimace beneath. The grubs and maggots followed, spewing out of Asher's urethra and onto his mother's torso. The larvae chewed her as if she were already dead, burrowing into her body to eat her from the inside.

Waving his left hand over his mother, the spell took effect instantly. Mom's eyes were shoved out of their sockets by a frenzy of black worms. Dangling on her cheeks, the eyes boiled in Asher's semen, but though she suffered and went blind, Asher would not let his mother die yet.

"Time to be born again," he whispered.

Asher spread his mother's legs wide. Already, his curse had infested her pubis with lice that crawled in and out of her. They did not deter him. Placing Mom's legs on his shoulders, he put his hands together as if in prayer, then drove them into her mangled vagina. He shoved harder, entering her up to his wrists. Pushing his arms in opposite directions, he used his Satanic strength to shatter her pelvis, shoved in up to his elbows, and widened the birth canal before diving into it face-first.

Mom's lower body split in half as her only child shredded his way back into the womb. His thick, black fingernails tore through her guts, and when a tube of intestines ripped, a deluge of larvae and insects spilled out. Asher dug deeper still, burying himself in the gore that used to be his mother, relishing in the sticky warmth, and once he was in up to her chest—as far in as he could go—he felt the warmth grow hotter and closed his eyes as his rebirth began, waiting to make his new father proud.

THIRTY

WHEN ASHER AWOKE, HE WAS standing naked in a valley of sand and withering trees. All was beige, including the sky, and the air was arid and foul. Barren soil stretched for miles into the horizon, where a tangerine sun hung low. Looking down at himself, Asher saw he was covered in his mother's blood. Her body was gone. Asher was no longer in his house. He doubted he was even in his world.

A hill of desert rock stood before him. Drawn to it, Asher started up the hill, passing burnt weeds and failed vegetation. Skeletal human remains were wedged in the earth, most small enough to have belonged to children. There was a droning noise, and the closer he got to the crest, the louder it became. A gravelly voice beneath the drone started as a murmur, then increased in volume and intensity as Asher trekked on.

"You serpents," it cackled. *"You brood of vipers. How shall you escape the sentence of Gehenna?"*

When he reached the hilltop, Asher saw a series of cave-like tombs dug into the rock. Stacks of human skulls and bones formed walls around them. The skull placed above the entrance to the largest cave was gigantic, looking barely human, and the Sigil of Lucifer was painted on its forehead in ash.

The voice went on. *"It is better to be born crippled than to have two hands as you're born into Gehenna, better to be born lame than walk into this valley with two good feet. Your tongue is a fire … it sets on fire the course of your life and is set on fire by Gehenna."*

Asher recognized these bible quotes because he could pull them from Rex's memory. They were slightly changed to fit his situation, but these warnings from the books of Matthew and James told him where he was, just as his Satanic intuition did.

This was the Valley of Wailing—Gehenna, the realm of divine punishment. Though it was an earthbound location in Jerusalem, Asher understood he'd not transported to the earthly realm but rather to the metaphysical one, the Gehenna of dark theological connotations—an abode of the damned. The remains of children made more sense now, for this place had been used to burn children alive as sacrifices to Moloch, the Ammonite god.

Asher approached the large tomb before him. It was a deep cave of impenetrable blackness, the walls forged of human remains like a catacomb. Here, he found Gehenna's only moisture in the blood trickling from these freshly flensed skulls. He stepped inside. Something moved beneath his bare feet, and when Asher looked down, he saw the floor of the tomb was swarming with scorpions. They did not sting him but crawled up his legs, clinging to him with a strange affection. The drone grew louder. Asher followed the sound, and as he rounded a curve, the darkness was split by hellfire.

The ground grew wet with blood that rapidly pooled up to his knees. Schools of rodents swam up to Asher, circling around his legs as the scorpions climbed his torso. He pressed on as the red light grew brighter.

The drone gave way to an electric guitar that burst into a heavy metal solo. The unseen guitarist showed incredible skill, as if they had more than two hands to play with, reminding Asher of the work of Glenn Tipton, Paul Chain, and Bill Steer, only even heavier and more ferocious. The howl of the music echoed through the cavernous tomb, a deafening explosion of noise that rose every hair on Asher's body.

A tall figure appeared within the rising flames.

Backlit by the redness, the figure was cast in shadow, but Asher could tell it was a man and could make out the guitar in his hands. Long, wet hair whipped as the man headbanged, flinging blood.

Asher called to him. "Rex ..."

There was a noise like thunder, and the glow flashed like a strobe light, fluctuating between crimson and darkness as the guitarist's flesh and hair fled his body in bloody ribbons, skinning him down to a skeleton. Still he played, his solo more elaborate even as it increased in speed. The darkness fell in full, and Asher was suddenly in a cemetery lined with cross-shaped tombstones on fire. A crumbling church tower smoldered at the rear of the graveyard, its bell chiming along with the music. Under the stars, the living skeleton shredded through his guitar solo, growing louder until all Asher could hear was amplifier fuzz.

"It's you," Asher said to his uncle's evil spirit. "*I'm* you."

The red light flashed again, transporting Asher back to the tunnel of human remains. The flesh had returned to the bones and skulls that lined the walls, and the severed heads screamed in chorus, sounding like a nursery of crying babies. He recognized Deanna and Paul's heads—the socket bowl still drilled into Paul's skull. The decapitated heads of Terry and his daughter wailed, cursing Asher as he passed by. Severed arms and legs writhed from their spots in the walls, slithering like tentacles through the sinewy gore.

Were these souls trapped in Gehenna to endure divine punishment? Asher didn't think so. Though some might have sins to atone for, Asher was the one who'd sent them straight into this Hell. The punishment they suffered was of his doing. His chest swelled with pride.

His mother's crippled hands reached out for him from the mass of human limbs, but she only had half of her face, the rest having been melted off by her son's acidic semen. The other victims of his death cult appeared amongst the rows of mangled bodies. Having been stabbed repeatedly by Ximena, Diego's face was a concaved wad of meat. Asher stared at his best friend, feeling nothing as Diego shrieked. Fernanda's head appeared in anguish, followed by the gelatinous skull of her fetus. It unhinged its jaws to scream like a hawk.

Asher shook with an inner heat, and the blood of his victims rained down from a ceiling of mutilated bodies, the red pool rising to his waist, and Diego and Fernanda's unborn child split down the center to projectile vomit its own afterbirth. As it coated his head and shoulder, Asher licked it from his lips, and then something tugged at him—an invisible force driving him toward the glow as it turned white—and though it blinded Asher, he refused to shut his eyes as he was reborn.

THIRTY-ONE

ASHER ROSE FROM THE RUINS of his mother's corpse.

Her intestines were wrapped around his torso in fleshy belts, ooz-ing bile. The room pulsed around him, warm and moist like a womb, and as he rose to his feet, the moldy afterbirth of the dead dribbled down his body. He snatched his mother's soggy panties, exited the room, and closed the door behind him, leaving a trail of bloody foot-prints as he returned to the kitchen for another breakfast beer. But the clock on the stove revealed it was now late afternoon. Lost in Gehenna, he'd been blacked out for hours. Now that he was back, he craved fluids, but he was also in the mood for something hot, as if the fires of Hell weren't enough. When he fetched his beer, he snatched the bottle of sriracha from the fridge and took a few sips. He paused when he caught his reflection in the sliding glass door to the patio. His hair was now down past his shoulders and black as soot. He grinned at his image and wiggled his unibrow.

"Happy birthday," Asher told himself.

Born again in the name of Satan, he was primed to become his true son. He was climbing the rungs of Hell's monarchy while still on this Earth, but as far as he'd come, he needed to push further into that fire, to continue his momentum by spilling more blood—much more.

Carrying the beer into the shower, Asher washed the nastiness away. He would have preferred to let it dry, but he was noticeable enough without being caked in the stinking gore of his dead mother. The thick new hair sprouting from his upper arms and shoulders told him he was becoming more animalistic—not just in behavior but in physical form—but his father, Lucifer, had schooled him on the importance of appearances. Asher stood under the hot water for a long time, plotting and planning, dreaming atrocities.

When he got out of the shower, Asher stored his mother's panties with the others he'd collected. Dressing in black, he sifted through a crate of Rex's records for something to listen to while he prepared for the night ahead. He selected Charles Manson's debut studio album, *Lie: The Love and Terror Cult*. It was one of the few non-metal albums in Rex's collection, along with Coven's *Witchcraft Destroys Minds and Reaps Souls* and the greatest hits of Sammy Davis Jr., who'd been known to have ties to The Church of Satan in the 1970s. Manson's stuff was a little too hippy-dippy for Asher's taste, but he appreciated the novelty of listening to a convicted murderer, even if Charlie sounded like a dollar store Bob Dylan, who was grossly overrated to begin with.

Asher wasn't sure what he wanted to do with his mother's carcass (or what was left of it). She was now as big of a mess as her bedroom. He could probably cleanse it all away with a wave of his hand but wanted to keep the room as it was, sensing his mother's remains would prove useful to him as a warlock. Sifting through her purse, Asher opened the billfold that held her wallet and phone. Behind a plastic frame was her driver's license, Mom putting on that big smile even at the fucking DMV. In another plastic frame was an old photograph Asher had not known she kept on her. In the picture, Asher was just a toddler, and he was sitting on his mother's knee. She had one arm around his waist and her nose in his hair as if sniffing him. Little Asher was laughing about something.

He laughed in a much different way now.

Retrieving her phone, Asher saw she had text message alerts. He tried to open it, but the home screen required face recognition. At first, he thought to just bring it to her corpse and scan her dead face, but then he remembered she didn't have one anymore. He chuckled at his own foolishness. Surely, his sorcery could open a simple phone.

He tapped it with his left finger, and the phone awoke.

The messages were from someone Asher didn't know, but based on what was said in them, Asher could guess who this asshole was.

He was listed under Mom's contacts as Sam.

I had an amazing time with you last night, Elizabeth, Sam's text read.

"I'm sure you did," Asher said to himself, "but not as amazing as the time I just had with her."

He read Sam's follow-up text: *I'm already excited to see you again.*

"Yeah, you should definitely check her out now," Asher laughed. "She's lost a lot of weight. Bitch looks better than ever."

Asher went back through their previous texts. Some were playful—even sexual without being too dirty—while others were typical inane messages about their days. It seemed Mom had been dating Sam for some time but had kept it secret. Had she been seeing him before she'd separated from Dad?

An idea came to Asher.

He texted Sam back, posing as his mother: *Hey, Sam. Personally, I think last night could have been better. You really know how to disappoint a woman.*

It didn't take long for the floating bubble to appear as Sam scrambled to find the right reply.

Sam: *Are you messing with me??? I thought we had a wonderful evening.*

Asher/Elizabeth: *You thought wrong, noodle dick.*

Sam: *Are you busy right now? Can I call you?*

Asher/Elizabeth: *Don't bother. I'm going back to the only man who has ever satisfied me—my husband, James.*

The phone rang as Sam tried to call. Asher sent it to voicemail.

Asher/Elizabeth: *I told you, I'm done, Sam. DONE.*

Sam: *Please, baby, talk to me.*

Asher/Elizabeth: *We've been over this and over this. I keep telling you James is the only man I could ever love. I told you I'm going back to him, and I meant it. Why can't you accept that?*

Sam: *This is the first I'm hearing of it! You seemed happy to be with me last night. Please, I don't understand this.*

Asher/Elizabeth: *You need to stop stalking me. I've told you that in person. Now I'm telling you in writing. You can't have me, you bastard. Not after WHAT YOU DID TO ME LAST NIGHT.*

Sam: *WHAT THE HELL DID I DO?*

Asher/Elizabeth: *If you don't stop this, I'll be forced to file a restraining order. You're scaring me and I'm sick of it. Just leave me and my husband alone.*

The bubble fluttered as Sam started to text something, then went still as he chose silence. It was a man's best move in a situation like this. It would also work to Asher's advantage.

He found his father in his mother's phone and read through their recent texts. Though they'd ended their marriage, the divorce process had been amicable, each of them showing respect and decency. It made Asher sick to see what a simp his father was even when his woman had screwed him over (and was already screwing a new guy). Dad deserved to be dumped, and he deserved what was coming.

Asher texted him.

Asher/Elizabeth: *Hi, it's me. I've been doing a lot of thinking. Do you have time to come over today or tomorrow? I'd love it if we could talk, and your son wants to see you too.*

There was a sudden knock at the door.

Asher figured it must be his girls having returned to their master after finishing the cleanup of the Vincent house. When he parted the curtains, he was flabbergasted by what he saw on the front porch. He opened the door just enough to stand in the wedge, his eyes gone dark to conceal their redness.

The pair of nuns were dressed in their habits, complete with hooded headpieces and large crosses hung around their necks by beads. The older one appeared to be in her late fifties, with wrinkles crinkling the corners of her mouth. The younger one couldn't have been older than twenty-five, and her skin was like that of a baby's, her chubby cheeks pink from the nip in the air. He couldn't see much of her shape under the habit, but the nun was plump in a way that excited him. Asher believed younger women could get away with a little extra weight until they hit their thirties, after which they were just fat. Even without makeup, this nun's youth made her attractive. The older one was carrying a sack on a sling like a postman, while the younger one had a purse. Their smiles were bright but somehow strained.

"Good afternoon, sir," the older nun said with the voice of a lifelong smoker. "I'm Sister Ernestine. This is Sister Rosemary. We're with The Sisters of St. Joseph convent, representing Our Lady of Mercy Catholic church. How are you today?"

Asher smiled, thinking of the last time he'd seen Our Lady of

Mercy. It'd been a furnace.

"I'm just dandy, sisters," he said, eyeing Rosemary. "Though I must say I'm a bit surprised. These days, you don't see many people going door-to-door to convert people to their religion."

Leaning with the door halfway open, a little of the house's stench must have drifted out because the nuns recoiled, and Rosemary briefly put her hand to her mouth.

"Forgive the smell," Asher said. "I'm boiling cabbage."

"Cabbage?" Ernestine said, forcing herself to keep smiling. "Seems like you're ready for St. Patty's Day, but it's nearly Christmas-time."

Asher blinked. He hadn't even realized the holiday season had come. He'd participated so little with society that he'd broken free from the world around him, preferring the one below.

"We just like cabbage here," he said.

"Of course," Ernestine said like an apology. "It makes for a fine side dish at Thanksgiving."

Was Thanksgiving approaching, Asher wondered, or had it passed? Mom hadn't mentioned anything, but things hadn't been going well between them, so perhaps she'd not mentioned it on purpose. Asher couldn't even say what today's date was. Calendars and clocks no longer held any meaning.

"Anyway," Ernestine said, "we're not here to convert, as you put it—though we are always happy to talk about The Lord. We're going door-to-door to ask for donations to rebuild our church, which was destroyed in a fire."

"My goodness," Asher said. "Isn't that just awful."

"It is very unfortunate, yes. A donation of any size would be greatly appreciated."

"How've you been doing so far? Have my neighbors been generous or stingy?"

"Well," Ernestine said, a little put off. "Everyone gives what they can."

"Hey, if there's one thing churches need, its more money, right? They're all a business and yet they pay no taxes, even as they spend their money on golden palaces instead of aiding the poor and the sick. I mean, can you really blame people for not wanting to help you build another gaudy eyesore?" He delighted in seeing Ernestine's face flush with outrage. Before she could reply, Asher pointed at her bag. "What's in the sack?"

"We can see we've bothered you," she said, turning to go.

"No, no. Wait. I apologize. I didn't mean to take out my frustrations with organized religion on you."

The nuns stopped.

"It's just that the only priest I listen to is Judas Priest," Asher said, "and the only Christ I've ever loved is John Christ."

"Who is John Christ?"

"Guitarist for Danzig. If you ain't heard them, you're missing out, Sister."

Ernestine forced that smile again. She opened the bag and drew out one of the many tote bags inside. Once unfolded, Asher saw it had the logo for Our Lady of Mercy stamped on one side, a golden cross on the other.

"We're handing these out with donations of ten dollars or more," Ernestine explained.

Opening her purse, Rosemary spoke for the first time. "We also have buttons and pins for less."

The inside of her purse was packed with pinback buttons with the same church logo, and acrylic pins of Christ on the cross.

"I always wondered why Christians focused on Christ's death like this," Asher said. "You'd think his crucifixion would be the last thing he'd want his symbol to be."

"The cross honors Christ's sacrifice," Ernestine said. "He suffered and died for our sins."

"Only because his old man demanded it. God could have just forgiven everyone and spared his only son all that pain and suffering, but hey ..."

Ernestine glowered, no longer trying to hide her frustration.

Rosemary answered Asher for her. "It's not for us to judge God. He works in mysterious ways we cannot fully understand. That's where faith comes in."

Asher smirked. The young nun's high voice made her seem even younger than she was. He wondered what she looked like under that unflattering habit, what she'd look like with his huge cock ripping her anus open, or what her final prayer might sound like if he slit her throat.

"If human beings can't fully understand God, then why do people like you claim to speak for him?" Asher asked.

"I do not claim to speak for God," Rosemary said. "I only preach his word."

"But you get those words from a bible admittedly written by men—Matthew, Mark, Luke, and John. If human beings can't fully understand God, then isn't it possible these men misinterpreted His message? Isn't it possible you're spreading false information?"

Rosemary swallowed hard. Clearly, she was not used to being confronted this way, for what kind of prick would harass a nun?

Ernestine seemed armored compared to her fellow sister, her years of experience suggesting she'd dealt with heretics more often. "The Holy Bible is God's word."

"Which bible?" Asher asked. "Every religion's got a different one. How do you know yours is the right one? I mean, you even have multiple versions of the Christian bible, right? New and Old Testament? Seems like a real gamble to commit to just one."

"We respect the religions of others," Rosemary chimed in, "but we embrace our own as the one true faith."

"So, you respect *all* religions? Really? Even fringe groups like Scientology or the bastardized Christianity of Mormonism? Even the stuff cults come up with?" he asked. Rosemary struggled to answer, so Asher went on. "You know what I often wonder is … what if all the cult leaders out there who claimed to have a direct correspondence with God were telling the truth? What if guys like David Koresh really are the second coming of Christ but we just keep killing them all? What if their strange beliefs really are what God wants?"

Ernestine took Rosemary's arm. "Let's be getting along now, Sister."

"I'm just asking questions," Asher said.

"If you need answers, I suggest you read the bible."

Asher hadn't, but Rex had, so all the information was there. Asher was eager to attack the nuns with conflicting quotes from their own holy book—especially quotes from the blood-soaked Old Testament, which was filled with wrathfulness and vengeance. But that wasn't the best route to take with the sisters if he wanted to keep talking to them.

"Will you forgive my cynicism?" he asked.

"Of course," Rosemary said, resisting Ernestine's attempt to pull her away. "Christ teaches forgiveness."

"Just how much sin can be forgiven?"

"All of it, provided you repent and accept Jesus as your savior."

Rubbing his chin, Asher looked skyward. "Hmm. You drive a hard bargain."

Rosemary furrowed her brow, not understanding but wanting to.

It was obvious the young nun was eager to save souls, even ones as black as Asher Benton's.

"Listen," he told them. "I practice a different religion."

"We understand," Ernestine said, tugging Rosemary's sleeve. "We'll leave you be. Thank you for your time and have a nice—"

"Hold on," Asher said. "I may not be Catholic, but I'll still help you out. Let me get a tote bag and one of those cross pins."

Rosemary grinned. "Thank you so much."

"Sure thing. I just need to grab some cash." He opened the door wider. "Why don't you come in while I fetch my wallet?"

Rosemary almost did, but Ernestine tugged her sleeve harder, drawing her back. The older nun's smile was more strained than before.

"We appreciate your kindness, sir," Ernestine said, "but we have a lot of houses to visit today."

"Look, if it's the cabbage, I'll light some scented candles. I know you sisters love your candles."

Ernestine had had enough. "Let's go, Sister Rosemary."

"I think Rosemary wants to stay," Asher said, staring into the young nun's eyes, allowing just the slightest hint of redness to flicker through his irises. "You did say you were always willing to talk about God, didn't you?"

Rosemary's eyes couldn't leave Asher's. Her lips parted just slightly, her tongue darting out to wet them. Asher smiled wide. The nun's faith would not save her.

"We really must be going," Ernestine said.

"Why don't you let Rosemary decide for herself?" Asher asked.

"Sir—"

"C'mon, Rosy," Asher said, ignoring Ernestine. "C'mon inside with me."

Rosemary wouldn't have broken eye contact with him if Ernestine hadn't shaken her arm. The young nun blinked rapidly, seeming to emerge from a deep, dark dream. She reached into her purse and handed Asher one of the crucifix pins. He nearly reached for it with his dominate left hand but didn't want Rosemary to see the Baphomet pentagram etched into his palm, so he accepted it with his right.

"I'll pray for you," she told him.

Asher chuckled. "How about a reverse exorcism?"

"A *reverse* exorcism? I'm not sure what you mean."

"That's when the demon tells the priest to get out of the kid!"

Ernestine started down the driveway. Rosemary remained on the porch. She seemed determined to do something, but Asher couldn't tell what. Looking at her, he suddenly realized what a treasure the sister was. Married to God, nuns tended to be virgins, depending on when they'd become a nun. He could only imagine the sort of power he'd be granted if he sacrificed a virgin this holy.

"C'mon, baby," he told her, still trying to lure her inside. "The old bat can sell those tote bags on her own. Why don't you come in here with me? I'll make it worth your while. Just check this out." He slid his tongue between his teeth. Like his penis, it had grown longer, and he wiggled it about like he was Gene Simmons of KISS. "I'll drive this tongue so deep it'll tickle your ovaries."

Rosemary actually *gasped*. She put her hand to her chest and gripped her cross.

There was no doubt about it. This one had never been fucked.

"You ..." the young nun said. "I never thought I'd say this to another human being, but ... you're an *evil* man. But I will still pray for you in the hope you'll detach from Satan."

"Do not talk about my father that way." Asher pinned the crucifix to his shirt upside-down. "Let me know if you come to your senses. I can help you pursue pleasure instead of piety. Don't waste your life trying to earn a better afterlife."

Rosemary finally started following Ernestine, who stood at the edge of the property with her fists pressed against her hips. Asher watched Rosemary, waiting for her to look back. She did, and Asher reveled in knowing he'd tempted her after all. Then the nuns walked down the street, not even bothering to go to Asher's next-door neighbors. Forget the donations; getting away from him was their priority.

Asher closed the door, knowing he'd see the nuns again. He would make sure of it.

Returning to his mother's phone, he saw his dad had not replied to the text yet. Dad was of an older generation and didn't neurotically check his phone the way people under fifty did, and he commonly answered texts with a simple *thumbs-up* emoji. Asher considered going to the Vincent house to see what his women were up to but decided it was better to make them come to him, so he laid out two rails of cocaine on the coffee table and snorted them up, then turned on the TV. Mom had been the last one to use it, so the true crime channel was on. Asher popped another beer and sat down to watch the show. It recounted the story of a stalker who'd kidnapped, raped, and tortured a woman he'd only gone on one date with. The show included reenactments as well as interviews, and Asher couldn't help but chuckle at how graphic it was. True crime was so popular, even with basic bitches like Mom, despite how sadistic and grotesque the accounts could be. It was ridiculous how so many people could enjoy that and yet complain about the graphic nature of heavy metal lyrics, scary movies, or horror novels. Even things as dorky as *Dungeons & Dragons* roleplaying games had been seen as tools of The Devil at one time. Meanwhile, the same parents who condemned all that stuff binge-watched hardcore murder porn like this.

He wondered if his killings would one day be dramatized in a true crime show. This led him to flip the channels until he found a news program. He didn't even have to wait. The slayings were all over the news—*four found dead in an apartment building, each of the victims brutally murdered and mutilated.* A police sergeant was being interviewed at the station and was telling reporters it was the worst crime scene he'd ever seen in his twenty-eight years on the job. Returning to the newsroom, the anchorwoman announced one of the victims had been pregnant but did not mention the missing fetus. Asher figured the police had decided not to share that gruesome information. There was an Amber Alert out for the little girl Asher had sacrificed. Her name was Nikki Parks, and she'd just turned twelve. Only Asher and his death cult knew she would never see thirteen. The news program showed family members, friends, and even the police still clinging to the false hope she would be found alive. The newscast then turned to a related story of two other missing people, Paul and Deanna.

Asher repeated what he'd heard in a hundred of Mom's true crime shows. "No body, no crime."

Without the hard evidence of a corpse, it was difficult for police to bring charges against someone suspected of murder. That covered Deanna, Paul, and little Nikki's deaths, but the four bodies at Diego's apartment had been discovered, which was to be expected. Asher had wanted them to be found. He and his acolytes had arranged the crime scene with that in mind, painting the walls with Satanic messages and symbols to drive fear into the community. He wondered if the police had linked this to the church burning yet, and if they had, would they take another look at the fire that killed Terry and his daughter, Maxine?

A spell of protection was in order, especially now that his mother was dead. Her coworkers were bound to notice her absence. She had an active social life, and people would come looking for her soon enough. Asher was again struck by the notion that he shouldn't discard the remains hastily, that they could serve some greater purpose. Rex was trying to tell him something.

Asher returned to his bedroom to retrieve the one thing that could answer his questions. He could have played the download of the album on his boombox but knew the best way to communicate with his uncle and the dark forces—and perhaps even Satan himself—was to go directly to the source material.

With a wave of his left hand, the wall rippled like a rain puddle, the drywall becoming fluid he could reach through to grab the record. It was warm in his hands, the edges of the sleeve glowing like embers. He put it on the turntable, and it spun blackly beneath the Baphomet, the sound of the guitars equally cyclonic. A bass drum made the walls tremble. The voice of his uncle was underlined by the whispers of females—souls Asher conjectured Rex had taken in life and kept as trophies in the afterlife. Instead of chanting, Rex gave instructions on how Asher could better use the new powers he'd earned by slaughtering his own mother. Rex taught him about spells, invocations, and talismans. Asher played both sides of the record to be sure he gathered everything required to be a master warlock.

Once he was finished studying, he went to the garage to test what he'd learned. He snatched a socket wrench from the toolbox, gripped it with both hands, and broke the steel in half as if it were a pencil.

"Nice."

He tossed the pieces and picked up a hammer. Holding it in his left hand, Asher focused, and the tool warmed up quickly, the metal turning red from the heat.

"Hot damn," he said. "I'm fucking Superman."

Going back into the house, Asher grabbed dishwashing gloves and his mother's apron from the kitchen cabinet, then entered her bedroom. One of Rex's lessons was how a witch could protect their home from outsiders. Nature—a warlock's kingdom—demanded rent just as any landlord would, for nature owned the soil. If one were going to protect their land, a sacrifice had to be entombed within the walls of their home. According to the Book of Kings, even the God of Israel once sanctioned burying people alive inside great buildings to attain their stability and permeance. Ancient castles sank and were rebuilt repeatedly until masons were brought in to bury innocent little girls alive within their walls.

With his newfound superhuman strength, Asher was able to dismember his mother's carcass using only his hands, snapping her tendons and breaking her bones. To keep investigators away from his house, he created another portal like the one he kept the record in and placed his mother's severed head into the living room wall facing the front of the house. He put the hands he'd busted with a nutcracker into another portal beside the patio's sliding glass door. Using his mother's blood, he painted Satanic symbols on every windowsill in the house, then shielded the garage with an inverted cross made by nailing Mom's legs together and attaching them to the inside of the garage door.

Asher threw the gloves and apron into the trash. He was about to pack Paul's skull with weed to have a few tokes, but there came another knock at the front door. His loins stirred from the possibility that Sister Rosemary might have changed her mind about getting her pussy tongued out, but when he opened the door, it was only Violet and Ximena. They looked exhausted.

"All cleaned up?" he asked.

"We had to rent a van to get the mattress out of there," Ximena said. "The mattress store Melissa ordered a new one from was willing to take the old one, but we didn't want the delivery guys to see all the blood on it, so we took it to the dump ourselves."

"Where's Melissa now? Getting her wounds taken care of?"

Violet shook her head. "Mom decided to tend to them herself. She told us she'd already had her privates stitched the other day, so she worried if she came to the hospital and they saw the stitches had been undone, they'd start asking questions. She didn't want to get you in any trouble."

This news made Asher beam, for his control over Melissa was now absolute.

"We helped her with her injuries," Violet said. "We had plenty of tampons and a first aid kit, plus some antibiotics left over from when Callie had bronchitis. We figured they could help if any of her internal wounds got infected."

"Well done," Asher said, proud of his girls. "So she's at the house, then?"

"Yeah."

"And what about your sister? At school?"

"No, it's Saturday. She's at home, but she doesn't know about anything. She slept in so late we were finished cleaning by the time she got up."

"So the sleep spell worked perfectly."

He stepped aside to let them in, and when he closed the door, his girls gagged from the stench. Even the snake around Ximena's neck seemed to recoil.

"What the *fuck?*" Ximena said. "It smells like an open sewer in here. Goddamn, is a grease trap being drained?"

"I like it," Asher said, leaving it at that.

"What happened?" Violet asked, her hand over her nose and mouth.

Asher allowed the question. "Well, first I summoned Beelzebub while fucking your mother in the master bedroom. That brought most of the filth you're smelling now. But then, just a few hours ago, I killed my mother in there too."

Violet's hand fell away from her face as her jaw dropped. Ximena stared into space.

"Don't worry," Asher said. "I'm not gonna make you clean it up."

"Why did you kill her?" Violet asked.

"Lucifer demanded it. Well, no, that's not exactly accurate. Lucifer didn't demand me to do anything. That's not how our father works. He merely suggested I couldn't be *everyone's* son if I wanted to be his."

"Hold up," Ximena said. "You mean you actually met with Satan?"

"Do you dare to doubt me?"

"No, Master. That's not it. This is just exciting news."

"Yeah," Violet said. "But killing *your mom?* Isn't that kinda ..."

She couldn't find a way to finish her sentence. Asher explained his motivation for his mother's murder and described his visit to the spirit realm of Gehenna.

"I have been born again," he told his girls. "I am destined to be a son of Lucifer, and I am here to do my father's work."

"And we're here to do yours," Violet said, caressing his chest as she stepped closer. "Anything you want, Master."

"That's what I like to hear." He patted her on the head. "Tell Callie she's coming out with us tonight. Make it like she's invited to a party."

"Okay. I'm sure she'd like that."

"Of course she would. Girls her age are gullible. In a way, women always are. Tell her we'll pick her up later tonight. Right now, I'm calling a meeting." He turned to Ximena. "Call the guys and tell them to meet us at the usual place."

"Yes, Master," she said. "Did you hear the news? They found the bodies."

"Yes, I know."

"When we went to get the van," Ximena said, "we saw missing posters for that little girl, Deanna, and Paul."

Violet nodded. "They were all over the place."

"Don't be afraid," Asher assured them. "Everything's going according to plan."

Ximena hesitated but had to ask. "Master ... what exactly is the plan?"

"That's enough questions," he scolded her. "If you need to know something, I'll tell you."

"Sorry, Master. I only want to serve you to the best of my ability."

"You do that by sucking my dick like you're Linda Lovelace. Now call the guys like I fucking told you to."

She bowed her head in shame and drew her phone from her pocket. As Ximena made the calls, Asher pulled Violet aside.

"When it comes to your sister," he told her, "here's what I want you to do. Be cool to her to get her to come along with us, but whenever all three of us are together, I want you to be mean to her. Not viciously cruel but belittling, bullying."

"But ... I thought you wanted me to be nice to her and show interest in her."

"Only until I'm around. Then get bitchy with her. I'll be the one who's nice to Callie now. I'll even defend her when you make fun of her. Think of it as playing good cop, bad cop."

"Um ... okay ..."

It was obvious Violet had more questions but was too afraid to ask them.

"Don't you get it?" Asher asked. "This will put me in the position to be Callie's friend and protector. She'll warm up to me by her own volition. That's what we want—for her to like and appreciate me so she'll be malleable in my hands."

"Yes, Master. As you wish." She cuddled close to him again, running circles on his chest with her finger. "Will you fuck me again? Please? I just want you inside me all the time. I dunno, it's just all I can think about anymore."

He kissed her cheek to keep his incubus spell strong, locking Violet's mental state right here where he wanted it. "Soon, my pet."

"Maybe just a quicky? I'll do whatever you want. I'm sure Ximena will too, if you want us both."

Asher smirked. "And what about Callie?"

Violet's face fell, her gaze going to the floor. "Um …"

Asher did not plan to fuck Callie, of course, but he wanted to test Violet's loyalty, especially after how she'd begged for her mother's and sister's lives the night before, having believed Asher intended to make her kill them.

He kissed Violet on the lips, and when her mouth opened, Asher stretched his tongue into the back of her throat, blowing his noxious breath into her lungs. His tongue wormed its way down her esophagus and into her stomach bile, making it bubble from his heat. Violet convulsed in his arms as her eyes rolled back, her incubus overlord invading her, slobbering his black magic into her insides to strengthen his hold on the girl. When he withdrew from her, Violet stumbled to the kitchen trash and vomited. Wisps of dark fog exited her nostrils as her black puke splattered the bin.

Asher patted her butt. "Just a little refresh for you, baby, so you remember who's in charge. If I want to fuck your little sister, you're gonna help me to do it. If I want to rape her, you'll gladly hold her down. In fact, you'll see it as an honor and a privilege."

Though still retching, Violet nodded in obedience.

"Remember what you said a moment ago, Violet: *Anything I want.*"

"Yes, Master," she said as she gasped for air.

"I am your family now. Not your slut mother or absent father or your teeny little sister, but me and your new father, Lucifer. Now praise his name."

"Hail Satan," she said, black spittle dangling from her bottom lip.

Ximena came around the corner but knew better than to ask what was going on. "It's all set up. The guys said they'll be there in half an hour to forty-five minutes"

"All right, then," Asher said. "Now get over here and kiss me, sweetheart."

THIRTY-TWO

"OUR NEXT TARGETS WILL BE religious people," Asher told his followers. "Not just people who believe in God but those who've dedicated their lives to the church."

The cult of five were gathered in the same clearing they sacrificed the little girl in the night before. It was a frigid afternoon, and everyone but Asher had their shoulders up and their hands buried in their coat pockets. Barney had on a new leather trench coat and wore dark eyeshadow with black nail polish, thinking it made him look spookier when it only made him look stupider. He also reeked of marijuana, so when he'd arrived in his new garb, Asher addressed him as "Drugula."

"Sounds good!" Barney said of Asher's new plan.

"Don't interrupt me," Asher replied, silencing his henchman. "The reason we're going to shift focus to the holy rollers is because they're the next logical victims for the sons and daughters of Satan. They'll be valuable sacrifices, especially those who're virgins."

"So, like, priests?" Ximena asked.

"Yes. And nuns too." He told them about the ones who'd come to the house. "Sisters Rosemary and Ernestine are religious refugees of the church we torched. I don't think it's a coincidence they were delivered right to my front door."

"The hand of fate?"

"The hand of Lucifer. He is always guiding us. To see that guidance, you just have to keep your eyes open."

Lenny lit a cigarette. "Do you know where we can find these nuns, Master?"

"As it turns out, Our Lady of Mercy has ties to a small convent called The Sisters of St. Joseph—a sort of school for aspiring nuns to go through a process called discernment, where they spend a few years with the nuns there to determine if they're worthy of becoming nuns too. It's also a refuge for wayward girls. Basically, The Sisters of St. Joseph is an all-female commune where nuns study scripture and help pregnant teens without family. It's not far from the church, and it's even more rural. You can bet your ass we'll find Rosemary and Ernestine there, but they're just the tip of the iceberg. Just think of it—a small community of young women and old nuns, isolated and completely defenseless against the forces of darkness."

"Namely us," Ximena said, playing with her pet snake as it coiled around her arm.

"This is brilliant, Master," Barney said, eager to gain favor. "When can we go? I hunger for blood again."

"Easy, Drugula. I want this done right. There'll be more people there than there were at Diego's apartment. We need to strategize and arm ourselves. I want a clear plan before we break into this nunnery. That's why you and Lenny are gonna scope it out from afar and get the layout down. I want to know every entrance and exit, every road leading in and out, including any trails through the surrounding woods." He looked at Violet. "And you're going to get a tour of the inside."

Violet blinked rapidly. "Me?"

"You're young enough to pass for a high schooler. Tell the nuns you're a pregnant orphan interested in joining the convent, but you want to see the place first, to decide if it's for you."

"You really think they'll give me a tour?"

"If you're pathetic and pregnant enough, yeah."

"But I'm not pregnant."

"Don't worry about that. I can make you look pregnant."

Violet started picking her cuticles but didn't voice her concerns.

"Don't go soft on me, now, sweetheart," Asher told her. "If you can kill people and get eaten out by demons, you sure as shit can lie to nuns."

"Yes, Master," she said meekly. "Whatever you want."

He turned to Ximena. "It'll be too suspicious if two unknown girls show up there at once, and besides, you don't look as innocent as Violet. So while the others work on this, I've got something else you can help me with, and I don't just mean draining my balls."

Barney snickered, but one look from Asher shut him up.

"As you wish," Ximena said, twirling the snake in her hands.

"Did you give your pet a name yet?" Asher asked.

"I call him Dragon."

"How do you know it's a male?"

"A mother knows …"

"What about us?" Lenny asked. "Do we have a name yet? Every cult needs a name. I'm sure the press will come up with all sorts of names for us, but it'd be nice to give one to ourselves."

"How about The Asher Family?" Barney suggested.

Asher sighed through his teeth. "Drugula, I swear to Satan, if you say one more moronic thing, I'll fill your mouth with possum feces with a mere snap of my fingers."

Barney looked at the ground. No one defended him, not even himself.

"We'll call ourselves The Reapers," Asher said. "That'll do. It's simple and scary, which will keep people from forgetting it, and it'll be easy for us to write it in human blood."

"That was my thinking too," Lenny said. "We create a brand and mark our work with it. Let the people know who to be afraid of! Rex called our old group Satan's Skulls. Always sounded more like a biker gang to me, but Rex knew best."

"He *still* does. I've been learning more from my uncle every day, and so far, he's been right about everything. Now I'm right too— *always*."

Lenny nodded. "Absolutely, Master. Absolutely. And I have some weapons that'll help with the mass killing you're talking about—an AR-15, a Glock 26, and even a chainsaw if we want to get crazy."

"Whoa," Barney said. "You've got an AR?"

"You're goddamned right I do."

"Beautiful." Asher said. "One thing to know about using a gun on someone is to just shoot them. No warnings—not even a warning shot. That just gives them time to attack you. So just fucking shoot your enemies and victims. Always." He addressed the whole group. "Gather whatever other weapons you can—knives, pepper spray, baseball bats. Zip Ties and rope will also come in handy. Ximena, I've been in your bedroom, so I know you have handcuffs."

She seemed a little embarrassed but agreed anyway.

"My grandpa's a deer hunter," Barney said. "He has a rifle case in his den."

"Steal them," Asher said. "And wash that stupid makeup off your face. You look like a fag in a goth bathhouse. We want to intimidate people, not make them laugh."

Barney looked away again. Lenny snickered.

"Yes, Master," Barney said.

"Good," Asher said. "Now, before we go, I have a treat for everyone, a reward for your service to Satan."

Asher drew the gallon-sized, plastic freezer bag from his coat. It almost looked like it was filled halfway with spaghetti, but opening it, the stench of human offal told a different story. He handed it to Barney first, the red goop slushing as he cradled the bag.

"This is the blood and flesh of my mother," Asher told his cabal. "Take a drink and pass it around."

Barney stared at the bag's contents with a pinched face.

"Don't just stare at it," Asher said. "You said you hungered for more blood. Now drink up."

Raising the bag, Barney angled it and opened his mouth to accept a mouthful of gore. A strand of Mom's hair dangled from his chin. Barney swallowed, and his belly shook as he forced himself to keep the human remains down. He passed the bag to Ximena, and she looked at Asher with haunted eyes.

"Even the doctrines of God's church promote cannibalism," Asher told his acolytes. "Christ's followers eat his body in the form of wafers and drink his blood in the form of wine. As with everything the Christians do, their ideas of sin and salvation were stolen from paganism and other pre-Christian religions, dating back to human sacrifices and the mystic rites of cannibalism. For as long as there have been religions, man has hoped to partake of immortality and divinity by devouring the flesh and blood of his incarnated God or some divine messenger. I am Satan's messenger, and my mother's blood is my blood. I have offered her, for every religion preaches salvation through sacrifice. Our salvation is found in the arms of Lucifer."

Ximena closed her eyes tight and drank, then passed the bag to Violet, everyone taking turns slurping the bloody stew.

"Trust me as your sorcerer," Asher told them. "My mother's flesh will protect you all, just as her skeletal remains protect my house. Through her death, I was born again. My power is beyond your understanding, but you must trust in it if you want it to work for you."

His followers agreed that they did.

As they started back to their cars, Lenny walked alongside Asher. "I love what you've been doing with the cult. We're on the right path here. It's really starting to feel like a family."

"Every one of us has a need for family. The ones we were born into failed us."

"Actually, in my case, I was the one to let my family down." Lenny drew a cigarette from the hard case in his breast pocket. "When I was a teenager, I was on acid all the time. I did it so much it started to feel weird to *not* be on it, you know? But somehow, I managed to keep my drug use from my folks. See, parents were different in the '80s. They didn't obsess over their kids the way people do now, and I came and went as I pleased. But my folks didn't want to leave my little sister, Joanie, alone. She was thirteen years younger than me, so sometimes when my folks went out, I was put in charge of watching her.

"One summer day, I was babysitting her but decided to drop acid. So I'm trippin' out listening to the new Overkill album, and it's not until an hour or so goes by that I realize I haven't seen Joanie in a while. Couldn't find her in her room or anywhere in the house. She'd been complaining about wanting to go swimming, so I went out to the above ground pool we had in the backyard, and there was my four-year-old sister, floating face down in the water. At some point, she'd snuck out to it, and I was too busy trippin' to even notice." He lit his cigarette, the orange glow of the lighter highlighting the age in his face. "Things with my family were never the same after Joanie died. My folks told me it wasn't my fault, but it was obvious they blamed me, and with good reason. I don't think Mom and Pop ever forgave me for what happened. So I left home when I turned eighteen. Soon enough, I met your uncle Rex. He was my gateway to Satanism, which I was drawn to 'cause it gave me a sense of belonging to something bigger than myself. Then Rex started gaining followers, giving me a new family. Now, thanks to you, I'm part of another one. That's something I didn't expect to have again, so thank you."

"Thank me by doing this convent thing right," Asher said. "This could be huge for us. Don't let me down."

"You don't need to worry about that, Master. I promise."

Asher took the girls with him and sent the men to scope out the nunnery. He had a text from his father on his mother's phone, agreeing to come by tonight if Mom was still open to it. Asher could sense his *birth father's* desperation. It was embarrassing seeing a man grovel at a woman's feet like this. It went against the natural order of things.

Posing as Mom, Asher sent a message back, telling Dad to come by at seven-thirty. Asher would have Violet and Ximena tidy up the house and make something to eat. Asher was not the soft simp his dad was. He was a real man, and real men dominated their bitches. Women and girls didn't just deserve to be controlled and abused; they also wanted it—especially the ones who said they didn't.

Girls like Callie.

THIRTY-THREE

THE MASTER BEDROOM WAS BEYOND repair, so Ximena and Violet were tasked with cleaning up the rest of the house before Dad's arrival. Asher told them not to touch any of the symbols he'd painted on the windowsills and doorways. On the way there, he'd stopped to pick up scented candles and other deodorizers to conceal the musk of death. The girls wore only panties as they washed the bloody footprints out of the carpet. Though they did this to keep their clothes clean, Asher enjoyed seeing their blood-splattered tits sway as they scrubbed on their hands and knees. Once the house was in passable shape, he had his girls wash each other for his amusement. Then he told them the plan, and the trio set everything up, hiding the proper tools in the master bedroom.

When Dad pulled into the driveway, the girls stayed in the bedroom to wait. Asher had already put his mother's car in the garage, where it would stay until he had time to dispose of it. He watched his old man from the window—the sunken shoulders, the protruding beer belly, the slow shuffle to the porch. Under the light, his hair looked even thinner, his wrinkles deeper. Asher was disgusted, ashamed to have come out of this pathetic man's dickhole.

"Hey, Dad," he said as he opened the door.

"Asher!" Dad said with a smile. "Is that you under all that hair? Boy, it sure grows fast when you're young. Not like mine." Dad stepped in for a hug that curdled Asher's stomach. "It's so good to see you, son."

"Yeah, you too."

Dad got a closer look at him. "You seem so different since I last saw you."

"Unibrows and sideburns are back in style."

"Okay," Dad said with a chuckle, in too good a mood to question his son's grooming. "Where's Mom? I didn't see her car."

"She's not here right now."

"Oh. Am I early? I thought she said seven-thirty."

"She got caught up."

"All right, then. Say, is that your Challenger parked out front?"

"Yeah. Ain't she a beaut?"

"A real gem. You know, I had a Mustang when I was in my early twenties. Seems like a hundred years ago, but damned if I don't still think about that car. We get sentimental as we get older, I guess."

"Is that why men your age go through a midlife crisis?"

Dad raised his eyebrows. "Only some do."

"You were just talking about how much you missed driving a muscle car. That's one of those things a guy in a midlife crisis always buys—a flashy car to make up for a limp dick."

Asher could tell he'd hit a nerve, but his father tried to laugh it off. "I drive a Volvo. That's enough for me."

"What about younger women?" Asher asked. "Dating any college students yet?"

Dad laughed again. "You must be joking! I'm fifty-four, son. I'm not rich or a celebrity, and I don't work in a field that involves any interaction with college students. I'm too busy to date women my own age, let alone chase some young thing."

"Mom hasn't been too busy to date."

The look that befell Dad's face assured Asher he'd been unaware of his former wife's active love life.

"She's been fucking this guy named Sam," Asher said. "You know him?"

"Jesus, Asher, don't talk about your mother that way."

"I'm just telling you the truth. She's probably riding him right now."

"Hey! That's enough. You don't talk that way about your mother, especially not to your father." Huffing, Dad turned to hang up his coat. "Your mom told me you were having some issues. Now I see what she means."

"Issues?"

"She's worried about you, son. Now that I see you in person, I can't say I blame her. You don't talk to her like that, do you?"

Asher smirked. "Not anymore."

"You ought to appreciate her. She took you in when you lost your job and Rebecca broke up with you. Not to mention her carrying you for nine months—and you were *not* an easy birth, Mr. Come-Out-Backwards. Her labor lasted nineteen hours. A boy should always love and respect his mother."

"And what about his father?"

Dad put his hands on his hips. "I would hope you love and respect both of your parents."

"I admit I wasn't any easy birth—either time."

"What?"

"Never mind."

"Look, son. Whatever it is you're going through, you know I'm always here to talk about it, right? You're old enough to understand that just because I don't live in this house right now doesn't mean I'm not still your father."

Only he wasn't Asher's father. Not anymore.

"You said you 'don't live in this house right now.' As if it's only temporary," Asher said. "I thought Mom left you for good."

"Things change. Your mom and I have a lot to talk about. That's why she invited me over tonight."

"You don't think you're clinging to false hope? Women love to mess with the minds of emotionally vulnerable men."

"Your mother has never been one of those types."

Asher smirked. "Things change."

Dad walked past Asher on his way to the kitchen, patting his son's shoulder. "Want a beer?"

"Always."

"Man, it reeks of bleach and air freshener in here. Your mother didn't have to deep clean just because I was coming to dinner."

Dad returned with two bottles, motioned toward the kitchen table, and they sat down across from one another.

"Nothing like a father and son bonding over a couple of cold ones," Dad said. "Why don't we talk about your love life instead of mine. How's the Vincent girl treating you? Veronica, right?"

"Violet. And she treats me the way I tell her to."

"You make it sound so one-sided."

"There's nothing wrong with a woman submitting to a man, especially when she wants to do it."

Dad shrugged. "Hey, she's your girl. I just know that, in my experience, a good relationship is built on mutual respect."

"*You're* lecturing *me* on how I treat my girlfriends? Your marriage was a failure, and you've not dated anyone since. Maybe if you'd dominated Mom instead of letting her dominate you—"

Dad slammed his beer down on the tabletop. "Watch it, buster! You're *way* out of line."

"Well, it's not like you can ground me now, is it?"

"Damn it, Asher—"

"Relax, okay? I don't want to argue with you, Dad. I just don't want to be told how to handle my relationships. I'm a grown man."

"I wish you'd act like it."

"Look, let's not fight. I really am glad you could make it tonight."

Dad simmered down, but his eyes retained irritation. "I am too. But you need to mellow out. I'm your dad, not one of your buddies."

"I know, and I actually have a surprise for you." Asher stood. "See, I was thinking about the whole midlife crisis thing. I know it can't be easy to be at this stage of life, so I got you a present, something that always makes middle-aged men feel better about getting old."

Dad chuckled. "I hope you're telling me that Challenger outside is really for me."

"Better," Asher said. He shouted toward the master bedroom. "Ladies!"

The door opened, and Ximena came out first, still wearing nothing but her panties with Dragon the snake draped around her neck, his tail covering one nipple. When Dad saw her, the beer slipped out of his hand, and he stumbled to right it before it could spill. Ximena drew closer, her bangs sweeping over dark eyes that locked on Dad's. She ran her hands down her thighs and back up again, cupping her breasts and pushing them together to increase her cleavage.

Dad's jaw dropped. He looked back to Asher. "Did … did you hire a stripper?"

"No. I don't have to pay to get women to do what I want. I simply demand it."

Dad was about to saying something but lost focus as Violet came walking down the hall. She wore only a black bra and panties with her leather boots. After washing each other, the women had also done each other's hair and makeup, and Violet's lips were red as summer tomatoes. Her lithe body was enough to silence any man, her skin flawless with youth, the exciting parts Barbie-pink. If Dad recognized her as the girl next door, it didn't show. Violet came beside Ximena, and they stepped closer to Dad, who only sat there, stunned. Asher wondered how long it had been since the old man had seen a naked woman in person. Had Mom been the last one, before she'd even gotten the new tits? What an utterly depressing thought.

"Aren't they nice?" Asher asked.

Dad was too nervous to say anything in front of the girls. He looked at Asher as if to ask what was going on, but then his gaze went right back to the nude nymphets standing in front of him, rubbing their crotches and playing with their nipples. The looks they gave him were innocent yet seductive. Ximena stepped to Dad's chair and slowly straddled him. Violet came around the back of the chair to play with what was left of the old man's hair, scratching him softly before licking her finger and running it over his bottom lip. Dad was visibly shaking. His eyes were huge with confusion.

"Go ahead," Asher told him. "You can touch them."

Dad hesitated, so Ximena took his hand and cupped it to her breast. She put her fingers over his and made him squeeze.

"Hooo, boy," Dad said, gently taking his hand away. "I don't know what's happening here, but whatever it is, I'm sure we shouldn't be doing it."

It was hard to tell who he was saying this to.

"C'mon, Dad," Asher said. "You can't tell me you don't want to fuck a hot, young piece of ass."

Dad mumbled. "I wasn't ready for any of this."

Violet leaned over his shoulders and unhooked her bra, putting one cup on Dad's head like a yarmulke. She brushed a tit against his cheek. Ximena started grinding on him in a silent lap dance, each of Asher's girls following orders. But Dad didn't know how to react to it. The women's sexuality excited but also intimidated him, making him sweat for a variety of reasons.

"Son," Dad said. "I'm here to see your mother. We don't want her finding us like this."

"Real men don't cower from women!" Asher snapped. "A real man sees what he wants and takes it, regardless of any consequences to himself or others. This is a lesson you should've taught me, but instead, I have to teach it to you."

Dad politely tried to get out from under Ximena, but she pressed her legs tight to pin him, and Violet pushed him down into the seat, kissing his neck. As they toyed with him, Dad's resistance weakened. There was no doubt this was the first time more than one woman was crawling all over him like this, and his arousal began to outweigh his delusions of nobility.

"A hard-on has no conscience," Asher told him.

As Ximena grinded on his crotch, Violet stepped out of her panties so her bare crotch was just inches from Dad's face. His eyes refused to close. His nostrils widened as he breathed in the perfume of her teenage pussy.

"Oh ... oh, my sweet heaven," he muttered.

Now, Asher knew he had him, so he gave the girls the signal. When they got Dad out of his chair, the front of his khakis was tented by an erection. Ximena grabbed him by it to lead him into the hall. The look on Dad's face made Asher wonder if the old man had just cum in his pants. Not that it mattered. It wasn't like Asher would really let the old man fuck his girls. Ximena and Violet were Asher's property, same as the Challenger or his record collection. He would tempt others with what was his but would never share anything again. In a world that only takes, only a fool gives. Charity is a tax on saps. He'd not brought his birth father here to get him laid. He'd brought him here to be seduced by the women but had a different result in mind.

"I don't know if I can do this," Dad told Ximena as they drew closer to the bedroom door. "I don't think I can have sex with you."

She smirked. "Then at least let us suck your dick."

Asher couldn't have been prouder of her. Having been a dirty girl before Asher even met her, Ximena was a better seductress than Violet, as more experienced women tend to be. Asher understood why men wanted to deflower cute virgins who had no idea what good sex was, but there was also something to be said for sluts. Asher believed they got a bad rap when they ought to be celebrated for not being cockteasers. As an incubus, he could turn any female into a cum-thirsty whore, but the ones who were like that to begin with were special, not just to him but also to Satan. Hell was full of sluts.

Clearly, Dad had never experienced the joy of fucking a dirty whore, and the women he had fucked he could probably count on one hand. He'd never had a girl ask to suck his cock; he always had to beg them for it. Perhaps he'd been handsome as a young man, but those days were far behind him. Now, he was just as saggy as women his age. His body was as soft as his personality. Asher wondered if the old man had popped a Viagra on the way over just in case Mom wanted to have make-up sex, and if that was the only way he'd been able to get hard with the girls. He couldn't imagine his father main-taining an erection on will alone.

"Your mother will be here any minute," Dad said to Asher.

"No, she won't. Mom isn't going to interrupt, and she'll never find out. Trust me."

"Yeah," Violet said, petting the old man. "Trust us."

As they reached the bedroom door, the lingering odor of death overpowered the air fresheners. Dad scrunched his face as the stink hit him, but he didn't say anything. He was too lost to the gorgeous ladies pawing at him for sex, as any middle-aged divorcé would be. They were young enough to be his daughters but behaved like they wanted him to put babies in them. Dad was trapped in a porn fantasy come to life. All he could do now was allow himself to be carried away.

Ximena pushed the door inward. The room was wallpapered with dried gore, and the floor was stained with Mom's blood. The waves of feces Beelzebub brought here during his last visit had now caked into every crevice of the bedroom. As he was led into this pit of hu-man waste, Dad stumbled back, but Asher pushed him forward again. Dad groaned in disgust as he was forced into the room, his eyes bulg-ing as he took it all in.

"What the hell happened here?" he asked.

Asher raised his left hand and turned the palm toward his dad. The wound of the pentagram suddenly reopened, the cuts weeping black blood. The skin of his hand began to ripple, and blisters ap-peared, only to pop immediately, spewing a foul custard rife with tiny insects that flew from the ooze. They formed a dark cloud that en-cased Dad's head, discombobulating him as Asher's minions dragged him to his soiled marital bed.

298

"Asher!" Dad cried for help. "What is this? Asher, stop this!"

But his son had only nefarious intentions. Whatever love the two once shared had been dissolved by time and distance, and what little affection remained had been tainted by Asher's diminishing respect for the man. He wasn't looking at his father anymore. He was only looking at James Benton, a man who could have been his son's role model if he'd only had an ounce of testosterone. If he'd smacked Asher's mother around instead of always caving to her, Asher wouldn't have wasted so much time being nice to girls who did not want or deserve it. From his parents' shitty example, Asher had been taught the wrong way to treat women. That's why Rebecca had left him. If it wasn't for his father being such a pusillanimous turd, Asher would have grown up with more strength and confidence of his own. It was a harsh realization to come to, but it hardly mattered now that Asher had a new father.

As the girls tore Dad's clothes off, he tried to resist them but was choking on the stinging insects flying up his nose. Ximena managed to get his shoes and khakis off, and Violet tugged his collared shirt in opposite directions, causing the buttons to pop free. His fat belly was graffitied by stretchmarks and moles, his man-boobs covered in wiry gray hair. When Ximena stripped him of his boxer shorts, Dad's dick had gone soft and lay draped over his pendulous scrotum like a salted snail. Looking at it, Asher could understand why Mom had chosen to fuck Sam instead. He had no idea what her new boyfriend was like, but Sam was bound to be an improvement over this flabby waste of life.

"Asher!" Dad said, coughing on bugs. "Please, help me!"

Asher opened the drawer of the nightstand to retrieve the rape kit and other tools put there while preparing for the evening. Withdrawing two sets of handcuffs, he climbed onto the bed with the others. He was stronger than his dad—especially now—and had no trouble cuffing his wrists to the bedposts so the old man was in a Y shape. Asher shooed the swarm of insects away to better see the terror in his dad's face. When he screamed for help, Asher took the wad of Mom's panties from his pocket and stuffed them into his old man's mouth, then sealed it in with duct tape. It amused him that this was the closest Dad would ever get to Mom's pussy again. Ximena sat on Dad's legs to keep him from kicking as Violet tied his ankles to the bottom posts with wires, tight enough to cut off circulation.

Then Asher brought out the nutcracker.

"I've realized something about myself," he told Dad as he hovered over him. "I enjoy genital mutilation. At first, I thought it was just a psychosexual thing, but that's only part of the reason I mangle vaginas. I see that now, because I have no sexual attraction to male genitalia, and yet I have the urge to destroy them too." He opened and closed the nutcracker as if he were playing with a butterfly knife. "Now, I understand that my affinity for genital mutilation stems from a deep-seated hatred for reproduction. I'm a proponent of human extinction. Did you know your son is a serial killer? I'm sure you've seen my work on the news—my new family's work." He delighted in the horror behind his dad's eyes. "I kill the living, but why stop there? I already prevented one fetus from being born. If I must perform the abortions myself, then so be it. In fact, I couldn't be happier. But back to ripping up private parts. I think I do it for a variety of reasons. It's shocking and vile, and with attractive women, it gives me a dirty thrill. But my hatred for humankind is the real driving force behind it. Genitals are gateways to more babies, and as tasty as a baby can be, I'd rather see them eradicated. So why not start at the source?"

Asher had Ximena lift Dad's low-hanging balls so he could set the clamp of the nutcracker around a testicle. Dad shrieked behind his gag even before Asher applied pressure—not that Asher could blame him. He gradually squeezed the handle, feeling the testicle's resistance, then suddenly squeezed *hard*. Crushing the ball, Asher twisted the scrotum with the nutcracker's steel teeth, cutting into the sack. Dad bucked and squealed but couldn't go anywhere. Watching the torture, Violet's smile went from humorous to sexual, aroused by the suffering of others. Asher had taught her well. Using the nutcracker like a vise, Asher pulverized his dad's other testicle, and Violet started playing with herself.

The room grew hotter as the walls of gore began to throb. They inflated and deflated like a breathing chest. Revived by horror, the dried bodily fluids grew moist again, slicking everything with putrescence. The ceiling drizzled red rain.

Drawing the knife from his rape kit, Asher handed it to Ximena. Pain had brought his dad to the edge of unconsciousness, but the sensation of a sharp blade against his penis brought him back, a nauseous dread awakening him.

"May I do it now, Master?" Ximena asked.

"As you please, sweetheart."

She cut into the base of Dad's penis and began to saw.

Blood gushed as a vein in his cock was opened, and Ximena bent over to suck it up in a gruesome blowjob. Still, she sawed. Excited by fresh gore, Violet crawled over and started lapping up the excess blood flowing from Dad's groin. Finally, Ximena severed the cock completely. She put the head of it into her mouth and used it as a straw, sucking up blood through the urethra. Violet ran her tits through the pooling gore and slicked her clit with it. Holding the dead dick in her mouth, Ximena came closer to Violet until they were face-to-face, and Violet took the stump end of the cock into her mouth. Asher smiled as his girls chewed his old man's cock like the dogs in *Lady and the Tramp* with a strand of spaghetti, inching closer to kissing with every bite. Blood and other penile fluids sprinkled their breasts as they pressed their bodies together.

Asher reached into the drawer for Ximena's kris dagger. He poked a hole through each of his dad's flabby tits but didn't go deep enough to puncture any organs. Angling the blade, he ripped the nipples in half from the inside out. When Dad didn't react, Asher realized he was out cold. He carved into the belly—a flesh canvas in the art of murder. When he was finished, the wounds formed a single word.

Leviathan.

It was appropriate that the beast's name be etched into human flesh, especially when that flesh belonged to a sacrificial father. Asher was sending out an infernal invitation. He put a stamp on this invite by carving a Leviathan cross into Dad's forehead. His only resistance was a fluttering of the eyelids.

Asher did not have to wait long.

The blood dripping from the ceiling became a steady drizzle. Finished with their little meal, the girls looked up and opened their mouths to the blood rain, their eyes widening as the ceiling became a vortex of gore. It began to boil and then burst into crimson flames that spiraled over their heads. Swimming in the fire were all the people the cult had killed. Their broken bodies were covered in wounds and severe burns, with large warts and skin tags distorting their features. Their eyes melted in their sockets. They screamed but could not speak with their tongues being devoured by centipedes. Asher and his death cult had sent these poor souls straight to Hell, and he delighted in knowing their suffering had only just begun.

Asher led the girls off the mattress, leaving their offering cuffed on the bed. He kissed Violet, then Ximena, and they cuddled to either side of him, planting little kisses on his cheeks and neck as they moaned in salacious rapture. Even as the godless beast Leviathan emerged from the cyclone of fire, the girls remained focused on Asher, caressing their master and begging him for sex.

"Feast," Asher told the hovering serpent.

Leviathan's massive jaws opened like a beartrap. Fangs the size of railroad spikes gnashed within its head as it descended over Asher's birth father. The beast made a sound like an avalanche, causing the entire house to vibrate, pictures falling from the walls and bulbs shattering in the light fixtures. Windowpanes cracked. Drywall fell like snow.

Leviathan bit into the sacrifice. With one tug, the beast tore Dad's torso free from the limbs cuffed to the bedposts. The severed arms swung as they dangled. It's many eyes rolling, Leviathan tossed the carcass in the air and snapped it in half, Dad's belly and groin landing in the bed as the great eel of Hell chomped on the head, shoulders, and ribcage. Guts dangled from its jaws in wet festoons as it retreated into the realm of fire, satiated by this Satanic sacrifice.

Asher put the girls back on the gore-soaked mattress.

"Now fuck me in my dead father's blood," he said.

THIRTY-FOUR

XIMENA WAS EXHAUSTED. ACCEPTING HIS acolytes needed sleep even though he didn't, Asher dropped her off at home, then drove back to the Vincent house with Violet. The night was still young.

So was her little sister.

Melissa opened the door before they could even reach the porch. Asher figured she'd been watching from the window, wishing for his return. Melissa wore a black silk robe that ended above the knee and had on more makeup than he'd ever seen on her before, making her look like a Paris whore. A pushup bra showcased her breasts, her blond hair ending in beautiful curls, the varicose veins at her ankles hidden by thigh-high stockings. The housewife had made herself up for him even though she'd had no idea when he might come back. *How marvelous.*

The moment the door closed behind them, Melissa pressed her palms to Asher's chest and wrapped a leg around his. She paid no attention to her daughter. Violet was no longer as important to her as Asher was. Patting the housewife on the butt, Asher walked to the kitchen for a drink, only to find a bottle of wine and two glasses sitting on the island block—the same place he'd first gone down on Melissa. When he turned to smile at her, he noticed how poorly she was able to walk. He'd almost forgotten how wrecked he'd left her last time, having allowed literal demons to have a go at her. It was amusing to see her stumble like a drunk.

"This is from my husband Joel's collection," Melissa said, holding up the dusty wine bottle. "I broke it out for whenever you were ready to come back to me. Joel's a real wine snob. He even made a little cellar in our basement, just like he turned our garage into a natural disaster bunker with all his stupid power banks and sleeping bags. Anyway, out of all of them, this bottle is his prized possession. It's the most expensive too. I was pissed when I found out what he'd paid for it."

Asher sighed. "Yeah, yeah. Where's Callie?"

Melissa's face went slack. "She's upstairs playing video games. Please, Master ... she can't satisfy you the way I can." Melissa pressed her palms to his chest again, looking up at him with a strange combination of desire and fright. "Please, fuck me. I don't care how torn up I am down there. I want you to destroy me all over again."

"In good time," Asher said, pushing her away.

"I'll do whatever you say. You can do whatever you want to me."

"I'm very aware of that. Now go fetch your daughter."

"Please," she begged. "Your love is like a drug. I *need* you inside me."

Asher smacked her across the face. "Don't be so fucking needy! You'll do as you're told, bitch, or I'll put an army of fire ants beneath your skin and have you shit rusty nails."

Tears streaming down her cheeks, Melissa dropped to her knees before her master, still pleading for sex. Asher put his hand on top of her head and pushed her back until she fell on her ass. Violet watched all of this with a cold expression, as if she were watching an infomercial instead of her mother's degradation.

"Violet," Asher said, "go fetch your little sister for me."

"Yes, Master."

Violet disappeared up the staircase. In the mood for something spicy, Asher grabbed a bottle of habanero hot sauce from the fridge. He drank it straight from the bottle as he glowered down at Melissa.

"I have no doubt you're dying to get fucked, but something tells me you have an ulterior motive … don't you, Melissa?"

"No, Master …"

"Bullshit. You know Violet is a lost cause—she's even more hooked on me than you are—but you think maybe you can spare Callie the same fate. You're begging me to take you instead of her."

"No! I mean … yes … but only because I want you all to myself."

Asher smacked her across the face again. Melissa whimpered, and he smacked the other cheek, whipping her head back and forth. He didn't stop until a drop of blood exited her nostril, then grabbed her by the hair and forced her head back to look up at him.

"You don't get to decide what happens to you, your daughters, or anyone else," Asher told her. "If you try to intervene, I promise I'll make your worst nightmares come true. You'll suffer, but not as badly as your little girls will. Do I make myself clear?"

Melissa nodded as he let her go, sniffling back blood and tears. "Yes, Master. I want only to serve you and make you happy. I love you so, so much."

"Love?" Asher said with a laugh. "You're a married woman who fucks her daughter's boyfriend. What the fuck do you know about love?"

Melissa wept softly. It was enough to make Asher reconsider fucking her right then and there—nothing was more stimulating than fucking a crying woman—but he had bigger plans for the evening. Besides, Melissa needed to learn her lesson.

Putting the bottle of hot sauce in his coat pocket, he grabbed Melissa's arm and raised her to her feet. "Go clean yourself up. You don't want your daughters seeing you like this, and frankly, I don't want to look at you either. Pitiful old whore, you disgust me."

Whimpering apologies, Melissa limped to the bathroom and shut the door behind her.

When Violet came downstairs with her sister, Asher stared straight at Callie, a faint crimson circling his pupils. Callie gave him a shy smile and waved. Though not as garish as her mother, she'd put on makeup in anticipation of a night out. She wore sneakers and re-laxed-fit jeans, and a powder blue sweater with sleeves that covered half of her hands. Her blond ponytail bobbed as she came down the last steps, and the Vincent sisters joined Asher in the kitchen.

He pinched Callie's chin. "Aren't you just a pearl."

The girl blushed, smiling. "Oh, shut up …"

"Ready for your big night out?"

"Absolutely! What're we doing?"

"Well, for starters, let's have a little drink."

He uncorked the imported wine and filled the glasses, handing one to each of them, then took a swig from the bottle. Joel Vincent may have been a cuck, but his taste in wine was superb. Seeing Violet drink, Callie shook her head.

"Are you crazy?" she asked. *"Mom's home.* If she catches us drinking, she'll—"

"Don't worry about your mother," Asher told her.

"I can't help it. She's been acting weird all day."

"I mean don't worry about her punishing you."

"Why not?"

Asher smiled. "Because punishing you is my job."

Callie gulped, her eyes never leaving his. When Asher pointed at the glass, she took a sip, her face souring as she swallowed. Clearly, she wasn't a drinker like her old man.

"Um ... what do you mean by punish me?" Callie asked.

"Just that bad girls need a spanking now and then. Isn't that right, Violet?"

Violet smirked. "She's a bad girl, all right. She doesn't need a spanking—she needs a swift kick to the ass with your steel-toed boot."

Asher gave her a subtle look of approval. Already, Violet was stepping into the role of her sister's bully so he could be Callie's savior.

"I'm not a bad girl," Callie said defensively.

"Oh?" Asher said, brushing her cheek with the back of his hand. "Does that mean you're a good girl?"

"Okay, now I *know* what you mean by *that.*"

"Then answer the question. Are you gonna be a good girl for me?"

Callie blushed so hard she looked like a beet. "Asher! Oh my God ..."

She looked at her sister as if to tell Asher she was standing right there. He was Violet's boyfriend, after all. As far as Asher knew, she hadn't told Violet about what had happened when he'd driven Callie to school, how he'd encouraged her to touch his dick. But Asher could tell she'd been thinking about it a lot.

"Listen to me," he told Callie. "We're taking you out tonight because I know you're ready for it. You're more mature than other people your age because you're smarter than they are. You're fifteen going on twenty-one. It's time to leave childhood behind, Callie. You're not Daddy's little girl anymore."

Callie smiled up at him with eyes bright as sunshine.

"Don't let us down tonight," Violet told her. "Don't fucking embarrass me."

Callie frowned with hurt. Her pink face was wrought with confusion, but she did not seem afraid, only nervous. This was her audition to hang out with an older, cooler crowd, and like any teenage girl, she wanted to be liked and seen as a young woman instead of a child.

"Don't worry," Asher said, leaning down so his face was level with Callie's. "I believe in you, sweetheart."

✚

Though she admitted she'd never done it before, Callie raised her tongue and let Asher put the tab of LSD in her mouth. He and Violet dropped acid too, but he'd given Callie a double dose from the sheet he'd found stashed in a brick of Terry's coke. As they drove into the night, Asher drank from the wine bottle, and Violet lit a joint and passed it back to her sister, coaching her on how to toke. One hit and Callie coughed like she was dying. Asher chuckled. Violet shook her head in disapproval. The drugs required time to kick in, so Asher took the sisters on a joyride, the music of Abramelin rumbling from the speakers.

Asher looked at Callie in the rearview mirror. "Your sister tells me you don't like metal."

"Oh …" Callie rushed for the save. "No, I mean—I like some of it."

"Liar," Violet said. "Fuckin' Bon Jovi is too much for you."

"I don't even know what that is!"

Asher laughed like hell.

Callie continued trying to sound cooler than she was. "I don't hate metal. I'm just not as familiar with it as you guys. I'd love to learn about some more bands."

"Yeah, right," Violet said. "You didn't like any of the ones I played for you."

"Well, maybe Asher has better taste in bands than you do."

Asher liked seeing the girl snap back at her big sister. He wanted Violet to taunt Callie tonight, but not so much that she would grow concerned about what was really going on here. Having her sister there gave Callie a false sense of security she wouldn't have if she and Asher were alone. The little fool thought she was safe, and Asher wanted to keep it that way for as long as possible, so when she finally realized the real reason she'd been invited out tonight, her terror would be bright and beautiful and absolute.

"I've got a record you really need to hear," Asher told Callie. "But I'm saving that for later." He changed the death metal to something lighter but equally good. "You just need to step into heavy metal gradually, Callie. Check this out. This band's called Icon. They're from the hair metal era but not as poppy as Poison or Warrant, who have some fucking nerve calling themselves metal at all. See, this kind of music is a nice gateway to the heavier stuff. Take baby steps, baby."

Callie bobbed her head to the beat. "*This* I like."

"Atta girl," he said, passing the wine bottle back to her.

Violet scoffed. "Callie, you'd say you like the sound of wet farts if you thought it'd impress Asher."

"I would not!"

"Your idea of good music is the Michael Graves era of The Misfits."

Asher groaned. "For fuck's sake, I'll take the wet farts over that garbage."

"Why're you being such a bitch, Violet?" Callie asked. "I thought you wanted me to come out with you guys, but all you've been doing is dumping on me."

Violet turned in her seat to snap back at Callie, but Asher gripped her thigh and spoke before she could. "Lay off her, Violet. Callie's cool. You just gotta give her a chance."

Callie smiled at him through the mirror. "Thank you, Asher."

"No problem, sweetheart. Besides, I love the sound of wet farts. The wetter, the better."

Callie laughed, her braces glimmering in the dashboard light. Asher was feeling the initial effects of the LSD, so he was sure the girls were feeling it too, along with the chasers of alcohol and marijuana. He drove deeper into the blackness of the backroads, through farmland with no houses or streetlights.

"Where are we?" Callie asked, leaning forward so her head was between the front seats.

"Never-never land," Violet said.

"I don't think I've ever been this far into the boonies. I figured you guys were gonna take me to Kirby's bar or something—though I suck at pool."

"Those places just don't excite me anymore," Asher said. "Only losers hang out in bars."

"Then where're we going?"

"I've got a special little place in the woods I want you to see."

"Like, a cabin?"

"Better."

"Is it far?"

He grinned back at her. "Enough with the questions. You don't want to ruin the surprise, do you?"

"No …" She rubbed her eyes. "Asher … I feel funny."

"Good."

"Everything's all, like, ripples." She wiggled her fingers in front of her. "It's like I'm underwater or something."

"That's exactly how I want you to feel."

"You do?" She scooted to the edge of her seat to put her head on his shoulder. "You're sweet."

"Sweet as candy."

Violet stared at them, her face pinched in jealousy, but she didn't dare protest. She knew Callie was falling right where Asher wanted her—*in his grip*—and would never do anything to go against his wishes, even at the expense of her own. Asher patted Callie's head and hummed along to the music to comfort her. She kept her head right on his shoulder until they reached the dirt lot, then looked all around as Asher put the car in park. There was nothing to see but dead trees, and when Asher turned off the headlights, the pitch blackness was all-encompassing.

"So where's your special place, Asher?" Callie asked.

"We have to walk the rest of the way."

They got out of the car, and Asher took a swig from the habanero sauce in his pocket. He wanted more heat, inside and out, compelled by a demonic force to make everything burn, even his guts.

He handed Callie the boombox. She seemed happy to be trusted with something that belonged to him.

"Oh, man," she said. "It's so cold out. I hope it isn't far."

"Trust me," Asher said. "It'll be worth it."

He stared into the girl's dilated eyes. He was tempted to use his incubus power to control her but knew that wouldn't do—not in this situation. Lenny was right when he'd said Lucifer was very particular about certain things, and now that Rex had taught Asher everything, he had no excuse to not get it exactly right. Besides, he understood why Lucifer wouldn't want the girl to be hypnotized into going along with this. That would diminish her terror and lessen the cruelty. Asher didn't want that any more than his new father did. Like Lucifer, he feasted on misery and horror, and the more innocent the target, the greater the reward.

Cloud coverage smothered the moon, leaving the woodland in complete darkness. All was silent. Asher put himself between the sisters and took their hands, guiding them into thickets of decay. The girls hunched their shoulders against the cold. Asher breathed it in deep, knowing it would soon be very warm. Violet must have known it too, because she was gripping his hand tightly. She'd been out here several times but was more frightened than Callie was to be in these woods tonight, having prior knowledge her sister didn't. Asher hadn't told Violet exactly what was going to happen, but he didn't have to. Her mounting anxiety was proof of that.

When they reached the clearing, Asher took the boombox from Callie and queued *Music to Sacrifice Virgins To*.

"This is the good stuff," he told her.

Callie seemed less interested in the music than she was in their surroundings. "What're we doing here? Where's the cabin?"

"I never said there was a cabin."

She looked all around, but whatever there was to see was shrouded by darkness and distorted by the hallucinogens she'd ingested. Callie hugged herself, and Asher knew it was more than the cold she was guarding against. The first tingles of dread were hitting her.

"But what're we doing here?" she asked. "It's so cold and dark."

"Don't worry. I'll make fire soon enough."

Asher turned up the volume of the Satanic record, the guitars crunching and whining with feedback, the voices of the dead roaring from the deepest pits. Stepping behind Callie, he placed his hands on her shoulders. They were taut as piano wires.

"Are we just gonna hang out here and listen to music?" she asked. "Is that really what you guys do for fun?"

She looked to her sister for answers, but Violet had gone silent and refused to look her sister in the eye.

Asher brushed Callie's ear with his lips. "You know, your big sister is into the occult. How about you?"

Callie stepped away, but not aggressively. When she looked at Asher, her enormous pupils made her cartoonishly cute, as if she'd stepped out of an anime comic book.

"Occult?" Callie asked. "You mean, like, Wicca?"

"Something like that. Here. Let me show you."

Asher took a long stick off the ground and started drawing a pentagram in the same patch of dirt Deanna, Paul, and the little girl, Nikki, had been sacrificed. Violet teared up and turned away before her sister could notice. She would do what her master wanted, but Asher couldn't make her like it or make it painless. It was a little disappointing to see this weakness in her. If Violet hoped to ever be a demon bride, she would have to jettison whatever humanity she had left. What better way to get her to do so than to force her to participate in her baby sister's doom?

When the pentagram was complete, Asher etched the Sigil of Lucifer into its center, letting his father know this would be in his honor.

"Is this, like, a séance?" Callie asked.

"In a way," Asher said.

"I've done Ouija boards before. Is it like that?"

"You really do ask too many questions."

Callie pouted. "Sorry. You're not mad at me, are you?"

Her eagerness to please came not from any influence he held over the girl but from an ingrained desire to please everyone. Callie's insecurity was clear. Asher wondered where it had come from, but ultimately, he didn't care. The teen's problems wouldn't bother her much longer anyhow.

"How could I be mad at a sweet pea like you?" Asher asked her.

He put his hand under Callie's chin to raise her face to his, then leaned over to kiss her on the lips. Asher could taste her innocence and smell her sweet dreams, but she didn't kiss him back. Instead she backed away.

"Whoa," Callie said. "What's going on here?"

"Relax," he said. "You're just trippin'. And stoned and drunk."

"But ... you *kissed* me." She looked at Violet, but her sister only stared at the ground. "Asher, why're you kissing me when you're my sister's boyfriend?"

"A good big sister shares with her little sister. Isn't that right, Violet?"

Violet murmured, "Yes, Master."

Callie's brow furrowed. "Did you just call him *master?*"

"She did," Asher said. "If you're smart, you'll do the same."

The apprehension Callie had been showing instantly evolved into real fear. She took a few steps backward as if she might make a run for it. Her dilated eyes scanned her surroundings, but they remained cloaked by an impenetrable darkness. She couldn't even find the trail anymore. Roused by Asher's evil presence, the demons hidden in the wild had closed the woods around the clearing, creating a barricade of thorny briar. There was no escape.

Callie turned back to Asher. "Wait a second … just wait a second, okay?" She looked at her sister but found no help there. "This isn't funny, you guys. I'm getting scared."

"You should be scared," Asher said. "But there's no sense delaying the inevitable, sweetheart."

"Delaying *what?* What're you talking about?" Tears filled the teen's eyes. "I wanna go home now. Will you please just take me home?"

"You are home," he said, pointing at the pentagram in the dirt. "Now lie down in the circle."

She shook her head. "No way. I don't know what you're trying to do, but no way."

Asher shoved her. Callie fell into the pentagram, dust fogging around her. She tried scurrying to her feet, but Asher was quicker, pouncing on her, straddling her, and pinning her arms to her sides when she tried to claw at him. She screamed, but there was no one to hear it. She cried, but there was no one to dry her tears.

"Why?" she bawled. "Why're you doing this to me? I thought you liked me, Asher!"

"Don't take it personally. I don't like anyone, kid. At least not anyone human who's beyond my control. Your sister and I manipulated you into liking me so you wouldn't be afraid to come out here, so you wouldn't fear me the way you should have."

"I just wanted to be friends …"

"And look where that got you. Here's a little tip, sweetheart—not that it'll do you much good now. *Never trust anyone.* The only real friend anyone ever has is themselves."

She wiggled helplessly. "Let me go! Please, just let me go."

"Fighting will only make it worse."

"Please!" she cried. "Please, Asher, don't rape me. Don't let him rape me, Violet!"

"Rape you?" Asher said with a chuckle. "Is that what you think I've brought you out here for? Just to rape you? I only wanted a little kiss. Sure, we had a naughty time when I showed you my dick, but that was just for kicks. I needed to see how pure you really were. If I wanted to fuck you, I could've done that back at your house. It's not like your sister or that whore mother of yours would've stopped me. No, I'm not going to rape you, Callie. I'm going to sacrifi—"

"No!" she bawled, cutting him off. "You *are* gonna rape me! I know it! Please, please, don't. I can't go through that again!"

Asher froze. He looked at Violet, but she seemed as confused as he was.

"What did you just say?" Asher asked Callie.

"Please ... don't rape me."

"No, you said you couldn't go through that *again*. What did you mean by that?"

Blubbering, Callie turned her head away, suddenly ashamed. "I ... I was ..."

"Callie, who raped you?" Asher demanded. She only wept, so he shook her. "Answer me. Tell me who raped you or I *will* rape you."

"Okay!" she cried. "It ... it was the pastor of our church."

Violet's jaw fell. "Reverend Bower?"

Callie nodded with her eyes shut tight. Asher released her arms and sat up, still straddling the girl as he considered the implications of this.

"When did this happen?" he asked.

"Um," Callie said, "about two years ago."

"Two years? He raped you when you were thirteen?"

"Twelve."

"What did he do? Did he just use his hands on you or make you do something to him, or did he go the distance?"

The way Callie's face scrunched at the memory assured Asher the pastor had taken full advantage of her. He rolled his hand over his head with a sigh of frustration. Here he thought he'd had the perfect virgin sacrifice, but Callie's cherry had already been popped by some pedophile preacher. The irony of it was not lost on him. But did rape really count against the girl's purity? If she hadn't consented to the sex, was she still a virgin in the eyes of God? More importantly, would Lucifer accept her as a sublime offering, or would she be just another victim of his death cult, which wouldn't earn him as great of reward?

"What happened?" he asked her.

Through tears, Callie explained she'd been part of the church's youth group and assisted the pastor's wife with Sunday school and fundraisers. Sue Bower was often alone with Callie, giving her plenty of opportunities to sneak the girl to her husband so the dirty bastard could live out his depraved fantasies. With Sue's assistance, Bower had sexually assaulted Callie on five separate occasions and convinced her no one would believe her if she told because he was a respected man of God, whereas she was just a kid, a nobody. Callie believed him, but when the abuse only escalated, she'd finally broken down and told her mother.

Violet started pacing. "Oh my god ... that's it, isn't it? That's why we stopped going to church. Holy shit, does Dad know?"

"No!" Callie said. "I didn't want anybody to know. I made Mom promise not to tell anyone."

"What the fuck? *Why?*"

"Because then I'd always be the girl who got raped by her pastor!" Callie shut her eyes tight again. "I was already hurt. I didn't want to suffer any more because of what happened. I didn't want to have to go to court and give a statement against him. He was right—people would believe him, not me. Everybody knows Reverend Bower and loves him."

Asher was floored by what he was hearing but had no doubt Callie was being truthful. She was shaking just talking about what had happened to her, the trauma still raw.

"Your mother really agreed to stay silent?" he asked.

"Not at first. She wanted to go to the police. I begged her not to, but she insisted, so I told her if she took me to the cops, I'd deny everything I'd told her. I threatened to hurt myself." She sniffed. "Mom was so mad about everything, but she was worried about me too. She saw what it was doing to me."

"So what'd you two do?"

"Mom made an anonymous call to the police station to report Reverend Bower. She left me out of it. I don't know if they investigated him or not, but nothing ever came of it. See what I mean? He was right when he said no one would ever believe he was a rapist. Mom didn't tell Dad why, but she got him to let us leave the church. He was only going to make her happy anyway. Now I won't have to see the Bowers anymore."

Asher glowered. "So that's it?"

"That was the end of it, yeah. Mom came around on the idea of keeping it quiet too. It would only hurt me more if we went after him."

"And what about the other children in that church? Surely, you weren't the only victim. If you turned him in, it might prevent other girls from being assaulted."

Callie looked away in shame. "There wasn't anything else we could do! I just *can't*. And I think it was more important to Mom to protect me."

Asher shook his head. "Your mom is a real piece of work, you know that? A real piece of work."

Violet huffed. "I can't fucking believe this. I can't believe Mom would ..."

"Please, let me go," Callie whimpered.

"Shut up a second," Asher told the girls. "I need to think."

This unexpected revelation put a serious damper on his plans. Should he kill the girl on the chance she still counted as a virgin? Should he kill her regardless because she was still young enough to be a more worthy sacrifice than an adult? Or should he cast his incubus spell over Callie, putting a stranglehold on her soul just as he had her mother and sister? Adding an underage girl to his cabal certainly had its appeal. Surely, Lucifer would be pleased if Asher transformed Callie into another devil worshipping devotee.

"I'm surprised you didn't resist when I had you touch my dick," he told her. "I would've thought you'd have a flashback of sexual assault and freak out."

Now that he wasn't holding her arms down, Callie was beginning to calm, even if she remained fearfully bewildered. "Yours isn't the first penis I've ever seen—I mean besides Reverend Bower's. I'm fifteen. I've fooled around with boys. I just never went all the way. I'm not ready to *give myself* to anyone yet."

"But your pastor *took*."

"Bower doesn't count. That was a whole different thing. It wasn't sex—it was an attack."

"And what about with me?"

"I ... I *liked* you. I knew we shouldn't be doing what we were—I kicked myself for it later because I felt like I'd betrayed Violet—but you just excited me, I guess. You're older. You're cool. I don't know why, but I just wanted to, you know, *touch* you. You made me feel ... different."

"Like a woman?"

"I guess so."

"Like a woman instead of a little girl."

She nodded, and Asher shook his head, grinning. Even when he wasn't deliberately utilizing his incubus abilities, his power drew in every female who had the misfortune of entering his orbit—even young girls. He wondered if it mattered if they were old enough to have sexual desires, if they had to reach puberty before his seductive spell could have any effect on them. Knowing Satan, Asher doubted there were such limitations.

He weighed his options. Though Callie's hands were free, she did not try to scratch or hit him. She was still pinned under him and wasn't going anywhere. The girl seemed to know this. Was she just trying to placate Asher to keep him from doing whatever awful things she believed he was preparing for? If so, what was she willing to do to get out of being hurt?

Asher called Violet over, and she got on her knees beside them. Callie slowly reached for her sister's hand. Violet held it but couldn't seem to come up with any words of comfort. She knew whatever was going to happen wouldn't be good for her little sister. Perhaps it wouldn't be good for Violet either. Though her love for Asher was stronger than anything else she could feel anymore, Violet maintained affection for her family. She'd shown that when they'd gone to her house the night of the slayings at Diego's apartment, when she'd begged Asher to spare her family's lives, not knowing he wasn't intending to kill them. She'd simply assumed that's what he would do. Violet cared about Callie but was trapped under Asher's spell, making it impossible for her not to put his needs first, no matter how evil. Such was the nature of being in any cult, but especially one with a messiah whose supernatural abilities weren't imaginary.

Maybe Violet wasn't cut out to be one of Asher's Satanic brides. Her capacity for evil was colossal but diminished significantly when it came to the people she cared about. She seemed incapable of stifling empathy the way Asher had. Now, he wondered if her weakness could be his fault. Had he not motivated her enough? Had he failed to push the girl beyond her boundaries so she could find bliss in the arms of Lucifer?

Asher came to a decision about what to do with Callie, one that had more to do with Violet than her little sister.

"Ximena proved herself," he said to Violet. "Remember how she stabbed Diego in the face dozens of times? He was the only family she had left. Still, she slaughtered him for me—*for Satan*. She's made a commitment to our family by removing herself from the restraints of her previous one."

Violet's eyes misted. "Master ... I am devoted to you. I'm totally committed to our family and to Satan. Haven't I shown you that with all the things I've done? All the people I murdered …?"

Hearing this, Callie began to squirm again. "No … no …"

When Asher pushed her flat onto the ground, Callie reached out and scratched his face—*hard*. The sting of her attack only heightened his arousal.

"Violet," he said, "put your knees on Callie's arms to pin her down."

Callie screamed, thrashing again, clawing at Asher without success. She could scratch him and make him bleed but was unable to really hurt him. The voices on *Music to Sacrifice Virgins To* became demonic laughter, mocking the girl's horror and egging Asher on. Violet hesitated only briefly before pressing down on her little sister's arms.

"Don't look so sad," Asher told Violet. "You had a pretty good idea what we were coming out here for."

She couldn't deny it.

"I bet you thought the reason I had you bully Callie while I was nice to her was because it would help me seduce her," Asher said. "But let me tell you the real reason, sweetheart. I wanted Callie to be fond of me because it would be that much more horrible for her when I killed her." Callie shrieked, so Asher put his hand over her mouth. "It's always better when your victims know and trust you, Violet, and best of all when they love you. Betrayal adds levels to their suffering, and human misery is The Devil's candy. Ximena understands that. You don't. It's high time I taught you."

A tear fell down Violet's cheek, and she quickly wiped it away, as if embarrassed to have emotions other than the rage, lust, and greed that drives a dedicated Satanist.

"Do you understand what I'm getting at?" Asher asked.

"Yes, Master."

"Good." He took a swig of hot sauce. "Now hold your baby sister down while I rape her."

THIRTY-FIVE

THEY PARKED DOWN THE ROAD from The Bower house, Asher choosing a spot far from any streetlamps. Having been to the house several times to help Sue Bower with church activities, only to be sexually assaulted by the woman's husband, Callie knew where to find her attackers. Asher insisted on going. He had Callie ride shotgun despite the risk of her being better able to jump out of the car than she would have been in the back seat. Now that he'd had his way with the girl, he was turning on the charm again, playing good cop *and* bad cop.

He'd decided to rape Callie instead of killing her, but he wasn't sure why. It was just what he'd been compelled to do after finding out she technically wasn't a virgin. Was Rex encouraging him to keep her alive, just like he'd convinced Asher to hold on to mementos of rape and murder such as panties and body parts, knowing they could be used for black magic? What special purpose could Callie serve? If Rex knew being raped didn't count towards Callie losing her virginity, he would have wanted Asher to make a human sacrifice out of her as initially planned. He wouldn't have coerced Asher into keeping the girl alive. But was it Rex who had gotten him to rape the girl instead of slaughtering her, or had Asher made this choice himself? It was getting harder to tell Rex's thoughts from his own. Though Asher couldn't point to a specific reason for sparing Callie, he knew he hadn't done it out of mercy. It was greed that motivated him. Something told him Callie would be more valuable to him alive.

At first, he'd planned to rape Callie and then have Violet murder her. It seemed like the logical step to take. When it came to killing, Violet needed to be shoved out of her comfort zone. She needed to be tested. So when Asher suddenly changed his mind about murdering Callie, he still wanted to test Violet's loyalty. He had her hold Callie down. This made her an accomplice in her sister's rape. Of course, Violet had obeyed. She was probably just relieved Callie wouldn't have to die tonight. As horrible as rape was, at least people could survive it. The same could not be said for being eviscerated.

He could have used his abilities as an incubus to make Callie submit willingly, but that would not only take away her pain and fear but would also defeat the purpose. The rape wasn't about fucking Callie—it was about getting Violet to participate in her sister's abuse and degradation. Violet hadn't enjoyed it, but she'd done it, and there was no coming back from that.

Callie's life had been spared, but Asher could not stand to be teased with a killing only to have a bloodless night. Someone had to die.

Driving to the Bower house, Asher had twirled Callie's panties in his left hand, sniffing the inside of the crotch. Now that the rape was over, he would use his powers of seduction on Callie after all. He had to keep her around—and close. It was the only way to find out what special purpose she would serve. She would make a fine addition to his death cult. As with the heavy metal music, he just had to break her in. *Baby steps.* Asher had to show her the family's way of life, what it meant to be a Reaper. The best way he knew to convert Callie to Satanism was to empower her. That's what had attracted Asher to the demonic forces. He'd quickly realized that, with Lucifer's power behind him, he didn't have to fear anything anymore. He didn't have to appease anyone but himself and didn't have to worry about money or women or anything else that stressed men his age. Best of all, he didn't have to take shit from anybody ever again. Uncle Rex had given him the greatest gift, and Asher had given this gift to his followers, to a lesser extent. He'd liberated them from society's rules and God's law. He'd shown them the light of hellfire. Callie would receive the same blessings—perhaps even more so if she truly were special—but would only attain them through the same sinister means as the others.

In short, Callie had to kill.

Asher could think of no better victims than the Bowers.

Nothing would empower Callie as much as getting revenge on the people who'd stolen her innocence, destroyed her faith, and scarred her for life. What better way to embolden a girl than to teach her to stand up for herself? The pain she felt right now from being raped by Asher was irrelevant because his incubus spell would erase those negative feelings from her mind, replacing them with stronger feelings of love for him. The memory of the rape would remain, but soon, she would see it as Asher doing what was best for her. Reflecting on it would even start to turn her on. But the pain the Bowers had caused Callie could not be erased, only avenged.

Losing her virginity didn't make Callie a woman.

Killing those who wronged her would.

Before they got out of the car, Asher leaned in for a kiss. Callie didn't fight him—she'd learned that lesson while he'd forced himself on her. His tongue was wet with black spittle, and he ran it along her braces, coating her teeth with his enchanting elixir. Their lips locked, and Asher released his foul breath into the girl's petite body, filling her lungs with a deleterious smog that drove his black magic into her bloodstream. The infection was instantaneous. Callie shut her eyes as the spell took seed within her soul. They were still closed when Asher broke the kiss. He raised her panties to his face again and licked the inside of the crotch. Callie's eyes snapped open. She bucked her hips. Asher licked the panties again, and the girl shuddered in her seat as she inched toward orgasm without Asher even touching her. The movement of his mouth on her panties was psychically transferred to her vagina, making her feel his tongue as if it were hitting her clitoris. Climaxing, Callie's entire body went taut. Asher wondered if it were the first time she'd ever had an orgasm outside of masturbation, or if she'd ever had an orgasm before at all. Asher put his hand around her throat, squeezing gently.

"You're mine now, sweetheart," he told her. "And you're gonna be a good girl for me. Isn't that right?"

Callie was trembling from conflicting feelings of pleasure and fear.

She did not resist as his incubus hold on her deepened. She wasn't as enthralled with him the way her mother and sister were but would be soon if everything went well. For now, Asher only wanted to bring out the darkness within her, to encourage her thirst for violent vengeance.

"Say it," he told her. "Tell me you'll be a good girl."

She whispered. "Yes, I'll be a good girl, Asher."

"Master," he corrected.

"I'll be a good girl, Master."

"Until I tell you it's time to be a bad little girl."

"Okay … Master."

He brushed a lock of that natural blond hair behind her ear. "How're you feeling now, Callie?"

"Nervous."

"And how do you feel about me?"

Her eyes met his. He saw no loathing in them now, only bewilderment—not over what was happening but how she was feeling. The spell of an incubus could work like dementia, giving the victim a happy thought, only to make them lose that thought, leaving them feeling happy without knowing why. Callie knew she'd been raped by Asher with her sister's help, just like Sue Bower had helped the reverend rape her. She understood why she should be hurt and terrified, but simply no longer was. Though not in love with Asher yet, her crush on him was slowly returning. It would only grow stronger with each act of obedience.

"I feel …" she said, unsure how to answer his question. "I feel funny."

"Must be the drugs in your system. But how do you feel about *me*, Callie?"

As she gazed up at him, Callie's expression transformed. Asher witnessed her love grow. Her eyes softened, and she batted her lashes. Her lips parted in a bashful smile, shoulders hunching up to her ears, as if she might giggle if she tried to speak.

"I feel … special," she said. "I mean … *you* make me feel special. I feel for you in ways I haven't felt for other boys. I can't even find the words to explain it. I mean, I know you're bad, but at the same time, it's like … oh, exciting isn't the right word for it … it's like you're bad but for the greater good."

"A necessary evil?"

"At least for me."

"And your sister and mother too. I am the beloved master of the Vincent women. I do know what's best for you, sweetheart. That's why we're here."

Callie looked at the Bower house across the street. "Are you gonna kill them?"

Asher smiled, knowing how this would go but also knowing Callie wasn't ready to hear it. So he answered her question with a question. "You want them to die, don't you?"

She wasn't quite there yet, but she was inching closer. "I just want them to pay for what they did. They shouldn't be allowed to just go on with their everyday lives after how they hurt me."

"I agree. Now what're we gonna do about it, Callie? What're *you* gonna do about it?"

Callie squinted, searching her mind for the answer. "I guess ... I guess I'll do what you tell me to ... Master."

"That's exactly right." He slipped the pocketknife out of his coat and placed it in her hand. "I want you to follow my lead, but I also want you to follow your heart. To achieve anything, you must want it. I know what's best, but I don't force you or Violet or anyone to do the things we do. Even if you don't know it yet, you already want to do these things. I just show you the way how."

She smiled at him like the schoolgirl with a crush she was. There was nothing left to be said now—there was only action. Asher got out of the car, and in an uncharacteristic act of chivalry, he opened the passenger door for Callie, and she and Violet exited the Dodge. He was thirsty again, so he took a sip of hot sauce to get an inner burn going. While extra hot to normal people, the habanero just wasn't cutting it for Asher anymore. He would have to find something with a bit more kick.

Callie had the knife, and Asher had his pistol, but Violet needed something too, so he popped the trunk and fetched the tire iron, handing it to her along with the rape kit.

The trio crept toward the pastor's home under the cover of shadows. It was a white single-story house on a small plot of land with no fence. A ceramic nativity scene was framed in the front window, illuminated by gold string lights. Asher led the sisters along the side of the house. They tested each window—all locked. Reaching the rear, they discovered a laundry room with a glass door. Asher put the nail of his left index finger to the glass, right beside the door handle, and dragged the fingernail down, cutting like a diamond. He made a perfect circle, then popped the pane out by wedging his fingernails around the edges and drawing the disc back. He reached through the hole to unlock the door from the inside. Callie watched all of this with wonder. Her older sister bounced on her toes, eager to get into the house.

As they entered the laundry room, Callie stuck close to Asher, holding his arm with one hand and the knife out in front of her with the other.

"No need to cling to me," Asher whispered. "That's what children do. After tonight, you won't be a child anymore."

She reluctantly released him and put both hands around the handle of the knife. Though Callie didn't say anything, Asher sensed she understood what he was trying to tell her. She didn't want to let him—or herself—down. Though intimidated to be here, the pure rage behind Callie's dilated eyes stemmed from deep within her, unaided by Asher's influence.

As they reached the kitchen doorway, Asher put his hand on the small of Callie's back. "Ladies first."

They stepped into the kitchen, and he softly closed the door behind them. The only illumination came from the night-light above the stove, leaving the rest of the house in shadows. The trio entered the living room. Above an impressive entertainment center hung a painting of Jesus on a black velvet canvas. Christ was looking up with his hands clasped in prayer, blood pouring from his crown of thorns, his face twisted in anguish. It looked more appropriate for an exorcism horror movie than a pastor's living room. Over the front door was a plaque reading *"Christ Shall Protect Me,"* a blessing for whenever the Bowers left home. The mounted head of a large buck looked down at Asher with dead, black eyes. It seemed the reverend not only liked to hurt innocent kids but also innocent animals. Framed photos decorated the walls, including some of the pastor with the church's choir children and Sunday school flock. Asher stared at a picture of the Bowers with a group of Girl Scouts, the pastor hugging two uncomfortable girls into him while his wife's hands were firmly planted on the shoulders of a very young blond girl with a corpse-like expression. Asher recognized the girl immediately but didn't bother pointing the picture out to Callie. Looking at it, the shadow of his reflection darkened the smiling faces of the Bowers.

There's evil everywhere, Asher thought. Evil had championed the human race a long time ago, mostly in the name of God. But Asher wasn't interested in vigilante justice. He didn't really give a shit about holier-than-thou child molesters, even ones who'd hurt his newest possession, Callie. The constant, perverse cruelty of church leaders was the only thing he liked about organized religion. He only wanted payback against the Bowers because they'd potentially ruined his virgin sacrifice. More importantly, he'd brought Callie here to facilitate her bloodlust, expediating her transformation from timid youth to sadomasochistic nymphet.

Dual snores came from the end of the hall. The bedroom door stood ajar. Asher figured Bower was the louder snorer, but when he peeked in on the sleeping couple, he saw it was the wife who sounded like a warthog trying to breathe underwater. With a pig like that in his bed, it was no wonder the pastor had turned to diddling preteen girls. The door to the attached master bathroom was also ajar, a small bit of light coming from somewhere inside, casting a yellow line across the bed—just enough light to see the Bowers snoozing. The man was skinny, the wife plump. Both were in their fifties. Hanging above the headboard was a statue of Jesus nailed to the cross. Asher wondered just how many children had stared up at this image of their savior as their pastor sexually assaulted them in his marital bed.

Raising his revolver, Asher gently pushed the bedroom door inward, and the Vincent sisters followed him in.

He woke the Bowers by shooting Sue.

THIRTY-SIX

HAVING CONNECTED HIS PHONE TO the stereo's Bluetooth, Asher put on the kind of music that had never played in the Bower residence before. The speakers of their entertainment center probably hadn't hosted anything heavier than Pat Boone. Now, they pulsed with black metal. It smothered the sounds of violence nicely, and with the windows closed, no neighbors would be alerted to the Bower's impending doom.

After shooting Sue Bower in one huge buttock as she snored on her side, Asher had turned the gun on the reverend, pressing the hot barrel against his head. Violet opened the rape kit, and the Bowers had their hands cuffed behind their backs before being ushered into the living room. Asher wanted them to suffer here for two reasons. One was so he could listen to heavy metal. The other was because the insipid *"Christ Shall Protect Me"* sign was in there. Asher wanted the pious couple to realize just how wrong they were about that.

Sue wailed about her wound, so Asher had Violet stuff the

woman's mouth with toilet paper and seal it with duct tape. The pastor begged for their lives, telling the intruders to just take whatever they wanted, lying about how they wouldn't even call the police if the trio left without causing any further harm. Asher pistol-whipped Reverend Bower, giving him one solid blow to the head that dropped the man to his knees. He squirmed over to his wife, who was in a fetal position on the floor, her fat ass covered in blood.

Callie was shaking, afraid and furious all at once as she tried to keep the knife steady in both hands. As conflicting emotions struggled for control of her, Asher pressed the palm of his left hand to her back and rubbed it up and down her spine, leaving trails of crimson light that vanished just as quickly as they had appeared. He whispered a lost language into Callie's ear, calming her while encouraging her darkest thoughts. Looking to Violet, Asher pointed at Reverend Bower, and she gave his torso several whacks with the tire iron. The pastor cried out in pain.

"You hear that?" Asher asked Callie. "Even the greatest guitar solo in rock history can never sound as sweet as your enemy's screams."

Callie stopped trembling.

"Go on," Asher told her. "Join your sister in the fun." Callie stepped forward a little too eagerly, so Asher held her back. "Just don't rush it. Take your time on this pig. We don't want him to go easily."

Callie did something Asher didn't expect. She kissed his cheek.

As Callie approached Reverend Bower, her sister pinned the man's shoulders down for her, just as she'd pinned down Callie's arms when Asher raped her mere hours ago. But so much had changed since then, and when they were through here, Callie would come out of this dark night like a caterpillar emerging from its cocoon as a butterfly. As she straddled the pastor, Asher sat on the sofa and took a sip of habanero sauce, having always preferred having a beverage while watching a show.

"Remember me?" Callie asked the pastor.

Reverend Bower kept his head turned away. "I haven't seen your faces ... you don't have to—"

He was cut short by Callie slicing open his cheek. It was only a nick, but it got his attention.

"Turn the other one," she told him.

He groaned. "Wha-what?"

"Christ teaches to turn the other cheek, right? So do it."

He mumbled something about letting him go, so Violet grabbed his head and forced him to turn it. Callie pressed the tip of the blade into the pastor's other cheek, then twisted the knife slowly.

"It's Callie, Reverend Bower," she said. "Callie Vincent. You used to call me Pinky ... because you liked to put your pinky up my ..." She struggled but managed to get it out. "You used to sing 'a pinky in the stinky for Callie,' remember?"

Violet turned his head back, making him look straight up at the sisters.

"Callie ..." the pastor said, blinking. "Is that really you, my child?"

"Shit, your glasses," Callie said. "I almost forgot. I need you to witness this."

"Don't get up," Asher told the girls as he rose from the sofa. "I saw them on the nightstand."

He fetched them from the bedroom, and while he was in there, he noticed the closet door was open. Something caught his eye. Asher drew the pastor's black shirt from its hanger. The white clerical collar was looped around the hook. Taking both with him, Asher returned to the living room, and Sue Bower kicked at him as he walked by. Asher stomped down on her foot and grinded her toes against the hardwood floor, making them snap. She wailed, and her husband called out for her, telling her everything was going to be okay.

"Don't make your last words to your wife a lie," Asher told him as he put the glasses on the pastor's face.

Looking at Asher with clear vision, Reverend Bower recoiled in horror. When he was committing acts of evil, Asher's ghoulish features were heightened. His cheekbones were more pronounced now, and his unibrow ended in devilish Jack Nicholson arches. His teeth were mustard-colored and jagged, sideburns like wire brushes.

"God in heaven," the pastor whimpered.

Asher smirked. "Guess again."

"You ... you're not a man ... you're a demon!"

"Look who's talking."

The pastor closed his eyes and began to pray. Asher looked to Callie, saying it without saying it. She stabbed the pastor in the belly. Bower's eyes shot wide open, and he gasped before making any sound of pain.

"Don't bother praying to God," Callie told him. "It sure didn't work for me. No matter how much I prayed, God didn't stop you from raping me. You made me think He was on your side. You were *my pastor* … I trusted you!"

Though he begged for his life, Reverend Bower did not accept responsibility for his criminal acts. He did not apologize to Callie, only cried for her to let him go. He wasn't even asking for his wife to be released anymore. With a knife in his belly, he was focused only on himself.

Callie drew the blade from the pastor's gut, releasing a steady flow of blood. She raised it with both hands, aiming the tip over Bower's heart, but Asher made a *tsk tsk* sound before she could dive in. He'd told her to take her time. She seemed to remember that as she lowered the knife and stared at him for further instruction. Asher took another sip from the bottle of hot sauce before handing it to her without a word. Now, Callie had the bottle in one hand and the knife in the other. Asher enjoyed seeing a revelation come over the girl. Her face brightened with malicious intent as she put aside the knife and removed the pastor's glasses.

"You know it's me," she told him. "You don't need to see me anymore. You don't need to see anything."

She upturned the habanero sauce into his eyes. The pastor screamed and tried to turn away, but Violet held his head in place. Callie kept dumping the contents of the bottle into Bower's face, prying his eyelids open with her fingers to better drench the eyeballs with the extra-hot fluid—a fiery combination of habaneros and jalapenos with a touch of ghost pepper. The acidity ate away his eyelashes and made his eyelids swell. The bottle had been halfway full when Asher handed it to Callie. When she was finished blinding the pastor, only a teaspoon's worth remained. She raised the bottle toward Asher in toast and drank the rest down.

Then she started stabbing.

Over two years of pent-up rage exploded out of Callie. She sent the knife in and out of her tormentor, puncturing his chest, shoulders, and neck, undeterred when the blade sputtered against bone. She just kept stabbing until she hit other soft spots and drove the blade deeper into the tissue, turning the knife inside him, screaming almost as much as the pastor. Watching her husband be murdered, Sue Bower sobbed and tried to get to her knees, but Asher kicked her in the face, and back to the floor she went. His freakish strength caused the woman's nose to break and both cheekbones to collapse, concaving her face, but still she gurgled, still alive.

The pastor was still alive too but was incapacitated. With every desperate breath, more blood spurted from his flooding lungs. Knowing the pedophile didn't have much time left, Asher yanked Bower's pajama bottoms down to expose his genitalia. It was all the hint Callie needed. She grabbed the head of the penis that had violated her, stretched it out, and started hacking. The castration was rough, involving as much tearing of the flesh as cutting. The pastor convulsed when Callie and Violet managed to rip his penis and scrotum free. They jammed the bloody mass into Bower's mouth, and Violet used the tire iron to shove it all further down his throat, silencing his final prayer. The only air he could get now was whatever came through the holes in his chest, but that didn't matter either way. Shock had set in, and the pastor was fading fast.

"Say hi to The Devil for me," Asher told him.

Callie stared at Reverend Bower as he died, savoring the moment, donning the same blank expression she wore in that living room photo. Asher put his arm around her shoulders, then slid his hand down to cup her tiny breast. She closed her eyes as he kissed her ear.

"That's my good girl," he told her.

She kissed him on the lips, and when she pulled back, there were tears in her eyes. "Thank you for this ... my master."

Asher drew his pistol from its holster and put it in Callie's blood-slick hands. He went to the stereo, turning up Deicide's first album so the roar of the Satanic death metal was all anyone could hear.

Callie stared at the revolver, turning it over in her hand.

Then she started toward Sue Bower, getting low so her face was level with her former Sunday school teacher.

"You know," she said to her, "I've thought about it a lot, and I think you're even worse than your husband."

Sue tried to speak, but her words were muffled, so Callie ripped the duct tape off and removed her soggy gag.

"No," Sue pleaded. "He made me do it. Honest! I'm a victim too!"

"I was just a little girl. You were the grown-up."

"Callie, please, don't do—"

Callie shoved the barrel of the gun into Sue's mouth, chipping a tooth. "Suck it. Suck it like you made me suck him."

Sue could only sob hysterically, so Callie shoved the barrel in and out of the woman's mouth, the pistol's jagged sight ripping the roof of her mouth open, filling it with blood. More teeth cracked as Callie effectively face-fucked the pastor's wife with a loaded gun. Thrilled by this, Violet went at Sue with the tire iron, shoving the pointed end into the bullet wound in the woman's ass. Sue tried to scream but could only gargle blood as she choked on the pistol. Violet got the woman's sweatpants and granny panties down to her knees, drew the oversized dildo from the rape kit, and attacked her anus with it. Asher picked up the bloody pocketknife and cut away at the woman's garments until they were out of everyone's way. He rolled her on her back and slid the knife between Sue's labia, then started spinning the blade—clockwise first, then counterclockwise, mutilating her flabby vagina until it looked like a gopher hole.

Asher knew if this had been any other couple, Callie wouldn't have taken to the violence with such gusto. It was only her hatred for the Bowers that prevented hesitation. His spell over the girl could only influence her so much, especially in this early stage of seduction. The anger that motivated her was purely her own.

Violet had been raging against these latest victims too, but now Asher led her away from Sue, withdrawing the dildo and knife from her twitching body. He wanted these final moments to be Callie's alone. Sue's mouth was now busted apart, the lips split, shards of teeth dangling from bloody strands of saliva. Callie had been going at it so hard her arms had worn out. She looked up at Asher only once, and he gave her a little nod—one last nudge onto the left-hand path.

Keeping the barrel in the mess that had once been Sue Bower's mouth, Callie pulled the trigger. The bullet came out the back of the skull, flying upward and hitting the velvet Jesus right between the eyes.

THIRTY-SEVEN

BEFORE LEAVING, THEY DECORATED THE Bower
house with Satanic symbols, fingerpainting the walls with blood. Below the brain-splattered painting of Christ, Violet wrote *"HAIL TO
THE REAPERS"* for brand recognition. Callie wasn't sure what she
was supposed to write, but Asher dipped her fingers in Sue Bower's
blown-out head and encouraged her to follow her heart. Callie fin-
gerpainted an image of a church with a cross on top and a stick figure
man hanging from it by a noose. Beneath this, she wrote *"VENGE-
ANCE."* Asher added two more words to quote the bible, making it
read *"VENGEANCE IS MINE."*

"I like it," Callie said.

The sign above the door claiming *"Christ Shall Protect Me"* was altered with blood too, Asher scrawling over the word "protect,"
changing it to read *"Christ Shall Rape Me."* It seemed the most appropriate. He was going to take Sue's panties with him, but she'd soiled
herself. He didn't need some dirty, wide-load granny panties

muddying his beautiful collection, so instead, he took one of Sue's socks, along with Reverend Bower's black clerical shirt and white collar. Looking up at the deer's head, he decided he wanted that too.

No neighbors had come knocking. No one had called 911. No one saw or heard anything. But they would smell something soon enough. It was usually the stink that led police to bodies. No matter how well a killer hid the remains of their victims, the foul odor of death eventually revealed all. It was a shame, really. Asher rather liked that smell.

As they drove away, Violet sat in the back seat with the buck's head and lit a joint. Asher put his hand on Callie's thigh. She'd been staring out the window in silence, and his touch seemed to awaken her from a trance.

"You don't have to be afraid anymore," he told her.

"I'm not afraid of you, Master," she said, "even though I know you're evil."

"Why is that?"

"Because I know you're only looking out for me." She glanced at the glow of the car radio, which was playing Venom. "Is it the heavy metal that made you evil?"

He chuckled. "No, sweetheart. Deep down, most metalheads are nice people—at least as much as any other type of person. Listening to this music doesn't make me an evil man. That was a separate choice, which I also made." He caressed her thigh, his hand moving higher. "But that's not what I was talking about when I said you don't have to be afraid anymore. What I meant was you don't have to be afraid of the Bowers anymore, or anyone else for that matter."

"How come?"

"Because they'll be the ones who are afraid—of you."

She stared out the window again, leaning her head against the glass. "Are we gonna go to prison for what we did?"

"No."

"Are we gonna go to Hell?"

"Because we killed church folk? The Bowers were about as Christ-like as Jeffrey Epstein."

"But we still killed people—a deadly sin."

"Sinning is winning. Remember that."

"Is that why you guys wrote all that Satan stuff on the walls?"

Violet chimed in. "We're Satanists, Callie. We worship The Devil."

"So we *are* going to Hell."

"I no longer fear Hell. I don't fear anything. That's what our master is trying to tell you—*don't be afraid.* There's no longer a need."

Callie stared at Asher, long and hard. "Are you a demon?"

"We all have our demons," he said. "At this point, I'm not exactly sure if I am man or beast, mortal or Hell-spawn. But I was born human. I've simply evolved."

Callie sighed. "I can't believe we murdered them …"

"They deserved it," her sister reminder her.

"I know that."

"You didn't seem to mind killing them," Violet said.

"I didn't mind. I wanted to kill them and have for a long time. I just can't believe we really did it."

"Do you regret it?" Asher asked.

Callie took a deep breath. "No."

He put his arm around her and pulled her closer. "That's my girl. You're free now. The Bowers no longer have any power over you because you took it back for yourself."

"Yeah. I guess you're right."

"I'm always right."

Callie's cognitive dissonance was to be expected. It was always an adjustment when you first start killing. Even with his hypnotic hold over her, she still had her own thoughts and emotions and had to come to grips with what she'd done. Despite the justness of her motive, being a murderer was a lot for a fifteen-year-old to process.

"So what happens now?" she asked.

"Honestly, I haven't worked all of that out yet," Asher said with a smile. "You were supposed to be sacrificed tonight, but instead, you've become part of the family. You must've done something in a past life that made Satan happy—I dunno. What I do know is there's something special about you. There's a rage in you, sweetheart—a dark energy stronger than anyone else's in our family. Now, it's been unearthed, and the streets will run red with blood."

She shook her head. "I don't know if I could kill again."

"Well, I do, and you will."

"But I don't have anyone else I want to get back at. Not *that* much."

"Revenge isn't the only good reason to kill a person."

Callie put her face an inch from his. "Master … may I ask what you want?"

"It's not what I want. It's what *all of us* want. As your master, my desires are your desires, my needs your needs."

"What do *we* want, then?"

"Sometimes, people get so focused on long-term goals they fail to live in the moment. Let me worry about where we're going. You just stay on the path with me."

She settled into him. "Yes, Master. I will. So ... where are we going right now? I mean, like, where're we driving to?"

"Home, silly. Your mom must be worried sick about you. It'll be good to let her know you're one of my girls now instead of dead. We're all going to be very happy together."

Violet leaned in. "One big, happy family."

The first blue hint of dawn cracked the horizon as they pulled into the driveway of the Vincent house. Melissa, still in her black lingerie, opened the door before they got halfway to it. Seeing her daughters were okay, tears of relief filled her eyes, but Asher was the first person she went to, wrapping her arms around the back of his neck, as if they were dancing.

"I've missed you so much, Master," she said. "I love you so deeply. I need you. Please take me inside and make love to me."

Her mother's behavior raised Callie's eyebrows. She and Violet were enamored with Asher too, but not to the obsessive degree their mother was. Only Asher understood why she'd been affected by his incubus magic more deeply than anyone else. Melissa had been love-starved too long, trapped in a marriage without affection, and was in dire need of male attention. This made her more vulnerable to Asher's touch, surrendering to him completely.

Saying nothing, Asher went into the house, and the Vincent women tailed behind him like puppies. He grabbed an apple from the fruit bowl on the kitchen counter but found no beer in the fridge. Telling Melissa to keep it stocked from now on, he grabbed a bottle of Cholula sauce and took a swig, the liquid peppers titillating his tongue. Still, he wanted something hotter.

"Your little girl is a woman now," Asher told Melissa.

She looked at Callie, but her gaze went right back to Asher, too enthralled with her incubus master to put anything before him, even the well-being of her children.

"Tonight, she did what you should have a long time ago," Asher said.

Violet spoke up. "Me too, Master. I killed them too."

"Yes, yes. We're all very proud of you. But I'm talking about Callie now."

Callie paled, shocked they were telling anyone what they'd done, especially her mother.

Melissa's brow lowered. "Killed who, Violet? What're you talking about? You didn't kill anyone, honey. You couldn't do something like that."

"Right now," Asher said, "all of my girls need to shut up and listen."

Bowing their heads, the Vincent women fell silent.

"Melissa, your daughters—*both of them*—are killers. You didn't protect them, so I taught them to protect themselves."

"Master, no," Melissa said. "I've always protected my girls."

"Don't you fucking lie to me. You knew what that dirty, old reverend did to Callie, but you just let him get away with it."

Tears returned to Melissa's eyes. "That's ... that's not really true."

"It *is* true."

"Not the way you describe it. I tried to talk Callie into going to the police, but—"

"Fuck the police. If you were any kind of mother, you would've burned the Bowers' house down with them in it."

She began to cry. "Master, please, I—"

"Don't bother. What's done is done."

"I would do anything for my girls—*anything*."

"Oh yeah? Let's see you prove that. Get your old ass upstairs."

Melissa would never disobey a direct order, but that didn't stop her from being confused. "Master?"

Asher started toward the staircase, and the women followed.

"I only want to make you happy," Melissa told him. "I'll cook for you and clean for you. I'll buy you whatever you want. My husband has a credit card with a fifty grand limit! I'll max it out for you. I'll be such a good girl, Master. I'll suck your cock on demand. You can fuck me any time—my pussy, my mouth, my ass. Rip them apart as much as you want. Cum on my face. Tie me up. Hurt me. Whatever you desire. Let me please you, Master."

When they reached the bedroom, Asher climbed onto the brand-new mattress, and the Vincent women followed, crawling with salacious hunger. They caressed his thighs and pushed up his shirt to kiss his belly. They twirled his greasy hair in their fingers and sucked his earlobes, whispering their devotion. Violet unzipped his fly, and she and her mother crowded their heads around Asher's pulsing cock, licking and worshipping it.

Asher smiled at Callie. "It's time to be a bad girl now."

She smiled back, seeming more nervous now than she'd been all night. Asher could tell she was worried she might disappoint him with her lack of experience, so he decided to give her a hand.

"Melissa," Asher said, "here's your chance to do something for your daughter. Show Callie how I like to be fucked."

The mother smiled, but there was a trace of pain behind her eyes. Once they got Asher's clothes off, Melissa guided her youngest daughter, showing her what Asher liked so she could repeat it. As the foursome commenced, the walls began to sweat, and the stench of sulfur permeated the bedroom. It was more than the pleasures of the flesh that motivated Asher tonight. His sexual prowess served a greater purpose now, one even he wasn't fully aware of. Rex was guiding him just like Melissa guided Callie, and Asher was just as eager to learn.

But while his control of the Vincent women left him drunk with power, Asher was experiencing a sexual ennui. Even the new addition of an underage girl didn't excite him the way new pussy had when he'd first become a warlock. The only way he could get aroused anymore was through abuse and domination, and his lust for murder had usurped his sexual lust. Suddenly, fucking three females at the same time wasn't as alluring as ripping one apart. But he needed to climax, so he was extra rough with the Vincent women without causing any permanent damage—just enough to get him there.

He ejaculated inside of Callie, but Asher just kept coming, so he climbed onto Violet and ejaculated inside of her too. The semen did not burn the girls or fill their vaginal canals with insects, but it was blacker than any he'd discharged before, and thick like raw honey. Asher could feel its evil intent. As the semen filled them, the girls shook as if being electrocuted, and their eyes rolled back as they murmured in dead languages, the warlock's seed further soiling their souls.

When he exited Violet, Melissa took hold of Asher's cock, sucked the last drops out, and licked his penis clean of her daughters' excretions. The taste of his cum was all she needed to have an orgasm of her own. She wrapped herself around his leg, keeping his dick in her mouth as her daughters cuddled into Asher, resting their heads on his chest.

That was when he realized what he was going to make the Vincent women do.

THIRTY-EIGHT

LENNY HAD DONE A GOOD job scoping out the convent, and Barney had assisted him without getting in the way. They showed Asher the digital pictures they'd taken, and Barney drew a map, exhibiting more artistic skill than Asher would have expected from him. Lenny had even pulled the building's blueprints from public records.

Sitting in the living room of the Vincent house, the men drank beer from the twelve packs Asher had sent Melissa to the package store for. Callie and Violet were sleeping off a night of murder and debauchery, but Asher kept Melissa up so she could wait on him and his disciples. As they went over the plans, she got to cooking the filet mignon and prepared a side salad just for Asher. It was made entirely of fresh peppers, including ghost, Scotch bonnet, and Carolina reapers she'd picked up at a specialty grocer.

"Everything's set," Lenny said, popping a can of beer. "Those nuns are like sitting ducks up there, all alone in their little commune. No security guards, no dogs ... not a man in sight—just nuns and

338

teenage girls."

"Beautiful," Asher said. "Once Violet gets inside, she'll give us the lowdown on the building's interior. Something tells me they don't allow smartphones in a place like that, so if there's just a landline, we can easily cut it and separate them from the outside world even more than they already are."

Barney nodded. "Man, I can't wait for this. You're gonna let me rape some of them, right, Master?"

"Why is everything about sex with you?" Asher said with a chuckle. "Not that I don't admire your salaciousness."

"It's just that it's been a while for me, and you said I could—"

"Yeah, yeah, I know. I told you there'd be women if you joined me. I suppose you've done a good enough job to deserve a small reward."

Barney wet his lips. "Oh, Master ... I would appreciate it so much."

Melissa entered the room with steaks and side dishes, and Asher popped a Carolina reaper in his mouth, chewing it raw. Seeing him eat something she'd prepared made the housewife smile, and last night's sex had left her with a happy afterglow. As instructed, she was dressed in her black kimono and matching high heels, and Asher's men couldn't help but notice her form—the way the heels made her ass pop and the pushup bra flattered her breasts. When Asher caught Barney ogling her, he slapped Melissa on the butt and gave it a hard squeeze.

"Not bad for being a hundred, huh?" he asked his men.

Melissa blushed, ashamed to be flaunted before them. Lenny gave an approving nod. Barney agreed, nearly drooling.

"Melissa," Asher said, "get on your knees and suck Barney's dick."

She turned white. "Master ... I ..."

Barney's shocked face made Asher laugh, but not as much as the dread on Melissa's.

"Are you deaf?" Asher asked her. "I said, get on your knees and suck Barney's dick. And do a good job of it."

"But, Master, I am loyal to you and only you."

"Then do what I tell you."

She looked around the room as if for a way out of this. Asher told Barney to stand and drop his pants. He did, and held his short, already-hard pecker, pointing it at Melissa, but he was too nervous to speak.

Asher smacked Melissa on the ass again. "Go on. Suck him off. Or would you rather I get Callie to do it?"

Asher would never allow Barney to touch Callie or Violet, but Melissa didn't know that. His bluff put her on her knees. This was all about control. He also wanted to keep his male soldiers happy before the siege on the nunnery so they would have no hesitations to do as he commanded, but Asher could have spellbound any female into having sex with Barney and Lenny. Using Melissa was just another way of breaking the woman down, keeping her where she ought to be—*in thrall.*

As Melissa fellated Barney, Asher continued his conversation with Lenny over steaks. "I had a virgin sacrifice that didn't work out, but this siege will more than make up for it."

"For sure," Lenny said. "It's gonna be metal as fuck."

In mere seconds, Barney moaned and trembled, on the edge of climaxing.

"Don't take him out of your mouth when he cums, Melissa," Asher reminded her. "I want you to chug that dick snot like you're starving and it's the last fucking morsel of food on Earth." He turned to Lenny and smirked. "My favorite pie is apple pie, but Melissa's is throat pie. Isn't that right, Melissa?"

Her mouth full, Melissa could only hum a "*mmmhmm.*"

Barney's face twisted, his legs shaking as he unloaded into Melissa's throat. An obedient slave girl, she kept bobbing her head even as her mouth overflowed with unwanted semen. Swallowing it, her face pruned in disgust. Asher praised her with a slow, sarcastic clap, then returned his attention to his steak.

"You want her to suck you off too?" he asked Lenny.

"It's tempting," Lenny admitted, "but maybe later."

"What if I give you free use of all her holes?"

Lenny eyed Melissa more seriously now. "I like it rough and nasty. Is that cool?"

"Do whatever you want to the bitch. I don't care. Her pussy is already like a dynamited mine."

Asher popped another pepper in his mouth as Barney stumbled back into his jeans. Lenny went to Melissa, staring down at her on her knees, malicious desire in his eyes.

"You like it rough, sugar?" he asked.

She was hesitant but agreed. "I like whatever my master tells me to like."

"Nice work on this one," Lenny told Asher. He patted the top of Melissa's head. "I've had a lot of coffee today, lady, and now I've had two beers. Get my drift?"

Melissa shook her head, her look of sadness deepening.

"It means I've got a maxed-out bladder," Lenny said. "I like to offer my bitches a drink before they eat out my asshole."

Asher laughed. "Damn, Lenny. You really are nasty. Don't do that shit in here, though. This house is my home away from home. Take the old lady to the shower."

Lenny helped Melissa to her feet, and she hung her head as she was escorted to the bathroom for further humiliation.

"Listen up, Jonny two-stroke," Asher said to Barney. "You've gotten your nut, so now I expect your head to be clear. Our mission at the convent is to kill, not get our rocks off. Rape will just be a bonus—and only when I give the okay. So don't go in there with your dick hanging out."

"Yes, Master."

They finished their meals, and Asher laid out rails of cocaine to start the day. His high was heightened by the sound of Melissa crying behind the closed bathroom door. Lenny was taking more time with her than Barney had and, from the sound of things, was treating her far worse.

"Did you raid Grampa's rifle cabinet?" Asher asked Barney.

"Sure did. I told him I was going hunting with friends—which is true, in a way." He snickered. "So he lent me two shotguns. One a pump action, the other a double barrel. They're in the car. I've used them both before, so I'm pretty good with them."

"Doesn't take a lot of skill to use a shotgun, but okay. What else have you got?"

"Mostly knives. Oh, and this." He drew a canister of pepper spray from his pocket. "Got it online."

He handed it over, and Asher popped the lock and squirted some in his mouth, smacking his lips. "Spicy!"

Barney stared in disbelief as Asher chased the pepper spray with a ghost pepper. "Holy Hell … I don't know how you can do that."

"Some like it hot," Asher said, handing back the canister. "This pepper spray will do just fine. I doubt the nuns will enjoy the taste as much as I do. I'll be taking that pump action shotgun from you, though."

"Okay, Master. You bet."

They heard hurried footsteps upstairs. When Violet came down and entered the living room, she was nearly unrecognizable.

"Asher!" she cried, holding her belly. "Asher, what's happened to me?"

"It's *Master*, remember?"

But she was too hysterical to comprehend. Asher couldn't blame her. Violet's stomach had swelled, looking like she was hiding a globe beneath her skin. Her shirt was incredibly tight on her now and showed half her belly. Violet had also gained a little weight in general, but the bulk of it was in her midsection.

"What's going on inside of me?" she pleaded.

Asher shrugged. "I'm no doctor, but you look pregnant to me."

"How could I be *this* pregnant?" she asked, pulling her shirt up to expose her rotund stomach. "I was skinny last night. Now, I woke up as big as a house."

"Easy now," he said, going to her and putting his hands on her shoulders. "I said you *look* pregnant. That doesn't mean you're gonna have a baby. Remember the plan? I told you I could make you appear to be with child so you could get into the convent, posing as a young, wayward mother."

"I thought you were gonna pad my clothes! I didn't think you would change *my body*. I don't like this. I'm scared."

He'd never seen the girl so panicked. Even when he'd first dominated her sexually and even when he'd first involved her in a murder, Violet had never been as frightened as she was right now. It excited Asher.

"That fear you're feeling will be useful at the convent," he told her. "It'll be that much easier for you to convince the nuns you're a pregnant teenage runaway."

"Okay, but … but this is my body and—"

"No. It's *my* body. It's mine to do whatever I wish with. You know that."

"I do, but … well, how long is this gonna last?"

"As long as we need it to."

"So I won't be like this for very long, right?"

He shrugged again. "Probably not."

"Once this thing with the nuns is over, my baby bump goes away?"

"If so, that just gives you more motivation to do this thing right. You get in there, find out everything you can, and assist us with the plan."

She nodded. "Okay … I just … oh, I've got to sit down."

As Violet sat on the sofa, she hissed with discomfort. "My ass is burning."

"Maybe you've got hemorrhoids. I've heard pregnant women get them. One of the magical things that comes with being knocked up."

"But … you said I'm not really pregnant, right?"

"We need this to be believable, Violet. That's why we couldn't just pad your clothes. Stop complaining. You should be honored to take in my seed."

She sniffled. "You came inside Callie last night too. I checked in on her, and she doesn't look like this. She looks the same."

"I do hope you're not questioning me."

"No, Master," she said quickly. "I would never."

"Lucky for you. Don't forget that with a snap of my fingers, I can make you bleed from your eyes and shit lava."

"Yes, Master," she said, too intimidated to look at him.

"Atta girl. Now get your ass back upstairs and get some rest. You're no good to us half-dead. We're all counting on you, sweetheart."

Violet looked down at her rotund belly, running her hands over it in stunned disbelief. She waddled back upstairs, struggling to adjust to the sudden increase in weight.

"You see that?" Asher asked Barney. "*That's* how you treat a woman. If you were more dominant with the ladies, you wouldn't go so long without one."

The bathroom door opened, and Lenny came out, still buckling his belt, grinning.

"See his face?" Asher asked Barney. "That's the look of a man who knows what women are for." He patted Lenny on the shoulder. "How was she?"

"Obedient," Lenny said. "I got a little carried away in there, but she took it all."

"No permanent damage, right?"

"No, Master. I wouldn't do that without your permission. She's just a little bruised is all. And you weren't kidding—that pussy was already a mess before I got to it. I don't know what happened, but it looked like a grenade went off inside the bitch. She's taking a real shower after her golden one, now that she's scrubbed my ass hair out of her teeth."

Asher shook his hand. He was starting to like Lenny, but even though Asher considered him his second in command, he still didn't trust him completely. But the same could be said for anyone. Humans were so weak. They folded at the first threat. That was how so many criminals ended up behind bars, because when their friends got caught, they ratted them out in exchange for a lighter sentence. Asher's incubus spell over the women assured the utmost loyalty, but he wasn't about to seduce his men. They were heterosexual, giving them a natural immunity against his incubus spell, but Asher didn't want them lusting after him either. He just wanted them to follow direction. Witchcraft could be used on the men, but Asher preferred to test their loyalty his own way. Barney was a lapdog. Lenny had an air of independence about him, leading Asher to keep a closer eye on the man. Lenny had been Rex's sidekick—or so he claimed—but that didn't guarantee he'd be as faithful to Rex's nephew. Asher liked to think Lenny would always serve him well, as he had so far, but as the leader of this cult, he had to maintain order. Therefore, he couldn't afford to call anyone his friend.

His only true friend was Lucifer. Asher hoped to see him again soon and was ready to do whatever it took to make that happen.

Asher went over the loose plans with his men until Melissa limped out of the bathroom, a purple bruise having already formed under one eye. Though she'd washed away Lenny's filth, she could never clean her mind of all the things her master put her through. Still, she smiled at Asher as she walked by in just a towel. It pleased him to see it. Melissa couldn't have looked more destroyed if she were dead.

As she headed to the staircase, Asher joined her.

"Violet's pregnant," he said

Melissa gave him a lost look. "How do you know?"

"Just wait until you see her."

"Is she going to ... I mean, are *you* going to keep it, Master?"

"Don't worry about that now. Just understand she's gonna need your help with this whole pregnancy thing. You're her mother, after all, and you've been through this before."

Melissa stared into space, zombified.

"You know," Asher said as he walked her to her bedroom, "I've grown very fond of your daughter. I have big plans for us."

"That's good to hear. I mean, I want you romantically too, but I'm happy to know you care about Violet and see a future with her."

Asher snickered. "I wasn't talking about Violet."

THIRTY-NINE

"YOUR HUSBAND," ASHER SAID. "YOU mentioned he was coming home soon, right?"

"Joel said he'd be home this afternoon," Melissa said. "Now, he says it'll be a little later, but he'll keep me posted."

"Then keep me posted too. I can't wait to meet this cuck."

Melissa seemed afraid to ask but did anyway. "What're you going to do?"

"It's not what I'm going to do. It's what you're going to do."

Now she *was* too afraid to ask. Sitting there in her towel, Melissa was white as a winter sky, and though she was looking at Asher, he doubted she was seeing anything at all. She was wandering in a mental fog, her mind shattered by sexualized torture, her soul rotted by Asher's demonic influence. He wondered just how much longer she'd be of any use to him.

"I promise this is the last time I'll say it," Melissa said, "but I just have to ask you one more time, Master. *Please,* consider releasing my girls. I'll take whatever you can dish out. I'll fuck who you tell me to fuck. I'll take whatever you or your friends want to do. If you'll just let my daughters go, I'll do anything you want."

"You'll do that anyway," Asher said.

Her eyes fell away again, what little hope she had left deteriorating.

Leaving Melissa and the girls to rest up, Asher returned to his house with Lenny and Barney and tasked them with cleaning up the bloody mess that had once been his father. Leviathan had taken its share, but scraps of flesh and bone remained.

"Don't just throw out whatever body parts you find in there," Asher told his men. "Bag them up. They just might prove useful."

To demonstrate this, he retrieved the bong made of Paul's skull, and the men smoked up, passing the severed head around. Holding his friend's severed head, Barney's face paled. He went to work on the master bedroom, and Lenny tidied up the rest of the house, ridding it of any substantial evidence. Asher preferred the place to look and smell like a slaughterhouse, but eventually, someone would come here looking for his parents. He couldn't have their remains dripping from the walls if police arrived to do a wellness check. It wasn't possible to return the house to its original condition, but if it wasn't an obvious murder scene, Asher wouldn't have to worry as much about a police investigation interfering with his plans to attack the convent.

Using his parents' phones to pose as them, he sent back and forth messages regarding the attempt at reconciliation Asher had fabricated. Then he created a dialogue focused on Mom's boyfriend, Sam, and how both Mom and Dad had come to fear him. As Mom, Asher wrote she was terrified of Sam's reprisal and that he'd been abusive and controlling in the past, saying if he couldn't have her, no one could. As Dad, Asher wrote that he wasn't going to back down to Sam's threats, that Elizabeth was his one true love and he would always protect her. While going through his mother's phone, Asher found new texts from Sam as well as several voice messages, all asking for an explanation for Mom ghosting him. He was growing increasingly agitated, each message more insistent than the last. Posing as Mom, Asher finally texted him back, saying she would go to the police if he didn't stop stalking her.

On both phones, Asher noted missed calls from his parents' places of work and texts from their bosses and coworkers. Their absences had been noticed. It was only a matter of time before someone looked into this. Asher had been too busy to concern himself with it before, but something had to be done. The protective seal of sorcery he'd put over the house could only do so much to keep his enemies away.

Using his own phone, Asher called his parents' phones and left similar voice messages.

"It's me again. I know you guys wanted some alone time together, but I just want to check in. I just want to know you're okay. I love you."

One thing at a time, he told himself.

Going to his car, Asher brought the deer's head he'd stolen from the Bowers back to his bedroom. His fingers glowed with a trace of flames as he deftly separated the buck's mighty antlers from the head with ease. With the heat radiating from his left hand, he welded the antlers to the forehead of Paul's skull bong. The skull began to warp, the cheekbones becoming more pronounced, the lower jaw falling off. The wrench socket he'd been using as a bowl popped out and hit the wall. Using one fingernail, Asher cleaved the skull in two at the sides, separating the front from the back, then molded the facial bones as if they were clay, his supernatural energy making them malleable. When he was satisfied with it, Asher brought it to the mirror and put the death mask over his face.

He stared at himself—at what he'd become.

What a horror to behold.

When the men had cleaned as well as they could, they brought Asher the garbage bag half-filled with parts of his father, as well as leftover scraps from his mother's carcass. Knowing what was best for them, Lenny and Barney did not ask whose remains they were, or even what had happened here.

"Where do you want this bag?" Barney asked.

"Just put a couple more bags on it and put it in the garage for now. Hide it under the work bench."

"Got it. Oh, and I put my grandpa's shotguns on the coffee table for you, just in case you need them for anything before the party at the convent."

"Good." Asher handed them the keys to his parents' cars so the men could dump them in the marsh on the outskirts of town. "Don't worry if the cars don't sink completely."

"You sure, boss?" Lenny asked.

"It's a remote location, but the cars will be found eventually, and I've got things all worked out. Take these too." He handed Lenny his parents' phones. "Leave their phones in their cars. You'll have to make two trips, so you can drive back in your car once the others are in the marsh. So that'll keep you boys busy for a while."

"Should we come back here when we're done?"

"No. I have other business to attend to with my lovely neighbors across the street."

Barney giggled. "They're lovely, all right. Specially that mama."

As they turned to go, Asher had a thought. "You boys have any masks?"

He raised the horned mask he'd made, putting it over his face again.

"Nothing that twisted," Barney said. "But I have some old latex masks from when I worked at the haunted house last Halloween."

"And I've got my old cult mask," Lenny said. "Rex always had us wear them when we were doing rituals."

"Perfect," Asher said. "We're gonna get back to those witchcraft basics. Besides, masks will scare the shit out of those nuns."

"Right, boss." Lenny looked at the crates of records on the floor. "So there's Rex's collection. Man, I haven't seen some of those records in years. Do you mind?"

Asher nodded, but only because he was curious what Lenny would do. He had a good idea what his henchman was after.

Lenny flipped through the vinyl. "Hot damn, he's got some great shit—or I guess you do, now." He looked up at Asher. "But then, Rex's a part of you, so ..."

Asher said nothing, waiting for the question he knew was coming.

"Say," Lenny said. "Could we listen to *Music to Sacrifice Virgins To* while we're here? I mean, I know we've heard the download on your phone, but I'd love to hear the actual vinyl play on Rex's sweet stereo."

"I'm sure you would, but not because of sound quality. You know as well as I do the album has more power when it's played directly from the record."

Lenny shrugged with a smile. "We could all use a little more power, right? What with the assault on the convent coming up and all."

"You're a good solider, Lenny, but you need to remember your place. If you're to receive more power, I'll be the one who decides when and how you get it."

"Sure ... it's just that Rex spent his whole life trying to make that album, and I was his right-hand man all that time—or left hand, in our case. I think I've earned the chance to hear it at least once. If you're able to talk to Rex, I'm sure he'll tell you—"

Asher backhanded Lenny, silencing him. "Rex left *me* the record—not you! He hasn't possessed me the way he planned to, but we're working together toward the same goal. I don't need you telling me what he would want—we share a brain, for fuck's sake!"

Lenny dabbed at the blood trickling from his nostril. "Yes, Master. It was my mistake to think I had any right to it, and I apologize. I'll be sure to mind my place going forward."

"See that you do," Asher said, grabbing the man's shoulder. "You worked your whole life for the rewards Satan offers. Don't flush all of that down the shitter by getting greedy."

Lenny nodded. Barney watched the whole scene in a daze, not knowing what to do.

"I gave you both a treat today," Asher said. "I let you get your rocks off with one of *my* whores. Now I don't want to hear you asking for any more favors until we get this job done. Got it?"

"Yes, Master," the men agreed.

They left with Barney driving Asher's father's car and Lenny tailing behind him in his own.

Asher placed his hand on the wall where the record was hidden. Perhaps Lenny really had just been excited to see it in person and hear it on the turntable, but the man had first come into Asher's life trying to take the record for himself. Lenny did excellent work—a true warrior in Asher's evil army—but being a more experienced Satanist made him a bigger threat than anyone else under Asher's command. He would have to watch Lenny closely. Any sign of dissention and he would skin him alive and bury him in a silo of salt. Once the attack on the convent was over, Asher just might kill him anyway, if only so he wouldn't have to worry about the son of a bitch anymore.

Having some time to kill, Asher took a ride to Ximena's house to collect her. Though her car was in the driveway, she didn't answer when he knocked on the door. He tried the handle. Locked. Slipping a fingernail into the keyhole on the deadbolt, Asher turned his left hand, and the lock slowly grew red from the heat. As the metal began to melt, his nail penetrated the tumbler, and the door swung open. The windows were blanketed by blackout curtains, leaving the house in gray shadows, concealing the clutter.

"Ximena?" he called out as he stepped inside. "Your master is here. Come and greet him appropriately."

Asher heard nothing. Perhaps Ximena wasn't here after all, but if that was the case, why was her scent so strong? Following the sweet smell of her flesh, Asher entered the bedroom. Ximena sat on the floor in the corner near the new tanks for all her snakes. She wore only socks and an oversized t-shirt with the demon baby from Black Sabbath's *Born Again* album on it. Her eyes were darker than ever, making her look harrowed and shrunken. Looking up at him, those eyes grew wet, and her lower lip trembled.

"Why the fuck didn't you answer the door?" Asher demanded.

Ximena opened her mouth but closed it just as quickly.

"Spit it out," Asher said. "What the hell's wrong with you?"

"I ... I can't sleep. Can't eat. I don't ... I ..."

As Asher came closer, Ximena pushed further back into the corner.

"Something bothering you, sweetheart?" he asked.

"I just can't ... I can't do this anymore."

"Do what?"

"This family. This cult. *You.* I just can't do it. I mean, my God, I've *killed people.*"

Asher smirked. "You wanted to kill them. You've *always* wanted to kill. I just taught you not to be afraid to run with that feeling."

"I admit I've always had a dark side—darker than most. Sure, I fantasized about murder sometimes, but that's all it was—*fantasy.* I never would've really murdered anyone, especially not Diego, if you hadn't made me."

"Don't pin your bloodlust on me, Ximena. Your hands weren't tied."

"But ... it's like I have no control over myself when I'm with you. I have no impulse control, no sense of morality or even consequences." She dabbed at her tears. "When I'm with you, everything's so grand and beautiful—the violence, the blood, the madness. But once we're separated, the guilt and horror set in. You have so much power over the rest of us. That's why I need to get away from you."

Asher squatted beside her. "You don't really think you have that option, do you?"

"I don't know what I believe anymore. I mean, what even are you? What are you *really?* You may have been a man once, but you're not anymore. You're some kind of crazy, evil thing."

"And you fucking love it," Asher said, leaning in for a kiss.

Ximena scooted away. "No! Don't come any closer. I can't ..."

"Oh, stop it. If you really wanted to leave me, you would have done it. You had all of last night to get away, but you chose to stay here and wait for me."

"Because I didn't know where to go! I felt like you'd just find me anywhere I went."

"I would. You belong to me, Ximena. You're my property."

"No ..."

"*Yes.* That's why you won't run off or call the police. *You can't.*"

"I didn't call the cops because, despite everything, I can't bear the idea of getting you in trouble. They talked to me, you know, about Diego and Fernanda, and I just played the part of grieving family member. I've come to realize I could never betray you even if I wanted to."

"I know."

He took hold of her chin and kissed her. Ximena tried to resist, but weakly. Soon, she wasn't resisting at all. Asher slid his hand down her bare thigh and cupped her crotch over her panties.

"Please," she whispered. "I don't want to be a demon too."

"That's just the stress talking, baby. Killing people isn't like anything else on this Earth. It's the most satisfying, natural experience, but society has conditioned us to feel sick about it. To normal people, it's the ultimate taboo. But we Reapers do not allow a society we never asked to be a part of to dictate our actions. You must not let them dictate your feelings either."

"But *you* dictate my feelings. Half the time, I don't even feel like myself when I'm around you. It's like the darkest part of me swallows everything else. All I feel is lust and rage and the need to please you at any cost."

"Because you love and worship me," he said, caressing her.

"I know I do, but sometimes, I think I shouldn't. I feel like I'm falling into a deep, dark pit I'll never be able to climb out of."

Asher pulled her panties to the side with one finger, then slid two others into Ximena. She released a shuddering breath.

"Enough of this nonsense," Asher told her. "Surrender to me, now and forever."

She rolled her hips against his hand. "I ... I ..."

"We can rule it all, you and me. You know you're my number one, don't you? My most special girl. Despite your nagging conscience, your inner evil has been there from the start. The moment we met at that diner, your black soul called out for me, asking to be dominated, begging me to show you the way. You were lost. I carried you out of the nothing. Together, we can have everything, Ximena. Be my princess of darkness."

Tears rolling down her cheeks, Ximena exhaled in sexual pleasure, a dichotomy that made Asher's dick hard.

"This is how Satan wants you," he breathed in her ear. "You're at the height of your beauty, and with my help, you're growing stronger every day. Each new kill adds to our power—power I want to share with you." As Asher fingered her, Ximena started shaking, fear and orgasm becoming one. "All you must do is submit— now and forever, or until Hell takes us."

Ximena climaxed and immediately started sobbing. Asher bit into her neck hard enough to make her scream, but once his black saliva hit her, her body went slack as incubus sorcery entered her pores, refreshing his hold over the girl.

Ximena's willpower was much stronger than that of the others. That's why Asher liked her so much. But it also made her a liability. The very trait that made her the worthiest of being his bride could also undo all he had wrought. He would have to keep a closer eye on her. If she gave in completely, Ximena would make for a fine companion in his reign of evil. But if she continued to pull away like this, he would have no choice but to discipline her. He was as prepared to kill her as much as any victim—more, even, if she tried to stand in his way.

"Get dressed," he told her. "From now on, you don't leave my sight."

FORTY

THE REAPERS WERE NATIONAL NEWS.

Thanks to the graffiti they'd left at recent crime scenes, the press was even calling them by their chosen name and emphasizing their devil worship, especially with the latest victims being a pastor and his wife. The FBI had taken over the case from the state police, but little information was being offered to the public due to it being an ongoing investigation. One thing they did stress was the continued search for Paul Mord and Deanna Butterworth. Demons had disposed of their bodies in the woods, so Asher knew the search was futile. The police had only located Deanna's car where Barney had left it the night of the murders.

Preferring to work in the shadows, Asher wasn't interested in being a celebrity, but the dread he'd caused fueled him more than any drug could. First, he'd rattled the town, then the state, and now the country, if not the world. While murder was almost a national pastime these days, with Americans having grown numb to school shootings and gang violence, a cult of Satanic serial killers captured everyone's attention. Murders were one thing, but when you added devil worship and ritual sacrifice, you tapped into the oldest, purest form of horror. Even in a country rapidly losing interest in religion, the old-world fear of Satan was deeply ingrained. Every news outlet was regurgitating what little they knew about the crimes and their ties to the occult. The Reapers were trending on social media and dominated newspaper headlines. They were public terror number one.

"We're the biggest thing since Manson," he said with pride as he watched the TV coverage.

"They keep comparing us to his family," Ximena said. "I've also heard people say we're the next Richard Ramirez, only worse because we're allegedly a group of Satanic killers instead of just one man. But other people really believe our murders are the acts of one person."

"Only because the idea of multiple killers is so much more frightening to them. They can't handle it."

Asher's phone rang. It was Melissa.

"Joel says he'll be home around eight-thirty," she told him.

"Perfect. That gives us plenty of time to set up."

"Set up what, Master?"

"His surprise party, of course."

Melissa breathed deep. "I don't know if I can go through with this, whatever it is."

"I'm getting pretty sick of hearing that. Do you love me or your husband?"

"Master, I love you more than I even love myself. Joel doesn't matter to me half as much as you do. But he's still the father of my children. He's still my husband of twenty-two years."

"He's a neglectful husband and father, and you know it."

"I do, but—"

"Listen, you old cunt! If you want to be blessed by my presence ever again, you'll strive to prove your complete and total devotion to me tonight. You must cast Joel aside in favor of me. You must put aside your children in favor of me. I am *everything*, Melissa. *I am God.* So you'll do what I tell you to and stop being so fucking wishy-washy."

Melissa lowered her voice. "Yes, Master."

"That's better. Now how are my girls?"

"Violet is just as pregnant as you said she was, if not more. She looks like she's ready to deliver any day. May I ask what's going on with her?"

"No. How's Callie?"

"She's ... I don't know. She seems a little dazed after last night. She's not saying much and is keeping to her room. Master ... what happened to Reverend Bower is all over the news."

"Don't talk about that on the phone, you imbecile."

"It's just that I think it's affecting her."

"Yeah, no shit. Callie had a life-changing experience last night. She's still adjusting. It's your job to keep her focused on what's important—*me*."

"I understand. You are my king, always. Whatever you want me to do ..."

"You're gonna wait until about eight p.m. Then you're gonna text Joel saying you and the girls are going out for a while."

"Well, okay, but he'll want to know why we're not going to be here to greet him after he's been away so long."

"Tell him that's exactly why you won't be there. Say you're sick of his lack of consideration for his family and how he doesn't show appreciation for you. Tell him it's time to face the consequences of his actions. But say all of this through text. If he calls, send him right to voicemail."

"Okay. Are the girls and I going somewhere with you?" she asked, sounding hopeful, almost excited.

"Straight to Hell," he said with a laugh. "But not yet, sweetheart. You and your daughters are staying home tonight. You're only *telling* Joel you won't be there."

"I don't understand."

"You don't have to. I'll be there in about two hours. I want you and the girls to look as sexy as possible when I get there, understand? Lacy panties, lingerie, whorish makeup—the works. Go shopping if you need to but be home on time. Got it?"

"Yes, Master."

Asher hung up. Ximena was looking at him but stifled whatever questions she had. Before leaving her place, Asher had her collect her raciest lingerie, including fishnet stockings and a collar attached to a chain leash. She also had a leather BDSM cat mask.

He called his mother and left another message asking where she was and why she hadn't returned his calls, putting a tremor in his voice to sound upset. Then he texted his father, pleading for him to make contact, telling him how worried he was getting.

"You've got me all excited again," Ximena said, rubbing Asher's thigh. "Just like I knew you would."

"Excited to kill again, you mean."

Ximena couldn't help but smile. She was under his spell again and happy to be there. "My family—not *our* family but the Falco family I was born into—are direct descendants of the Mayans and the Incas. They used to kill thousands of people just to celebrate the openings of new temples. Human sacrifice was my people's offering of nourishment to their gods and goddesses. Nobody does human sacrifice better than a Mexican."

"There's my girl," Asher said. "I was worried I'd lost you there for second."

"I'm so sorry to have worried you. I don't know what came over me. It's a big adjustment, like you were saying. I guess I was overwhelmed."

"Lucky for you there's a way to make it up to me."

That's when he told her the plans for the evening and what her role would be in them. Ximena's smoky eyes warmed with anticipation, eager to prove herself to the master all over again. She caressed his chest and draped one leg over his lap, nuzzling into his neck to plant little kisses.

"Save that for later," he told her.

"Please, I need you now. Let me show you I'm sincere."

She tried to kiss him, but Asher shoved her away. "No sugar for you until you've done as I've commanded."

"Oh, just a quickie, Master? Please, I need you inside me. Your choice of holes."

Asher grabbed her by the throat. "My boot will be inside your ass if you don't fucking listen! Access to my cock must be earned. Now stop begging and start thinking about the task at hand."

Ximena slinked off him. Asher's phone buzzed with a text message from Lenny, saying the job was done. Both of Asher's parents' cars were gone when he'd come home with Ximena, so he knew what his henchman meant. Lenny asked what else he could do for him, but Asher's plan for the evening didn't include the male members of his cult.

Tonight was all about his harem.

✝

With the Vincent women in the master bedroom of their house, Asher closed the door and went to the second-floor landing overlooking the stairwell. He shut off the overhead light, blanketing himself in shadows, and used the same power of camouflage he'd used on Barney the night of Paul and Deanna's murders. To anyone looking up from below, Asher wouldn't be there at all.

Melissa had gone to great lengths to doll up herself and her daughters. The mother was dressed in a new vinyl corset, with tall heels, black stockings, and a garter belt with no panties. Her makeup was garish but somehow worked for her. Though huge with her "pregnancy," Violet had also been given a whore's makeover and wore a teddy with no bra cups, leaving her swelled breasts exposed. But it was Callie that stole Asher's eye. The petite blonde wore what was likely her first lingerie—a frilly, blood-red ensemble that flattered her young body. Her budding female form was practically gift wrapped for her master.

They awaited him in bed while Ximena stood at the bottom of the staircase, facing the front door. She would be the first thing Joel Vincent saw when he returned home, and what a sight she was, dressed in those crotchless panties, fishnet stockings, and a one-size-too-small bustier that accentuated her hourglass figure. She'd thought Asher wanted her to wear her cat mask, but he had her heighten her beauty with full makeup instead, and the leashed collar was in her hand rather than around her neck. Knee-high hooker boots added several inches to her height. Though she could not see Asher now, Ximena knew he was up there, and she stared up at the balcony with adoration. She was ready. She was eager. She was *his*.

Headlights swept through the front window as Joel Vincent arrived in his minivan. Ximena posed provocatively. When Joel opened the door, she was on full display for him, and Asher had never seen a man so surprised.

"Who ... who're you?" he asked, putting down his suitcase. "What're you doing in my house?"

Joel Vincent had a paunch and short, curly hair that was going gray. Though they were the same age, he looked at least a decade older than his wife, who'd taken better care of herself over the years. His face was lined by the wrinkles of exhaustion and defeat. While shocked by the scantily-dressed young woman before him, he couldn't keep his gaze off her most delicious bits.

"I'm a friend of Violet's," Ximena said. "We've met before, don't you remember?"

It was a lie but a believable one. Joel looked around nervously.

"It was a while ago," Ximena said. "Back when we still had slumber parties. I've *blossomed* since then."

She stepped closer to Joel, and he did not step back.

"Why're you dressed like that?" he asked, no aggression in his tone.

Ximena bit her bottom lip when she smiled. "I wanted to look nice for you when you came home."

"I'm sorry ... what?"

Ximena pressed her palm against his chest. "I've always had a crush on you, Mr. Vincent. But I know you're a good man and wouldn't make love to me until I was of age."

He blinked rapidly. "Make ... make love?"

"I'm legal now. And I'm all yours."

She guided his hand to the opening in her crotchless panties, grazing his fingers to feel her wetness. Joel's eyes went wide. He withdrew from her, looking for any sign they weren't alone.

"Where is Violet?" he asked. "Is she here?"

Ximena shook her head and put her arms around his neck, pressing her breasts into him. "It's just you and me here, Mr. Vincent. We've got the whole house to ourselves."

"How did you get in here?"

"Violet left her window unlocked."

"That doesn't sound like her. What's *really* going on here?"

Ximena silenced him with a kiss, rubbing his crotch as she slid her tongue into his mouth. Joel hesitated to kiss her back, but he did not try to get away. He was a middle-aged businessman who struggled to get an erection with his wife, making him a prime target for a midlife crisis. This made him easy prey for any young female, just like Asher's old man, but Ximena had a special seductive magic to her on top of her exotic good looks, penetrating Joel's resolve. Her heavy flirting catered to his starved ego, making him lose sight of his doubts, of reality itself. As Ximena grinded on him, his hands slowly reached for her buttocks, the thong panties giving him easy access to her supple flesh. The touch seemed to electrify him.

"This can't be happening," he said. "I mean, who are you? I don't even know your name."

"I'm Ximena," she said. "And I'm here to do something I've wanted to do since the ninth grade."

"What?"

Ximena slipped the collar around Joel's neck, tightened it, and clutched the other end of the chain leash. "I'm here tonight to fuck your brains out."

Joel's mouth hung open. Even from this distance, Asher could smell the man's sweat. Joel stammered, unable to follow through on a thought, let alone find words. He just stood there trembling as Ximena got down on her knees in front of him and undid his belt. She started fellating Joel just as Asher had instructed her to. He'd experienced her deepthroat skills enough times to know Joel would be unable to resist her once she started. Even a man suffering from impotence couldn't refuse a hands-free blowjob so deep the woman's tongue lay flat against his balls. It was also possible that a new sexual partner was all Joel needed to get it up again. Maybe it was his shrew of a wife that caused his little problem. Thinking back on what a bitch Melissa had been when Asher first met her, it was not difficult to imagine. Nothing takes the lead out of a man's pencil like a disrespectful woman who doesn't appreciate all he does for her.

Ximena sucked on Joel for a minute, but his penis only got semihard. If it hadn't, Asher guessed the shlub would have cum right away. Joel's stress over his inability to perform showed on his face. Clearly, he wanted to be fully erect for Ximena and was embarrassed to only make it half-mast. Asher almost felt sorry for the guy. But whether Joel rose to the occasion or not, Ximena knew what to do with him. She would show patience, understanding, and desire unlike anything Joel had experienced from a woman before, including his wife, and soon, she would lead him upstairs.

Asher went into the master bedroom and softly closed the door. Melissa and her daughters were sprawled out on the bed, waiting for him with hungry expressions. The Vincent women had been told what needed to happen tonight, what they needed to do to prove their loyalty to their master. Asher climbed into bed, and his girls helped him out of his clothes. Their collective desire was palpable—lips and hands and tender parts swarming Asher's body, every moist void aching to be filled by his anaconda cock, every inch of their bodies available for even his most depraved sexual urges. By the time the door opened again, the orgy had already begun, and his girls were pleasuring him in a variety of ways.

Joel Vincent was saying something about having Viagra in his medicine cabinet as Ximena led him into the room. She flicked the light switch, revealing Joel's wife and daughters crawling all over Asher as he degraded them with his perversions, changing partners and orifices with every other thrust. Joel froze. Asher stared straight into the man's eyes, delighting in his look of shocked horror, a look that would worsen before the night was through.

Melissa took Asher's cock out of her mouth to smile at her husband. "Welcome home, honey."

Joel choked on his words, unable to process all he was seeing— his cheating wife, his underage daughter in lingerie, and his other daughter looking eight months pregnant. Catching Melissa having sex with another man shouldn't have surprised him, but Joel couldn't be blamed for being dumbstruck by this sick orgy. The mother of his children was not only sharing a man with them but doing it at the same time in the same bed—Joel and Melissa's marital bed. The hurt of betrayal was eclipsed by flabbergasted disgust.

Asher went right from Melissa's mouth into Violet's rectum, making the girl groan as his giant penis drove deep into her colon. He waved at Joel, the pentagram in his palm glowing like a lit cigarette.

Joel didn't charge at Asher. He didn't curse or scream. He just stood there stunned, his jaw slack and his limp dick still dangling out of his trousers. Looking at the girls, Asher detected a hint of shame in Melissa and Callie. Though they were obeying him—and clearly *wanted to*—they retained enough affection for Joel to feel remorse over what they were doing. Only Violet seemed completely detached from the pain she was causing her father. Having been under Asher's spell longer than anyone else, her love for him overpowered any other emotion she could experience. Making him happy made her happy. No one else mattered anymore. She looked her father dead in the eyes as she begged Asher to fuck her ass even harder.

With a face as red as his youngest daughter's thong, Joel suddenly lunged at Asher, and though Ximena tried to restrain him with the leash, the man's rage was explosive, and she was unable to hold him back.

"You son of a bitch!" Joel yelled. "Get the fuck away from my family!"

When Joel's hands landed on him, Asher grabbed him by both wrists and swung him in the air like a child, utilizing his superhuman strength. Joel was in midair when Asher released him, and he flew into the wall, fracturing it and knocking a framed wedding photo off its nail. Joel hit the floor, groaning in drywall dust. His face twisted in pain as he put a hand to his lower back.

"Ladies," Asher said, addressing his four females, "the time has come for you to put me above all others, forever."

The Vincent women were still, none of them seeming to want to make the first move. Asher could feel the resistance of their souls as their lifelong love for the family patriarch fought against Asher's Satanic hold over them, even Violet.

He put his arm around Melissa. "Remember what we talked about earlier. If you want your girls to ever be free, first you must offer this sacrifice."

Melissa reached under the pillows and withdrew the four butcher knives she'd been told to hide there. Still, she showed hesitation, so Asher increased the dosage of her love potion by breathing a cloud of black vapor into her face. Her eyelids fluttered as Asher's sorcery stripped away her last morsels of affection for Joel, leaving only the anger and heartbreak her husband had caused her during these last few years of their marriage. Asher kissed her and bit down on her bottom lip, giving her just enough pain to remind her how brutal the consequences would be if she disappointed him. When he released her, Melissa got out of bed and handed a knife to each of her daughters, then gave the last one to Ximena, keeping the largest butcher knife for herself as she approached her husband.

"Melissa," Joel said, looking up at her from the floor. "What're you doing? What is all this? Please, you have to—"

Melissa drove the blade into her husband's shoulder so quickly he didn't have time to process what had happened before she stabbed him again, sending the blade into his chest. Joel screamed and fell to the floor on his stomach.

Violet rolled out of bed, struggling with her extra weight. The hardwood floor creaked when she planted her feet on it, and she waddled toward her father with the knife, her face expressionless, eyes cold and gray. Joel's pleas went unheard by his oldest daughter, and as he tried to rise to his hands and knees, Violet stabbed him in the back. Joel let out a deafening screech. Instead of stabbing him again the way her mother had, Violet put both hands on the knife's handle and put all her body weight onto it, the force sinking the blade deeper through her father. Joel slipped in his own blood as he tried to get away.

Ximena approached Joel next. She kicked him in the face, and he fell on his side, Violet's knife still stuck in his back. Getting on her knees beside him, Ximena pulled on his penis, hacking at it before Joel managed to punch her, making her tumble backward. A white-hot fury made Ximena snarl. She dove into Joel's crotch headfirst and bit down hard on his bleeding member, shaking her head back and forth like a wolf with a critter it its mouth. The ensuing struggle triggered Melissa and Violet, and they came to Ximena's aid, Violet grabbing her father's head and driving her nails into her eyes. Melissa stabbed him everywhere, splitting his hands as he tried to block her attack, puncturing his torso, and opening an artery in his leg. The women writhed on top of him in an orgy of murder, their lingerie soaking up blood, their pretty faces spattered with red droplets.

Asher looked to Callie. She was still on the bed, watching the violence in a daze, tears welling in her eyes. She'd dropped the knife, and her face had lost all color, leaving her a ghost of a girl. Crawling back into bed with her, Asher planted little kisses on her neck, sending goosebumps across her skin.

"Don't be afraid," he whispered in her ear. "You know what to do."

Callie shuddered in his embrace. He rubbed his hand up and down her back, softly hushing her when she whimpered.

"This isn't like the Bowers," he told her. "This isn't about revenge. This is about devotion. It's your chance to prove yourself to me. I believe you're worthy of my love, Callie, but only you can earn it."

The other women had been instructed not to kill Joel tonight, only wound him, so now that he was down, they backed off, leaving him bawling in the growing puddle of blood. The women all stared at Callie.

Asher whispered to her again. "You hate your father as much as your mother and sister do. If they didn't, they wouldn't be doing this, no matter how much I influence them. I'm only building on the anger they already have toward him. Think about it, sweetheart. He's always gone. He's never here for you. His bullshit job means more to him than any of you ever could. Even now, he was about to cheat on your mother with Ximena. Obviously, he doesn't love any of you."

Callie wept, but when Asher put the knife in her hand, she gripped the handle so tight it shook.

"I'm here to give you all the love you deserve," Asher told her. "I wouldn't stand for the Bowers hurting you, and I won't stand for your deadbeat dad hurting you either. You'll find freedom and security in my arms, Callie, but before I can fully embrace you, I need to know you love me as much as I love you. You need to show me I'm the most important man in your life—the *only* man."

Callie looked to her mother, but Asher had instructed Melissa and Violet not to sway Callie either way, so Melissa only stared at her daughter, saying nothing, her face as lifeless as a corpse's. Callie looked to her sister but found only the same stoic emptiness.

"You do love me, don't you?" Asher asked her.

Finally, Callie spoke. "More than anything in the world."

"That's what I thought," he said, kissing her cheek. "Now be my good girl by being bad."

Callie slowly got out of bed and stepped barefoot through her father's blood. She put both hands around the knife's handle, but it continued to shake in her unsteady grip. She looked so small and fragile in this moment. Asher licked his lips as she approached her father. Joel was bleeding out from a small opening in his femoral artery and was going to die whether Callie attacked him or not, but that didn't matter to Asher. What was important here was that Callie made the gesture, and the better she did it, the greater her reward would be. If she failed to be totally subservient, there would be swift punishment, but she didn't know that, so it wouldn't affect her decision.

What surprised Asher was how much he cared about the outcome of this. He wanted Callie to succumb to his evil more than he had anyone else. He was even *nervous* she might fail. The sense that she served a greater purpose than his other acolytes was too powerful to ignore. Asher believed Callie was a key rung on the ladder of his Satanic ascension, even though he wasn't quite sure what her ultimate role would be.

"Go on, sweetheart," Asher told her as she got on her knees beside her dying father. "Show everyone how much you love me."

Callie raised the knife over her head. She remained in that position, frozen, until Joel tried to say something. The sound of his voice hit some ignition switch hidden within her. Callie went into a blind rage, driving the blade in and out of her father in a frenzy, sobbing and screaming as the only life she'd ever known was destroyed forever.

FORTY-ONE

THE NEXT MORNING, ASHER AND Ximena took Violet to the convent, dropping her off half a mile down the road so his car wouldn't be seen. Violet dressed in old clothes to look less mature than she was, facilitating the teenage runaway illusion. Asher even got her a cross necklace and a used bible to carry with her to the front door. Violet had detailed instructions. She was to report back to him by phone, if the nuns permitted personal calls. She would also send Asher letters detailing the routines of the nuns and the interior layout of the convent, paying close attention to who stayed in which rooms and where the inhabitants congregated at specific times of day.

To assure the nuns wouldn't turn her away, Asher concocted a sob story for Violet. She would tell them she'd been raped by her stepfather, and when he found out she was pregnant, he tried to force her to get an abortion so her mother wouldn't find out what had been going on, but Violet saw such a procedure as equivalent to murder—a belief the nuns shared and would gobble right up. When contacting

Asher, she would pretend it was her mother she was keeping in touch with, but would tell the nuns that, while she still loved Mom, she was an unfit parent, always in and out of jail and court-appointed rehab centers. Most of all, Violet would stress the lack of religion in her household and how the relationship she'd formed with God on her own was the only thing that kept her going.

"Talk with Sister Rosemary and Sister Ernestine as much as you can," Asher told her. "Those two brides of Christ are the ones I'm most interested in. Ernestine's a bit crusty, but Rosemary's a doll baby. She'll be easy for you to befriend."

"Yes, Master," Violet said. "As you wish."

As they drove off, Ximena gazed at Asher with admiration. "I wish I could control men the way you do women."

"You can. Look at how easily you lured Joel Vincent to his death. Men are easy because they tell you what they want, whereas women always feel the need to be ambiguous."

"Men are also huge liars."

"Absolutely, but so are women and children. Everyone is full of shit. You just have to dig through it to discover what they're really after. Then you've got them. Men all tend to want the same three things—power, money, and pussy—and the first two are really just methods to obtain the third."

"I've definitely used my sexuality to get what I want from men, but you have a power over women that is out of this world."

"You're not hearing me. If you want to control men, you just have to convince them you're not just one of their goals but that you're the key to achieving their other goals. Men have this irrational idea that the world owes them something, like a birthright just for being born with a dick. They're all the little boy having a tantrum when he doesn't get his way, only in larger bodies. If you feed their delusions, I promise they'll do whatever they can to kiss up to you. People often talk about alpha males, but guys like that wouldn't exist without desperate sycophants singing their praises in the hope their king will share his riches. That's how billionaires are made and presidents are elected."

"I'd vote for you," Ximena said with a smile.

Asher laughed. "Oh, sweetheart. I don't want to be president."

"Why not?"

"There's not enough power in it."

Ximena's smile faded. It seemed his words had given her a chill. They were entering Asher's neighborhood when his phone rang.

He didn't recognize the number but answered it anyway.

A nervous voice greeted him. "Hey. It's me, Barney."

"What's up? You sound like you're about to shit your pants."

Barney breathed heavily as he tried to get it out. "The police brought me in for questioning."

Asher pulled over on the side of the road to give the call his complete attention. "Listen to me, Barn, and listen good. If you're calling from the jailhouse phone, we're being monitored and recorded right now."

"It's okay. I'm not at the station anymore."

"So they didn't arrest you?"

"No, they just asked me to come in and answer some questions about Paul Mord and Deanna Butterworth. The FBI was even there. Someone who was at the party told police they saw me leaving with Paul and Deanna the night they disappeared. It's weird … they seem to think they're the ones involved in the Reaper murders. I guess 'cause they're known members of The Temple of Satan."

As dumb as Barney often seemed, he was choosing his words wisely, speaking of Paul and Deanna in the present tense to suggest they were still alive, just in case someone was listening. He also didn't call Asher "Master" or suggest he was anything other than a close friend.

"Where are you calling from?" Asher asked.

"I'm at home on my house phone. I figured it was more secure than a cellphone."

"All right. So what have you told them?"

"Just that Paul and Deanna gave me a ride home that night, and that was the last I saw or heard from them."

"How soon can you get to my place?"

"About twenty minutes."

"Good. If the police try to pull you in for questioning again, tell them you've already told them everything you know and you'll need legal counsel before you say anything else."

"Won't it look suspicious if I ask for a lawyer?"

"If they're questioning you repeatedly, then you're already a suspect. Anyone in your position with any sense would exercise their right to an attorney."

Beside him in the passenger seat, Ximena's eyes grew large, hearing only half of the conversation.

"Okay," Barney said, sounding less rattled now that he had his master's advice. "I'll see you soon."

"Don't bring your phone with you or use a GPS or anything else that can be tracked, understand?"

"Right. My car is ancient, so there's no built-in navigation system."

"Good. Don't stress about this." Then Asher said something just in case the phone was tapped. "Maybe Paul and Deanna are involved with these terrible crimes, but you're not, and law enforcement is smart enough to realize that."

They ended the call, and Asher hit the road again.

"They're closing in on us, aren't they?" Ximena asked.

"Nonsense."

"What're we gonna do?"

"Just shut up and let me think."

The Japanese sludge metal band Boris hummed from the speakers as he sped up, the droning music helping Asher process everything. Barney had become a liability. He was obedient and loyal, but would he remain that way if the police charged him with murder? Or would he accept a plea deal, receiving a lighter sentence by turning in Asher and the others? Having Barney in the interrogation chair was one step closer to police putting Asher in that chair too. Even if Barney made every attempt to protect the cult, that didn't mean he wouldn't slip up. The FBI had interrogation techniques designed to make suspects do exactly that. Barney was a decent stooge but was hardly worth taking risks for. Asher couldn't let one member of the family jeopardize the rest. He needed a plan.

That law enforcement suspected Paul and Deanna were *involved* in the Reaper slayings, rather than being victims, was an interesting development. The couple's history with Satanic organizations, combined with the timing of their sudden disappearance, made a compelling case they might be the killers law enforcement were searching for.

Barney was known to be a friend of Paul and Deanna. Violet had been more of an acquaintance, and no cops had come to question her—yet. The rest of the Reaper cult had no ties to the missing couple. Though Asher had been at the party where they were last seen, as the newcomer, no one there really knew who he was. The only thing that could link Asher to Paul and Deanna was Barney.

A plan started forming.

"Funny you should mention controlling men," Asher said to Ximena. "You're about to see it in action."

Returning to his house, the first thing Ximena did was light the scented candles to cover the lingering odor of death. It had faded since Lenny and Barney cleaned everything up, but decaying human flesh was a powerful stench that didn't leave easily. To further cover the smell, Asher sent Ximena into the kitchen to cook him some lunch, filling the house with the strong aromas of beef, garlic, and hot peppers. He drew a bottle of beer from the fridge, drank half of it in one swig, then refilled it with tabasco sauce, giving the brew heat. Asher opened a brick of cocaine and sniffed marble-sized clumps from the edge of a pocketknife. Once she'd brought his meal to him, Ximena was allowed to gorge herself on coke too. She filled a tablespoon with it, snorted it up, and went in for a refill. Asher liked to see it. Regardless of his powers, drugs still played a role in his control over his followers, for they altered their brain chemistry and hindered their good judgement. The emotional toll of committing heinous murders needed some sort of numbing agent. If Asher could keep his family high, they'd be less likely to relapse into morals and decency.

"That's right, Whitney Houston," he told Ximena. "Dig right in."

Melissa and Callie could probably use some sort of sedative right now. Asher wondered how things were going with the burial. After murdering her father, Callie had gone cold and silent, all traces of human emotion having fled to some dark inner chamber of her heart. Asher praised her for making the final death stroke, but she was too distant to be consoled. He had to accept he'd been pushing her too far too fast. Despite her Satanic potential, Callie was still a fifteen-year-old girl. The transition from school studies to brutal patricide had been a short and furious whirlwind. There were limits even to Asher's power. If he wasn't careful with the young girl's mind, he might accidentally destroy it, and if he didn't handle her soul gently, he might never capture it in full.

After Joel Vincent was dead, Asher had cast another sleep spell over Callie to give her a break from the violent chaos her life had become. The other girls were not given this reprieve. Violet's reaction to her father's murder had been surprisingly enthusiastic. She'd draped over him on her belly, using his corpse as a sex pillow to prop her ass up, and begged her master to fuck her in her father's blood—a nod to how Asher had demanded to be fucked in his father's blood. Asher granted her wish and took her from behind, Melissa resting her head on her daughter's lower back so Asher could go from Violet's snatch to Melissa's mouth with ease. Ximena had crawled through the blood puddle beneath Asher to lick his scrotum, and the foursome had only grown more perverse from there, with Joel's body parts being used as dildos and his guts as bondage rope.

The task of disposing of Joel's eviscerated carcass had been left to Melissa. Asher told her to keep it simple by burying him in the backyard. Melissa almost questioned him about this, hinting that he would be better equipped to dispose of a corpse than she was, but Asher shut her down. Joel was her husband, making him her responsibility. Asher had more important shit to do. Though he wanted to check on Melissa's progress, meeting with Barney took precedence.

When his henchman arrived, Asher got right to it. "Barn, how dedicated to the family are you?"

"One thousand percent," Barney said without hesitation.

"And what about me?"

"You?" He smiled. "You're my master. My idol. My savior. Before you, I was just a fat loser. My life had no direction. You changed all of that."

Barney sat at the table, and Asher had Ximena fetch their guest a beer. Then she sat with the men, observing, Asher teaching by example.

"Barn," Asher said, "do you love me?"

The unexpected question made Barney's cheeks flush. "With all my heart and soul."

"*Soul.* What an interesting choice of words. Does your soul belong to me?"

Barney's eyes darted in confusion. "If that is your wish, Master."

"Make me believe it, Barn."

"My soul is in your hands. I swear to you."

Asher smacked the table. "Swear to Satan!"

"I swear to Satan!"

Asher put his hands on either side of Barney's head and pulled him in close. Asher rested his forehead against Barney's. "There's much more to our existence than life in these bodies, these *flesh prisons.* Our time on this Earth is infinitesimally small compared to our infinite existence after death. This life is but a trial. It's our chance to prove ourselves worthy of Satan's blessings. And how do we do that?"

"Through murder?"

"Through *sacrifice.*" Asher patted Barney's cheek. "Sure, human sacrifice is a huge part of it. But it's not just the spilling of blood that pleases the Prince of Darkness—it's the risks we're willing to take to glorify him. By killing our fellow man, we put ourselves in jeopardy, don't we?"

Barney nodded, squinting as he tried to understand what his master was driving at.

"When you kill people—especially the children *you* killed, Barn— you risk losing your freedom, your reputation, your friends and family. You even risk eternal damnation. You're sacrificing not just your victim but yourself, and that's the greatest tribute of all. It shows Lucifer you've accepted him as lord and you're willing to do anything— and give up anything—to spread his glory. Now … you are willing, aren't you?"

"Absolutely, Master."

"That's exactly what I told Lucifer." Praising him, Asher saw light flutter through Barney's eyes. "When Satan asked me which of my disciples showed the most promise, I had to be honest, so I told him it was you. Isn't that right, Ximena?"

Ximena blinked, surprised to be part of the conversation, but she went along with the lie. "That's right. Our master was singing your praises to Lucifer himself."

"Wow," Barney said, grinning. "So, like … Lucifer knows who I am?"

"Of course!" Asher said. "He loves every one of us Reapers. We're doing his work, and he doesn't want anything to stand in the way of that. I'm willing to do whatever it takes to keep our family strong. I know you are too."

"For sure."

Asher patted his shoulder. "That's my boy! I knew we could all count on you! That's why Lucifer and I have decided you're going to make a huge sacrifice for the good of our family's mission."

Barney beamed. "Awesome! Just name it, Master. I'll sacrifice whoever you want me to. Just give me a name."

"All right." Asher put both hands on Barney's shoulders. "Their name is Barney Kaplan."

Barney's smile vanished. "But … that's my name."

"Exactly. Now, before you get freaked out, understand that we're not asking you to kill yourself." Barney exhaled with relief, and Asher continued. "The sacrifice you must make is to turn yourself in."

Barney's mouth hung open. "What do you mean?"

"I mean, you're gonna return to the police station and make a full confession. You're gonna tell the FBI that you, Paul, and Deanna are the ones behind the Reaper killings, and no one else. It must be you, Barn, because they already suspect you. If the police link the rest of us to these killings, our family is finished, and we won't be able to go through with the attack on the convent, which Satan has declared our ultimate goal. By taking the fall, you'll be protecting the rest of the family as well as our dark lord's mission. You'll be a hero."

Barney stared at nothing as the magnitude of this fell over him. He was beginning to sweat.

"I know this is a lot to ask for," Asher said, "but the loss of your freedom in this short life is a small price to pay for the rewards you'll find in the next. I'm poised to be the next Great Duke of Hell, and I want you by my side, Barn. But you must show you're truly worthy. You must make this sacrifice."

Still, the henchman was silent.

"Understand this is a great honor," Asher told him.

"Oh," Barney said, coming out of his daze. "I am honored, Master. Really, I am."

"With honor comes reward, my friend—reward and *power*. You'll be idolized by all Satanists. You'll be a fucking celebrity amongst the denizens of Hell." Asher cut into his rare steak and poured hot sauce inside of it as well as on top. "What's a few years in prison compared to an eternity of bliss? Forget about raping women—they'll be *lining up* to spread their legs for you. You'll be the king of your own circle, master of your own stable of sex slaves, a fucking immortal demigod!"

Now, Barney was smiling again. "Yeah. I mean … *fuck yeah!* I know I could be a great leader. I've learned so much from you, Master."

"You do this, Barn, and you won't be calling me Master anymore. You'll be calling me brother."

Tears of joy flooded Barney's eyes. "You really mean it?"

Asher bit into the dripping piece of steak. "C'mon, brother. Would I lie to you?"

FORTY-TWO

SMOKE ROSE FROM THE PENTAGRAM, the black plumes choking the sky.

They stood in his favorite wooded clearing, Asher etching the symbol into the dirt where Paul and Deanna had been slaughtered, their remains dragged down to Hell by demon claws. Though it was midday, a storm was moving in, casting a pall over the forest. The air was frigid and damp, but the red flames in the lines of the pentagram radiated intense heat. Ximena and Barney were sweating.

On the drive over, Asher watched for any police tails, driving in circles to test the cars behind them until they turned away. Confident they were alone, Asher brought his disciples here for the ritual.

He chanted and guided his followers to repeat after him. The words came to Asher as if yanked out of some distant memory. Ximena and Barney struggled to pronounce some of the words from dead languages, but the incantation was successful, and the soil began to stir as if being shifted by invisible backhoes. The pentagram became a pit of magma, the stones in the soil busting from the sudden heat, creating a volcanic vortex for blistered claws to rise from. The demons' jaundiced hands were covered in lesions that wept pus, the droplets boiling upon the hot flesh. The claws tossed bones out of the pit. Some still had morsels of decayed meat attached. A cracked ribcage was hurled into the dirt, and Deanna's skull rolled past Barney's feet. As the fire grew redder, a familiar stench permeated the surrounding thicket.

Ximena suddenly screamed.

Asher looked up from the pit to see the horned beast drifting amongst rows of withered trees, its black horns twisting clockwise atop its misshapen head, its tusks slick with green liquid feces. Beelzebub's eyelids opened and closed, flashing chipped baby teeth in empty sockets of festering meat. The mighty snout pissed maggots. Horseflies covered the demon like an extra layer of skin.

Gazing upon the Lord of the Flies, Barney dropped to his knees in worship, and Asher snickered, wondering if the fool thought this was Satan himself. Despite everything she'd seen before, Ximena stared in horror at the grotesque demon and got behind Asher, clinging to him.

"Don't be afraid," he told her, though even Asher had not expected Beelzebub to appear.

Ximena stammered. "I just … I didn't know …"

Asher shushed her and raised both arms to salute the foul demon. Now, both his hands were engulfed in crimson fire. The flames spiraled around Asher's arms, then wrapped around his neck and spread down his torso in waves.

"Hail!" Asher shouted.

The demon's eye-mouths widened, releasing a sound like a tiger's roar. The noise became almost musical, and the maggots that fell out of its snout chimed like bells as they hit the ground.

"Praise the Lord of the Flies," Asher told the others.

Together, they hailed, throwing up their hands in the horns salute. Asher removed his inverted cross necklace and held it high. Beelzebub closed its mouths, but still a strange sound emanated from the beast's rotted husk—a metallic drone that echoed through the forest, sounding like an old motor running in the bottom of a well.

"What does it want?" Ximena whispered over Asher's shoulder.

But Asher didn't know. He'd come to the clearing to unearth the corpses as evidence but had not anticipated the demonic entity.

Seeing Beelzebub now, he realized how much he'd been missing his interactions with The Evil Trinity. Though Asher was a warlock confident in his witchcraft, he still embraced whatever guidance the great ones offered. Just as his disciples lived to please him, Asher only wanted to impress his overlords with worship, sacrifice, and slaughter, so to further forge the stairway to his infernal throne.

Had he summoned Beelzebub without realizing it? Had Rex made him say the words that would draw the demon from the abyss? Or had it come without being called?

"How may I serve you, my exalted dark one?" Asher asked.

The malignant entity huffed, its breath like an open sewer. "It is I who have come to help thee. You continue to serve us well, Asher Benton. Thou art a true son of Hell."

"Thank you, my excellence. I am eternally grateful for your Satanic blessings."

The beast raised its trunk with a roar that echoed through the woodland, spooking crows from the treetops and silencing the scurry of critters. Beelzebub stomped its massive hooves, shaking the ground as it approached the bones within the pentagram. It's eye holes widened to twice their normal size, and black blood gushed out of them, sluicing through the gaps in their baby teeth. Its snout spewed fire, scattering burning maggots, and as the tar-like gore spattered onto the human remains, the flesh the lesser demons had devoured began to reform upon the bones. The tissue did not return to its pre-death state but rather to a stage of decomposition appropriate to the length of time the corpses would have been there, exposed to the elements.

Paul had been stabbed to death by Barney that night, and now all his stab wounds reappeared, along with the stump of his neck where Asher had severed his head. It was black with rot. The carving Asher had made in Deanna's belly returned, and her eviscerated torso writhed with what looked like tentacles, her intestines being resurrected only to be splayed out in the dirt. Her face reformed on her skull in a gray death mask. Asher's thoughts turned salacious, fantasies of face-fucking necrophilia stirring his loins, but he knew the remains were being altered for more than his amusement. By erasing the damage the lesser demons had done, Beelzebub was making the story Asher concocted for Barney's confession more credible. The demon barfed again, spewing houseflies and more grubs onto the carcasses to continue their transformation.

Beelzebub stretched out its trunk and wrapped it around Asher's neck like a noose, but he felt no fear, only ecstasy. Flies buzzed about, crawling on his face, their wings flicking drops of filth in a Satanic baptism.

"Thou must take the convent," Beelzebub said. "The brides of Christ must suffer and die. Your cult must not fail, Asher Benton. To fail is to fall."

"I won't fail, my dark lord. I swear it to you and Father Satan. Every nun will *intimately* know pain and horror before their executions."

"Thou hast been granted the power of a demigod. But Lucifer tasked me with giving power to the disciple of thy choosing, so thou wilt have a minion with access to black magic."

Asher considered this. He looked to Barney, who was still bowing in the dirt. Barney gazed up at him hopefully, almost pleadingly. The fool should have known better than to even think he had a chance of being gifted sorcery. Barney only filled one role now—that of stool pigeon. With the convent attack ahead of them, the killing would start right up again after Barney surrendered to the police, proving he wasn't the last of the Reaper killers. Asher could have forgone turning him in but wanted to create a sense of calm and relief for the locals before the convent attack so people would be less on guard, making the sudden bloodbath even more terrifying.

Asher looked to Ximena. He'd appreciated her inner darkness from the start, but while she was devoted to him, Asher consistently had to keep her spellbound so she wouldn't dissent. Her moral guilt was concerning. It would serve him well to have a witch for a hench-woman, but could Ximena be trusted with such power?

Perhaps he could choose a disciple that wasn't present, but Asher wouldn't have time to explain new powers to Violet before the raid on the convent, and despite her previous interest in paganism and the occult, Asher felt she was too immature to master witchcraft. Melissa was more of a slave than a disciple, too expendable to be special. And Asher certainly didn't trust Lenny enough to grant him any kind of power. He was too power-hungry as it was.

Asher didn't trust anyone anymore. He was no longer interested in bonding with people, other than to work with them to get what he wanted. He'd killed his parents and best friend. What sort of com-radery could a man like that ever experience?

"Ximena is the worthiest," he told the demon. Ximena stared at

Asher with a face that was hard to read. "But she's had her doubts about what needs to be done."

Ximena shook her head. "No, Master. Not anymore. I am with you all the way."

"You say that now, but let's not forget the depressive state I found you in at your place." He turned to Beelzebub. "If there's one thing I might ask for, it's for my incubus hold on her to be absolute."

Beelzebub released Asher and shot its elephant trunk toward Ximena. She gasped, and the snout entered her mouth, filling it with flies and liquid excrement. Her eyes rolled back as she was lifted off the ground. Beelzebub's trunk snaked down her throat. Despite her oral sex skills, Ximena gagged as the appendage entered her esophagus, bile spraying from her nostrils as she convulsed and peed herself. She glowed like a ruby in sunlight. When the demon released her, she collapsed in the dirt, twitching and struggling to regain air.

"She has been granted witchery," Beelzebub explained, "but may only use her powers to serve thee. From this day forward, her life's dream is to do thy bidding. Thou will witness nothing but unwavering servitude. At thy command, she will kill people without remorse or hesitation—including herself, if it be your will."

Asher hailed the beast, and it slunk back into the thicket, the dead shrubs coming to life to embrace its horrid form, caressing Beelzebub like the hands of lovers.

"There shall be great death," the demon said as it retreated. "And then there shall be great rebirth."

When Beelzebub was gone, Asher stood over Ximena, watching her cough up waste that had been pumped into her like so much semen.

"You've been preparing for that deepthroat all your life," he said with a snicker. "All those cocks in your mouth were just to prepare you for Beelzebub's mammoth trunk."

Ximena spat up festering goo. "Yes, Master."

"Help her up, Barn."

Barney got Ximena to her feet, but she was too dazed to stay on them, so Asher scooped her into his arms, pressing her chest to his.

"Your will was the strongest I've met yet," Asher told her. "You know I liked that about you, but sometimes, even the prettiest things must be broken."

A maggot crawled out her nostril as she gazed up at him in a delirium. "I love you so much."

"Of course you do. But I realize now that I mistook your depression for evil. They're so similar in appearances. Still, I've watched the darkness inside you blossom. Now, you'll be evil without that pesky remorse."

"Please let me kill for you." Ximena motioned toward Barney. "I'll feed you his heart, Master, if it be your will."

"And what about your heart?"

"If it is your wish, I'll tear it out with my bare hands just to see you smile."

Asher gave her a pat on the butt. "Good girl. Obedience is of the essence, as is time."

Ximena draped her arms around his neck, her eyes black and lost, likely forever.

"Barney," Asher began, "you are to go directly to the police station and confess. You'll tell the pigs that you, Deanna, and Paul committed all the Reaper murders together. Shortly after, Deanna started breaking down from the stress and convinced Paul they needed to turn themselves in. You tried to talk them out of it, but they'd made up their minds, so you called them out here on the pretense of discussing how you were going to surrender to police. But all you really wanted to do was kill them." Asher drew the folded knife from his pocket—the same one that had been used the night of the murders—and put it in Barney's hand. "It really was you who stabbed Paul to death, so you won't even have to lie about that. But you also must tell them you were the one to rape, suffocate, and gut Deanna."

Barney nodded. "Yes, Master. It was all me."

"When the cops ask what made you change your mind about turning yourself in, tell them Jesus came in his flying saucer, and he and the seven dwarves took you on a journey through time and space to show you the error of your ways."

Barney's face twisted in confusion. "Huh?"

"If they think you're crazy, they'll deem you unfit to stand trial. You'll end up in a sanitarium instead of a prison. Won't that be better?"

"Oh. Okay, yeah."

But Asher didn't care where Barney ended up. He just didn't want the police to believe anything Barney said if he changed his mind later and decided to rat out Asher and the others. He considered making Barney confess to killing Asher's parents too, especially seeing as there were still some of their remains in a bag in his garage, but that would only bring police to Asher's door sooner. He wanted to avoid that until after the convent, and besides, he already had another fall guy in mind for his parents' murders.

FORTY-THREE

THE HUMAN REMAINS HE'D BURIED inside the walls were proving to be effective talismans. Amazingly, they'd seemed to have kept police from coming around in search of his mother and father, because law enforcement posed a threat to Asher.

Mom's coworkers didn't.

The morning after Barney confessed to the Reaper killings, the doorbell rang, and Asher grabbed his pistol in case it was the police. Instead, when he looked out the window, he saw an older woman with very short hair. Excited she might be another nun, Asher sent Ximena to his bedroom, then opened the front door.

"Hello," the woman said, pushing her glasses up the bridge of her nose. "You must be Asher."

"Who wants to know?"

"I'm Bea. Bea Martin. Your mother works with me. I'm her supervisor."

Asher moved aside. "Please, come in."

Bea stepped right into the house, but her face soured when she got a whiff. Asher closed the door behind her and put his back to it, blocking the exit.

"Is, um …" Bea said. "Is Elizabeth here?"

"Not in the sense you mean."

Bea lowered her eyebrows. "I don't understand."

"I don't understand that hair. You think a mop like that is gonna land you a husband? Men want a woman who looks like a woman, not Moe from *The Three Stooges*."

"I beg your pardon?" she said, face burning with indignation. "I'll have you know I've been married for twenty-nine years and have five children."

"My condolences, Butch. That's worse than a prison sentence. What's your wife's name?"

"Young man, I didn't come here to be insulted! I'm looking for your mother because she's missed several days of work. She's been a no-call-no-show all week, hasn't logged into her work laptop even once, and won't answer her phone. Now, if she's not here, I'd like to know where she is so I can get ahold of her. If she wants to keep her job—"

Asher grabbed Bea by the throat and squeezed, making her eyes bulge. She tried to break free, but he was far stronger, his fingers closing around her neck like a noose. When she tried to breathe, Asher covered her mouth with his left hand, and red light made her skull glow from the inside out.

"My mother went on an extended vacation," he told her. "You're cool with that, aren't you?"

He released the woman. She coughed and caught her breath, and when she looked up at Asher again, her whole demeanor had changed. Bea stared at him with salacious longing as she started undoing her blouse.

"No one wants to see your saggy old tits," he told her. "Man, you're even more desperate than I thought. I guess that's what three decades of marriage will do."

"Please … I'll do anything …"

"Yeah, yeah, yeah. How well do you know my mom? Do you two get along?"

"We do! We've worked together for seven years or so and have a good relationship."

"What has she told you about Sam?"

"Her boyfriend? Sam Sutherland?"

Now Asher had a last name. "Yeah. Tell me what you know."

"Sam used to work with us before he left for a position with Docu-tech. Elizabeth told me she'd run into him again a few months ago and they'd started dating."

"I'll bet that whore was fucking him long before that. She was probably gargling his cum while they were coworkers and she was still with my father."

Bea pawed at Asher's chest. "I'd like to gargle your cu—"

"Shut up and listen, Jurassic cunt. You're gonna go back to work and tell everyone my mom is fine, that she took some time off to rekindle the flame with her husband. If you're the supervisor, you must have access to employee files. That's how you got my mom's address, right?"

"Yes."

"You're gonna pull Sam Sutherland's old file and call me with his address." He gave her his number. "Do not call me for any other reason. You're gonna get out of my house and fetch that address immediately."

"Then you'll make love to me?"

"Fuck no. I'd sooner put my dick in a blender. Now get that eighty-pound lump of cottage cheese you call an ass out of my house. And if you tell anyone about this, I'll crucify every one of your children in your front yard and set them on fire."

Bea was so lost to his spell she didn't even flinch at the threat. She was focused solely on her passion for the incubus. No one else mattered.

"Sure," she said. "Whatever you say. I can give you everything you want."

She kept babbling about her love for him as Asher shoved her out the front door. Bea fell, skinning her hands on the pavement. Still, she smiled warmly at Asher as she got to her feet. Once in her car, she blew kisses to him as she drove away.

Asher decided to check on his other old biddy.

With Ximena being fully spellbound and endowed with sorcery, he was no longer concerned about her being out of his sight, so he walked across the street to the Vincent house and let himself in with Joel's key. This time, Melissa wasn't waiting in the window, and she didn't come running when he closed the door. She did try, though. Melissa came limping out of the living room, using a cane for support.

Weeks of abuse had taken a serious toll, but that wasn't the only culprit. According to tradition, repeated sexual activity with an incubus could be disastrous to a woman's health. Melissa didn't have the immunity granted to Asher's female cult members, so she took the curse head-on. Her hollow eye sockets and scrawny arms suggested she either couldn't keep food down or hadn't bothered eating at all. Asher's black semen had slowly poisoned her, deteriorating her body as well as her mental state.

"Welcome home, my master," she said, smiling despite it all, overjoyed to be in his presence again. "How may I serve you today? Should I fix you something to eat and suck your dick?"

Asher pursed his lips. "Is he buried?"

"Yes," Melissa said, her sad eyes drifting. "We moved the little shed out back, buried him, then moved the shed back over the spot."

"Who's we?"

"Me and Callie."

"Where is my baby girl? How's she doing?"

"Upstairs in her room. She hasn't come out much. I couldn't let her go to school in the state she's in. I don't think she can take all this the way I can."

"If you ask me one more time to let your daughters go—"

"No, no. I'm sorry, Master. I just—"

"Just shut up. Is there any beer?"

"Yes, Master. I stocked up the garage fridge for you."

"Go fetch."

Melissa shuffled to the door leading to the garage. It swung wide open, offering Asher a glimpse of the tools and supplies she'd told him about when describing her late husband's obsession with storm preparedness. There was a generator and a smaller power bank, and plastic shelving holding lanterns, bottled water, and canned goods. Melissa drew a bottle of Asher's favorite beer from the packed backup refrigerator. Taking it, Asher unscrewed the cap, gulped down half of it in one chug, then handed the bottle back to Melissa. He went upstairs to Callie's room and found her sitting by the window, staring out at a sky of slate. She didn't even turn around to see who'd walked in.

Asher came behind her and put his hands on her shoulders. "How is my princess today?"

She didn't reply, so Asher squeezed her shoulders harder, delivering a stern warning. Callie looked up at him with a ghost-white face.

Her blond hair appeared platinum in the natural light, and her small body seemed so fragile in its girlishness. It was as if he were looking at a living porcelain doll. Asher was struck numb. He'd never seen anything so beautiful, so deserving of corruption.

"Sorry," was all she said.

"I'm not mad. Your mother tells me you helped her bury Joel. So now you've killed and fucked and disposed of a body. You're making great progress."

"Toward what?"

Asher kissed the top of her head. "I'm still not sure. I just know you're very special."

"Yes, Master."

Asher kissed her cheek. "You know what? You can just call me Asher."

"Are you sure?" she asked, nervous.

"I said you were special, Callie."

The girl blushed, her long eyelashes batting as her worries fell away.

Then Asher took his favorite girl to bed.

✝

Three days after she'd entered the convent, Violet's letter arrived in Asher's mailbox. It contained a map she'd drawn of the interior and broke down the daily routines and room assignments. Violet confirmed Sisters Ernestine and Rosemary were there, and she'd struck up a rapport with the younger nun. Overall, she'd gathered more information than Asher would have expected this soon. Perhaps she was more valuable than he'd realized. He could even sense the rising bloodlust in her words. Being in the convent and knowing what was coming had filled Violet with anticipation.

Asher was eager too. He was tired of waiting. The time had come.

He and Ximena had been staying in the Vincent house so Asher could sleep with Callie in her parents' bed. Each night, she cuddled into him, her soft body like an elixir. When he wasn't with the girl, he was teaching Ximena how to use her new abilities as a witch—telekinesis, fire-starting, and other forms of Satanic magic. All she did was practice, forgoing sleep and barely eating. She lit candles using only her mind, then worked her way up to setting logs ablaze in the fireplace. A wave of her hand sent dishes flying into the walls. Her irises were the color of boiled lobsters, and she'd carved an inverted cross into her forehead with her kris dagger. The wound flickered whenever

383

she used witchcraft.

Eating the breakfast Melissa prepared, Asher had Ximena read through the letter while he watched the television coverage of Barney Kaplan's surrender. As expected, Barney was being painted as an unhinged psychopath—a rapist killer of women, the elderly, and even children. It was a hell of a news story. The police had swallowed his lies because they confirmed the bullshit they'd already been running with—that Paul and Deanna were Satanic killers. It amused Asher how much cops loved to be right and how they valued catching criminals over helping victims. Barney's bail had been set at two million dollars, so he'd be staying in the county jail until his trial, which could take years to happen. According to the news, police were still investigating, but Asher wasn't concerned. He felt as invulnerable as a superhero.

He called Lenny and told him tonight was the night. His henchman was thrilled. So was Ximena. A fierce excitement was pulsing through the death cult, making their stomachs grumble for blood. Even Melissa was given a role in this. Asher had specific instructions for everyone, catering to their strengths.

He was no longer a solider in Satan's army—he was a five-star general.

FORTY-FOUR

THEY CREPT THROUGH THE VEGETABLE garden under cover of a moonless sky, their black clothes concealing them deep within the shadows of the night. Asher wore his motorcycle jacket over Reverend Bower's clerical shirt, the white collar hugging his throat above the inverted cross necklace. He carried the pump shotgun that belonged to Barney's grandfather. On his belt, he had his largest hunting knife in its sheath and the .38 pistol in its holster. From a shoulder strap, the portable boombox hung like a purse, and four sets of handcuffs were stuffed into his jacket pockets.

Lenny gripped his AR-15 like a member of a SWAT team, the Glock stuffed in his coat pocket along with extra magazines. Ximena had her kris dagger only, because Asher wanted her to break in her new powers through murder. She wore her pet snake Dragon around her neck, the serpent's eyes the same tomato red as its owner's. Melissa was parked at the edge of the property in her late husband's minivan as lookout and getaway driver. Sticking close to Asher's side was Callie, carrying the double barrel shotgun Barney had donated to the cause. Asher had taught her how to use it by taking her to the woods and lining up empty beer bottles, but it was more for Callie's defense than anything else.

Not that he expected the nuns to have the means to protect themselves. They would leave that up to Christ, and as always, the Lord would disappoint, this time fatally. Callie had been given pocketknives with serrated blades so she could unleash the same fury she'd exhibited at the Bower house. That was the sort of violence Asher wanted from her—not shootings but intimate stabbings and mutilations.

"These nuns are part of the same religious system that hurt you," Asher had told her. "Just like the Bowers, they take in young girls only to abuse them. They believe suffering is the path to righteousness, so let's send these bitches to the afterlife for that great reward they're always babbling about."

Despite the daze she'd been in lately, Callie seemed to agree with Asher and even expressed interest in killing again, provided the victims were Christian, and especially if they were religious leaders. She saw it as retribution. Callie's bias against the faithful had become a bitter prejudice, one that demanded bloodshed.

Asher chose the convent because he couldn't think of a better way to slaughter virgins, and holy ones at that. The celibacy and sanctity of nuns made them the most valuable of sacrifices. Lucifer must have felt the same way if he'd sent Beelzebub to give powers to another member of the cult. His true father would be proud, and that was all Asher wanted.

He'd also decorated his cabal. Ximena wore her BDSM cat mask. Lenny brought along his half-mask from his days in Rex's cult—a black latex piece like a Batman mask without the ears, with 666 painted on both sides of the head. Before his arrest, Barney had come to Asher with Halloween masks. Callie wore one of them now—a cartoonish devil mask resembling Hot Stuff from the old comic books—and carried a mask for Violet in her backpack, right next to Asher's trusty rape kit.

Asher wore his homemade mask, forged of deer antlers and the front of Paul's skull. He'd painted the horns and the top half of the mask black, and around the horns, he'd wrapped bloody threads ripped from his many victims' panties. Combining this with his burning red eyes, long greasy hair, and the clerical shirt and collar, the result was a terrifying visage, as Satanic a face as any beast from the beyond.

The convent was a large brick building, the dormitory taking up most of the space. There was a small chapel, a kitchen and dining hall, and a workshop. Outside, the vegetable garden stretched out a full acre, and there was a small manmade pond in a sort of Japanese garden—a special spot for prayer, bible study, and creativity, such as painting and poetry. Soon, it would be nothing more than a famous murder house no one would ever want to inhabit. Once a bastion for the brides of Christ, now it would be seen as a haunted place, cursed forever by its violent history, like Auschwitz, Jonestown, or the homes of the Tate-LaBianca murders.

Some might say the brutal slaughter of nuns and teenage girls was a sexist attack—like Asher could give a shit. His loathing was not specific to any group. His violent hatred was all-inclusive. Certainly, he despised some groups more than others, with religious types being his number one enemy, but no one was safe from his wrath, and he had no qualms about the murders being perceived as sexist, racist, homophobic, or anything else. People could misconstrue his motivations all they wanted. Society's opinions held no significance. All that mattered was that he left everyone afraid.

There were two main entrances. One was at the front of the dormitory, while the other led into the dining hall. Violet's map, along with the blueprints Lenny had obtained, noted other exit doors throughout the building. Asher and Ximena split up to cover those doors, using their gifts of fire to melt the metal locks in place, sealing every exit but the main two. Asher cut the only phone line. He didn't notice any security measures—no cameras, guard dogs, or alarms. The convent seemed to exist in another time, focusing on commune simplicity and rejecting modernity. The huge cross mounted over the front doors was the only security these wives of Jesus invested in. It was archaic. It was reckless. It was stupid.

Asher gave the orders. Ximena and Lenny would come in through the dining hall exit and barricade the doors behind them using Ximena's telekinetic powers. Asher and Callie would come in through the dormitory to fetch Violet.

"Don't just exterminate," Asher told his followers. "Make your victims suffer. Leave the most heinous crime scene imaginable. The only people who are off limits are Sister Rosemary and Sister Ernestine." He'd given them rough descriptions, and Violet's map pinpointed the room the nuns shared. "I want those cunts for my-self."

As they climbed the front steps, Callie took Asher's hand. She looked so tiny to him then, so young and fragile. He bent down to kiss her, coating her lips with a thin layer of blackened spittle—a touch of evil to give her strength and focus. Asher grabbed the handle of the dual doors. The metal went pink from the heat he radiated. He twisted it, causing the wooden door to crack, and when the lock popped out, both doors swung inward. No alarms sounded, but the noise of the busting doors echoed through the hallway. It didn't mat-ter. Soon, there would be gunshots, and that would awaken everyone.

As they entered, Asher's left hand became a torch, and the doors slammed shut behind them. Raising his mask just enough, he un-hinged his jaw and projectile vomited a tarry sludge that reeked of sulfur. It splattered over the entire doorway. The wood expanded, pressing the doors against each other and sealing them to the brick frame. The vomit was alive with hundreds of angry scorpions and black widow spiders that crawled over every inch of the exit.

"What's going on here!?" a woman shouted.

Asher spun around to see a short-haired woman in a baggy night-gown. She didn't look pregnant—Asher guessed she was too old to carry a child—and she had a demeanor of outrage, suggesting she was some sort of authority figure here.

"Who are you?" she demanded.

"I'm from Hell," Asher said.

Seeing the firearms, the nun's anger gave way to dread. She stared at this ghoulish invader in his skull mask and clerical collar, then looked at the cute devil girl with bewilderment. "You get out of here … I'm calling the police!"

But she didn't have a phone in hand. Violet had confirmed cellular phones were forbidden here. Voices murmured from the other rooms, doors opening a crack as otherwise homeless teenagers won-dered what the matter was.

Asher pointed the shotgun at the short-haired nun. "Every leap of faith you've ever made has led you to this moment." He pumped the weapon, filling the chamber with a slug. "Renounce God or die."

The nun's jowls went pale. "I will do no such thing. The Lord is my savior. You cannot come to this holy place with such hostility. God will punish you."

"Oh, the vanity to believe that, in an infinite universe, God would be focused solely on one species—let alone on just this place."

Instead of running, the nun crossed herself and began to pray. The sound of young women panic-crying in their dorm rooms made Asher salivate. One of the doors flew open, and Violet waddled out in her nightgown, holding her belly. It had swelled even more since Asher last saw her. He motioned her to come to him. As she passed by, the nun grabbed her arm.

"Don't!" the nun told her.

Violet shoved her away. "Fuck off, you penguin." She reached into her sister's backpack and put on her plague doctor mask.

The look of hurt on the nun's face was delicious. "Violet?"

But Violet didn't answer her. Face hidden behind the long beak and shaded goggles, she'd transformed from helpless, pregnant teen to intimidating madwoman.

"Last chance," Asher told the nun. "Renounce God."

Tears welled in her eyes. "Hail Mary, full of grace ..."

"Hail *Satan!*" Asher said.

Then he pulled the trigger.

The shotgun's spray covered the nun in bloody pockmarks, her face coming apart in a sinewy mist, chunks of flesh freeing from her fractured skull. One eye blew out of its socket and bounced off the wall. The nun's nose disappeared. Her lower jaw had detached at one end and was left dangling from the other, her tongue hanging out, dripping red. As she fell limp, Asher pumped another round in the chamber and fired again, the buckshot making the nun's body burst before she could hit the floor. Muscle tissue and bone fragments blew out of her back, and she collapsed into the mess.

Gunshots echoed from the other end of the building. Ximena and Lenny had made their way inside. The dormitory became a chorus of screams, but as much as Asher loved the sound of it, he had tunes to play. Putting on *Music to Sacrifice Virgins To*, Asher blasted the boom-box at top volume, the screeching guitars and snare drums joined by a chorus of chanting of demons, led by Rex's deep voice.

"For the Lords of Hell," Rex chanted from the album, "*we come bearing the wrath of Satan!*"

The voices branched off in several different chants, lapping over one another, accompanied by barking hellhounds and banshee shrieks—the sounds of Hell. All the victims Asher's cult had taken cried out from their circles of fire, screaming in eternal agony, and he was delighted to keep adding to that chorus.

A teenage girl ran out of her room. Asher blew her hip apart. She tumbled to the floor, howling in pain, and Asher stepped up to her, pumped the shotgun, and removed one of her kneecaps. Seeing the cross hung around her neck, Asher yanked it free and stabbed her in the face with it until she went still.

Pandemonium.

Doors slammed shut as the teen runaways tried to hide, but there were no locks on these bedroom doors. Asher guessed some would try to climb out their windows to safety, but those who were pregnant would be slow to escape, and the few who did would only live to tell the tale, spreading the word that The Reapers' reign of terror was far from over.

Asher handed the shotgun to Violet. "How many?"

"Eight more girls," she said. "Plus seven—no, six nuns with this one killed."

Asher drew his hunting knife from its sheath. "Let's rock 'n roll."

Violet entered a bedroom. Spotting a young girl hoisting herself to the window, she shot her in the back. Gushing blood, the girl crawled across the floor as if there was somewhere to go. Cackling, Violet bashed in her skull with the butt of the shotgun.

Callie took the next room and did not hesitate to open fire, unloading both barrels on a girl curled into a ball on her bed, hiding under the blanket. The shotgun's kick made Callie stumble, but she quickly regained balance. The sheets bloomed red as a rose garden. Watching his girl take human lives made Asher's dick hard.

"Make her suffer," Asher reminded Callie. "Make her *pay*."

Callie ripped the blankets back, revealing the girl's annihilated arms. She'd been hugging her swollen belly, trying to protect the fetus within. Asher guessed her to be at least seven months pregnant, despite looking no older than fourteen. Handing the shotgun to Asher, Callie flicked open a pocketknife, pounced onto the mattress, and stared slashing the girl's face. With her arms now useless, the girl couldn't block the attack. Her cheeks opened, lips splitting, the tip of her nose coming off. If not for the incubus kiss he'd given her on the front step, which endowed her with evil intent, Asher doubted Callie would be so relentless, but still, he was overjoyed to see such blood-lust in her. He had influenced Callie, but her rage was all her own.

When Callie's arms gave out, her victim's face was shredded meat, but she still gasped for air, still alive. Asher handed Callie his revolver, raised the teen mother's nightgown, and yanked her panties from her body, stuffing them in his back pocket.

"Now take her," he said.

Callie got between the girl's legs and forced the barrel of the .38 into her vagina. She pulled the trigger again and again, ending two lives. She did not snarl or cackle like her sister. Instead, her face was a cold blank, eyes glossy and loveless. Seeing the body jerk with each shot made Asher grin beneath his mask, and when gun smoke exited the destroyed pussy, he couldn't help but snicker. He took the pistol back, trading it for the shotgun so Callie could reload. The barrel of the pistol was hot against Asher's demon tongue as he licked away the vaginal blood. He reloaded and exited the room.

Another nun appeared, making a courageous effort to rescue the girls, but she came down the hall without a plan. Her only weapon was a broom, which she'd brought to a gunfight where she was outnumbered. Asher didn't need to draw his pistol. He tossed his hunting knife from one hand to the next, taunting the middle-aged woman as she took a desperate swing. Asher didn't try to dodge the blow. He let her hit him just so he could see the disappointment and terror in her face when it had no effect. Then he made the broom burst into flames.

"Burn, baby, burn!" he shouted. "*Hail Satan!*"

The nun dropped the broom, but the fire had already coiled around her arms. Her nightgown became a furnace. Falling to the floor, she tried to roll out the flames but was quickly engulfed, her skin charring as her hair withered away. The fire spread across the floor and climbed the wall beside her as she cried out for a God that never came.

A young ginger burst out of her room to make a run for it. As well as freckles, her panicked face was covered in acne, eyes wide as silver dollars when she saw Asher in his costume. Horror froze her in place. Asher made a fist, then opened it so the pentagram in his palm faced the girl. Her glasses reflected the flames rising from it.

"Ugly," he said, casting the spell.

The girl grunted as her zits grew larger. New blackheads appeared on her forehead in a sudden rash. Boils climbed her neck. Cysts appeared and ruptured. But it was her zits that overtook her. They swelled to the size of golf balls, weeping yellow fluid. The swelling broke her glasses and forced her eyes shut. She reached out blindly, pawing the air as her skin tore with fresh lesions.

Asher closed his fist, and every blemish on the girl's head burst at once. This explosion of bloody pus tore her face apart. A mustard-like discharge exited every hole in her head, including her ears and eye sockets, creating a waterfall that soaked her as she crumpled. Asher stepped over the ginger, leaving her to suffocate on pus as he headed to the nuns' quarters at the end of the hall. Lenny ran by, already covered in blood, laughing like a kid at a carnival. The glow of hellfire around the corner assured that Ximena wasn't far behind. Screams came from everywhere at once.

Using Violet's map, Asher had burned the location of Rosemary and Ernestine's room into his mind. But even if he hadn't, he could sniff them out like a bloodhound. He smelled Ernestine's weathered flesh and Rosemary's untouched cunt, underlined by the salty phero-mones of their terror-sweat. He tried to open the door. The nuns had pushed something in front of it. Annoyed, Asher let out a death metal growl that blew the door off its hinges, the force driving it into the room like a battering ram, freeing the doorway. Inside, Rosemary had snatched a crucifix off the wall and was brandishing it like an exorcist. Dread left her as white as her nightgown. Sister Ernestine was des-perately trying to get her landline phone to work. Seeing Asher, she gave up on it.

"God in Heaven ..." Ernestine muttered.

Asher stepped into the room. "God has abandoned you, Sister. In fact, He has abandoned all of humankind ... but Satan never will."

The old nun clutched the rosary beads wrapped around her wrist. All Asher had to do was look at the desk and it swiftly scooted across the floor, slamming into Ernestine's thighs to drive her into the wall. The nun cried out as she was pinned, calling for Jesus, and Asher increased the pressure, driving the desk into her legs and shattering her femurs. Focusing on the desk, Asher made it move side to side, the edge sawing into Ernestine's thighs, and when she began to droop, he pulled the desk away just to drive it into her pelvis. He did it so forcefully the desk cracked as well as Ernestine's bones, and he left her pinned to the wall, still alive.

Sister Rosemary stared up at Asher, the shadow of his horns cross-ing over her face in a dooming omen. Her hands trembled around the crucifix. The silver Christ was a useless talisman. Asher could have melted it in her hands but decided to let her keep it. False hope would only sweeten her suffering.

To accommodate two people, the room was twice the size as the others and had a large window. The nuns could have escaped, but instead, Ernestine had kept trying the dead phone. They knew better than to run out into the hall with all those guns going off, but they hadn't wanted to leave the young girls behind. Their kindness would be an unwitting act of suicide.

As he stepped toward her, Sister Rosemary backed toward the window too late, and Asher roared at her, the soundwaves creating a gust that lifted the nun off her feet and tossed her onto her bed. Still, she clutched the crucifix to her chest. Rosemary closed her eyes tight, rambling prayers until Asher snatched her by the ankle. She kicked in a panic, but he locked a handcuff around her ankle and attached the other end to the bedpost, put his knee on her stomach to pin her, then used a second set of cuffs to attach her other ankle to the next bedpost, leaving her legs spread. He had two more sets for her wrists but decided to let her hold on to her precious crucifix a bit longer.

With his favorite nuns trapped, Asher left the room to see what was happening in the rest of the convent. He heard Lenny yelling at someone in the next room—another one of the nuns' quarters. When Asher came to the open doorway, he saw an elderly nun on her knees in front of Lenny, giving him a forced blowjob at gunpoint, tears streaking her cheeks. When Lenny saw Asher, he gave him the horns salute with his free hand, keeping his Glock pressed to the nun's skull-cap with the other.

Asher found the Vincent sisters in the hall with two hostages. The captive girls had their hands on their heads, one sobbing uncontrollably while the other stood catatonic from the shock.

"I said take 'em off!" Violet shouted at the crier.

The skinny girl began pulling her nightgown over her head, and Callie yanked on it, forcing her to disrobe faster. She wore only panties underneath. She clutched her flat chest, as if there were something to hide.

"What is Catholicism without shame?" Asher said.

Seeing his costume, the skinny girl shrieked. Violet shoved the shotgun under the girl's chin, commanding her to shut up, but she was too hysterical to take orders and just kept screaming.

Asher dug into the backpack on Callie's shoulder, snatching his rape kit and a piece of a wire coat hanger. He had snipped off the hook and flattened it, making the curve narrow, then sharpened the end of the hook to a fine point. Grabbing the crier by throat, he choke-slammed her into the wall and raised her off her feet. Her sobs became croaks.

"Let me tell you how you're going to die," Asher told her. "I know what you must be thinking—that this can't be happening, that something will come along to save you, some fucking miracle or divine intervention. But it's stunning, isn't it, to know you're about to be murdered?" He held the wire hook before her eyes. "Have you ever seen a mummy? Not the movie ones like Boris Karloff, but a real mummy? The whole process was quite an ordeal for the ancient Egyptians. It took a hell of a lot of work. One of the things they had to do was remove the brain. They did this by inserting a hook up the dead person's nose."

The girl kicked and punched at Asher, but she wasn't going anywhere. Her friend stared into space, lost to horror.

"Every culture has their dark gods," Asher told the skinny girl. "My favorite Egyptian deity is Anubis—the jackal-headed god of the dead. Allow me to introduce you two."

Asher inched the end of the hook into the girl's nostril, shoving it high like a Covid test swab. She screamed silently, muted by strangulation, and Asher thrusted the wire deeper until he hit brain. The girl's eyes rolled. Her dangling feet danced. Twisting the hanger, Asher felt the resistance of the gray matter as he hooked a section of it. He yanked it from her nasal cavity. The brain tissue came out in soggy clumps as the girl went limp, and Asher threw her down the hall, his braindead victim sliding fifteen feet across the floor.

Lenny screamed. Leaving his girls to tend to the other victim, Asher went to the room his henchman was in. The old nun Lenny had been orally raping fled from the room, and Asher shot her in the back of the leg, dropping her. He found Lenny clutching his bloody penis, his face bright with pain.

"Fuckin' bitch bit me!" he yelled.

"Well," Asher said, "I left her waiting for you."

Wincing as he put his wounded pecker back into his jeans, Lenny limped into the hallway, then straddled the nun and pounded her face until her nose broke. Then he started biting her.

"How do you like it, bitch?" he snarled between nibbles.

Bruising the tissue, Lenny drew blood from the old woman's cheeks and neck. When she tried to defend herself, he sank his teeth into her forearm and tore a hunk of wrinkled flesh from the bone. In a frenzy of revenge, he gnawed at her ear, ripped half of it from her head, and spat it in the nun's face.

Another hysterical female ran out of her room and bolted toward the front door. Asher watched as she was swarmed by the hellish sea of spiders and scorpions. The Vincent sisters were now butchering their hostage. Lenny was practically eating his alive. Asher wasn't sure what Ximena was doing at the far end of the building but trusted she was being equally merciless.

The leader of the Reaper cult savored the violent chaos all around him.

The convent had become a nightmare.

Asher returned to the room where he'd left the two nuns. He pulled the desk away from Ernestine, and her legs fell out from under her, having been severed at mid-thigh. The stumps gushed, adding to the huge blood pool beneath her. Ernestine fell forward onto the desk. It was obvious she'd gone into shock. Sister Rosemary remained cuffed to the bed by her ankles, which had gone pink from her efforts to pull them free. Using his knife, Asher grabbed Ernestine by the hair so she was facing Rosemary, then carved her eyes out of their sockets. The old nun was too destroyed to resist.

Asher approached Rosemary, twirling the eyes in his hand like stress balls. He'd never heard such a terrified scream as the one that came out of her now. Asher shoved Ernestine's eyes into the younger nun's mouth, gagging her with them, but when she started to choke, he dug in with an elongated finger to plunge them down her throat, forcing her to swallow. She breathed deep as her windpipe was cleared, then retched in disgust.

Asher turned the music off so she could hear him better.

"Men like it when a girl swallows," he told her. "You'd know that if you hadn't committed to a life of celibacy."

He crouched beside the bed and sniffed at her exposed thighs. Rosemary squirmed as Asher pressed his masked face against the front of her panties, his nose pushing into the cleft of her labia.

"I can smell your virginity, sweetheart," he said. "I'll bet that pussy tastes like sugar water."

With her hands still free, Rosemary grabbed hold of Asher's horns and tried to twist his head.

Asher only chuckled. "What're you, trying to snap my neck?"

She swung at him with both fists but was unable to cause damage. Asher took every blow, never flinching or resisting, as Rosemary sank deeper into helplessness, into hopelessness, into her own living hell. She punched his skull mask so hard her knuckles came back bloody. When she finally gave up, she lay back on the bed, crying softly.

That's when Asher removed the mask. "Remember me?"

Rosemary stared at him for a long time before answering. "Yes."

"I just stopped by so we could continue our conversation."

"*What?*"

"When you came to my door, you said you were always willing to talk about God."

Rosemary didn't say anything. Her pallor said it all.

"You also said you'd pray for me, Sister. How's that working out?"

Her voice trembled. "You ... you're a tool of The Devil ..."

"True, but remember what you told me? You said even though you considered your faith the one true religion, you still respected other religions. It hardly seems fair to exclude Satanism."

Rosemary closed her eyes and murmured prayers.

Asher gently smacked her. "Hey, hey, hey! Stop wasting your breath. If God has let all these other people die tonight, why the fuck would he spare you?"

"*The Lord is my shepherd ... yea, though I walk through the shadow of death, I shall fear no evil—*"

"Oh, you'd better fear evil, Sister. You'd be a fool not to be afraid of me, and you seem pretty sharp for a Christian."

"Why're you doing this? *How* can you do this?"

Asher revealed the flickering pentagram in his palm. "According to you, I have no reason not to. You said it yourself that all sins can be forgiven if I offer a death bed repentance. Why be good if Santa Claus is just gonna bring you presents either way?"

"God knows what's in our hearts. He will not be swayed by your phony acceptance of our savior."

"That's okay. I had no intention of doing that anyway. But to answer your question, I'm doing all of this because it's part of *my* religion. Show some respect."

"No. I only respect religions based on compassion and love."

"Well, that leaves out *all of them*," Asher said with a chuckle. "Centuries of torture and mass murder are the legacy religion has wrought, and you Catholics are some of the biggest offenders. You're the ones who literally put people on the rack. The Catholic Church sided with Hitler during World War II, and even now, you protect your pedophile priests. Funny how a religion that forces its leaders into celibacy creates such high levels of sexual deviancy."

"Please ..." she whimpered.

But Asher wasn't finished lecturing. It amused him too much. "It seems like all priests and pastors like to fuck children. Even Stephen Collins is an admitted pedophile, and he only played a pastor on TV in *7th Heaven*. When's the last time you heard about a Satanic priest being arrested for hurting a kid? Yeah, the Christians rape children, the Muslims enslave their women and throw acid in the faces of girls who try to read, and the Mormons practice polygamy with grown men marrying underage girls. Which of these things best reflects the love and compassion you speak of, Sister?"

But Rosemary had no answer to that. "What are … what're you going to do with me?"

Asher drew the other handcuffs from his jacket. "Let's start with this."

Rosemary struggled but was no match for his strength. Her wrists were quickly cuffed to the posts of the headboard, leaving her spread-eagle. Asher tore her nightgown open, revealing a naturally curvaceous figure. She wore only panties. Asher squeezed one meaty breast. Rosemary shut her eyes and mouth tight. Asher continued to grope her with bloody hands.

"What a waste," he said. "A young, ripe body like that and you take a vow of celibacy?"

"Please … don't …"

"Oh, hush. I'm not gonna rape you—at least not while you're still alive."

Her eyes shot open. "God in Heaven …"

"Don't get me wrong. I'd love to fuck you blue in the face and show you what you've been missing, but I need to keep you a virgin."

She didn't ask why, but her teary expression did.

Asher grinned. "You're my virgin sacrifice, Rosemary."

"Please … you don't have to do this."

"But I want to. I'm not just taking your life—I'm taking your soul."

"No!" she said, defiant. "You might take my body, but you'll never take my soul! *Never!* God watches over me."

"For fuck's sake, how can you say that given all that's happened here tonight? I am going to *devour* your soul, sweetheart. It belongs to me!"

"It belongs to God and always will."

"Don't you get it yet? Either God is incapable of stopping me or he simply doesn't give a shit."

She closed her eyes again. "*I shall fear no evil, for thou art with me …*"

"The thing about evil is there must be someone to stop it, but everyone is too tired, fat, and distracted to fight anymore. Sure, they complain and commiserate, but they don't fight. They just hope someone else will—like God, for example. That's how evil prevails."

"I will always believe goodness prevails in the end."

"Face it, sweetheart. Goodness lost a long time ago. Look at all the evil in the world compared to all the good. It's not even a close race. Evil always wins because *evil does whatever it takes to win*. It isn't held back by laws, conscience, empathy, or honor. It doesn't give a fuck about your laws or commandments. That's why evil runs the world. It buries good people beneath its feet, taking no prisoners. The villains and maniacs run things now, Sister, and they do everything they can to keep decent people hopeless and broken, just as you are now."

The grief that befell Rosemary transformed her very essence. Fear morphed into a somber dread that was incredible to witness. Asher could see her heart breaking—for herself, for the world, and perhaps even for Asher. He'd yet to take her life, but he'd taken something even more precious away.

"Tell you what," he said. "Since you've been so much fun, I'm gonna give you a taste of life before you die—a taste of *real life*, the kind you gave up to waste what little time on this Earth you had in a convent." He reached between her legs and cupped her vagina in his left hand. "I can't penetrate you, but I can still make you cum."

Asher's arm rippled with sorcery, black vapor spiraling around him, and Rosemary started breathing heavy. She writhed against her bindings as her toes curled and her eyes rolled back. Asher licked his lips, and the nun shuddered in the ecstasy of his dark energy, tasting sexual pleasure for the first time. He felt her panties dampen. Rosemary moaned. She gasped. She cried out in an intense orgasm. But Asher didn't stop. He gripped her vulva harder, the foul mist funneling from his palm, through her soggy panties, and into her vaginal canal. One orgasm followed another in a relentless tidal wave that made the nun buck her hips and scream. She was still cumming even when he released her.

Asher put his mask back on and hovered over Rosemary in an ominous shadow, watching her quiver in an endless climax. Orgasm after orgasm after orgasm. It amused him to think of leaving her like that forever, a nun driven mad by an intense sexual pleasure she could not stop. Part of him was tempted to seduce her, to see if his incubus

398

power would work on such a pious heart. Maybe he could even brainwash her into joining his cult. What a glorious victory it would be to add a nun to his Satanic cabal.

But that wasn't what Asher was here for. It wasn't what Lucifer wanted.

He pressed PLAY on the boombox, and *Music to Sacrifice Virgins To* returned in all its heavy metal decadence. As Asher said the incantation, the demonic voices on the album chanted along with him.

"I offer this virgin sacrifice in the unholy name of Lucifer!" he said. "Father Satan, I am here to do your will. May all the churches burn. May every holy man, woman, and child suffer for your amusement. I shall make them bleed and burn, my dark lord! For the glory of Hell, I capture this bride of Christ and take eternal possession of her soul."

He placed his left hand between Rosemary's breasts.

"Hail Satan!" Asher shouted.

Rosemary burst into flames.

She shook against her cuffs as the hellfire consumed her. Flesh bubbled. Her long, brown hair became a pyre as her face blackened. But even as she was cooked alive, Rosemary continued cumming.

Asher flicked his fingers, springing claws like a cat, and stabbed them into the center of Rosemary's chest. Her ribcage cracked, and Asher slipped his hand into the cavity. He pawed upward until he clasped her racing heart, and once he'd expunged it, he took a bite before it could stop beating, filling his mouth with the sweetest blood he'd ever tasted.

FORTY-FIVE

"WHERE THE FUCK IS XIMENA?" Asher asked the others.

"Haven't seen her for a bit," Lenny said, dabbing someone else's blood from his face with a bandana. "After she closed off the dining hall exit, we got separated."

"How'd she close it off?"

"Same as you, only with snakes instead of spiders. It was *wild*. She opened her mouth, and the fuckin' things just came pouring out, one after another, like she was a Pez dispenser."

Asher addressed the group as the smoke of burning flesh obscured the hallway. "I'll head to the dining hall. The rest of you, check every room, under every bed, and in every closet. Leave no one alive."

The Reapers searched as Asher journeyed through the hall of corpses. Mutilated and defiled, these broken bodies were covered in blood and carved up with occult symbols, mostly on their foreheads and bellies. It pleased him. As he approached the dining hall, Asher heard hissing and rattles, and he stepped inside to find the place

400

swarming with black snakes. Dozens of them covered the tables and benches. Even more made a living carpet of the floor tiles. Asher stepped forward, and the serpents parted for him, a Satanic Moses in a reptilian Red Sea.

There was a mound at the center of the dining hall, and Ximena lay in the middle of it, flat on her back in the snake pile. She'd stripped nude, and snakes weren't just coming out of her mouth, vagina, and anus—they were coming *out of her flesh*. Purple tumors coated her limbs like tentacle suckers, and when Asher drew closer, he saw the tumors move and realized they were snake heads burrowed beneath her skin. Some had burst free, leaving holes in her resembling bullet wounds. Additional snakes had branched off her scalp like she was Medusa. Her favorite pet, Dragon, remained around her neck like a scarf, its eyes as fully crimson as Ximena's as she stared at the ceiling, at nothing. Her body convulsed as the snakes kept coming, a serpent-producing machine.

"For Christ's sake," Asher muttered.

With one wave of his left hand, Asher ended this mass birthing. The last of the snakes either popped free from Ximena or retreated into her body to hibernate, stored there by black magic until they were needed again.

"Looks like you got too much power too quickly," Asher told her. "Practicing is a lot different from using your powers against someone, isn't it?"

Ximena coughed up one final tiny snake before blinking her way back to reality. The redness that had taken over her eyes began to dim, the black pupils showing beneath, but the inverted cross she'd carved into her forehead continued to glow, the flesh surrounding it singed black. When she sat up, Asher realized she was holding someone's severed arm.

"Where's the rest of this victim?" Asher asked.

"The snakes got her," Ximena said, her voice husky from her throat's interior bruising. She nodded toward a slithering pile. "She's somewhere under there."

"Away!" Asher told the snakes.

They obeyed, and as they slithered off it, the corpse was revealed. It was so covered in snake bites and bruises it was impossible to tell the victim's age or whether she was a nun or a runaway. Venom left her swollen, and the snakes had chewed their way through her like rats, burrowing in and out of her torso, and as they fled, the exit wounds belched blood.

"Once I called on them, they just kept coming," Ximena explained.

"I gathered. Your power is stronger than you are. It's *darker* than you are."

It was disappointing. Asher had hoped Ximena would prove herself worthy of the sorcery he'd helped her to possess, but she'd gone weak on him again, even as she was trying to kill people. Asher had to accept Ximena wasn't the evil queen he'd hoped her to be. He understood that now. She was not Nancy to his Sid. She was a minion, nothing more.

"What's with the arm?" he asked.

Ximena looked at the limb as if she'd forgotten she was clutching it. "I tore it off the bitch's body ... with my *bare hands*. She'd come running down the hallway, so I grabbed her as she tried to escape, and her arm ripped off her shoulder like it was Velcro."

Asher shook his head. "You have no control. You're not ready, Ximena, and looking at you now, I doubt you'll ever be."

She gazed up at him with eyes full of pathos. "I'm trying, Master. Really, I am."

"Grovel later. Right now, get off your ass. We're leaving."

Ximena stood. Despite the holes torn in her skin, the birth of the snakes had not seemed to harm her. Already, her wounds were closing, her flesh gifted with a witch's regeneration, leaving her with only bruises and quick-forming scars. She started looking for her clothes, but Asher was impatient and ushered her out of the dining hall without them. Her pet snake was her only article of clothing when they rejoined the others, its head and tail covering her nipples, and seeing her nude, Lenny bit his bottom lip with a smile. Ximena was too dazed to care. The cult left together through the front door, Asher dismissing the armies of spiders and scorpions, leaving them and Ximena's snakes for whoever found the corpses.

The night air was crisp, making every breath taste clean. Asher stopped on the front steps and cracked his neck, savoring this moment of victory, but his pride was cut short when he noticed Melissa's minivan was not where they'd left it down the road. Instead, it was on the convent's property, still running. Trails of tire marks had ripped through the grass and dug up the dirt.

Asher shook his head. "What'd the silly old bitch do now?"

He led the others downhill where the minivan idled with its

headlights on. As they drew closer, Asher spotted tan legs sticking out from under the rear of the vehicle. They were short and thin and bare, the legs of a young girl. Streaks of dirt covered them. The knees were skinned. One foot had been turned completely around, the ankle snapped, a hunk of bone protruding through torn flesh. The windows were up, but Asher heard Melissa sobbing inside the van. He ignored her and had Lenny turn his flashlight toward the body for a better look.

The girl was about Callie's size, but it was hard to gather much more about her with one of the rear tires covering her face. The weight of the van resting on it had forced her skull deeper into the dirt before busting it. A single tire track covered her nightgown, which was bunched up around her waist.

Asher knocked on the driver's side window. Melissa rolled it down. Her face was a tight ball of pain, pink and wet with tears. She clutched the steering wheel so hard it paled her knuckles.

"I had to do it," Melissa whimpered. "I saw her escape through a window and ... oh, God, I ... I just *went after her.*"

"Nice job," Asher said and meant it.

"Oh, God ... oh my God."

"You said that already. I keep telling people he's not gonna answer."

Melissa wept. "I ... I killed a girl! A *teenage girl!*"

"She may have been pregnant too. It's hard to tell since you flattened her like a pancake."

"Oh, God, no." Her face pinched. "I'm never gonna get into Heaven now. Never. Oh, God ..."

Asher rolled his eyes as he opened the door. "Scoot over. I'm driving."

She started sliding to the passenger seat, and Asher shoved her impatiently. Everyone loaded into the van. Asher put on Alastor's *Blood on Satan's Claw* EP and took a celebratory drink from his bottle of ghost pepper sauce before hitting the gas. Violet and Lenny were still flooded with adrenaline, telling Asher about all the vicious things they'd done tonight. Callie and Ximena stared out their windows— silent, dead-eyed, emptied. Lenny had given Ximena his coat to cover up with, leading Asher to wonder if he was just trying to fuck her. No one consoled Melissa, not even her daughters. It would have been a waste of effort.

"I couldn't let the police come and arrest my girls," Melissa said, rationalizing. "I didn't want to kill that girl. I only meant to stop her."

"You stopped her, all right!" Lenny cackled. "Stopped her *dead in her tracks*, I'd say."

Sobbing, Melissa stammered when she tried to speak.

"Shut up already!" Asher told her. "Fuckin' women. You never shut up. It's just yap-yap-yap all the time."

"I just want this all to be over," she whimpered. "I ... I can't do this anymore."

"It'll be over for you when The Devil comes to drag you down to Hell. Until then, your soul belongs to me."

"I just ... God, I just wanna die ..."

"Didn't I tell you to shut the fuck up?"

Melissa kept bawling. "I wanna die! *I wanna die!*"

Asher backhanded her. It didn't stop her sobbing, but at least she quit talking.

"Look, bitch," he said. "We just had a great night. I am in too good a mood to listen to some old lady complain. Maybe your cuck husband put up with that shit, but you know better than to expect me to give a fuck about what you want. Now, if you say another word, I'm gonna rip out your tongue and make you eat it."

Melissa buried her face in her hands to muffle her sobs. Asher wondered just how much usefulness she had left, if any. Perhaps she wasn't the only one who should want her dead.

He looked through the mirror at Ximena in the back seat. The night of horrors had struck her dumb. Mouth open, she watched the world go by outside the window, entranced by the black blurs of night. Asher steamed. At least he'd never expected Melissa to amount to anything. Ximena's failure was far more irritating. Asher had been wasting his time on a woman too weak to stand by his side. She was undeserving of being a witch and unworthy of being his companion.

Asher looked to Callie. Her eyes met his in the mirror and did not look away. He was proud of how far she'd come, how ruthlessly she'd killed. Beside Callie was Violet. She was still dressed in the robe the nuns had provided her. Though the mission was over, her stomach remained swollen as if with child. Blood-stained and hollow in the eye sockets, the sisters appeared utterly insane. Perhaps they were now.

The cult arrived at the Vincent house, which had been serving as their headquarters. Asher checked his phone. Bea Martin, his mother's boss, had left a voicemail with Mom's boyfriend's address.

Sam Sutherland lived only two towns away. Asher realized he must have some residual resentment over his parents' separation, because part of him wanted to murder Sam with the same ferocity he'd attacked the nuns. But that would spoil his plans.

There were two showers in the Vincent house, so the death cult had to take turns washing up. In the master bathroom, Asher had Callie scrub him down in the tub. It was big enough for two and even had jets, with decorative soaps and other White woman decorations Melissa had bought when her life was basic. Callie shampooed Asher's hair. The gore was caked in so thick it was like undoing dreadlocks. A frosted window just above the tub offered a faint hint of daylight as dawn broke. Asher propped his phone up in an oversized coffee mug labeled "World's Best Mom," using it to amplify the audio file of *Music to Sacrifice Virgins To.*

The music was more distorted than ever, heavy and archaic, and already, the screams of the convent victims made a chilling chorus. The sound pleased him, but he was really playing it for Callie, to help her understand, to guide her deeper into the abyss he'd come to call home.

On the recording, a man cried out in agony, calling to God, and when a woman shrieked, he called out her name. "Sue! *Sue!* No, no, please, God, help us …"

"Hear that?" Asher asked Callie. "The Bowers are burning for you. We put your tormentors in a place of torment for all of eternity. They're our prisoners forever. Their pain will never end."

"Good," Callie said.

"You've been awfully quiet, sweetheart. What's going on inside that little head of yours?"

Callie's soapy fingers ran down his spine before she pressed her breasts into his back. She sighed and placed her chin on his shoulder. "Asher … what's gonna happen to my mom?"

"I haven't decided yet."

"What about my sister? Violet's still pregnant, but … *with what?* Is she gonna be okay?"

"I guess we're gonna find out."

She fell silent again, and Asher turned to face her. He booped her nose, leaving bubbles on the tip. "You're just cuter than a dog's dick, you know that? But you need to chill out, kid. It's better to focus on your own fate before you worry about someone else's. That's why activists are such miserable people."

"And what will my fate be?"

"Relax. I told you you're special."

"More special than Violet and my mom?"

"Way more."

"But don't you love Violet? She was your girlfriend first."

"Things change."

Callie took a deep breath. "Do you love me?"

"A man with my amount of power has no need for love." He caressed her, cupping water and pouring it over her, expressing tenderness physically rather than offering empty platitudes. "As long as you have something to offer me, and as long as you take direction and always look good, I'll take the best care of you. That's as close to love as anyone can get these days. It should be enough for any woman."

"I always do what you tell me to," she said. "Most of the time, I even like it."

"That's my girl."

"I wanted to kill those women tonight. I don't know why, but I just felt so much hate for them, especially the nuns."

"Part of that is my influence, but I'm only capitalizing on the hatred and anger that's already within you, just like I did with your mother's sexual neglect and your sister's desire to date a bad boy just to piss off her parents. Your hatred for religion is justified and personal. I'm just the key that lets it all out."

"So then, what makes me special?"

"Every king needs his child bride," Asher said, putting his arm around her.

Callie's eyes brightened. "You really mean it?"

"Sure. Even Elvis took a child bride, and he was just the king of rock 'n roll."

"I don't understand …"

"Look, the point is, it's not just what I want, Callie. I believe it's what Lucifer wants."

She kissed him on the lips, and when Asher's hand went to her belly, he sensed a bizarre heat brewing within her. He remembered how he'd been strongly compelled to ejaculate inside Callie and her sister. The next morning, Violet had swelled like a balloon, but Callie seemed unaffected. But Asher knew something was happening to the sisters that he had not anticipated and couldn't quite explain. In some ways, he was merely a vessel for The Devil's work.

"Father Satan must be pleased with you," Asher told Callie.

She stared into the bathwater, the brightness leaving her eyes. "Asher … is my real father down in Hell too? Is he suffering? I don't want to hear him on that record."

"Don't get weepy on me now. Not for that asshole. Any father who puts his job before his wife and children deserves to have his family turn on him."

"But … he was my daddy."

"*I'm* your daddy now, sweetheart."

"I still can't believe what we did to him."

"Like I said, I was only encouraging a rage that was already there, in all three of you."

Callie nodded reluctantly. "Yeah. I know."

"You haven't started a new chapter in your life, Callie. You've started a whole new book." He placed his hand flat against her stomach. "Forget about the family that failed you. You have a new family now."

FORTY-SIX

"THE BAG OF HUMAN REMAINS in my garage," Asher told Lenny. "You know, the one from when you and Barney cleaned up the place. Fetch it and bring it to this location." He gave Lenny the address Mom's boss had given him. "The dickhead's name is Sam Sutherland. You're gonna plant the remains on his property. In the trunk of his car or buried in his backyard—doesn't matter. Just plant them."

"Okay, but … what is this about?"

Asher didn't like being questioned, but it was better for Lenny to know every detail so he could take care of this accordingly. "My parents are in that garbage bag. Now, before you offer condolences, understand that I'm the one who killed them. Well, me and Rex. He really had a thing against my mother—his sister. You and Barney cleaned up what was left of my folks. It was their cars you guys dumped in the marsh."

"I see. So this Sam guy is …?"

"My slut mother's lover. I left a series of text messages from my parents' phones that'll lead police to believe Sam killed them in a jealous rage. We're framing him for their murders, see? I suppose it's not important in the grand scheme of things, but I've found it's the little things that give life its humor, haven't you?"

"Whatever you say, boss." Rising from the Vincents' sofa, Lenny grabbed his phone and attached his chain wallet to his belt beside his gun holster. "What do I do if Sam happens to spot me? I mean, I'm good at sneakin' around, so I don't expect him to, but how do you want me to handle it if it comes down to a confrontation?"

Asher scratched his burly sideburns. "Shit, you know what? Now that you bring it up, maybe a confrontation is even better than a frame-up."

Lenny smiled, proud but uncertain. "So what should I do?"

"Break into his house and hide the remains in a tote or some luggage—something that belongs to Sam. Put a bunch of air fresheners around it so it looks like he was trying to cover the smell. When he comes home, kill the bastard, but make it look like suicide. No beatings. No torture. But if you can get him to do it, have him write out a confession, saying he was in love with Elizabeth and couldn't bear the thought of her going back to James. Then hang him or cut his wrists—something like that. Whatever. Suprise me."

Lenny nodded. "Thy will be done."

As he started to leave, Asher stopped him. "One more thing. Last night, you gave Ximena your coat. I want to know why."

"Oh," Lenny said, caught off guard. "I mean, it was cold, and she was naked."

"Come off it, man. The cold had nothing to do with it, but her nakedness had *everything* to do with it. I saw how you looked at her—like she was lunch."

"Okay, yeah. What can I say? She's hot."

"She's also *mine*. They all are. You understand that, don't you?"

"Of course."

"Then keep your distance. Nobody takes what's mine. I see you doing nice things for my girls and it makes me think you're trying to fuck them behind my back."

"No way, boss. I wouldn't dream of it. Not ever. Even with Melissa, I only did her 'cause you told me to. I never would've made a move on her otherwise. Ximena is nice to look at, but I only gave her my coat 'cause we're a team—a *family*—and we need to look out for each other, right?"

Asher leaned forward. "Sure. But above all others, you look out for *me*. This cult is about what I want, and that's the way Satan wants it too."

"Absolutely, boss."

"*Master.*"

"Sorry. Absolutely, Master."

"That's better."

"I'm dedicated to you, Master. I hope my actions have shown that."

"I must admit they have. You've been a solid henchman for me, as I'm sure you were for my uncle. I take all of that into account. That's why I want you to be my lieutenant, so to speak. Barney never had a chance to be my second-in-command. He was too dense and too much of a newbie to Satanism. Decades of devil worship have given you wisdom I'd be hard-pressed to find in another man."

Lenny smiled. "Thank you, Master."

"However, while credentials and performance are of the utmost importance, without trust, they fly right out the fucking window."

"You can trust me, Master. I live to do your infernal bidding. I've killed for you before, and I'll kill for you again, starting with this Sam asshole. And I fully understand the girls are off limits. There's plenty of other pussy out there for a soldier in Satan's army, even an old fuck like me."

"Apparently, there are plenty of elderly nun mouths too."

Lenny snickered. "Hey, you said to make them suffer. That old crone went some seventy years without sucking cock—a lifetime of celibacy just to dedicate herself to Christ. I took that away from her in seconds by shoving my sweaty hog down her throat."

"Well done. It's just too bad she didn't know the rule about teeth."

"Yeah, that bite hurt like fuck. I'm all right, though. Just a little sore. And I paid her back real good."

"I'll say. You chewed her up like a wolf with a bag of jerky. Now *that's* the kind of initiative I like to see, Lenny. Keep making me proud."

"I will, Master. You can count on me."

"Okay, then. Now go take care of this. The bag is right where you guys left it, stashed under the work bench." He gave him the keycode to the garage door. "Report back when you're finished with Sam. I'm planning a ritual, and I want everyone here for it."

"You got it. What kind of ritual?"

Asher pursed his lips. There hardly seemed any reason to hide the truth. "The Satanic Rites."

Lenny's eyes widened. "So it's something *big* then."

"We just slaughtered an entire convent, some of which were pregnant girls. It was the ultimate mass sacrifice—virgins, holy women, and the unborn. I'd say that warrants the Satanist's equivalent to Easter mass."

"I couldn't agree more."

"Hell yeah."

They gave each other the horns salute.

Lenny left the house smiling, encouraged by Asher's pep talk, and Asher watched from the window as he crossed the street, noticing the first strings of Christmas lights on neighboring rooftops. At the garage, Lenny punched in the code on the keypad, and the door slowly rose. Asher sipped his bottle of hot sauce, watching, waiting. The shadows of the garage seemed to engulf Lenny, making him difficult to see the deeper he went in, but Asher didn't have to see the man to know what he was doing. When the garage door started coming down with Lenny still inside, Asher's suspicions were confirmed.

He'd given Lenny the brotherly pep talk for two reasons. One was to reinforce the rule that nothing of Asher's was to be coveted by his minions. The other was to remind Lenny what the rewards would be if he continued to honor Asher and put his wishes above all others, including Lenny's own. He'd deliberately put a positive spin on it, telling Lenny—quite truthfully—that he would make him his second-in-command if he remained loyal. But even with these reminders of the importance of trust, Lenny was trying to deceive him. He'd been deceiving Asher all along.

The closing of the garage door was proof of guilt. There was no reason for Lenny to close it when he was just going into the garage for the bag full of Mom and Dad. He should have picked it up and walked right back down the driveway, closing the door behind him. Instead, he'd closed himself within the house, away from prying eyes. Asher's wasn't stupid. He hadn't given Lenny the key to the door leading from the garage into the house. But that wasn't going to stop Lenny any more than threats or promises of reward would.

Stepping outside, Asher whispered a cloaking spell to prevent Lenny from spotting him if he peeked out the window. It didn't make him invisible but kept him out of view with tricks of the light, and obscured by trees, parked vehicles, and shadows. He crept along the side of his house to the sliding glass door at the back. He unlocked it quietly, but with the noise going on inside, he realized he hadn't needed to. A slamming sound was making the walls shudder. As expected, the noise was coming from his bedroom.

The door leading to the garage had been busted open. He walked down the hall, his hand aglow with vengeance. The door to his room was halfway open, and he could see Lenny swing the hammer into the wall. The toolbox from the garage was at his feet. Asher seethed. He didn't know how Lenny knew where it was, but there was no doubt what he'd come here for.

As Lenny reared back with the hammer, Asher made it explode. The steel and wood shattered into hundreds of pieces, spraying shrapnel that cut into Lenny's face and body. Shards of hot metal peppered his skull. The hand that had been clutching the hammer was punctured by large splinters that went in his palm and out the back, and half of his index finger had been severed by the blast. A mist of the tiniest fragments blinded him as he howled in pain.

Stepping into the room, Asher cast a heavy shadow over Lenny as he clutched his mangled hand to his chest and plopped down on the bed. Blood drops bloomed from his face lesions. There was a small hole in the wall, but while Asher could see one corner of the album sleeve, *Music to Sacrifice Virgins To* had not been expunged or damaged. He could hear snakes hissing behind the drywall, ready to strike if Asher hadn't struck first. Despite the shock of his injuries, Lenny didn't seem surprised to see Asher, only disappointed he'd been caught.

Asher shook his head. "And here I thought Barney was the stupid one. You didn't really think you could take my album away from me, did you?"

"It's *Rex's* album!" Lenny said, finally dropping the charade.

"You know, I almost believed you'd be a worthy lieutenant. I wanted to believe it. I'd hoped to form my own evil trinity—me, you, and Ximena. But she's too broken and you're a fucking rat."

"No. I serve my master. My true master."

Asher had to laugh. "Fuck, man, you're *still* stuck on Rex. You could've been after the record to give power to *yourself!* Instead, you're trying to give all that power back to your dead leader. Even in your own dreams, you're the fucking sidekick! Pathetic! How did you even know where I hid it?"

Lenny gestured to the crates of records. "I put tiny cameras in there when you let me look through the collection. When me and Barney left with the cars, you went to this wall. I saw it on video."

"So you really have been trying to steal from me all along."

"Look, I wasn't trying to hurt you. Honest. I was just trying to give Rex what is rightfully his."

"You mean possession of my body."

"It would be for the greater good, Asher! He's more experienced, more powerful. If you truly want to serve Satan, you'd let your uncle take over. He's the master warlock."

"No. *We* are the master warlock. When two souls inhabit the same body long enough, they eventually become one."

"If you really are one with Rex, you'll understand why I did this. I still serve my original master."

"But you also betrayed your new master." Asher sat beside Lenny and put his arm around his shoulders. "You tried to do Rex's bidding and were willing to fuck me over in the process."

"No, I didn't mean to—"

"You just can't accept that he's not coming back—not in the way you remember him. He didn't possess me like he'd planned but is still serving Satan through me. Can't you see that? My uncle recruited me, and we became partners—not you and him but him and *me*. That just eats you up inside, doesn't it?"

"No. No ... that's ..."

"It's not the eighties anymore, Lenny, no matter how much you want it to be. Your time has passed, old man. Perhaps Rex understood that better than you do. Maybe that's why he sacrificed himself to be born again through me, someone from the next generation who could bring Satanism back into the modern world."

Lenny hung his head. "It's just that ... *fuck* ... Rex and me had it all, man. Sex, drugs, and rock 'n roll. We lived like Mötley Crüe in their heyday! Every night was a *Headbanger's Ball* video. We were the true sons of Hell! We were supposed to reap all these fuckin' rewards in the afterlife. Instead, Rex self-immolated, the cult disbanded, and I was left alone. I didn't know what to do with myself. None of us did! I thought if I could just help him possess you, everything would go back to how it was in the good ol' days. Even when it seemed like it was too late, I just couldn't stop trying, couldn't stop hoping."

"I offered you a place in a new family."

"It's just not the same. Man, I miss the twentieth century. Nothing makes sense anymore."

"Nostalgia is a mental cage. The past is the past, and that's where it's going to stay. We all must learn to move on. Otherwise, we get left behind and are forgotten—or worse. In your case, much worse."

Lenny turned to him with tears in his eyes. "I only wanted the record 'cause I thought I could communicate directly with Rex that way. C'mon, man. Rex—if you're really sharing this body—you won't let Asher do this to me."

"You're just never going to understand, are you?" Asher gripped Lenny's shoulder harder, making him wince. "Rex is the passenger, not the driver. He's my Rick Rubin, see? I'm the star quarterback now, and my uncle is my coach."

"Please ... just let me talk to him."

"You are."

"I mean let me talk to him alone."

"There is no lone Rex any more than there is a lone Asher. There is only the demon we have become." He applied more pressure to Lenny's shoulder, bruising it as he went for the bones. "And we all agree we can't have dissenters to the throne."

"Please!" Lenny begged as his shoulder joint crackled. "I was just trying to serve my master—to better serve Satan! I'm sorry, I just fucked up!"

Asher released him just before Lenny's bones could snap. "Apologies are fine, but what is repentance without atonement?"

"What do you mean?" Lenny asked, clutching his shoulder.

"A chick can say she loves you, but if she's not putting out, it doesn't mean much, now, does it? It's like that gay-ass monster ballad 'More than Words' says. If you really want to show me how you feel, it's gonna take more than a simple apology. I need an act of contrition."

Lenny nodded. "Just tell me what you want me to do, Master. Tell me who to kill or rape or both. No act of evil is off limits! I'll sodomize an infant in front of its parents if it be your will, and then I'll make them eat it."

"An act of atonement can't be something you'd enjoy doing anyway. If you want to prove you're sorry, and if you want me to believe you're dedicated to me, you'll need to do something to help the cause. You must make a personal sacrifice for the greater good of the family."

"All right. Just name it."

Asher saw how earnest Lenny was being, but he also knew the man was more interested in saving his life than anything else. This wasn't remorse for betraying Asher; it was only self-pity. Lenny was a death row inmate trying to prevent his rendezvous with the firing squad.

Reaching into to the toolbox, Asher handed Lenny pliers.

"You can use these to pull all that shrapnel out of you," he said, "but first, you're gonna do something to protect the family, including yourself. I was just watching the news. The slaughter at the convent is on every channel. That's a good thing, of course. I mean, that's what I wanted—to instill fear. But you left behind a clue that could land us all in prison. You left bite marks all over that old nun. Those may as well be fingerprints. Did you know that's how they pinned Ted Bundy? He left bite marks on all his girls, and prosecutors matched them to molds of his teeth. We can't have that happening if the cops bring you in. You've just shown me you can't be trusted, so why would I trust you not to squeal if the cops corner you with proof they're your bite marks? The only way they won't match your teeth to the nun's wounds is to eliminate the evidence."

Lenny paled as the horror hit him. "You ... you're not saying you're gonna pull my teeth out, are you?"

"Of course not. Don't be silly. *You're* going to do it."

"*What?* I can't do that!"

Flames swirled around Asher's hand. "Then you're dead."

"Wait—"

"I'll send you straight to Hell, sweetheart, and you'll not find any great reward in the circle that turncoats are cast into. You'll suffer for eternity with the rest of the backstabbers and snitches."

"Please, don't do this, Asher—or, I mean, Master. Please don't."

"The choice is yours. Hurt yourself to protect the family or burn forever—after I torture you to death, of course."

Asher reached for Lenny with his claws, his arm flushing red as Satan's potion coursed through his veins. Facing Hell, Lenny backed into the corner where the bed met the wall. He did not try to fight. He did not draw the pistol at his hip, for he knew it would be no match for Asher's demonic power, and even if he did manage to shoot him, Asher wouldn't be the last demon to come for Lenny. His soul didn't belong to him anymore, and to fight against Asher was to betray The Devil himself.

There was no other choice.

Closing the pliers on one of his front teeth, Lenny squeezed the handle tight, shut his eyes tighter, and took several quick breaths to steady himself.

Then he yanked.

The tooth pulled free, dragging strands of gum tissue with it. Blood poured generously, spilling from Lenny's screaming mouth.

"One down," Asher said.

Lenny tore another free, shuddering in pain. He tried to remove the third one too quickly, and it snapped in half. His gums swelled like inflating balloons. Tears and snot muddied his grimace as he ripped one of his canines free. As Lenny disfigured himself, Asher took a joint from the nightstand and lit up. Weed always made everything funnier. Soon, Lenny had removed eleven of his front teeth, from canine to canine on the top and bottom rows. He groveled to Asher, but his mouth was so destroyed it was difficult to understand him. It seemed like he was asking if he'd done enough.

Asher pondered what to do with the bastard. His first thought was to get the girls over here so they could torture Lenny to death. It would show them what happens when a minion betrays the master. But with Lenny dead, Asher would need another way to plant his parents' remains on Sam Sutherland's property. Making matters worse, he couldn't shake the feeling that police would be closing in on him soon, that his sorcery could only protect him so long. Plus, he had to compose The Satanic Rites for the evening ritual and figure out his long-term goals for Callie and the others. He wasn't overwhelmed, but he was getting annoyed by tasks.

A voice came from behind. "You're overthinking it."

Asher turned to see Lucifer standing in the bedroom doorway, framed by psychedelic redness. The Prince of Darkness was as asexually handsome as ever, his hair lush and golden, his goat eyes like cherries in cream. Instead of the crimson robe he'd worn during his last visit, Lucifer was adorned in a cloak stitched from human flesh. It was not dried and tanned but soft and moist and young, as if the skin were still attached to its original hosts.

"Father ..." Asher said, awestruck.

Lenny stared at Lucifer in disbelief, mumbling with his mangled mouth. Entering the room, Lucifer stepped past Asher and placed the tip of his finger between Lenny's eyes. The touch caused Lenny to faint. He collapsed in a puddle of blood and tooth fragments.

"He'll be out for a while," Lucifer told Asher. "I could have given him an aneurism or something more permanent, but your disciples are your responsibility."

"Yes, Father. I was just correcting his behavior."

"So I see. Not a bad job. You could make a necklace out of all those teeth. But again, you're overthinking it, my son. Not just Lenny's fate but everything." He put his hand on Asher's shoulder, warming it. "I respect your efforts to frame an innocent man for your parents' murders, but it's a moot point. Planting evidence on Sam Sutherland is beneath you now, and trying to escape suspicion is a futile exercise, despite how successful you've been at it so far. You have more important things to tend to, and besides, the police coming for Asher Benton is inevitable. You're worried about Asher Benton as if you're still him. You must realize he no longer exists."

Asher swallowed hard. "I don't understand."

"Really?" Lucifer snickered, an airy, musical sound. "Just look in the fucking mirror, son. You said it yourself that there is no self, only the demon you and Rex have become. No one would ever recognize you as the Asher Benton you were just a month ago. The long hair, the unibrow, the dog-like fingernails—not to mention eyes that fluctuate between different shades of red, or the way your skull has changed shape, giving your face sharper angles and a stronger jawline. You didn't just gain your uncle's spirit and wisdom. His soul transformed you on the outside as well as the inside. Now, you look like a demonic hybrid of yourself and Rex—which, of course, you are. Asher Benton no longer exists. Now, you can truly live, because you've already died."

Asher took a deep breath as this sank in.

"The police will come to this house soon," Lucifer said. "Even if they don't link you to the other murders, they'll come around looking for Asher's mom and dad, right?"

"Yeah. That's why I was trying to set up Sam and—"

"You needn't explain your train of thought. What I'm telling you is a warlock of your stature should fear nothing, especially not human beings. Any cop would be totally useless against you. So just take what you need here and leave this house for good. And don't forget your uncle's record. You'll want to play the real thing when you perform The Satanic Rites, not just some digital download."

"Yes, Father."

"Don't get me wrong, now. You can still toss your folks' remains in Sam's yard, just to fuck with him and the cops. You're right that

417

it's good for a laugh. But your focus shouldn't be on Sam or even punishing Lenny. Your focus should be on your bride."

"Callie …"

Lucifer nodded. "Ximena let us down. Most people will do that. Callie is the better choice, but she's not quite ready for The Satanic Rites. Before she can be the bride of a warlock, she, too, must be reborn in my name, just as you were."

Asher thought back to how he'd been born again through his mother's mutilated corpse and how he'd visited a metaphysical Gehenna before returning transformed. He was about to ask Lucifer if it should be he or Callie who kills Melissa, making the mother a portal for her daughter's Satanic baptism, but Lucifer changed subjects.

"I must say, that business at the nunnery was a five-star slaughter. You really did your old man proud. You've sacrificed so many virgins, sent me so many souls. Now, it's time to enjoy the rewards. You have the power within you, my son—more power than you realize. Always remember that I seek not followers, only collaborators." The Devil's flesh cloak grazed Asher's arm, warm and soft like children. "You've also collaborated with that little girl of yours. Her womb has been infected by your evil seed."

"A baby?" Asher asked.

"You could call it that."

A chill ripped through Asher. "You mean … the Antichrist?"

Lucifer smirked. "People speak of an antichrist as if there can only be one. But even in The Bible, the truth was revealed: *As you have heard that the antichrist is coming, even now many antichrists have come.* My children are legion. Genghis Khan, Napolean, Hitler, Pol Pot, Stalin—all antichrists. This country of yours has more than one antichrist in its government today. My glory days were the entire thirteenth century. *Everything* was attributed to me back then. Now, the pendulum has swung back in my direction. This century is going to be *very* interesting."

"My child could rise to such greatness? It could really be an antichrist?"

"You're a warlock who knocked up a child. A demon spawn is inevitable. But if your baby is to be an antichrist, Callie must be reborn before the baby is born."

"What about her sister? Violet is pregnant too."

"Not exactly." Lucifer plucked a bit of lint from Asher's shirt. "She *looks* pregnant, and you certainly pumped her full of enough of your seed, but even a devil child doesn't grow *that* fast. You needed her to look pregnant to get into the convent, and your black sperm worked. That's all."

"So what happens to her now?"

"That's up to you. The fates of *all* your minions are up to you. Violet is your flesh puppet, son. I'm sure you'll find a use for her bloated womb."

Suddenly, having the girls torture Lenny seemed pointless. Of course Lucifer was right about Asher's power and status. He was more demon than man now—much more. The little people that had assisted him in his rise to power had always been expendable, but with Lenny being a backstabber, Melissa falling apart, and Ximena failing as a witch, the cult had become more of a hassle than they were worth. It was time to trim the fat.

Only Callie held value. Asher had sensed this for some time. Now, he understood her purpose.

"One more thing," Lucifer said. "If The Satanic Rites are to be performed correctly, you'll need another sacrifice, and it needs to be special."

"Another virgin? Maybe a priest?"

"That would do for most witches, but a sorcerer like yourself can do better than that. These rites will be your wedding ceremony. Make your sacrifice a grand gesture." Lucifer patted Asher on the back. "You've become a son of Satan. A *true* son of Satan. Now deliver me a true grandkid—the hell-spawn of a demon and a human child, an antichrist."

Asher bowed his head. "Yes, Father. I am your loyal son, and the baby shall be yours. May they be the pride of Hell."

"That's a good lad."

Lucifer pointed to the stash Asher had stolen from his first victim, the drug dealer Terry. That night seemed like years ago now. It was another life completely.

"Just look at all that cocaine and cash," Lucifer said. "That's enough for any man to make a new start in another town. You already bought a new car and clothes and such. There's just one more purchase I'd recommend."

"And what is that?"

Lucifer winked. "A guitar."

FORTY~SEVEN

LENNY AWOKE JUST AS LUCIFER vanished into a plume of sulfurous mist. He blinked with confusion, then groaned when the pain in his gums and the direness of his situation returned to him. As Asher sat beside him, Lenny cowered back.

"I suppose I can't blame you," Asher said. "I can imagine the temptation the *Music to Sacrifice Virgins To* album gave you. Who can blame a loser for trying to win the lottery? Who can blame a lonely man for raping his teenage daughters? Who can blame a sidekick Satanist for reaching for that brass pentagram in the hope of becoming a warlock himself?"

Lenny shook his head. His words were garbled by his injuries. "Mahsta, pwease, I—"

"Don't worry, Lenny. You'll have an eternity in Hell. That's plenty of time to ask Satan for another chance."

Asher stabbed him in the stomach with the fingers of his left hand, driving them in past the knuckles while sinking the thumbnail into his

420

side. The heat was instant and intense, coursing into Lenny's blood and stomach bile, making them boil. Twisting his wrist, Asher surged hellfire into his henchman's guts. The intestines peeled, spewing waste into his torso, and as the heat permeated his insides, Lenny's bladder burst in a spray of bloody piss. His liver turned black and imploded. Bodily fluids poured from the ruins of his mouth, choking Lenny as he was boiled alive from within.

When Asher spoke, it was in Rex's voice. "Tough break, dude. But a new master is a new master."

As Lenny melted from the inside out, Asher called Callie and told her to gather the others and come over. Together, they transported Asher's belongings to the Vincent house, including Rex's stereo and crates of records, the dope, and the cash bundles. The garbage bag full of Mom and Dad was put into the back of Joel Vincent's minivan.

When the girls saw the puddle that had once been Lenny Casella, none of them recoiled. They'd been desensitized to such things, and it seemed no love was lost with his passing. Melissa sneered down at the man who had violated her and spat in what was left of his face. She had calmed since her hit-and-run murder but was now a waste of a woman, broken in every sense. Her hundred-mile stare was as empty as her heart. She still obeyed Asher but did not engage with him, shuffling around like a zombie instead of trying to reason, bargain, or beg.

Violet waddled and huffed, unable to carry much in her bloated state. Her face was chubby and pale green, and she kept trying to pull Asher aside to talk with him, but he told her she had to wait. Dressed in Melissa's clothes, Ximena seemed the most eager to please, which was no surprise given her recent incompetence. She was smart enough to understand the situation her ineptitude had put her in and longed to return to her master's good graces. Asher decided to give her the opportunity.

"Take the minivan here," he said, giving her Sam Sutherland's address. "Then find a way to plant the contents of the trash bag somewhere on this man's property. You're powerful enough to create a cloaking spell to prevent people from seeing you, but you're also a fuck-up, so be careful. Just dump the crap and come right back. It's all just a practical joke anyway."

Ximena did not ask questions. She was off in the minivan before the others even got Asher's stuff into the Vincent house. Callie took Asher's hand as they shut the front door behind them. Violet narrowed her eyes at her sister, and the jealousy put a smile on Asher's face. Violet shuffled off. Melissa asked if Asher wanted something to eat, but he had another task in mind for her.

"Do you still have your wedding dress?" he asked.

Melissa frowned. Asher imagined the memories of that special day raking through the widow, torturing her with thoughts of her late husband, reminding her how he was rotting in a shallow grave of her own making. Sometimes, the emotional pain Asher caused was far sweeter than anything physical.

"It's in the attic," she said.

Asher gestured to Callie. "Think it'll fit her?"

Melissa's face grew impossibly sadder. "It might be a little long, but I was slim like her back then."

"Can you sew? Do you have a machine?"

"Yes, Master."

"Good. Callie, go with your mother to be fitted."

Callie's eyes were bright as suns. "Asher ... are you asking me to *marry* you?"

"No, I'm *telling you* you're marrying me." He gave her a pat on the ass. "Now run along, you little scamp."

Giggling, Callie joined her mother, and they went upstairs. Asher grabbed a beer from the fridge on his way to the living room to set up the stereo, but an idea led him into the garage. Checking the Vincent family's supplies, he noted the portable power bank, the kind of unit used during blackouts. It wouldn't be as strong the generator, but he didn't need it to be, and it would be easier to cart around. Returning to the living room, Asher found Violet sitting on the sofa with her face in her palms, crying quietly. Her gut was enormous.

"What's with you?" he asked.

She sniffled but did not speak or even raise her head.

"Answer me, goddamn it."

Finally, she looked up, her face pink and swollen. "You don't love me anymore."

"What the fuck are you talking about?"

"You're supposed to be *my* boyfriend. I know you're our master. I wasn't mad about you fucking other women—even my own mother and sister—because I thought *I* was the special one. But now here I am, pregnant with your child, and you're proposing to *Callie* instead of *me!*"

Asher sat beside her. "Don't get so worked up. You're not

carrying my child."

"Then what the hell am I carrying?" She looked down at her belly, holding it with shaky hands. "What is happening to me? I feel so sick. Am I gonna die?"

"Eventually, yes. But right now, you're simply changing. You're becoming something I need."

"But *what?*"

"That doesn't matter. Your only reason for living is to please me. You should be grateful for the opportunity to do so. There are thousands of other women out there who would literally sell their souls just to sit at my feet."

"I am grateful. So, so much. I just … I just want to know what's happening. With me, with us, with you and my little sister. I've done so much for you, Master. I've killed people for you—including my own father. It was your will, and I trust your judgement."

"Then keep trusting me, sweetheart," he said, wiping a tear from her cheek. "I know what's best for all of us."

"*But why are you marrying her instead of me?!*" she shouted.

Violet's sudden outburst surprised him. That she was enamored with him was to be expected, but he'd thought he'd worn her down enough to make her completely submissive. It seemed his spell over the girl was a double-edged sword. It made her crazy about him— perhaps too crazy. Though Violet would do whatever Asher said, her love for him had transformed into a romantic infatuation strengthened by her perceived pregnancy. Her human emotions were so strong they were chipping away at his incubus hold.

Asher snatched Violet by the hair, pulling her in so they were face-to-face. She flinched but looked him dead in the eyes. He'd almost forgotten how pretty she was. Sorrow brought out a unique brand of beauty in a young woman.

"Before me, your idea of magic was moon water and tarot cards," he growled. "I brought actual magic to you, Violet. You were fucking around with make-believe—I showed you the real thing. *I am Satan's son!* You're merely one of my goons. You could never understand sorcery like I do, you stupid bitch, so if I say we're doing something, you don't ask me why, you just go along with it. That's the natural order. That's how you serve me *and* Satan! Now, I am marrying your goddamn sister and you're gonna be there for the ceremony, and when the time comes for you to serve your purpose, you're gonna do it with a big smile, got it?"

423

Finally, Violet closed her eyes, freeing tears. "Yes, Master. I'm sorry. I love you."

Asher released her. "Get out of my sight."

Violet struggled to rise from the couch. Asher did not assist her. She started toward the stairs, stopping when she reached the banister to look at him with puppy eyes.

"I really am sorry," she said. "Your happiness is more important to me than anything else. Whatever you need me to do for the ceremony, I'll do it, my master. That is my place, my purpose. I just want you to know *I'm* happy to do whatever it takes to make *you* happy, even if that means you're marrying Callie instead of me. It's not what I want, but that doesn't matter as much as what you want, and deep down, I've always known that. I'm here for you, Master. Do what you want with me."

Asher sipped his beer. "Get upstairs and find something to make you look sexy. It won't be easy with you being so goddamn fat, but at least it'll keep you busy for a while. Don't come down until I call for you."

"Okay," she said, trying not to cry. "I love you."

"You said that already. Move your ass."

Cradling her misshapen belly, Violet struggled up the stairs, huffing and sweating. Asher put his feet up on the coffee table and turned on the TV, flipping through the channels in search of any stories about the convent. He'd been lying when he told Lenny he'd seen it on the news. Had the bodies been discovered yet? While Asher didn't find anything about the mass murder at The Sisters of St. Joseph, he did find another story that grabbed his attention.

Barney's face filled one side of the TV screen while a newswoman shared the information.

"The man believed to be the leader of The Reapers—a Satanic cult suspected in multiple murders in New Hampshire—has died. Twenty-seven-year-old Barney Kaplan, seen here in a mugshot taken the day of his confession, was being held in Mortson County Jail, the largest facility of its kind in the state. Yesterday, Kaplan was found unresponsive after another inmate pushed him over the railing of the second tier of the jail. Authorities tell us that Kaplan struck the concrete floor below and was pronounced dead at the scene. Information is sparse at this time, but prison officials believe Kaplan was targeted by other inmates because of his involvement in the brutal slayings of several children."

Howling with laughter, Asher slapped his knee. The newswoman went into the details of The Reapers killings but was only going over the same information the networks had been regurgitating for days. It was good for ratings. People love their panic porn. But even the newswoman suggested there was more to this series of crimes than what little information the police were releasing.

"Here at Channel Six, we're bringing you the latest as this story continues to develop."

Asher laughed so hard he coughed. While his girls took to their tasks, he unwound with cocktails of beer, marijuana, and cocaine. He wrote notes for the ritual, filling a notepad with incantations, chants, and vows, putting The Satanic Rites together like a word puzzle. More than an hour passed as Asher got things just right. He was still drafting when Ximena returned.

"It is done, Master," she said. "A car was in the driveway. I used the craft you taught me to unlock the trunk and poured out the human remains into it, then closed it and took off. I figured that'd make for a nice surprise for this guy."

Asher patted the couch cushion bedside him. "Come."

Ximena obeyed but did so timidly. She put her hands in her lap as she sat down. They were trembling.

"You're afraid," Asher said.

She nodded.

"Why?"

"Because … because you're disappointed in me."

"You could still serve a purpose," Asher said, glancing at his notes. "Perhaps the most important purpose of all."

"But I'm not as good at this witchcraft stuff as you are. I know I've only just begun, but I feel like … I dunno, like …"

"Like your heart isn't in it."

Ximena shook her head. "No, Master, no. I serve you."

"Bullshit. You *have to* serve me. That doesn't mean your heart is in this. You've shown me that time and again. You're just not cut out for this work the way I thought you were."

Her eyes grew wet. "I'm so sorry I disappointed you. Really, I am."

"When we met, your life was dog shit. You were just another small-time drug dealer in a dead-end town, going nowhere fast. But you've rejected the new life I've tried to give you."

"It's not a rejection. It's just more than I can handle."

"It *is* a rejection, and I'm warning you not to argue this with me."

She hung her head. "Please … tell me what I can do."

"It's too late to turn back, sweetheart. It's not like you can return to who you were before you met me. You're a murderer now. And without my power protecting you, you're going to find yourself behind bars, doing life without parole."

"Oh God …"

"Don't despair. New Hampshire abolished the death penalty years ago, but they might make an exception the way Massachusetts did for the Boston bomber—Tsarnaevo or whatever that raghead's name is. If the state will gas an Islamic terrorist, I'm sure they'll have no qualms about offing a Mexican serial killer, even if you are a woman. Nothing attracts punishment like killing kids. Just ask Barney."

"You mean because he's in jail?"

"Because he's fucking dead. I just saw it on the news. Our Drugula was executed by fellow inmates. Even convicts hate people who kill children. They'll lynch you too. Seeing as you're Mexican, someone will probably deem you an illegal immigrant who came to this great country to murder kids because you hate our freedom, or some such shit."

"No … I was born in America."

"Like anyone will give a fuck."

"I didn't kill those kids …"

"You tore your cousin Diego's baby from its mother's womb. Have you forgotten?"

"No! I *can't* forget! I see it every time I close my fucking eyes!"

"That's because you're weak." Asher grinned. "You're one of many goth girls who thinks she's so damn spooky, but when she's confronted with true darkness—with real evil—she crumbles just like any other whiny bitch." He grabbed Ximena by the chin, forcing her to face him. "And I was foolish enough to believe in you. I gave you powers beyond imagination, and still you whimper with guilt over every little murder. I had such high hopes for you, babe. At one point, I thought you might be the Satanic queen to my king. But you have squandered my gifts. You're lazy. You're selfish. You're incompetent. You're a disgrace to our family and a complete waste of my efforts."

Ximena wept as Asher berated her.

"I should've seen it coming," he said. "Diego was your family, and you betrayed him, so why wouldn't you hurt our family too? Letting people down is the only thing you can be counted on for, Ximena. I see that now."

"Please," she said through sobs. "I'll do anything to make it up to you."

426

"Horseshit."

She slid off the couch and got on her knees before him. "I'm begging you. I have nowhere else to go. You're right—there's no turning back from this. If I'm condemned to Hell anyway, I'd rather go as one of Satan's soldiers than—"

"You're just trying to escape punishment. Your dedication is not to Satan but to your own sorry ass."

Ximena groveled. "No, please, Master—*please* forgive me. I'll do anything." She caressed his thigh. "Anything you want."

He batted her hand away. "You've reached the limit of what your body can buy you. This is about *your soul.*"

"Please ... just tell me what I can do, and I'll do it."

Asher stroked his chin, pretending to mull it over, though he already had plans for Ximena. "All right. As I said, you might still serve a purpose. But returning to Lucifer's good graces does not come easy. You say you'll do anything, but are there limits to what you'll sacrifice?"

"No," she said, choking on the word.

Ximena was in too deep and knew it. Unfortunately for her, Asher knew it too.

"What will you sacrifice?" he asked.

"Anyone. Men, women, or ... anybody you say."

Asher brushed her cheek with the back of his hand, then curled a lock of her hair in his fingers. Ximena's tears aroused him. Sex had become less about desiring females and more about hurting them. Now when he saw a beautiful woman, his first urge was to brutally kill her, with carnal lust coming second. Anything soft had to be hardened. Anything fragile had to be broken just for the crime of being fragile. Any soul with the slightest chance of redemption had to be taken while the getting was good.

"I'm getting married tonight," Asher said. "The Satanic Rites will make Callie my unholy princess. But we need a human sacrifice, one grander than any we've made before."

"What could be grander in the eyes of Satan than the sacrifice of children, nuns, and the unborn?"

"Well," he said, bending over so their noses were almost touching. "The greatest Satanic sacrifice is for someone to go willingly."

As the heaviness of what he'd said struck her, Ximena's shoulders fell. Her lower lip trembled, but no words came out, only childlike whimpers.

Asher cupped her face in both hands. "If you want to save your soul, you must be willing to offer your body."

"Asher ..."

"*Master.*"

"Master ... I ... I'm afraid to die."

"Yeah, well, you'll just have to decide what frightens you more—death, which is inevitable anyway, or eternal damnation, which you can avoid with this one grand gesture. Trust me, it's much better to go out like this. This way, you'll rule in Hell instead of burning there until the end of time. This life is but a transition—a test run. What you chose to do with it will decide your true fate."

Tears slicked her cheeks. "I'm only twenty-six. I can't die now."

"Now is the best time to die, sweetheart. You're dying at the height of your beauty and abilities. You're dying as *a witch*. That makes your suicide a more meaningful sacrifice. Lucifer will notice, and your rewards will be plentiful. You may return as a Satanic sorceress with even more beauty and power than you could ever obtain on this plain of existence."

"But, Master ..."

"It's only a body, Ximena. Let's not pretend you're unfamiliar with the desecration of your flesh. Not only do you have tattoos and piercings, but you were also a cutter. If making yourself bleed made you feel better, just imagine what fully bleeding out will do for you."

"But I—"

"Better to die with honor than live in shame. The Japanese understand that. The samurai had a practice called *seppuku*——ritual suicide by disembowelment. This allowed them to die with honor instead of falling into the hands of their enemies. People think this was just some ancient, medieval practice, but even Japanese officers in World War II committed forms of ritualistic self-sacrifice. Kamikaze pilots were common. The Vietnamese set themselves on fire as a form of protest. Islamic terrorists make suicide vests and fly planes into buildings for their god. Are you unwilling to do the same for yours?"

Ximena couldn't speak, but beneath her sobs, Asher detected the first signs of acceptance. Like someone falling from a great height, Ximena would be better off accepting her fate rather than flap her arms in protest of the inexorable.

"Don't worry, sweetheart," he told her, soft and gentle like a father. "I won't make you disembowel yourself. This will be much easier. All you have to do is offer your life at the ritual. Just say 'kill me.'

I'll take care of the rest."

Eyes shut tight, Ximena nodded.

"That's my good girl," Asher said, planting a kiss on her forehead. "Now get upstairs until I call for you."

She rose and took a deep breath. "Is there anything I can do in the meantime?"

"Sure. Pray to Satan."

FORTY-EIGHT

THE LIGHT OF DUAL BONFIRES gave the woodland a Halloween glow. The skies were black and starless, but a crescent moon hung low on the horizon like the clipped toenail of a giant. They'd come to the same clearing he'd used since the beginning. Asher had his remaining followers carve different symbols into the earth. At his command, the women cut the meaty parts of their palms and squeezed out blood to rain down into the engravings. Asher made a large Leviathan Cross with Ximena's kris dagger, the serpentine blade gleaming from the residual glow of his hand.

Before the Leviathan Cross, Rex's stereo was arranged like an altar, connected to the portable power bank Joel Vincent had kept in the garage in case of power outages. They'd needed a dolly and wheelbarrow just to get everything out there, but Asher wanted everything to be perfect.

Music to Sacrifice Virgins To spun on the turntable, sounding less musical than ever, a collection of hollow screams and groans, the desperate cries of the damned and the cruel laughter of those who tormented them. The sounds of gunshots, breaking bones, and axe blades entering flesh were underscored by screeching electric guitars and a thudding bass drum, accompanied by a perpetual doom metal drone. The result was a nightmarish symphony of noise—the soundtrack to Hell itself.

Melissa and Ximena wore black lingerie, their flesh exposed to the frigid breeze. Unable to find any that fit her in her engorged state, Violet wore only her mother's black kimono. It had to be left open so her cauldron belly could poke through. It'd grown impossibly large. She looked less like she was carrying a child and more like she was about to give birth to a sea lion. It was amazing she could even stand. The women were barefoot and wore excessive, whorish makeup. Ximena's pet snake was coiled around her arm. Melissa's panties were crotchless, revealing she'd shaved for the occasion.

Asher was adorned in his demon gear. The horned skull mask he'd worn at the convent was stained by the blood of nuns. The clergy-collared shirt was covered by his leather jacket, with studded leather armbands on his wrists. His skin had taken on a crimson sheen. The metal of his inverted cross necklace had turned orange from his radiating heat, and yellow fangs filled out his grin, each tooth coming to a jagged point.

But Callie was the best dressed for the occasion. Melissa had manipulated her old wedding dress to fit her teenage daughter, and it clung to Callie's lithe form, highlighting how small and thin and young she was. The gown was flowery white with lace sleeves. It would not stay pristine for long. Her hair hung about her shoulders in golden curls, her face half-hidden behind a sheer veil.

Looking at this cherub of a girl—this *child*—Asher felt no love or affection. In Callie, he saw only opportunity. This marriage was an offering, same as any slaying or sacrifice, a ritualistic act meant to appease dark, unknowable forces. Joining with the girl under Satanic vows assured their baby would be born evil, making it the ultimate offering to Lucifer. But while the wedding was not based in love—because Asher was now incapable of love—that didn't mean he couldn't enjoy himself. Taking a child bride was a special brand of sin reserved for the most diabolical of rulers. Callie was a prize he'd earned through horrific deeds, a trophy of flesh and blood. She was not just his princess but a possession, a jewel in his crown.

Melissa stood beside Callie, arm in arm, poised to give her

daughter away to the greatest evil she had ever known. Most mothers would break at this, but Melissa had been broken a long time ago, so now, she was silent in defeat, her face long, waxen, corpse-like. They walked along the path of occult symbols etched into the dirt, their bare feet wetted by blood as they approached the stereo altar at the Leviathan Cross. The flanking speakers pulsed with Hell's heavy metal, creating short bursts of air that fluttered Callie's bridal gown. Serving as groom and officiant, Asher went to the bridesmaids first. The fingertips of his left hand were oozing a black fluid like beads of sweat. He dragged his index finger down Ximena's forehead, branding over her scar with another inverted cross in a reversed Ash Wednesday. Then he ran his fingertip along the curvature of Violet's belly, coating it with a pentagram of runny, black discharge. She winced as it irritated her fair skin. Returning to his place at the altar, Asher cupped Melissa's groin, prodded the gap in her crotchless panties, and shoved two fingers into her dry, then pulled her toward him by her pubic bone.

"You've been a good whore," he told her. "I'd love to paint a jizz pentagram on your face, just for old time's sake, but tonight is about your little girl."

Releasing her vagina, Asher planted his left hand over Melissa's face. She shrieked, and the air filled with the smell of burning flesh. When he released her, the flaming pentagram in his palm had branded Melissa's forehead.

"Kiss the goat," he told her.

Whimpering, Melissa kissed Asher's skull mask, her lips pressing to Paul's teeth. Through the gap in the mask's jaws, Asher's long, warty tongue came out and entered her throat like an enormous worm, his black saliva coating the inside of her mouth. It was a refresh of his love potion, an incubus kiss that would keep the mother obedient as her youngest child was taken from her. Melissa's eyes rolled, limbs shaking as she pissed uncontrollably. Her pupils turned white as she swayed in place. Black slime drooled out of the corner of her mouth.

"Congratulations, old girl," Asher told her. "Tonight, I'm finally giving you permission to die."

Melissa grunted. It was all she could do.

Asher addressed everyone now—not just his harem but all the demons of the wild, every ghoul tucked into every dark corner of the world.

432

"We gather here today to celebrate the black union of the girlchild Callie Vincent and the warlock Asher Benton. Theirs has been an unholy passion, forged in the forbidden and the taboo, matured in the shedding of innocent blood, and honored by the slaying of Callie's father, Joel Vincent. Ours is a marriage made in Hell. Tonight, we join in the name of Father Lucifer so that we may continue to do his work with greater strength and focus. Hail Satan."

The women chanted in unison. "Hail Satan."

The bonfires reached higher, and the blood within the symbols began to boil. A foul stench wafted from the black forest, announcing the presence of Beelzebub, though the demon remained unseen.

"Let The Satanic Rites commence," Asher said, extending his arms as if crucified. "Glory to Lord Lucifer, for The Morning Star is our guiding light. What is dark within us, illuminate. Praise to Beelzebub and Astaroth, who walk between worlds and bless us with witchery. Satan—lord of terror and destruction, king of infinite wrath and despair—thy will be done on Earth as it is in Hell. Deliver us unto pure evil. Usher us into the void of your being so that we may spread darkness across this world and beyond, so that we may assassinate God and collapse Heaven. We torch His bible of lies. We vomit upon the cross of the false prophet of Nazareth. Why should all mankind be condemned for one man's faults? The left-hand path is primed for the final hour. With this union of man and child, we shall usher in Armageddon in the form of an unholy infant—an antichrist!"

Hearing his plans for parenthood for the first time, Callie gazed up at Asher with love and adoration. She didn't realize he'd already inseminated her but would find out soon enough.

Asher went on, quoting occult texts and blending them with his own poetic sermon. Rex spoke through him with Satanic verses pulled from his era, and their voices became as one as they recited ancient incantations.

"In the name of Lucifer, the scourge of all mankind, we offer these sacrifices!"

Asher gestured to Ximena. She stepped forward. Her eyes were lifeless, as black as the lingerie she started to remove. When she handed her panties to Asher, he stuffed them into his coat pocket with the others, having brought along his collection for this black mass. Ximena was now nude but for the snake wrapped around her forearm, its red eyes shining like andesine.

Asher drew the kris from his belt and held the blade up between his and Ximena's faces. He didn't say anything to her. He didn't have to. She knew what was coming. She'd prepared herself for it, and in a way, she'd been moving toward this end her entire life. All her drug use, cutting, and other self-destructive behavior were merely preludes to the sweet, final exit of suicide.

Their eyes locked one last time, and Asher savored the hopelessness in her gaze.

"Kill me," Ximena said. "Kill me now."

Asher did not hesitate. He'd always thought Ximena was special. Now, he realized he hadn't been wrong. She was precious, just not in the way he'd first believed her to be.

"Your soul *belongs to me,*" he told her.

Ximena gasped as the kris pierced the flesh just below her breastbone. Then Asher drove it home. The curved blade made quick work of his human sacrifice, sorcery helping it cut through Ximena with the ease of tissue paper. The first streams of blood were the normal shade of red, but as it kept coming, the blood grew darker, turning purple on its way to black. Asher punctured her organs and split her intestines, and as the cavity in her torso opened in curtains of flesh, dead snakes spilled from her guts. Lifeless grubs sailed to the ground on streams of fetid ooze. Ximena buckled. Melissa came up behind her, keeping her on her feet as Asher sawed downward, opening Ximena's lower belly and mutilating her genitals. He shoved the kris up her bleeding vagina, using the dagger like a dildo, fucking Ximena to death. Dead lice poured out of her like the foulest afterbirth. The witchery Asher had blessed her with had turned Ximena into a living nest for Hell's critters. With the death of their queen bee, Ximena's hive perished too.

Asher reached for the pet snake around Ximena's neck. He'd forgotten what she'd named it. Giving it a new moniker would solidify his ownership. As he placed the serpent around his neck, it flicked its forked tongue like a gentle kiss, embracing its new master.

Branches snapped. The enveloping stench worsened, skunky and rotten, and dead leaves crackled under the stomp of approaching hooves. Beelzebub's tusks emerged from the thicket's dead womb, gleaming in the firelight, its mighty horns raking the sky. The demon's monstrous form dripped waste, swarms of insects coating it in a living shawl. Gazing upon the black god of the Philistine city of Ekron, the women were frozen in terrified awe.

"Welcome, Prince of Devils," Asher said. "Lord of the Flies, you honor us with your presence at my wedding. Hail the brother to the Hesperus star. Hail, horrors, hail!"

The mouths of Beelzebub's eye sockets opened. "I have come on behalf of Lucifer, to bless this unholy union, and to accept this sacrificial soul."

The demon's snout rose with an elephant's trumpeting that rumbled the ground. Melissa released Ximena, and she collapsed before Beelzebub in a deluge of gore. Her throat made clicking noises as she struggled for her final breaths. Beelzebub lowered his snout and pushed it inside Ximena's eviscerated torso. She convulsed as the beast channeled a current of black fecal matter into her insides. Her skin shriveled as every drop of moisture was sucked from her body to be replaced by sewage. She aged rapidly, seconds working like decades, transforming Ximena into a decrepit, emaciated crone. Her eyes melted and dribbled down her sunken cheeks. The sockets were refilled with shit. Her breasts sagged into fatty plantains, and her teeth fell out as her gums turned black like an old dog's.

A seal must have opened with Beelzebub's arrival, for the cold air became dry and hot, and distant thunder sang. The sliver of moon was swallowed by strange clouds. Swarms of insects buzzed overhead, and black worms fell from the treetops.

Wrapping its trunk around her waist, Beelzebub hoisted Ximena into the air, her withered body flopping about, brittle bones snapping. Still, the black magic kept her alive. Her body was dead, but her soul lived on, suffering in this spiritual intermission, so she was able to scream as the great demon hauled her into the black belly of the forest, dragging her to Hell.

Asher returned his attention to his remaining harem—the Vincent women. Though they'd always been fair-skinned, horror left them ghostly pale. Witnessing Ximena's destruction, Violet had retched and was now soaked in sweat. She cradled her expanding belly with trembling arms. Callie had gone still and silent. Though still dazed, Melissa had returned from her spellbound zombie state, and her dread was clear to see. She stood between her daughters, holding their hands, the Vincent women huddled together as if that would help them, as if they could be saved, spared, or loved.

Asher pulled Melissa away from her daughters. To his surprise, she took his hand and cuddled into him, trembling like a child. Despite everything, she was still enamored with him, the effects of his incubus hold everlasting. Though her terror was palpable, she could not resist him and hardly seemed to want to.

"Tell us why you're here tonight, sweetheart," Asher told her.

"I'm … I'm here to give my daughter away."

"That's right. Callie's place is by my side. You know that, don't you?"

"Yes. She'll have a better life with you. No other life can compare now."

"So you give us your blessing?"

"I do, Master. After you, I love my daughters more than anything in the world. I want Callie to have a good life with you. And I still love you, Master, and want you to be happy with her, for you both to find happiness together. That's why I've prepared a wedding present." She reached into the breast cups of her lingerie and produced a folded letter. "This is my confession to the murder of my husband. I claim full responsibility, so Callie and Violet are protected. I hoped that, with you marrying my daughter, you would finally release me. I've been ready for death for some time now. I can't go on like this any longer. So I wrote this as both a confession and a suicide note. You said you'll let me die tonight. I'm ready, Master. And if it helps my daughters and my new son-in-law, I, too, am willing to be sacrificed."

The surprising gift gave Asher pause. He'd been planning on sending Melissa straight to Hell tonight, for her death was needed for Callie to be reborn, but he'd not expected her to give in so willingly. Yes, she'd been asking for death—and who could blame her, given all he'd put her through—but Asher had not anticipated this level of submission. One willing human sacrifice was a big win, but two was a Satanic jackpot.

"I've already discussed it with Callie," Melissa said. "She's prepared to make the offering as part of her wedding vows."

Asher's eyes locked on Callie's baby blues. His bride nodded and gave him a small smile, her love for him breaking through her last shreds of humanity. Asher raised his mask and took the letter. He kissed the pentagram burned into Melissa's forehead, and it sizzled with his saliva.

"You have served me well," he said.

"Thank you, Master." Tears rolled down her cheeks, but her voice remained steady. "It has been my honor."

Asher studied the Vincent women standing before him. One by one, he'd taken possession of their hearts and blackened their souls.

They were dedicated to him to the point of being willing to die for him. He held absolute power over these women—the greatest aphrodisiac of all. Their souls were in his palm of flames. Tonight, their eternities would be determined by him alone.

He recalled something Beelzebub had told him. *"There shall be a great death, and then there shall be a great rebirth."*

He'd offered Ximena—a willing sacrifice—as part of these Satanic Rites. He'd planned to have Callie murder her mother as her offering to Lucifer and be reborn through her just as Asher had been reborn through his dead mother. As for Violet, Asher was going to wait to kill her, to see why her belly had swelled to such proportions. He'd known there was a purpose to it but hadn't known what. Looking at her now, it was Lucifer's words that returned to him.

"The fates of all your minions are up to you. Violet is your flesh puppet, son. I'm sure you'll find a use for her bloated womb."

Asher's breath caught as the revelation struck him. The answer had been in front of him all along. It was his power that had caused Violet's stomach to blossom so grotesquely, not Satan's. Asher had been carving out his own path. His sorcery had him planning ahead without even realizing it.

Asher extended the dagger's handle toward Callie. She accepted it, holding up the blade before her face, admiring the beauty of the blood on the kris. Melissa turned her back on Callie and got down on her knees before her, raising her chin to expose her throat. As Callie pressed the tip of the kris against her mother's neck, she gazed up at her groom.

"I've prepared vows, my love," she said before she began. "In the name of Satan, in the presence of all the forces of darkness, and before my mother and sister, I, Callie Vincent, take you, Asher Benton, as my husband and master. All that I am, I give to you. All that I have is yours. Whatever the future holds, I will love you, serve you, and stand by you, in this life and the next, on Earth and in Hell. This is my solemn vow."

Then Callie stabbed her mother in the throat.

"Hail Satan!" Callie shouted.

Asher flashed his fangs. "Hail Satan!"

Violet hailed as well. Even Melissa did, though her voice was muffled by the wound.

Pushing the kris deeper, Callie punctured her mother's veins. Blood rushed out in a waterfall as Callie dragged the blade from one side of her mother's neck to the other. She left the dagger sticking out of her neck as Callie got on her knees in front of her, grabbed Melissa's head, and rubbed against her open throat, drenching the front of her wedding dress. The fabric sponged up the blood, turning the gown into a red nightmare. Callie ran her sleeves across the slit throat and raised the hem of the dress to coat it too, then spun around, grinding her butt against her mother's throat to decorate the back.

Watching his baby bride dye her wedding gown with gore, an evil heat swirled within Asher's scrotum. This sacrifice was the perfect gift, unexpected and earnest, and bound to gain him even more power. The butchery awed him.

Melissa crumbled into herself as she exsanguinated. Callie drew the dagger out of her only to drive it into her back. She hacked and sawed, digging to pop hunks of flesh from her mother's body. She raised the chunks above her head and squeezed them, ringing them out like sponges, raining blood upon herself while dancing on the tips of her toes. With two wads of wet flesh in hand, she approached her groom and gave him one to hold. Then she raised the other to his mouth. Taking her lead, Asher raised his chunk of flesh to Callie's lips, and they fed each other in a gruesome recreation of the standard cutting of the wedding cake.

Violet's wet groan pulled them out of the romantic moment. She had slid down the tree and was holding her huge belly. The pentagram Asher had put on it now seemed twice as large. Wincing with pain, she'd gone green in the face and was drenched in sweat.

"Damn it, Violet!" Callie snapped, pointing the kris at her. "This is *my* day! Can't you just be happy for me?"

But Violet wasn't ruining the moment out of some petty jealousy. Her stomach was continuing to expand, the cauldron of protoplasm inflating to a mass larger than the rest of her body. She could no longer stand. She could barely breathe. All she could do was suffer.

Callie huffed and returned her attention to her sacrifice. Melissa was almost gone, but Asher wouldn't let her go just yet. The blackness he'd spat down her throat would keep her alive a little longer—just enough time for what happened next.

The forest rumbled. Cracks appeared in the ground as it shuddered beneath their feet, the etched symbols glowing white hot. Red-eyed rodents and serpents burrowed out of the bloody dirt. Fire ants scrambled. Buzzards bleated in the distance. *Music to Sacrifice Virgins*

To came to a distorted crescendo as one of Hell's gates came open, releasing jaundiced goblins that cackled as they vanished into the shadows, their sores weeping as they cheered the new couple. The night sky throbbed with pink lightning, the clouds pulsing crimson against a moon like a skinning tool, and as Asher and Callie gazed up, the winged demon swooped down from the dire heavens.

Astaroth landed hard, hammering its feet and fists into the ground, sending tremors through the valley. Its greasy, nude body was that of an adonis but for pendulous breasts with nipples that dripped rancid cream. The demon's face was just as Asher remembered it—billions of faces shifting and undulating, warping the head with the speed of a candle's flicker, so the Duke of Hell was everyone and no one all at once. Its ossicones spun, and its wings fanned the bonfire flames. Its giant phallus unfurled like a question mark, the serpent head of the penis turning to the bride and groom and flicking a forked tongue out of the urethra.

Standing tall, Astaroth's wings spread out like a bat's. With the demon's presence, the snakes and lice that had fallen dead from Ximena's stomach stirred back to life. Astaroth scooped Melissa into its arms, and its scaly skin sprouted snake heads like thorns on a rose stem. They sank their fangs into Melissa as she rattled in the moist throes of death. Astaroth's screech echoed through the woods, a funeral bell announcing another soul's carriage into the underworld.

The Duke of Hell gazed down upon them with fire reflected in its goat eyes.

"The demon comes but must be born," it said with a husky, feminine voice.

Astaroth launched into the sky, its body a totem of mad serpents, its cardinal wings smoldering as it ascended into clouds of blood. A brief flash of lightning silhouetted the beast and the remains of Melissa Vincent, and then they were gone.

Callie stared at the sky. The ferociousness she'd displayed while slaughtering her mother had dissipated, and the look she wore now was one of shattered innocence, a child saying goodbye to her mother for the last time. With her father, there had at least been anger for his absence and emotional distance. The girls did not harbor this same fury toward their mother. Their problems with her were trite, the typical clashing all mothers and daughters experience during the teenage years. Callie and Violet were too lost to Asher's spell to resent their mother for allowing him to do what he'd done to them. Despite

Melissa's sacrifice—or perhaps because of it—Callie's mourning was immediately apparent. Perhaps some small part of her—that last shred of her humanity—even felt remorse.

Asher turned his bride to face him and removed her veil, snapping her out of sorrow with a passionate kiss. Callie blinked away her tears as her smile returned.

"Now then," Asher said, "I, Asher Benton, take Callie Vincent as my wife, disciple, and worshipper. For the glory of Satan, I take you as my possession. All that you are, I rip from you. This is my solemn vow—*your soul belongs to me.*"

Swooning, Callie put her head against Asher's chest. "I love you so much. You have my heart, and you have my soul."

They kissed to seal their union.

Asher lowered his mask back in place. Ximena's snake had climbed up it and was coiled around one of the horns. "It's time for us to start a family." He pressed his left palm against Callie's stomach. "My demon seed burns within you, but first, it is you who must be born. You have baptized yourself in your first mother's blood. Now, you must be born again in Satan's name."

"Yes, my darling husband," she said. "Show me the way."

Asher took Callie's little hand. Her other hand still clutched the dagger. He led her to Violet, moaning in the dirt, her stomach a hot air balloon of flesh, graffitied with stretchmarks and busted capillaries. The pentagram had warped out of shape. Violet's fat gut covered most of her outstretched legs. She stared at Asher and Callie as if she were blind, looking through them, past them, into the vast direness of this mortal coil.

With a wave of his left hand, the pentagram Asher had painted on Violet's gut glistened as the black mucus turned into tiny shavings of steel. They shifted at his command, sawing into her like millions of microscopic razors. Her skin opened, forming a new pentagram of blood, and then the shavings grew molten, burning deeper inside. Violet screamed as her belly split open like a cracked eggshell, erupting with gore.

"Open her wider," Asher told Callie. "Your sister is the gateway."

She stepped to Violet with the kris in both fists. Though her body language was timid, Callie's expression was cruel, a dark shadow passing through her.

"He's mine now," she told her sister.

Callie slipped the knife into the gap of Violet's flesh, using it like a crowbar to pry the belly open. Amongst the normal-sized guts was an enormous uterus like the skull of an oxen. It throbbed at Callie's approach as if it had been expecting her. She poked it with the tip of the knife, and Violet's uterus opened with a wet belch. Prying it with his nails, Asher peered inside. The largest part was the amniotic sac, the protective bubble that houses fetuses. Asher knew it was empty, but it wouldn't be much longer. Instead of his semen fertilizing one of Violet's eggs, it had tricked her body and mutated it, transforming her into the monstrosity she had become.

Taking the blade from Callie, Asher gestured to the amniotic sac. "See you soon, sweetheart."

Callie gave him one last kiss, then punctured the sac with her fingernails, digging inside and sinking in past her elbows. Violet convulsed, bile dribbling from her nostrils, but Asher couldn't tell if she were alive or dead. It didn't matter anymore. Callie entered her sister's womb headfirst, swimming into the amniotic fluid, and as she wiggled deeper, the tissue stretched over her in a pulsing dome. Her feet vanished, and the dome closed, sealing her into the huge amniotic sac, and with another wave of Asher's hand, Violet's eviscerated torso slowly started to mend, wrapping over the exposed womb in a blanket of gnarled flesh, closing it.

Asher stood back, drew a joint from his jacket, and sparked it up. He did not know how long Callie's trip through the metaphysical Gehenna would take in Earth time, so he turned the record to side B, sat on the tree stump, and got high listening to his favorite music, which was no longer music at all. The hellish cacophony was unlike any sound from the human realm, an otherworldly audio experience made with pride in Hell. As it played on, tall shadows emerged from the forest, and when they came into the firelight, Asher saw Beelzebub and Astaroth had returned. The demons entered the circle and stared at Violet, watching her belly rise and fall as Callie writhed within her sister. Neither Asher nor the demons spoke. All that needed to be said came from *Music to Sacrifice Virgins To*. The words were from dead languages, spoken on devil tongues, not understood but *felt* by Asher, an invocation that riled him.

A bloody hand burst through Violet's belly. Slowly, Callie emerged from her sister's corpse, making slop of its insides as she clawed her way out. She was caked in gore, her wedding gown dripping with the blood of her former family. When she opened her eyes, they were red and goat-like. But what grabbed Asher's attention most was Callie's protruding belly. It was not massive as Violet's had been, but a normal baby bump that tested the limits of her wedding dress, splitting it at the seams. Asher's seed had rooted itself. He guessed her time in Gehenna must have passed faster than the time here on Earth, giving her the nine months needed to swell with their child. Satan's power was a wonder to behold.

Asher went to his bride and took her hands, helping her step out of Violet's ruins. The surrounding trees crackled as fire burst from beneath their bark, and suddenly, the clearing was encircled by hellfire. The flames came for Violet, engulfing her, the heat so intense she melted down to a blackened skeleton almost instantly. As Asher and Callie returned to the stereo altar, he noticed another figure standing between the towering demons. The handsome man came forward. His suit was the same shade of red as the flames and had a hole in the back to allow his hairless, pointed tail to poke through.

Lucifer clapped. "Cheers to the bride and groom."

"Father," Asher said. "You've come."

"What kind of dad would I be if I missed my son's wedding? I realize I'm a little late, but at least I'm here in time for the important part."

Lucifer approached Callie and slit the midsection of her gown with a long fingernail, exposing her pregnant belly, and rubbed his palm over it and smiled. Callie's mutated eyes made her hard to read. Asher wondered how much of the teenage girl he'd once known remained in this demonic husk.

"We're all here," Lucifer said, gesturing to Beelzebub and Astaroth. "The Evil Trinity has come to witness the birth of the next antichrist. We're like the three wise men come to see baby Jesus get shat into this world, but instead of bearing gifts, we take gifts—in the form of souls."

As Lucifer spoke, the jaundiced goblins emerged through the enveloping flames and watched on with dozens of spider eyes, dragging their knuckles and genitals through the blood on the ground.

"Who needs camels and jackasses when you have hellions?" Lucifer said. "Christ was born in a manger like a fucking loser. My grandchild will be born into the great wealth of Hell, just like its siblings. This is a new dawn."

Callie leaned over with her hands on her stomach. Her water broke, splashing over her bare feet. The snakes slithered toward it and the grubs wiggled into the puddle, and Callie cackled, showing her rotted teeth. Asher had only ever heard that sort of laughter on *Music to Sacrifice Virgins To*. Coming out of little Callie, the sound was even more chilling, for in that laughter, he observed the madness of a mind poisoned by his own black magic. His bride frothed at the mouth, crying blood as she laughed and laughed until she keeled over.

Lucifer placed his hand on Asher's shoulder. "Time for deliverance."

Asher got on his knees between Callie's legs, putting the hem of her gown around her waist. Her panties were soaked, and he tore them off and put them in his pocket with the others. Callie's cackle became musical, and she serenaded in harmony with *Music to Sacrifice Virgins To* as it returned to a dirge of heavy metal. Her vagina dilated, emitting a droning noise, black mist rising from the percolating canal as it wept a russet discharge.

Asher watched as Callie's labia parted, the infant leading with its face. Its eyes were half-closed, yellow slits under a black unibrow like its father's. It had an overbite of two small fangs and an upturned pig nose, its fine hair coming to a point on its forehead. Asher reached in and cradled his newborn as it oozed out of its mother, dragging its tiny talons against the lining of Callie's vaginal canal. The umbilical cord was the body of a serpent, covered in black scales that reflected the firelight, and at its end was the misshapen placenta. Bubbling afterbirth followed the baby's exit. The fluid and tissue was filled with strange insects not of this world. As Asher lifted the child, it snagged hold of the placenta and sank its fangs into it. It ripped through the mass like a piranha, fast and feverish, compelled by an instinctual hunger for blood.

"It's a boy!" Lucifer shouted. Below the umbilical cord was a penis nearly half the size of the infant's legs. "Don't mind his appearance, Asher. He'll learn how to mask his true form, just like his dear ol' grandpa."

Asher cradled his son close to his chest, watching it feast on the placenta. He was not filled with instantaneous unconditional love the way other parents always described this moment. Though proud of his achievement, he had no interest in raising a child. He was too focused on his own path to take on such a responsibility, and looking at Callie, he doubted she would be much of a mother. She was still cackling in the dirt, limbs bent at odd angles, goat eyes whirling in her skull.

"What's to become of her?" Asher asked Lucifer.

"Well, Astaroth and Beelzebub took Melissa and Ximena's souls, and I snatched up Violet's the moment you two cracked her open like a coconut. They're all burning in Hell as we speak. I'll let them cook for a few years, as is my way, but don't worry, they'll be rewarded for their evil deeds. All their souls will be made into demons. Lowly demons—servants, really—but demons nonetheless. The Evil Trinity has gathered these gifts you've given us, my son. But Callie's soul is another matter entirely."

They stared down at the beast of a girl as she writhed in filth.

"She's not with us, is she?" Asher asked.

"Not in the normal sense. Her time in Gehenna was long and cruel. That infernal place wears down on the soul, weakening it so demons can invade it more freely. They've tortured her for months, mangling her spirit and mind beyond repair."

"She's possessed, then?"

Lucifer shook his head. "More like demonized. The soul is still there, but it's been so blackened and diseased it barely resembles the Callie you knew. I won't have to drag her to Hell. This poor girl already lives there."

Asher shrugged. "It's just as well. I don't need a wife."

"Who does?" Lucifer nudged Callie with his boot. She mewled as blood continued gushing from between her legs. "Callie's human body is done. You only need look at her to see she's transforming. Soon, she'll look more like her baby—a full-fledged demon."

Lucifer whistled at her, and Callie shot up on her haunches. Her long, decaying tongue came out and licked the entirety of her face, clearing away the blood to reveal jaundiced skin. Lucifer nodded toward the goblins lurking at the edges of the circle, and Callie galloped over to join them, flailing like a chimp.

"So what happens now, Father?" Asher asked.

"Lucky for you, I'm interested in the newborn in all the ways you are not. He'll come down to Hell with me to be raised right. Check your left pocket. I've made something for him."

Asher reached into the same pocket he'd been storing the panties of his victims in, and when he drew the wad out, they'd been stitched together into a quilt. He wrapped his son in it, warming the infant with the filthy undergarments of the slain and the damned. Lucifer reached out, and Asher placed the child in his grandfather's claws.

"You've done well, Asher," Lucifer said. "Producing an antichrist is no easy feat, even for a warlock as determined as you. Your rewards will be plentiful and sublime. Power beyond human imagination or understanding. All that you desire will be placed at your feet. No man, woman, or child can resist you, for you are my blackest witch—you and your uncle as one. As such, you will continue my work in the form of *your own wants and needs.* Do what thou wilt."

The Devil's left hand cupped Asher's cheek, and he felt a surge ripple through him as he was imbued with all the sorcery of Hell. It burned deep within, and Asher closed his eyes as his soul was raked across spiritual coals. It was pain but also pleasure, almost sexual in its sting. When his eyes shot open, their redness flickered, and power rattled his bones and blackened his insides, flooding him with the warmth of concentrated evil.

Lucifer kissed Asher's other cheek. "Welcome to bliss, my son."

FORTY-NINE

WITH EVERYTHING LOADED IN THE Vincent's minivan, Asher left the woods just as daylight broke. He put Samhain's "Let the Day Begin" on the radio to celebrate the dawn of a new era of evil, remembering how this was the first album he'd pulled out of Rex's collection and how Violet had been drawn to him because of this kind of music. The song triggered one of Rex's memories too, and Asher flashed back to a time before he was born—1987—watching from Rex's point of view as he fucked a punk rock girl with a Leviathan Cross carved into her left tit. Asher knew she was Luna, the girlfriend who had taken the fall for Rex so long ago, sacrificing herself for the good of her master, just as Asher's women had given themselves to him. They were all gone now, but there would be more women—many more. He was an even more powerful incubus than he'd been when seducing them, a warlock of the highest order, nearly as great a tempter as The Devil himself.

His demonic appearance slowly faded as he drove on, making him appear human again, though his face was now a flattering combination of his former looks and his uncle's, angled with the handsomeness of a male model. Arriving at the Vincent house, Asher took a long shower, cleaned his skull mask and wiped down his leather jacket, and tossed his clothes in the wash. He noticed something odd about his hands. The swirls of his skin had changed shape, creating pentagram-shaped scars on his fingerprints—another blessing from his Father. Asher carried the totes of Rex's records out to the van and loaded them in with the stereo. Using Callie's and Violet's school bags, he packed up the drugs and weapons, then stuffed the bundles of cash into Melissa's largest purse.

He turned on the TV as he waited for his clothes to dry. The morning news was supercharged with more talk of the Satanic slayings plaguing Mortson County. The chief of police was answering questions from a podium in front of dozens of reporters, and though he tried to assure citizens things were under control, every answer he gave further assured Asher the police were completely lost. But he wasn't going to push his luck by sticking around. Eventually, someone was going to come to this house as well as his mother's, and besides, there was a whole world out there to explore and defile. A successful killer is always on the move. There would be new victims and minions. His next cult would be bigger, and he would be less of a leader and more of a god. His journey as a Satanic prophet had only just begun. Churches would burn, the holy would be raped and destroyed, children would suffer, and babies would die screaming. Just thinking about it tickled him.

After the press conference, the news anchor delivered breaking news.

"Local man Sam Sutherland has been taken into custody."

Asher leaned forward at the mention of his late mother's boyfriend. He hadn't been sure if Ximena really had done with the bag of bones what Asher told her to, but now he was hopeful.

"The sheriff's office reports that Sutherland came to the Mortson County Police Station with human remains in the trunk of his car. Sutherland claims to have no knowledge of how the remains got there, saying he discovered them yesterday and went straight to police. The identities of the human remains have not been released at this time."

Asher chuckled. He had all the time in the world. For a warlock, death had no substance.

He gathered his things. It pained him to leave behind his new

Dodge, but he needed the van to haul all the heavy metal records, and nothing mattered to him more than those. Soon enough, he would have to dispose of the Vincents' van anyway. It would be easy enough to upgrade to something sexier. With everything loaded up, Asher was about to start the van when he spotted a police car pulling up to his mother's house across the street. He gripped the wheel tight, watching through the rearview mirror as a second police car arrived. There was a slight twinge of fear as Asher wondered if he'd been caught, even though he knew he could annihilate a handful of pigs without much of an issue, but then he realized what was really going on.

Mom and Dad's remains had been identified. The police must have discovered Sam Sutherland was involved in a love triangle with them. All the evidence was there, including the phony text messages Asher sent from his parents' phones. Once investigators opened the door to that house of horrors, Sam would be asked hard questions he had no answers for. Whether or not he was convicted of murder, a whole new level of terror would infect the state, the nation, the civilized world. Soon, everyone would know there was more to these Satanic serial killings than anyone had realized. They did not end with the deaths of Barney Kaplan, Deanna Butterworth, and Paul Mord. Once the bodies at the convent were discovered—if they hadn't been already, only to be kept quiet as law enforcement investigated—a crippling dread would curse this town.

After seeing the bloody ruins of his mother's home, police would begin searching for Asher, but finding him would be impossible, even if he were standing right in front of them. The Asher they would look for no longer existed. Even in human form, he did not look the same. To facilitate his seductions of the innocent, Asher was much better looking now, though his flesh reflected the two evil souls that had become one within his body. Even his fingerprints had been distorted by pentagram scars to further obscure his identity. As always, Lucifer was right. This was a new dawn.

Pulling out of the driveway before law enforcement could close off the area, Asher headed west, leaving the neighborhood he'd grown up in for good. But before leaving town, he was going to stop by his old girlfriend's place. Rebecca had dumped him, and there was nothing more satisfying than showing your ex what a success you'd become. When they'd been together, all Asher had wanted was her heart. Now, he could take it literally. It'd also been too long since he'd raped someone, and nothing was more sexually gratifying than violating a woman and making her beg for her life when you knew you were going to take it either way. Rebecca's brutal death would be the perfect period to place at the final chapter of his former life.

His new life awaited. Having Lucifer's blessing, Asher would be focused on hedonistic sin, savoring the Satanic bliss his infernal father spoke of. Everything he wanted or could ever want was in his grip. He was ready to bleed the world to nourish himself, feeding his narcissistic desires with impunity.

But he did have one task in mind.

He and Rex wanted to make a second album, and with all the money Asher had stolen from his first victim, getting in the studio would be easy. All he needed now was a guitar, as Lucifer suggested. Rex had the musical skill. Asher had the financial means. With their combined powers as a master warlock, *Music to Sacrifice Virgins To: Volume II* would be even more hellish than its predecessor. More records would follow. Asher and Rex hoped to one day create heavy metal louder than 1,100 decibels, a noise so colossal it would create a black hole to destroy this worthless galaxy. But for now, the conjoined Satanists would approach human genocide one ritual slaughter at a time. There were many more virgins out there, each with fresh, nubile bodies awaiting a sacrificial blade.

Asher drove on in victory, passing by Christmas decorations and plastic nativity scenes. He smirked at them in his newfound knowledge.

The Christians have it all wrong, and karma is a myth. Justice does not prevail. To get everything you want, you must be incorrigible, selfish, and ruthless. Nice guys finish last for a reason. It's the same reason wealthy liars run the world. No one cares how good of a person you are, because in the end, that doesn't matter. Only accomplishments matter, and good leaders are burdened by scruples, while those of moral vacuity conquer all. The meek have already lost their inheritance of the Earth. Thoughts and prayers hold no power. Peaceful protests bring no changes, for violence is the only tool that can craft a better personal future in this dog-eat-dog world. God is dead, powerless, or just doesn't give a damn about his pathetic creations. Villainy is the golden key that unlocks all victories, and because he understood these truths, there would be no comeuppance for Asher Benton, no punishment in this life or the next. The demon he'd become would only know glory.

The bad guys always win.
Hail Satan.

ACKNOWLEDGMENTS

Thanks to Lisa Lee Tone for her dutiful editing work, Tery Ramdhany for his incredible cover art, and C.V. Hunt for her wicked cover designing and formatting. You all made this book presentable. Thanks also to Chandra Claypool for always being my beta reader. Additional appreciations to Aron Beauregard, Daniel J. Volpe, Gregg Kirby, and Brian Keene. And special thanks to Tom Mumme—always.

ABOUT THE AUTHOR

Kristopher Triana is the Splatterpunk Award-winning author of *Gone to See the River Man, Full Brutal, They All Died Screaming, The Old Lady,* and many other terrifying books. His work has been published in seven languages and has appeared in many anthologies and magazines, drawing praise from Rue Morgue Magazine, Cemetery Dance, Scream Magazine, and many more.

He lives in New England.

Get signed books at: TRIANAHORROR.COM
Visit him at: Kristophertriana.com and on Substack, Instagram, Facebook, and TikTok.

www.ingramcontent.com/pod-product-compliance
Lightning Source LLC
Chambersburg PA
CBHW060214030726
47499CB00004B/1042